Have a Heart

GENNY CARRICK

Cover Design & Illustration by Melody Jeffries

Edited by Zee Monodee

ISBN (e-book) 978-1-957745-04-6

ISBN (paperback) 978-1-957745-05-3

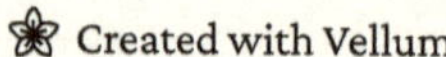 Created with Vellum

content

This book contains themes of familial pressure, a manipulative ex (past), and includes implied intimacy.

For Rob
wish you were here

eliza

ANYONE WHO SAYS there's nothing better than a nice dinner with your family has never been served what's on the menu at mine.

Steaming helpings of concerned parental commentary on my life choices, with a side of light bragging from my successful older sisters, all topped off with general dismay and hand-wringing over my iffy future.

At the moment, I couldn't think of anything I'd rather endure less.

I dragged my feet across my parents' front porch, breathing in the last of the free air before this week's PressureFest could begin. I just needed to get through a few hours of interrogation before running right back to my apartment to slip into my PJs and listen to Taylor Swift's latest album while finishing off a box of chocolate chip cookies. I could handle a few hours of soul-crushing family time.

It should be pretty standard stuff. I could predict my parents' gentle nudges and helpful hints down to the last *If it's too tough out there, you could always move back in for a while.* My childhood bedroom was ready and waiting for me, I only had to ask.

Just give up my pride, admit the big, bad world was too much for me, and ask.

Yeah, right.

"I'm doing great," I said to the creepy smiling scarecrow wreath on the door. "I don't need that childhood bedroom and all its rent-free glory."

No matter how loudly my bank account disagreed.

I squared my shoulders, plastered on a smile, and pushed open the door.

"I'm here!" I shouted into the old Craftsman as though my mother hadn't sensed it the moment I turned down their street. "Webb Family Dinner can officially commence."

"If it isn't our very own Pippi Longstocking." Caught on his way to the dining room with a platter of my mom's honey chili chicken, my father Joel tracked me with wide eyes as if my completely expected arrival were a minor miracle.

For the record, I had almost perfect Sunday dinner attendance, despite my aversion to their pushiness. It would take a Godzilla-storming-town type of situation to keep me away from my mom's cooking. My talents in the kitchen didn't extend much beyond cookies and ramen so family dinners were practically mandatory for my stomach, but showing up more than once a week was a no-go. Too many impromptu meals with my folks only raised their suspicions about my meager grocery budget. I didn't need more care packages dropped by *just in case*.

Well. I did need them. Still. The principle of the thing, you know.

"Pippi's hair is red." I flounced my mostly-blond hair over one shoulder, showing off the bright underlayer. "Mine's pink."

He pulled me into a hug until my nose itched with the faux-lemon scent of the industrial-strength soap he used between patients at his vet clinic. "Close enough."

My hair color of the moment had become a favorite conversation piece during these weekly torture sessions. A little shot of purple or blue could keep my family's attention diverted from my work life, or worse, my love life, for hours at a time. The bright pink had been a necessary change after my experiment with turquoise faded to a sickly green. A diversion during Sunday dinner was all well and good, but I didn't want to look like a zombie Monday through Saturday. A girl had to have priorities.

I found the rest of the usual suspects in the kitchen. Eden, my oldest sister, and her husband, Booker, shuttled plates to the dining table while our middle sister, Harper, checked on a pie in the oven. My mother Darlene presided over it all like the fading but still graceful former beauty pageant queen she was.

In looks, Eden and I took after our mom: blonde and blue-eyed, with heart-shaped faces and generous hips. Harper took after our dad, nabbing the auburn hair, brown eyes, and lithe frame. In everything else, though, I was the odd girl out. My sisters had good jobs and paid their bills on time. Me? I scraped rent money together at the last possible second and probably had expired yogurt in my fridge just hanging around to give me E.coli.

Loving them proved easy. Living up to them...let's just say I hadn't figured that one out yet.

"Where have you been, Eliza? I was about to text you." Eden flashed a glare as she carted a platter of green beans to the table.

The woman couldn't make a move without her planner—it drove her crazy when I breezed in after seven. I didn't do it on purpose, but disrupting her rigid timelines still brought some perverse satisfaction to my youngest-sister heart. She needed to lighten up before she gave herself a coronary.

"I'm ten minutes late, it's not like I drove into a ditch."

"Don't give them new things to worry about." Booker's deep voice came from behind me. "Try to keep it simple."

I turned around and craned my neck to look up at him. Booker was roughly ten feet tall with a personality that sparkled laughter and joy. He grinned down at me until his dimples stood out on his dark skin.

"Come on, what could be simpler than driving into a ditch?"

His grin morphed into an unimpressed frown, but his attempt at scolding barely lasted three seconds. I liked to think I was just too lovable to bring out his true irritation, but probably he was just too big of a softie to ever show it.

The newest addition to our family, Booker had swept Eden off her feet and married her in a gorgeous little ceremony over the summer. I never would have predicted our town's star high school basketball coach for my sister, but here she stood with a ring on her finger and that generous hunk of man in her bed. He fit right in with our family, and had set up shop as the teasing but protective brother-in-law we never knew we needed.

"Besides," I told him, "I don't give them things to worry about. They do that all on their own."

He shot me a knowing look. Yeah, yeah. Every move I made gave my folks something to worry about. The curse of the youngest child. They didn't really want me to grow up, and I complied by making one bad decision after another. I had good intentions, I swear I did, but things just kind of fell apart in my hands.

"Hi, Mom." I wrapped an arm around her shoulders and pecked her on the cheek. Sweet notes of vanilla and hibiscus perfume mixed with the harsh tang of hairspray wafted around me, a smell I would forever associate with good posture and well-meaning but incessant meddling.

"Hi, baby." She spooned out the last of the roasted veggies from the baking dish and passed the serving plate to me. "Did you get that wholesale deal you were hoping for?"

I swallowed down a groan. What a way to kick things off. They weren't supposed to bring up my work problems until at least halfway through dinner. How was I supposed to share my latest failures on an empty stomach?

I considered lying straight to my mom's face but couldn't do it. Anyway, lies would just lead to more questions, and I wanted to move on from this topic as quickly as possible. "That didn't work out."

"Oh, Eliza, did the Countryside deal fall through?" Harper asked.

Wisps of hair trailed out of her long braid, and she still had on the pumpkin-printed scrubs she wore at her job as a physical therapist over at Magnolia Ridge's retirement community. A few months ago, they'd added alternating weekend shifts to her schedule, and now every other week she looked like she needed a glass of wine and a bubble bath rather than chicken and pie.

Well, she probably needed the pie. Everybody needed a slice of my mom's pecan pie.

I stomped down the disappointment bubbling up in my chest and forced my smile wider. "It's no big deal. It was a long shot, anyway."

"What's this about Countryside?" my dad asked from the dining room.

Geez. I should have dyed my whole head pink. Doubtful even a rainbow-striped mohawk would have let me avoid the looming mess of a conversation.

Confessions about my career missteps were the literal

worst. With all the practice I'd had at making them, they shouldn't still bother me as much as they did. Tendrils of nerves twisted through my stomach, drying out my mouth and smothering my appetite.

Turning around to face the others at the table, I held the platter of veggies in front of me like a shield. "Countryside ended up rejecting my bid."

There. Easy. Simple and to the point.

I set the dish next to the sweet and spicy chicken and took my seat beside Harper. Pretending getting rejected by one of the biggest home decor stores in Central Texas didn't deserve further discussion, I reached for the bowl of rice, but it only took seconds before the questions started. My family wouldn't let a remark like that go even in my wildest dreams.

Okay, my wildest dreams were mainly of the naughty Chris Hemsworth variety, but in my more normal dreams, my family didn't pry into my every move like my own personal NSA.

"I thought that was as good as done," Eden said over the clatter of serving spoons.

So did I.

"Turns out that one was a *nope*. Pass the sweet tea, please."

"Now wait a minute," Dad said. The gentle, disappointed look in his eyes sent my heart sinking straight through the floor. I hated that look, and yet I always seemed to bring it out in him. "I thought you needed that contract. What happened?"

I'd been asking myself the same thing for the last week.

Six months ago, I'd started selling cold-process soap as a side hustle. I experimented with scents and colors until I developed *Sunshine Soul,* a custom line of luxe-rustic soaps I sold at the local farmers markets. It'd seemed as though I was on the fast track to becoming Central Texas's reigning Soap Queen, and I *might* have quit my day job too soon.

Like, immediately.

Now, my profits had leveled off, and I didn't know yet how to get them on the climb again. I still clung to my hopes of small businesswoman badassery—I just needed to find new ways to market and sell my soaps. The sooner, the better.

Not that I had any intention of admitting that to my family over dinner.

I tried for indifference. "They weren't interested. Harper, how are things over at Siesta Village? Everybody still old?"

She shot me the tiniest glare at my nickname for her workplace. I'm sorry, but naming a retirement center *Fiesta Village* just invited jokes. I couldn't be blamed for voicing them.

"What do you mean, they weren't interested?" Mom cut in. "What did they say?"

I played innocent and gestured at my mouth stuffed full of yummy chicken. Good manners, and all.

She leveled me a look, her lips pursed tight. I knew that look well, too, although it didn't usher in quite as much guilt as my dad's. Her every day, garden-variety underwhelm had long ago lost the sharp edge it once held.

"Eliza."

It'd been worth a shot.

I swallowed hard as a familiar phrase spun through my brain, dragging down my pretend cheer. The rejection email's words were burned into my mind, I'd read them so many times.

"Their merchandiser said she liked my soaps, but she didn't love them enough to bring them into their stores. That's all there is to it."

As simple as that. I'd been naive to think her initial enthusiastic interest when I showed her my soaps would lead to a big contract. A wildly popular chain of down-home gifts and accessories dotted throughout Texas, Countryside probably got a lot of people through their doors who wanted to sell with them. They had to be selective.

Didn't mean that bitter pill hadn't knocked me on my rear.

"I've still got the farmers markets. I'm stocking up bars for the winter markets as we speak, with new scents for the holidays."

"All you ever do is make soap," Eden said. "Your apartment was full of the stuff last time I was over there. How could you possibly make more? Are you going to hire someone to help you?"

The problem had never been how many soaps I made—I could knock out hundreds of bars in a day. Finding enough people to buy them to keep my bills paid? That's where things got trickier.

"Are you looking for a job? I thought things were pretty good for you over at the library, but I'll see what I can do. I'll need to see some references, though."

I considered her answering frown another win for me.

"Is that why you're working at Irwin's again?" Harper asked.

I choked back every last curse word that sprang to mind and cut my middle sister a death glare. "Seriously? I've barely had that green vest on for a week."

"What? I saw you Thursday night on my way home from work."

She seemed completely unaware of the bomb she'd just dropped on my *nice family dinner*. Embarrassment squirmed through me as every Webb turned their eyes on me like I sat on display in a museum of human disasters. Thank God for Booker, who didn't know the history there, and kept his attention on his meal. I'd make sure to serve him extra ice cream with his pie as a thank you.

"Wait." Mom threw one hand to her forehead as if trying to force her thoughts to make sense. "You're working at Irwin's again?"

I tossed one last glare at Harper but bobbed a shoulder. Not like I could have kept the news secret if I'd wanted to. Everybody knew Irwin's, and I wasn't exactly a closed book. I'd just figured I would get around to telling them on my own time. Like maybe after I'd got my soap business on solid financial ground and quit Irwin's yet again.

"Are you done with soap now?"

"I'm not done with soap." I didn't know yet what I was, but now wasn't the time for impulsive decisions and sweeping declarations. In general, I enjoyed impulsive decisions, but not while my whole family looked on like they'd just caught the tail end of a horror movie—they didn't understand what they were watching, but it sure was horrible to see. "Grant Irwin called me last week and asked if I would be interested in picking up some hours. It's no big deal."

Thankfully, no one reacted to that understatement. I'd spent my teen years and college summers wearing the Irwin's vest, and here I was wearing it again at twenty-six as if the intervening years had never happened, *Failure to Launch* personified. I hadn't been able to make any of my jobs since college stick, and now I was back working retail to try to keep my small business afloat.

Working at Irwin Outdoors again was the biggest of deals.

"Why didn't you tell me you needed a job?" Dad asked. "You could always come work with me again."

"And hold bull semen while you get a bunch of cows pregnant? No, thanks."

A tiny frown touched his mouth. "There's a bit more to being a vet tech than that."

"Not how I remember it. When handling bull semen is an actual job requirement, it kind of blurs out the rest."

He shook his head as if my aversion to bull semen made *me* the weird one.

"Is it full time at Irwin's?" Mom asked, a note of hopefulness in her voice. She'd probably love it if I took a permanent position there. Working for a good company with steady income and benefits—every mother's dream, right?

"Part-time, and just temporary until Grant can hire a new crew. I guess he lost two sales associates at once. They fell in love and ran off to climb mountains together."

"That sounds romantic," Harper said.

I cringed. "Does it?"

"Shared interests and travel? I'd be in."

"Now all you need is a guy who likes canasta and the Bingo Palace."

She must have been too tired from her shift to even roll her eyes. I gave her a hard time about it, but she needed to broaden her social circle beyond the over-seventy set. She'd supposedly been seeing a guy up in Waco, but none of us had met him yet, and I'd begun to doubt his existence. I couldn't remember the last time she brought someone home to meet the fam. Not that I'd been doing any better in that department, but I much preferred casting stones to fielding them.

"The right man will come along for both of you."

That hopeful desperation in my mother's voice again left me with a bitter aftertaste. I knew she only wanted me to be happy, but I wasn't an old maid at twenty-six. I was young, vibrant, constantly teetering on the edge of an eviction. The works.

"This is all your fault." I pointed a finger at Eden and Booker, who faked an appropriate level of guilt. "If you two weren't so disgustingly happy, the rest of us miserable singles could live our lives in peace."

"I'm not miserable," Harper said.

I grinned at her. "That's nothing a set-up can't fix."

"Speaking of," Mom said with a sly little look. "Frannie's nephew is visiting for a few weeks. He's a software engineer in Dallas." Her grin turned devious, like the Grinch plotting to steal Christmas. "He might be worth meeting."

I subdued a sigh. Really, this was all my fault for bringing up Grant's happily paired-off job deserters. What could I expect with that kind of opening? Mom's wedding-fever hadn't been satisfied with Eden's ceremony over the summer—now she wanted Harper and me to stroll down the aisle, too.

I waved a hand in Harper's direction. "He sounds like a perfect match for that one. Software engineers aren't really my speed."

"What kind of guy *is* your speed?" Booker asked. "Just as a frame of reference."

Dad hunkered down over his dinner. "I think I'm better off not knowing."

I shrugged as if I'd never given the men of Magnolia Ridge a second thought. Oh, I'd thought about them all right, but I'd never let it progress to more. My motto was, I could look, but I couldn't touch, and so far, it had worked well. The last time around had proved my radar for decent guys was completely busted, and I didn't trust myself to try all that again.

"I saw a guy in town the other day who looked interesting. He rode a black motorcycle, had tattoos down his arms, and a big old beard. I think he'd be about my speed."

Predictable as ever, my family erupted into a chorus of laments over my poor dating choices just as I'd hoped. I ignored their criticisms, since they weren't based in anything close to reality. Much easier to talk about a dangerous-looking biker I had no interest in than deal with Mom's increasingly desperate offers to set me up. I could just imagine the kind of guy she would find for me. Probably someone who wore a tie to the office every day, drove a sensible car, and was a verifiable Nice Guy.

I had no intention of making that mistake twice.

TWO

dean

I ADJUSTED the knot on my tie while looking over the quarterly financial report. I'd been through the figures top to bottom already today but went through them again to be certain. I'd never turned in a sloppy report and wasn't about to start.

Outside my window, the afternoon sun had begun to set over Magnolia Ridge. From my second-floor office on Center Street, I looked across the town's brick storefronts sprawling out toward pasture and farmland in the distance. As far as office views went, mine wasn't too bad.

Not that I did much more than look at it these days.

My older brother walked in and slumped into a chair across from me. "God curse coworker affairs."

"Grant." I kept my eyes on the report, scanning through the numbers. "You had a good day, I take it."

He groaned in answer. "Ever since my two best sales associates ran off to explore the world together, I've been pulling double shifts on the sales floor. Maybe I should put a *No dating* stipulation in the employee handbook, what do you think?"

"You could," I said without glancing up. "It's probably illegal, though."

"At least Eliza Webb agreed to come back for a while. She's seriously saving me."

My fingers paused on the keyboard, numbers momentarily erased from my mind. "Eliza's working in the store again?"

"Yeah, but she's adamant it's only temporary." He sighed, sinking lower into the chair. "She asked for Saturdays off, and I gave her a raise over last time, but she's worth it. I've got ads in all the usual places, but the only applicants so far don't want to work evenings and are completely deluded about the going rate for retail pay."

I only halfway listened to my brother grouse about his poor job applicant pool. Eliza Webb was back at Irwin's? Interesting, but not unusual. Irwin's was already on her resume at least four different times, but job stability didn't seem like a high priority for her. As far as I could tell, she seemed proud of her spotty work history. She made sure to stand out among the women of Magnolia Ridge, too, rotating through absurd hair colors and talking too loudly everywhere she went. She was like the human version of snapping bubblegum—irritating but weirdly hypnotic.

Perhaps most irritating of all, Eliza had zero regard for me. I didn't care that she'd utterly dismissed me as a man—I couldn't think of a woman less suited to me than Eliza Webb—but she had no respect for me within the company. She showed my parents a docile appreciation, Grant she respected as her sometime-boss, and she even gave a friendly deference to my youngest brother, Rhett. But for me? Nothing but snark. Considering our conversations usually featured some sort of jab from her about spreadsheets, I chalked it up to a wholehearted disdain for the nerdy numbers guy.

"You're not even listening. Why do I come complain to you, anyway?"

"I don't know," I said, pulling my unruly thoughts away from Eliza Webb. I'd spent too much time wondering just what she disliked about me as it was. *Not my problem.* "You have plenty of other options available."

One of those other options walked into my office carrying a package.

"The *Explore Texas* issues arrived!" Rhett shouted into the outer hallway.

Our parents shuffled out of their shared office, ready to see how this feature had turned out. Grant hopped up to give them the two seats in front of my desk while Rhett opened the package and passed around crisp magazines that still smelled of the printer.

Our family had been interviewed by media outlets in honor of Irwin Outdoors' thirtieth anniversary next month, and print copies of newspapers and magazines had been rolling in for weeks. Most of the articles focused on my parents, Nathaniel and Patricia, founders and co-CEOs of one of the most successful independent outdoor outfitting chains in Texas. A few reporters had wanted to talk to my brothers and me, too, to amp up the family business angle, and *Explore Texas* had been one of those few.

I left my copy unopened on my desk. I didn't have to read through it to know what I'd find inside. A pithy feature on my parents, who found love on a camping trip gone wrong during college and turned their mutual affinity for the outdoors into a thriving business. Something highlighting Grant's mountain climbing obsession and his latest ascent, and Rhett's goal to raft every Class V whitewater in the lower forty-eight.

A summary of the nonsense I'd spouted.

For a few minutes, the only sound came from my fingers

tapping on the keyboard, and pages flipping. I finished the report and sent it out to the executives, most of whom currently crowded my office. Preparing myself for the worst, I logged out of my computer for the day.

Rhett spoke first. "Dean, you really knocked this one out of the park."

His lopsided grin proved I hadn't.

"Oh, hush." Mom had apparently read my little sidebar, too. I hadn't confirmed it this time around, but my interviews never rated the kind of space my brothers' did. Considering what I'd had to contribute, no reason they should.

Grant's eyes were glued to his copy. "Seriously, Dean, this is painful."

I fought the sigh that wanted to groan out of me. I wished I'd never spoken to that reporter.

Usually when someone approached me for an interview, it was to brag about the little Texas company that could. As Irwin Outdoors' controller, I could talk sales, profits, and the company's financial future for hours. This reporter hadn't cared about the financials—he'd wanted anecdotes and first-hand experiences. What were my favorite products, my favorite sports, my favorite places to 'just get outside'? I'd come up empty. I was the numbers guy, not the person you went to when you wanted flowery descriptions of scenery and rave gear reviews.

"'The Hill Country Natural Area is one of my favorites,'" Rhett read out loud, stifling laughter. "'The West Peak Overlook is a steep climb, but it gives spectacular views of the Hill Country that are well worth the effort in the end.'"

He peered at me over the magazine. "You've never been to the West Peak Overlook. Where did you get that?"

I'd blanked during the interview. They were supposed to ask me about financials, not fitness. I ran five miles every morning, but I logged my distance on the treadmill in my townhouse, not a local trail. If I wanted to work out, I used the punching bag in the garage or maybe hit the gym. The last time I'd spent any quality time outdoors was in high school, and I didn't think half-remembered stories of stumping around the trails of Camp Yaupon would impress *Explore Texas*'s readers.

I never thought flipping through the tourism magazines in my dentist's waiting room would save my behind, but here I was.

Judging by the reactions in this room, my quick thinking had only *mostly* saved my behind. *Explore Texas* readers might accept my regurgitated garbage as proof of my deep and abiding love for the outdoors, but my family knew me better than that.

"'My favorite piece of gear is the Vireo 25 day pack.'" Rhett read in a stilted monotone as though emulating me. *The numbers guy is an emotionless robot.* That joke never got old.

"'It holds everything I need for a day on the trails, but is light and comfortable on my back. I can rest easy knowing it's made from recycled materials, so I'm helping the environment while exploring it.'" Rhett barked out a laugh. "Talk about recycled materials, you recited directly from the mailer."

Pushing back a flare of irritation, I grumbled something under my breath I'd rather my mom didn't hear. How was I supposed to wax rhapsodic on the merits of a day pack I'd never used? If the reporter had asked for a recap of the Vireo's profit analysis, I would have aced it. I shifted in my seat while my parents stared at me like they might turn me to stone. My generic answers might have flown with the reporter, but it hadn't impressed them.

"You didn't get to my favorite part," Grant said. "'The best thing about Irwin's stores are the people. When you walk into an Irwin's, you know every associate is there because they love using the gear and know it inside and out. They answer customer questions from experience, not from a practiced sales pitch or reading off a brochure.'"

"He said, after reading off the brochure," Rhett added with a chortle.

I closed my eyes, praying their gloating would be short-lived. It could have been worse. Probably the only people who would ever realize I'd been out of my depth were right here in this room. I opened my eyes again to find my family watching me with a disturbing combination of aggravation and amusement.

Perfect. Just where I liked to be—the butt of the family jokes.

"You had a lot to say about what it's like in an Irwin's store when you never worked in one," Grant said.

"I did in high school." I stopped there. No point in bringing up the rest. Not when they were already laughing at me.

Rhett rolled his magazine into a tube and knocked it against his knees. "That's right, didn't you last two whole weeks?"

I straightened the pencils on my desk. That story made my mess of an interview look like a slam dunk. "Three."

Grant snapped his fingers. "I remember now. The backpack guy."

Yes, the backpack guy. As though Grant had ever forgotten.

I'd never been as sociable or customer service-oriented as the rest of my family, but I'd tried to help out in the store. I'd lost my cool when a customer demanded I detail the differences between two identical backpacks. When the man pressed for more information, I gave him a refresher on the differences between green and blue, prompting him to lodge a complaint about my 'condescending attitude'. Not one of my finer moments, but I'd been hot-headed at seventeen. I didn't need to defend mistakes from fifteen years ago.

"Is that really all the time you ever worked in one of our stores?" Dad asked. "Three weeks?"

Again, I didn't see how it could be surprising to anyone. "I've spent the last eight years here since I got my MBA."

"Right here?" Grant gestured around my spartan office. "Because from what I've seen, you've practically spent the entire time in this room."

The accusation annoyed me, mostly because it hit too close to home. "I haven't summited any mountains lately, if that's what you're getting at."

"If you need more time on the sales floor, I could use the help. Our schedule is wide open at the moment."

"I'm calling an Irwin Executive Meeting." Dad's voice had lost its amusement, now speaking with the weight of co-CEO behind him.

I smoothed my tie and sat straighter out of sheer habit.

"I think it's time we make some changes."

I froze, the annoyance in my gut hardening into something too close to anger. Was my father seriously going to take some sort of action based on one lousy magazine? "I know I didn't come off very well in that article, but I wasn't expecting questions like that."

"That much was clear. Improvising's not your strong suit." Dad laced his fingers together as if formulating plans. Normally, I loved plans, but not when someone else made them about me. "When was the last time you did anything more than walk through an Irwin's store?"

I drew in a breath as I thought back.

"We're going to fix that." Dad rightly interpreted my silence. Even when I did drop into the store, it wasn't to move stock around or make a sale. "You've been up here in your office too long. You can quote all the numbers, but you don't know what Irwin's is about."

"That's not entirely—"

He raised a finger, silencing the rest of my protest. Irwin Executive Meetings might be family affairs, but they were still serious business. "You need a crash course on what it's like on the ground floor. You're going to work as a sales associate."

I stared at my father as every thought in my head ground to a halt. As much as I prided myself on control nowadays, it currently teetered at the edge of a cliff.

"You're demoting me?" I couldn't keep the insulted tone out of my voice.

"I want to promote you to CFO."

Grant and Rhett turned stunned eyes on me. One minute our father wanted to send me to the sales floor, the next he wanted to essentially make me partner? My stomach lurched in ten directions at once, my career target suddenly at my fingertips.

"You're making me CFO?" I tested out the words. Even if I'd hoped the position would eventually come to me, I didn't take anything about the family business as a guarantee.

"No. I *want* to make you CFO."

I kept my expression calm even as my exasperation cranked up another notch with every sentence he spoke. My father wasn't usually this inscrutable. His way was direct, often to a painful degree.

"With our store expansion progressing, it's time we hire another accountant and bring in a Chief Financial Officer."

That he no longer referred to *me* as the CFO shot tiny spears of panic in my chest. All this because of one interview that by all rights, nobody but us would know was garbage?

"You've proved you're more than capable of handling the financial side of it, the accounts and budgets. But without ground-floor experience of our stores, how will you know how company money should be spent? How will you be able to make long-term plans?"

My brothers watched in absolute silence, front-row spectators to the job interview from hell. Mom stayed quiet, too, but her eyes had grown thoughtful. My brothers, on the other hand, looked like they wished they'd brought popcorn.

I'd given everything I had to this company since I earned my MBA, and now one article managed to call my entire ability into question? I took deep breaths, trying to soothe myself with a calming mantra, but *This too shall pass* couldn't make a dent in the frustration brewing inside me tonight.

"What do you want from me, exactly?"

"You know why your mother and I started this store. We want to pass our love for the outdoors on to everyone who walks through our doors. You need to have that love if you want to step up to help run this company."

I ground my teeth together, my unruffled façade worn paper-thin. The indoorsy one in a family of outdoors enthusiasts, I'd always stood out, but Mom and Dad never much cared what I did in my free time before. Now my CPA and MBA weren't enough?

"So, what, you want me to go to summer camp?"

His slow smile didn't reassure me.

"Something like that. Your expertise has earned you your title, even if you don't know the first thing about what we sell. If we ran a big corporation, maybe it wouldn't matter that you don't have experience in one of our stores."

Seriously? I fought to keep my face neutral after that back-handed compliment. I worked damn hard for this business to have it summed up as so much nothing.

"But?"

"But we're not a big corporation. People come to us because we're small. We're a family business who know our products inside and out, that's the draw, just like you said in that interview."

And what a mistake that had been. Next time a reporter wanted a few words, I'd give them two: *Get lost.*

"You're skilled at your job, no one's questioning that. We wouldn't be where we are today without you, that's a fact. But this interview made clear you don't know the first thing about the products we sell or the people who use them."

"That's a little unfair. I spend fifty hours a week in this office. I don't have a lot of spare time for hikes in the park or kayak trips down the San Gabriel river."

"That's part of the problem, honey." The Good Cop to my father's Bad Cop routine, Mom's soft voice was meant to gentle the blow. "We knew you were putting in a lot of time, and we love your dedication, but we want you to have a life outside of the company, too."

Since when? I wanted to shout, but I swallowed the words down.

"Here's what I propose." Dad paused, and the rest of them might as well have leaned forward in their chairs, ready to watch the hammer fall. "I want you to beat your previous record on the sales floor. Work for four weeks as a retail associate, get a feel for what it's really like in an Irwin store, what we sell, and why our customers choose us. Then we'll make you CFO."

I held my breath a beat. I liked the sound of becoming CFO before I hit thirty-two. That title had been the carrot at the end of the stick for years now, and I finally had it within reach. But what my dad wanted me to do for the next month poured a cold glass of humiliation on any celebration. "You want me to just walk downstairs and get to work?"

"I've got space on the shift calendar. You can start tomorrow." Grant looked far too satisfied by this turn of events. He'd have more help on the sales floor *and* get to boss me around. Every older brother's dream.

"Tomorrow?" I laid one hand on my laptop out of instinct, my overcrowded work calendar flashing in my brain. The situation had spiraled so far out of my control, I didn't know how to shift it back. "What about my actual job? I can't leave for a month."

"You don't take much vacation time," Mom said. "You could use some time away from this desk."

I failed to see how working downstairs would qualify as a vacation.

"Don't say that." Rhett pressed a hand over his heart as though it pained him. "He loves his desk."

"We're in the middle of a three-store expansion." I kept my voice even, but I couldn't be the only one who saw the problem in what they were wanting. Logic said my corporate duties trumped any experiment in working on the sales floor. "I'm up to my neck in budgets, and new bills come every day. You need me up here."

"Then split your time," Dad said as though he wasn't asking the impossible. "But I want you logging actual hours in the store. Part time or better, that's the deal."

His ridiculous stipulation mowed down my pride, then backed over it for good measure. How was this happening? I had the promotion of my life within my grasp, and I was being sent back down to the minor leagues. Or worse. Working the sales floor in the small Magnolia Ridge flagship store was more like being knocked down to bat boy.

"Just to confirm, you want me to work the sales floor, keep up with my regular tasks, and take time off. Do I have that right?"

He just blinked at me, unfazed by his preposterous demands.

"How about this," Mom said. "For the next four weeks, you put in the hours Dad's asking you to downstairs. When you're up here, treat your job like a regular employee would. No overtime, no weekends, no staying at your desk for twelve hours a day. Do what needs to be done, and go home."

Little did she realize that usually meant working overtime, weekends, and staying at my desk.

"And when those four weeks are up," Dad said, "as long as we're sufficiently satisfied, you'll be promoted to Irwin Outdoors' CFO. Do we have a deal?"

Becoming CFO was what I'd wanted ever since I'd finished my MBA. The reason I put in so many hours, the reason I triple-checked my work when twice would do. Was I really going to get this close and try to argue my way out of it?

I could handle four weeks on the sales floor if it meant I'd be CFO in the end.

"We have a deal."

eliza

THE MIDDLE-AGED WOMAN shifted one way then the other in front of the mirror as if preparing to strut her stuff on a runway. She'd been trying on rain jackets for the last twenty minutes, carefully examining her reflection in each one before discarding it for the next. I didn't like to bother customers who hadn't asked for help, but she clearly needed a little advice.

"Is there anything I can do to help you make your choice?" I asked.

"I'm going to move my daughter in to the University of Washington later this month and I need a good rain jacket while I'm there." She continued to twist in front of the mirror as if she might be able to see herself from all angles at once. "I can't decide which one is best."

I glanced over the selection of brightly colored jackets hanging haphazardly from the mirror. Her first problem? She'd pulled one of each rain jacket we carried. One thing I'd learned working here was too many choices breeds indecision, and she was riddled with it.

"There's no such thing as a bad choice here at Irwin's, but I can help you narrow down your options. These two," I said, pulling aside a couple of the hangers, "you won't need unless you expect to be out in hurricane-force winds and rain."

She laughed. "I've heard it rains a lot in Seattle, but probably not that much."

"And this one," I said, snagging another hanger. "It's designed to fit super snug to the body. That's great if you're exercising in the rain, but not necessary for normal activities."

The woman gave the jacket a dark look. "I didn't realize that."

I held up my picks. "Any of these three options would be good. If you want my advice, try on each one without worrying about how you look in the mirror. How it feels on your body when you move is important, too. My favorite rain jacket makes me look like a grape, but it keeps me snug and dry."

"Thank you, I'll try that."

I wandered away to let the woman try the jackets on in peace, adjusting stock while walking through the back clothing section, putting hangers in proper size order and refolding shirts strewn on top of their displays. Even if being at Irwin's again felt like moving back a space on the great *Sorry* board of my life, I did love the store. Open and bright, with light wood cubbies displaying everything from foldable walking sticks to water purifiers, it had a modern but still homey feel. Shopping at the much larger Irwin's in Austin was like walking through a cold and impersonal warehouse.

I noticed a man in the front of the store and headed his way. Shouldn't judge a book by its cover and all that, but this guy's suit said he probably wasn't a regular. The ones who weren't quite sure what they wanted always made things easier than the seasoned adventurers who felt the need to prove they knew more about Irwin's products than I did. Nothing like mansplaining to make a shift drag.

"Welcome to Irwin's."

The man turned around, and I sucked in a breath. Not just any man, this was Dean Irwin, the middle Irwin brother. All three worked for the store, and all three were delectable in their own way. Grant, the oldest, managed the Magnolia Ridge store. Tall and lean, with a responsible streak that rivaled either of my sisters', but tempered with a generosity that made him a great boss. Rhett, the youngest brother, did all the marketing and promotions. Shorter and stockier than the other two, with a bright smile that never left his face, he had the flirting skills of an overeager puppy.

Then we had Dean, the low-key hot accountant who took professionalism and icy stares to weapons-grade levels. A few years older than me, he had dark brown hair and gorgeous hazel eyes. Those always threw me off. Pale brown irises with a flare of green around the pupil I rarely got close enough to see, those beautiful eyes killed me. He could be high-key hot, except he kept his dress shirts buttoned all the way to the top. Nothing said starchy and joyless like buttoning your shirt all the way.

"Hello, Eliza." The small, weird smile that briefly crossed his face reminded me of my mom's expression whenever I changed out my hair colors. A little grimace of dissatisfaction I wasn't meant to see, covered up by a thin smile. "Back with us again."

I pushed my pink-highlighted ponytail over my shoulder and immediately scolded myself for it. I didn't need to hide from anyone, especially Dean Irwin. "It's an addiction. I keep coming back for more."

"It's good to know you think Irwin's is such a great place to work."

"Hey, you should see my blog."

He tilted his head toward me. "The pink is subtle."

Of course he'd seen it. Those stupid gorgeous eyes caught everything.

I flashed a prim smile. "It fits with my subdued personality."

His mouth twitched but no more. No full smile, no laughter. Typical somber Dean. Rolling my eyes probably would have earned me a scowl for my impropriety. He really needed pearls to clutch or something.

Luckily, Dean was rarely my problem for long.

"If you're here to see Grant, he's in the office."

Normally, Dean didn't do much in the store. As far as I knew, he stayed squirreled away in his office upstairs most days. Sometimes, I spotted him around town, but he always looked busy, as if perpetually on the clock. Probably had something to do with the suits, which should have tipped me off when I saw him across the store.

While the other Irwins kept to business casual with a healthy dose of sportswear, Dean wore dress shirts, slacks, and ties no matter the weather. I suspected he didn't want anyone to forget he was a big shot businessman. If that was his plan, it worked. Every time he walked through town, some middle-aged woman sighed over his MBA. *That man is going places.*

He didn't impress me so easily. Sometimes, I caught him watching me with a strange look on his face, like he'd tallied me up and found me lacking. Maybe I didn't go seeking his approval, but I resented his obvious scorn. I didn't quite know why—he wasn't exactly alone in his disapproval. Still, when he looked at me that way, I wanted to hold him down and tighten the tie on his throat until he begged for mercy.

He was looking at me that way now.

"Actually, I'm here for a Vireo 25," he said.

Okay, that was unexpected. He'd come here to *shop*?

"Do you want me to..." I gestured behind me to the backpack displays. Irwins didn't usually need customer assistance when they came into the store, but Dean wasn't your average Irwin.

He raised his eyebrows as though the answer should have been obvious. It wasn't.

I guess we were really doing this. "Follow me, then."

I led him to the backpacks and pointed out the pricey one he wanted. "It has padded straps and a soft inner frame, with plenty of organization pockets inside, and four pockets on the outside. It also has an integrated rain cover and comes in three colors. We're out of the red right now, but we can order it for you."

Not that Dean was a *red* kind of guy. He leaned more toward colors like soul-sucking gray and bummer beige.

"You know a lot about it."

"That's my job." I'd probably gone overkill with the sales spiel, though. He had to know more about the products they sold than I did. "Do you want to try it on?"

"Sure."

I loosened the straps on one of the packs to fit Dean's big shoulders while he slipped off his suit jacket. He was tall, a feature I liked when scoping out eye candy, but on a man as off-putting as Dean, his height just made him look like a grizzly stuffed in a suit. Standing so near him fired up my nerves, a strange, tingling sensation coiling higher and higher through my ribcage. If Dean was a grizzly, I was definitely prey.

That thought barely swirled through my brain before I ushered it out again. To heck with that. I might not be an executive, but that didn't make me salmon. Or whatever grizzlies ate. I stood straighter, silently chastising myself for letting him get to me.

Even though I always did.

He slipped his arms into the pack and let it hang loosely on his back. "This feels pretty good."

"You need to adjust the straps." I stepped closer and tugged each of the straps down snug. I kept my fingers moving so I wouldn't accidentally touch him, and I refused to make eye contact. Against my will, I had to admit he smelled good. Very non-grizzly-like. The warm, fresh scent of some expensive cologne hovered around him. I knew it was expensive because being this close to him didn't make my eyes water. The smell only made me want to get closer.

Ha, no. This was as close as I would ever get to Dean Irwin.

I took a step back and glanced him over. He still looked slightly awkward and out of place, but probably because he was wearing a suit with a hiking backpack in place of the blazer. "How does it feel?"

"Comfortable."

He didn't look or sound especially comfortable but when did he ever? "The pack's empty. We have a twenty-five-pound filler to give you an idea of an average load for this size bag."

"Then fill away."

I hefted the weighted bundle out of its bin. He slipped the pack off, I shoved the bundle into it, and he put the backpack on again. He didn't seem to notice the difference in weight as he walked around a few displays to get a feel for it. He ran his hands over the straps like a kid who couldn't stop touching a new toy. It was almost cute.

No. Not cute. That was salmon talk.

"This is good. I like it. I should get this."

I nodded without expression. Vireos were crazy expensive, and Irwin's commission was pretty good. If this were a real sale, that extra money would pay for soap supplies, groceries, maybe even a dinner out. Since Dean was basically an owner of the company, I wouldn't get a commission. He'd buy it with his discount or, who knows, comp it and walk right out the door with it.

"Dean, what are you doing here? I told you I have an appointment at one." Grant strode across the sales floor to stand beside his brother, two sides of the same gorgeous coin—one a smiling Patagonia model, the other a gloomy J. Crew ad.

Dean slipped out of the backpack and hung it on the rack still weighted down. On autopilot, I pulled the weight from the pack, stowed it where it belonged, and straightened out the display.

"You said you wanted me here at one." Dean pulled out his cell phone, called something up, and turned the screen to Grant.

Grant grimaced. "Fine. I screwed up. I have to go out for an hour or two, I can't get out of it."

Dean's shoulders eased down a touch, and he seemed to relax for the first time since he'd walked through the door. To be fair, I didn't know what Dean actually looked like when he was relaxed, but he looked less constipated, and that was a start.

"No problem. I can come back later. How about tomorrow?"

"No, you're here now. You might as well get your time in, right?" Grant grinned over something, and I had the weirdest feeling I wouldn't like whatever he said next. "Eliza can show you around."

Dean turned to me as though surprised I was still here. Oh, how I wanted to tighten that tie.

"I can show Dean around what?"

"The store." Grant paused, his eyes drifting from me to his brother. "Dean is going to help us out on the sales floor for a while since we're short-staffed. Do you mind giving him a tour, getting him set up with a vest, basic stuff?"

"I don't mind."

I *so* minded. Being alone with Dean Irwin featured rather prominently on my short-list of Things to Avoid at All Costs.

Historically, Dean and I didn't get on well. Technically, he was pretty high up there in the Irwin's chain of command, but nothing about our rapport was especially professional. Our interactions in the store didn't deviate much from his snappy assessments of my job skills and/or attire, followed by my sassy, inane retorts about his spreadsheets. We banter a little, he glowers until his eyes glow red, and I glory in those silent wins. The pattern goes on like that until I get bored of retail and take a different job, only to return again months later with my tail between my legs. The circle of life.

Outside of Irwin's, I didn't know much about him. What did he do? Where did he go? Did he apply product to his hair or was it naturally that thick and wavy? I had no leads.

Grant grinned again. "Treat Dean like any other trainee on their first day. Pretend he doesn't know anything about what we sell."

Dean's withering look would have made another man's knees quake, but Grant just laughed it off.

"I have to run, but it's going to be great. You're going to do fine, don't worry."

I couldn't tell if Grant's reassurance was for me or for Dean. He gave us each one last glance before he took off out the door.

I turned stony eyes on Dean. "You're looking for a Vireo, huh?"

He almost looked chastened. Almost. "I lost my train of thought."

"Really."

He blinked as if conveying important information in code. Sometimes, we had whole conversations where all he did was blink condescendingly. Frankly, I preferred it when he gave voice to his patronizing. Hard for me to come up with a sassy comeback to a blink.

"I was distracted."

Right. I didn't buy that one bit. Dean was the least-distractible guy in Magnolia Ridge. He probably passed dogs on the sidewalk without petting them, the monster.

"So," I prompted, "you're going to try your hand at sales."

"Just until Grant can hire a couple more people."

"That sounds...nice."

His brothers spent loads of time in the store, and even Nathaniel and Patricia sometimes popped in to answer questions and chat with customers, like a benevolent king and queen communing with their subjects. But I couldn't imagine someone less suited to customer service than Dean. Sure, he had brains, and confidence wasn't a problem, but he could also be blunt and, like now, rarely smiled. Those traits never made for a winning combo on the sales floor.

"It is nice."

He tried for a smile, but it had no warmth to it. It reminded me of the way my boss at my sole corporate job after college used to smile at her underlings. Indulgent but fake, as if she hadn't quite heard what I'd said.

Out of the corner of my eye, I saw the woman with all the rain jackets make a beeline for the registers. "Excuse me a minute."

I walked across the store, leaving Dean with his false smiles and fancy outfit behind. Coming back to Irwin's should have been easy and low-stress, but I hadn't factored in working with Dean. He was supposed to stay up in corporate, like usual. Hopefully, Grant would hire a new crew on lickety-split, and I would be free of Mr. Morose.

"Did you find something to keep you dry in Seattle?"

The woman laid the jacket across the counter. "I did just what you told me. I tried it on without looking at it. This one was the most comfortable, *and* I like how it looks."

"I bet the blue looks great on you." I rang up the sale and

put the jacket into her reusable tote. "Thank you for shopping at Irwin's."

As soon as she left, I turned to find Dean closer than I expected, watching me like he was getting ready to write a performance evaluation.

"You're good with the customers."

His unconcealed surprise turned a perfectly fine compliment into something rude.

"Well, I am a nice person." I laid on more than a touch of sarcasm.

Dean didn't seem to find the remark as cutting as I'd intended it. His eyes traveled over me as if *nice* wasn't quite the right word. My back stiffened, and I glanced down at my outfit —jeans, a neon pink camp shirt that matched my highlights, and hiking boots. The ensemble proved way too warm for our sweltering fall weather, but well within the confines of business casual. His gaze skimmed to my hair again, and I pushed it back over my shoulder.

Standing in front of Dean in his pressed shirt and shiny shoes, I looked like a sloppy soccer mom in comparison. I had nice clothes, but they were better suited to going out with friends than impressing someone at work. Not that I believed I could ever impress *this* particular someone. I dressed more or less like Grant did, and he'd never asked me to wear something different.

"There's nothing wrong with what I'm wearing." As though telling him that would stop the inspection.

"I never said there was."

No, but an unimpressed once-over was worth a thousand words.

Shaking off his easy dismissal of me in true Taylor Swift fashion, I spun on my heel.

"We should get you a vest. Come with me."

I took a quick look around for customers and led him across the store and through the stock room into the back office. Pulling open the closet full of dark green Irwin vests, I tossed him one. He hung up his suit jacket before shrugging into his vest and buttoning it to the top, of course.

Instead of helping him fit in, it only made him look even more out of place. You can take the man out of the suit, but you can't take the suit out of the man.

No, wait. *Not* where my thoughts needed to go.

Ignoring my dumb brain, I got out the temporary name tags, stickers, and a Sharpie. "Put your name on there."

He wrote *Dean* in the neatest script I'd ever seen. Pinning the name tag onto his vest, he managed to get it perfectly straight on the first try. He probably ironed his underwear, too.

And now I'm thinking about Dean's underwear. Well done.

"Look at you. You're officially a sales associate." I slathered on the fake cheer extra thick.

His mouth pulled down at the edges, apparently less than thrilled with the title. I couldn't really blame him, since I wasn't all that excited to be a sales associate right now, either. Still, he'd volunteered. Probably.

"I'm a little confused why you're down here." In all the time I'd worked at Irwin's, Dean had never taken a shift on the sales floor. True, he'd been away at college and grad school most of the time I'd originally been on staff, but in the years he'd been back, I'd never witnessed it.

"Grant said he needed the help."

"Ah. So he called in the big boss." I gave him a finger gun because I'd apparently become a twelve-year-old boy. He lifted an eyebrow.

Moving on.

"What happens with all the spreadsheet stuff upstairs while you're down here?"

"The spreadsheets will be fine."

I nodded as though something had clicked into place. "So you're saying your job's unnecessary. Interesting."

His mouth twisted, as if maybe holding back a smile. He did that a lot around me. It was either the most he allowed himself to enjoy life, or his default look of reproach. Probably a two birds-one stone situation.

"I have to find a way to do both."

I frowned at his matter-of-fact attitude. "You have to do your corporate job and retail, too? That sounds like a lot. Don't you sleep?"

"Are you worried about me, Eliza?"

His voice curled until it sounded almost teasing. I refused to be fooled. Dean was not a teasing sort of man. Antagonizing yes, but teasing implied humor and affection. Those didn't really seem in line with Dean Irwin. Not when it came to me, anyway.

My ponytail swung in an arc as I turned my back on him. "It will pass."

I gave him a quick and dirty tour of the store, pointing out the main sections. Camp gear, clothing, shoes, accessories. Irwin's stores' bigger branches catered to a wider variety of activities, but the flagship stayed with the basics. I hooked a thumb at the backpacks as we went by. "You know where the Vireos are."

He must already know what they carried in his family's stores, but Grant had told me to give him a tour like he was a new employee, so that's what I would do, complete with introductory speech. His gaze darkened as I really rubbed in the newbie treatment. Typically, I found myself on the receiving end of Dean's condescension, so it was kind of a power trip to give a little back.

"Here at Irwin's, we put our customers first. You might be

the outdoors expert—" I glanced him over, unsure he qualified. "But first and foremost, we're here to serve our customers."

"That doesn't sound rehearsed at all."

"I've mentored my fair share of trainees."

That frown reappeared. Obviously, Mr. Top Button saw this job as a step down from whatever he did upstairs. Okay, it definitely was a step down from corporate, but he didn't have to act so sullen about it. We were in the same boat now.

Although to be fair, I'd never had a *step up* job yet.

"How long have you worked here?" he asked.

"A week."

"I mean cumulatively."

I pulled my bottom lip against my teeth, pushing the months together in my mind. "A couple of years, maybe. I'd have to write it all down."

"But you never decided to stay."

"There are a lot of fascinating jobs out there."

"And you intend to try them all."

He looked at me like I had the word *Failure* tattooed across my forehead. I fought the impulse to defend myself and explain away every job I'd quit or lost. He didn't seem like he'd be all that sympathetic to my story, anyway.

"How long did it take you to find your way around the store the first time you worked here?" he asked.

"In high school? I don't know, probably a couple of weeks."

His expression brightened just noticeably. "That doesn't sound so bad."

"There's a lot to learn but you seem like a smart guy, I'm sure you'll catch on." I flashed a saccharine smile. "Eventually."

dean

I WASN'T sure I could tolerate four weeks on the sales floor if it meant Eliza Webb giving me the Sass Queen treatment the whole time. I thrived on orderly work environments based on structure and control. Eliza was the least controlled woman I'd ever met. Her boldness got to me until I wanted to provoke her just to see what she'd say in return. I wasn't proud of it.

I wasn't stopping, either, but I wasn't proud.

Whenever she came on staff, my visits to the store were punctuated by her flip comments pointing out how stiff and unappealing she found me. Somehow, that hadn't stopped me from walking through the doors to find out what she'd have to say. I'd come downstairs, shake the hornets' nest, endure whatever stings she saw fit to throw my way, and go back to my office. I didn't like the masochism this fascination implied, but I hadn't managed to keep away, either.

Again, not proud of it.

I hovered at the edge of the store as she rang up a customer's hiking poles. As much as she seemed to enjoy being mouthy with me, that didn't carry over to the customers. Her edgy appearance wasn't very customer-friendly, but I couldn't fault her demeanor. Professional, courteous, and kind, she smiled at everyone who walked through the doors like they'd made her day just by existing. She could be wholly charming, but that charm had never extended to me.

Being the exception to her rule irritated like an itch in the center of my back. Impossible to ignore, but I couldn't do anything about it, either.

"Excuse me, where are your headlamps?"

I glanced between the scowling man standing in front of me and Eliza, who chatted with the woman buying poles at the registers. I had two choices here. I could ask for Eliza's help, or I could handle this myself. Interrupting her to ask where headlamps were would be slightly ridiculous, given the size of the store. Based on her tour, the headlamps should be with the camping gear.

"Right this way." I took the man to the camp displays, scanning shelves on the way. I passed bins full of first aid kits, bear spray, and fire starters. Crates crammed with cookware, stoves, and tiny bottles of propane. I stopped at the front window crowded with books, technical clothing, and sleeping bags, but still no luck.

"I think they're over here." I walked to the other side of the camp area, heat crawling up my neck with every step. How hard could it be to find headlamps? The first thing I was asked to do at my new "job" and I couldn't even do that?

"I could have searched the store on my own," the man said, sounding as frustrated as I felt. "I might as well go to Sport Outlet for all this hassle."

"Sport Outlet?" I spun to face him, the calming mantra I needed nowhere to be found. "With their shoddy knock-offs? Why don't you just throw your money away?"

"I'm sorry, sir." Eliza materialized between us like a retail angel, complete with beatific smile. "Dean is a trainee, it's his first day here with us. What can I help you find?"

The man glared at me. "Headlamps." He said the word like he'd rather be cussing me out.

"Of course, they're right here." She grabbed my arm and pulled me three feet to the left.

I turned my head to see a rack of headlamps right where I'd been standing. *Dammit.* Could I have looked more ignorant?

"Was there a particular one you wanted?" Eliza asked.

She and the customer talked headlamp specs while I silently fumed at getting called out for being a trainee. A CPA with an MBA and eight years in finance, now I was being treated like I couldn't find my butt with both hands. This whole experience was beneath me. Was this really what my father wanted me to do for the next month? Most CFOs didn't work their way up from the ground floor. My time would be better spent doing literally anything else for the company.

Eliza chatted away, but I wasn't sure she realized she still held onto my bicep. Her hand on my arm proved oddly comforting, like she was siphoning off my frustration. She seemed to be doing the same thing to the customer, soothing him in a soft voice as she discussed the merits of one headlamp over another.

"I'll take this one," the man finally said. His scowl had faded until he looked almost pleasant.

How did she do that? The guy had been agitated from the moment he first spoke to me, yet she'd not only appeased him, but reassured him enough he wanted to spend money. Left to fend for myself, I would have made the guy storm off to leave an angry one-star review.

Eliza let go of my arm, taking all the warmth that had been building inside me with her. Against my will, I missed that warmth.

I hung back and watched while she rang up the sale. The

man smiled at her when he walked away with his purchase, but he cast a contemptuous glare at me, as if I'd screwed him over on purpose.

Once he'd gone, Eliza sauntered up and leaned a hip against a wooden display case full of sleeping bags, her eyes glinting up at me. "Well. That was not excellent."

Her remark settled over me like an ill-fitting suit, and I frowned down at her. I wasn't used to floundering, especially not while a woman like Eliza looked on. Read: a woman who would notice and comment on that floundering without restraint.

"Like you said, it's my first day."

"Yeah, but haven't you worked in the store before?"

Admitting the truth would only add to my discomfort. "I haven't logged the kind of time you have."

Her mouth curled into the smallest smirk. "You probably haven't heard, but one of the first rules is, don't fight with the customer."

"I wasn't fighting."

"Oh, I saw it. That was your version of fighting."

An insult hid in there somewhere, but contesting it could only prove her point.

"It's perfectly fine to say you don't know where something is, or you need to get someone else. You can always use *Hey, it's my first day* for the first week. Or in your case, maybe a month."

"Funny." At least I wouldn't have to stay down here any longer than that. From where I stood, it would be a rough four weeks.

She looked me up and down, openly assessing me. "You're nothing like your brothers, you know that?"

I clenched my jaw, well aware of my outsider status in the family. "Why do you say that?"

Her saucy little shrug needled me, just one in a long line of quirks seemingly designed to annoy.

"They've just got a definite vibe, and you don't fit in with that."

She made a circuit of the store and I followed, unable to let the remark go. "What vibe do my brothers have?"

As if I didn't know. Women adored my brothers and weren't afraid to show it. Grant and Rhett's good looks and charisma had made them magnets for women since our teens. In adulthood, their varied prowess in extreme sports turned their charm up to full blast. Me—not so much. Increasing profit margins by four percent didn't turn anybody on. I wasn't unattractive, but I bore no delusions my skills with accounts matched my brothers' reputations.

"They're more laid back. Relaxed. People-person...people." Eliza touched things as she walked, her fingers lightly trailing clothes, tapping book spines, shifting bags. Maybe she was mentally tallying inventory.

Or maybe she was just very tactile.

That thought should not make my chest heat the way it did. She was my employee.

Well, technically she wasn't *my* employee. Even if I were CFO, I wouldn't be her boss. Still, a high-level corporate officer and a sales associate added up to a sketchy combination. She didn't often stick around long. Maybe, if we ever spoke outside of this store, we could actually get to know each other...

I tossed that thought away. None of that mattered, because this conversation made it clear she'd never entertain any of the ideas trying to catch hold in my mind.

"I'm a people person." A ridiculous thing for me to say after what she'd just witnessed, but it popped out anyway.

"Ha. No."

One customer interaction went down in flames and she

knew everything about me? To be fair, it wouldn't take much observation for anyone to come to the same conclusion, but I didn't like her marking me down so fast. Or, more likely, yet again. "What's your definition of people person then?"

Her casual shrug wormed straight under my skin. "Someone who is friendly, outgoing, easy to talk to. Someone who doesn't pick fights with grouchy customers. Someone who doesn't stare at other people like he's looking for reasons to fire them."

"I don't have the authority to fire you."

She smiled in scathing sarcasm. "That's super comforting."

"I might send you to an HR seminar about non-antagonistic methods of interacting with coworkers."

"I was doing just fine before you showed up. Maybe the problem isn't with me." Her tone had more bite to it than the friendly one she'd been doling out to customers.

"Where else have you worked that you honed this stellar attitude?"

"Let's see, I worked in communications, I did promotions for a real estate developer, I was a bartender at the Broken Hammer." She ticked off the jobs on her fingers. "I've been a web content manager, a vet tech, a truck dispatcher, and a receptionist at a day spa."

I opened my mouth but shut it again. I stared, trying to figure out how she could have had so many jobs in what couldn't possibly have been many years. I knew she hadn't yet settled on anything like a career, but I hadn't realized just how often she'd moved around. It didn't say much about her loyalty or dedication if she'd quit all those jobs. Worse, she might have been fired from some of them.

"Currently, I make and sell soap, but it's, uh…" She scrunched her nose. "It's complicated."

"It sounds that way. I guess you never finished your degree."

"What? Why would you say that?" All her easy charm disintegrated as she scowled up at me. "I have a Liberal Arts degree, not that it's your business."

"How did you lose all those jobs in four or five years?"

I recognized my error too late. Her scowl turned ferocious. If I had to guess, the only thing saving me from a string of profanities was Grant walking through the door. She broke her stare down and stepped away, crossing her arms over her chest like she needed to stop herself from taking a swing at me.

Grant walked over, blissfully unaware of the tension swirling around us. "Did Eliza get you settled in?"

She wiped her expression clean of the murderous glare she'd been using on me, but hints of a frown lingered around her mouth. I tried for a casual smile but pretty assuredly failed.

Grant slowly looked between the two of us, understanding dawning, before settling an incredulous gaze on me. "Everything good here?"

Polite lies ran through my head, but Eliza answered first.

"We're good. He's had a tour of the store, he's got his vest, and he even helped his first customer." She smiled as if she were oh so proud of me.

"That sounds...good." He didn't sound especially convinced.

"I think Dean's going to do great here," she said. "Really, really great."

"Fantastic." Grant watched me, clearly dreading whatever my response would be.

"Well, I am a people person," I said.

Eliza laughed but covered it up with a cough. "It's time for me to clock out, if that's okay, Grant."

"Sure thing."

"It's going to be great working with you, Dean. Really

great." She cast a sweet, patronizing smile my way before walking off toward the back office.

I had the crystal-clear realization we were having a Princess Bride moment, except when Eliza said *Really great*, what she actually meant was *Screw you*.

"Seriously?" Grant hissed at me. "You're having problems with *Eliza*?"

"This isn't my fault."

"If you're having issues with Eliza, it is one hundred percent your fault. I expected you to be bad with customers, that's a given, but I thought you were past fighting with coworkers."

"We're not fighting—" I shut my mouth as Eliza walked back out and through the store.

"See you tomorrow."

She waved goodbye to Grant, and for half a second as she turned away, I got the full force of her true, open smile. When she wasn't glaring like she wanted to strangle me, Eliza was beautiful. I'd caught fragments of that free-spirited beauty from a distance in town, but seeing it up close knocked the feet out from under me.

As soon as she'd gone, Grant turned his own glare on me. "Looks like you're doing great down here so far."

I ran a hand over the back of my neck. "It's my first day. Eliza and I just got off on the wrong foot. We'll be fine."

"You'd better be. I'm relying on her for backup. If you make her quit, I will punch you, honest to God."

"I'm not going to make her quit." As though I had any power over Eliza Webb.

"I'm serious. If she complains about you even once, I will send you back upstairs, screw Dad's deal."

Pretty sure he didn't have that kind of authority, but I didn't need to argue and make the situation even worse. "Understood."

He glanced me over. "You look ridiculous. Did you pick out the biggest vest you could find?"

I tugged at the billowy green vest all Irwin's sales associates wore. "Eliza picked it out."

His mouth twisted into a smile. "I like her even more."

I unbuttoned the vest and pulled it off.

"So how far are we taking this?" he asked. "Are you getting associate pay for the month? Do I need to set you up with a commission account?"

"Don't do that, I don't need to earn commission." Puzzle pieces clicked together, and I blew out a breath. *Commission.*

I'd inadvertently dangled a hefty commission in front of Eliza, only to snatch it away. No wonder she'd been so pissed with me from the get-go. Following that up with my tussle with the headlamp guy and my thoughtless comment about her work history had probably cemented her opinion of me as a jackass, if she'd ever thought me anything else.

All in all, I was off to a banner start as an Irwin's sales associate.

FIVE

eliza

"YOUR APARTMENT always smells so good. Whatever you're making now, I need a bar when you're done."

Harper sprawled across my couch, a wine glass tilting precariously in one hand. She'd dropped in after work with containers of Chinese food and a bottle of wine. I wasn't anybody's charity case, but I could make exceptions now and then. Anyhow, turning her away would have been rude.

We'd already demolished the noodles, and Harper was getting lightly buzzed while I whipped up a batch of soap. Containers of coconut oil and shea butter, bottles of essential oils and colorants piled up in my tiny kitchen, covering every inch of counter space. I blended the lye solution into the melted oils, stirring and mixing while waiting for the magical moment the concoction turned into soap.

Most of Harper's visits played out this way—she hung around and watched while I worked. If it bothered her, she never said. I figured sometimes she just needed to socialize with people under a hundred years old.

"This one's lavender and lemon," I told her. "Feel free to order a bar from my website."

Dear God, someone needed to.

"How is the web commerce going?"

I made a face. Why did every conversation have to weave through a minefield of humiliation? "My website exists. That is an unequivocal fact."

"And sales?" she pressed.

"Not a problem at the moment." At least the website didn't cost much, but I couldn't exactly afford to throw money around. I needed to find a way to make my website stand out but I hadn't landed on it yet. The result? A pretty website with zero sales. "Think I can get in on Siesta Village's fall craft fair?"

"You have to be a resident to get a booth. And for the millionth time, it's *Fiesta* Village."

"I'm not totally convinced that it is. They've been pretty snoozy whenever I've stopped by."

They were sweethearts over there at the retirement center, though, and they loved Harper to pieces. Every holiday, she had at least thirty grandmas shower her with cards and baked goods.

"What if I sleep on a couch in the lobby for a month, do you think that would qualify me for the craft fair?"

"It would qualify you for something." She bounced a foot in time to the women of country music mix playing on her phone. "Can't you get in on another farmers market?"

"I'm already doing the two in town. I'd have to go all the way up to Waco to find a market on a different day, and that's Joanna Gaines territory."

"You could hire somebody to sell them for you. You have plenty." She gestured at the three metal shelving units that lined my small living room. Soap bars crowded every shelf, all labeled with their scent and the date they'd been poured. At this point, my apartment was approximately seventy percent soap.

"Not all of them are ready to sell yet. And I don't really think I'm at the *hire somebody* stage of my business." Unless I could find someone willing to be paid in the sarcastic memes I hoarded on my phone, which seemed like a long shot.

"Are you trying to get into more stores?"

My shoulders slumped, and I slowed my stirring. "Not yet."

After things with Countryside fell apart a couple of weeks ago, I hadn't worked up the courage to try again. I had all my samples and scent lists ready—I just hadn't managed to get them out the door. The only store I'd successfully convinced to stock my soap so far was Fine & Dandy, the home decor shop owned by my cousin June's step-mother-to-be. The two worked together, June doing interior decorating and Marilyn selling all kinds of fancy throw blankets and table lamps I couldn't afford. Having my soap on display in there gave me a thrill, but I suspected they'd mostly agreed to it because I'm family.

"So what's next?" Harper asked.

"Next," I said, kicking away the melancholy, "you need to take another batch of my business cards and spread them around to everyone you rub up on at work."

"You make my job sound so glamorous."

"They're the perfect market, I just need to find a way in."

"That's literally why they have the No Soliciting sign."

"I'm not a solicitor, I'm just a concerned citizen who wants to be sure the hygiene situation over there is top-notch."

"At a price," she snorted.

"Details." I kept my eyes on the soap as it whirled in the big bucket, pausing now and then to check the consistency. If I got distracted and waited too long to pour it, I could ruin five pounds of soap all at once—ask me how I know. I couldn't risk throwing soap in the trash again, hence the need to be careful.

"Hey, I saw that guy you told us about at dinner the other

night. The motorcycle guy? I thought you made him up, but there he was, walking into the diner in all his bearded glory. Unless *I* imagined him."

"Oh, he's real all right." I'd seen him a few times around town now, with his bulging, tatted-up biceps and skin-tight jeans. Magnolia Ridge was small enough that when a man like that moved in, people noticed. And in his case, *all* the women noticed. "I'm guessing you didn't stop to talk to him."

"Um, no thanks to that. I've got enough on my plate without worrying about a biker."

"What exactly do you have on your plate? Aside from spending your days with your buddies at the old folks' home, this is what you do." I gestured around the apartment with my soapy spatula. "You hang out here and mooch off my soap fumes."

"I do love the fumes."

Finally satisfied with the texture in the bucket, I poured the thickened soap into waiting molds and decorated the tops with the back of a spoon. I made swirls and gentle waves until they looked just right, then put the lids on the molds and heaved them onto a shelf. They would have to sit for two days before I could cut them, and then the bars would need to cure for over a month before I could sell them. The one big drawback to making cold process soap was how long it took before they were ready to sell.

That, and trying to find people willing to actually buy them with any regularity.

"Motorcycle Guy hangs out at the diner, huh? I might have to go down there and introduce myself." I winked at my sister.

Her sarcastic laugh held a challenge. "You will do no such thing."

I shot her a glare. "I'm a big girl. You can't stop me."

"Oh, I won't stop you. But you'll never go down there to talk to him. I've got your number."

I didn't like the sound of that. I threw my bowl and spatula into the kitchen sink and wiped off my hands. "What do you mean by that?"

"I mean you talk a big game, but that's all it is. Talk. There's always somebody you're threatening to throw yourself at, but you never do."

I scooted Harper's legs off the couch so I could sit down. "Maybe I throw myself at dozens of men I never tell you about."

"You don't."

"I've done things that would curl your hair."

She laughed again, and I was kind of starting to hate it. The fact that she was right just aggravated me even more.

"You're such a liar. When was your last date? Actual date, not sitting in the Broken Hammer watching guys play darts from a safe distance."

So I had some gaps in my dating history, big deal. A four-year gap seemed a little excessive at this point, but I'd made my peace with it.

I shrugged rather than give her the satisfaction of saying it out loud. She knew the answer anyway, and I didn't have the energy to keep up the attitude. This was the third batch of soap I'd made for the night. Add my day at Irwin's into the mix and I'd lost my mojo.

"We're quite the pair," Harper said. "Me with my ladies and gents at the retirement home, you with your soaps. Mom's going to have a breakdown if she can't get one of us paired off soon. She's addicted to weddings now, all it took was the one."

Didn't I know it. My stomach curdled as I thought about her increasingly unsuitable suggestions for who I might match up with. Matching up wasn't in my game plan. That was the way of betrayal and heartbreak. Ogling hot guys I would never talk to? Now that was more my department.

But at this point in the night, I didn't have the mental band-width to discuss either my intentional lack of a love life, or our mother's desperate hope another wedding might be on the horizon for one of us.

"Don't forget, I do more than just soaps. I also sell camping gear and deal with stuck up businessmen." Just thinking about the snooty attitude he'd given me this afternoon made my pulse kick up.

Harper stretched out to put her feet on the coffee table. "Who's stuck up?"

"Dean Irwin. He's working in the store for some reason."

"That's weird. I thought he did the finances."

"He does, but I guess he's going to help out until Grant gets a full crew back."

She took another swallow of wine. "That's nice of him."

"So you would think. He doesn't really seem like he's doing it out of the kindness of his heart. He acted more like he was there on court orders." His family owned the whole chain, but from his attitude, you'd think spending time in the store was a punishment.

Or maybe spending time with *me* was the punishment.

"I think we would have heard about it if Dean Irwin had been arrested."

"Their family would hush it up. He's probably the head of some bootleg bookkeeping software cartel. It's always the ones you least suspect."

She rolled her eyes. "It really isn't."

"My question is, why didn't Rhett offer to help out instead? He's a natural with people. Not like Mr. Surly Pants."

"Do I have to add Rhett Irwin to the list of men you admire from afar?"

I ignored the jab. Rhett was adorable, but he'd dated half the girls in my high school class. Hard pass. "All I'm saying is, if you put all the Irwins together in a room, aside from similar hairlines and shoulders for days, you would never know Dean was related to the rest of them."

"Every family has their weirdo. You're ours."

"No kidding."

I knew Harper meant it as a joke, but an ache twisted somewhere deep in my chest anyway. *The family screw up.* Leaning into that role hadn't made it hurt any less. Someday, I would get myself together. I just kept choosing the wrong thing to hang my hopes on, that was all. I wouldn't add Soap Queen to that list of failed ventures.

"Dean's got this whole *better than you* attitude that just makes me want to..." I mimed throttling someone. "He reminds me of Carter."

I didn't like to bring up that miserable wound, but today's interactions with Dean had picked at the scab. *Carter.* Just thinking his name still turned my stomach. I'd been so naive. So sure I knew what I was doing. But his big smiles and showy attention had drawn me in like a dummy anyway. When he stabbed me in the back and stole my work, I'd drawn my lines.

No dating coworkers.

No dating suits.

No dating, period.

"Dean's not that bad," Harper said, proving just how much she'd been drinking.

I made a sound of disgust. "Fancy suit, big-shot businessman, out to get me. I'd say they're pretty close."

Carter had gone all-in with the nice-guy routine, where Dean didn't try to hide his condescension, but I still saw the similarities.

"Out to get you?" Harper nudged me with her shoulder. "Since when has Dean Irwin been out to get you?"

"Since we started working together this afternoon."

"Eliza, not everyone who wears a suit is a jerk."

"Excuse me, Carter was not a jerk. He was a manipulative, job-stealing, heartbreaking jerkface."

"I think I'm falling in love with you."

That stupid line, with the big heart-eyes and the fake tender voice, was all it took. My tough-girl attitude had dissolved, I'd taken his bait, and had given him everything he wanted. Only later had I realized it'd all been fake. I still hated him for what he'd done, but sometimes, I hated myself more for believing his empty words.

"At the risk of sounding like Mom, there are nice guys out there."

I didn't want nice. Polite smiles and affected interest were easy to fake. I wanted good—good intentions, good actions, good heart. But *good* was a lot harder to find than *nice*. And after Carter, I'd basically stopped looking.

"Do not start quoting Mom. She still believes in love at first sight." I downed the last of Harper's wine. "Is hate at first sight a thing?"

"It definitely is at Siesta Village." She smacked me on the arm. "Now you've got *me* doing it."

I cackled and did a victory shimmy at her little mistake. One point for me.

"New residents move in, and they automatically have friends *and* enemies. It's so weird."

"That's what Dean and I are. Automatic enemies."

Harper lifted her eyebrows. "How long are you going to be working together?"

I sighed against the couch. "For the foreseeable future. At least I've still got my Dean-free farmers markets to look forward to. If he opens a stall next to mine selling bespoke financial reports, I'm out."

dean

WHEN I USED to envision how I'd be living at thirty-one, this wasn't it.

"This place is a sty."

I drank a beer while Rhett ate ramen noodles on the couch as if he were making one of those speed-eating videos. The room was littered with various pieces of detritus he couldn't trouble himself to pick up and put away, or throw out.

Usually, I did all the cleaning, but a week ago, I'd started an experiment: I'd refrain from picking up after my brother to see how long it took him to realize he needed to do it himself. It had seemed genius at the time, an easy way to teach Rhett a lesson and lighten my load.

By this point, the experiment had only proven I'd been stupid to think he might notice the difference.

He slurped up a long noodle. "Don't tell me you're getting the chore chart out again."

That had been a pointless endeavor. He couldn't be bothered to see dirty dishes on the coffee table—he'd been completely oblivious to the chart.

"You're getting soup on your shirt."

He brushed at his T-shirt, spreading the stain. I didn't understand how he could live like this at twenty-nine. He excelled at his job, and was more or less responsible in all other ways, but at home, he turned into Jabba the Hutt, lazing on the couch covered in filth.

"How did your first day as a sales associate go? Did you threaten to punch anyone?"

I winced as the headlamp guy popped into my mind. One shift in and I already had a failure under my belt. That situation had only been saved by Eliza's quick thinking and ability to soothe an irate customer. And I was supposed to keep returning to the sales floor for the rest of the month? That had disaster written all over it as surely as the chore chart had.

I tried for a poker face and took a pull from my beer. "It went fine."

Rhett pointed at me as if I'd made a gory confession. "I saw that look. What happened?"

Abandoning the straight face, I gestured uselessly. "Some fool threatened to go to Sport Outlet."

"I guess that would do it."

"Eliza had to step in and calm us both down." The memory of her soft touch warmed me all over again. Probably not a place I should let my thoughts linger, considering her actual feelings for me leaned closer to ice cold.

Grant walked through the front door without a knock.

"Did I miss anything? If you already gave Rhett the play by play, just give me the highlight reel. I'm easy." He strode across the living room, brushed a granola bar wrapper off a chair, and sat down. "Well? I want to know what I missed this afternoon."

"I finished out my shift with you. What do you think you missed?"

Rhett stood with his empty ramen bowl in hand. "He got

mad at some guy who threatened to go to Sport Outlet. That's all he's admitted so far."

He disappeared in the kitchen. For a second, I ignored the humiliation of my brothers glorying over my new, diminished, work role, and simply stood in awe of Rhett thinking to put a dish in the sink. But when he came back, I saw my mistake. He'd only got up for more noodles.

He resumed his place on the couch, loaded a spoonful of ramen into his mouth, and made a spinning motion with his hands. "Spill the rest."

"We're not doing this." They'd already witnessed the demeaning meeting that necessitated this whole endeavor—they didn't need to hear about every mistake I made on the sales floor as a bonus. "Watch a football game or something."

"Look," Grant said. "I would love to sit at the registers and watch you flail all day, every day, for the next four weeks, but I have things going on. I need a recap."

"If you're looking for a detailed list of all my failures today, you'll have to ask Eliza."

From the way his eyebrows tugged down, that wasn't the right way to steer the conversation.

"I still can't get over you having issues with her."

"I maintain that's not on me."

"Eliza *Webb*?" Rhett said, as though we knew another Eliza. "Leave it to you to not get along with her."

"We got along fine." I willfully ignored her frustration with me at the end of the day, and the way she had needled me every chance she got. It wasn't outside the ordinary for us, so it hardly counted.

"I can see how you might not," Grant said, eyeing me a little too critically. "Eliza is outgoing and personable. You are more..."

I waited, both wanting and dreading to know how he would

end that sentence. At this point in my life, I'd heard it all. Demanding. Aloof. Unfeeling. And those were the nicer terms.

"Reserved," he finally finished. "And she's a lot more business-savvy than she lets on."

"What's she doing working retail, then?"

"When did you become such a snob? We all work retail."

Grant managed the Magnolia Ridge store, but he also acted as the General Manager of the whole chain, overseeing the daily operations of all eight branches. Only a matter of time before the company made him Chief Operations Officer. Rhett covered a shift in the store now and then, but he really worked his magic in marketing, and designed our website and social media presence, along with every scrap of promotional material Irwin's put out. Saying we all worked retail was a gross over-simplification, but splitting hairs would do me no favors.

"I'm not looking down on her, I'm curious. She's had a lot of jobs for someone so young, don't you think?"

Grant hitched a shoulder. "No more than the average college grad who's realized their degree hasn't prepared them to make actual money. Just because you figured out what you wanted to do with your life when you were in the womb doesn't mean everyone else has to."

"Point made." I still wasn't sure about all her job-hopping, but clearly, Grant disagreed.

"By the way, I'll be in and out of the store again tomorrow. Rhett and I have some appointments for the anniversary party."

Each of the branches had anniversary parties in the works to commemorate the day. Magnolia Ridge's celebration would be a little different, since this was where everything had started. Grant and Rhett had plenty to do organizing what would essentially be a block party. I didn't know what all they had planned beyond the invoices I'd already signed off on, but if Rhett had a hand in it, it would be memorable.

He raised a beer in toast. "Ain't no party like an Irwin's party."

"Will I be working with Eliza again?" The thought intrigued me more than was reasonable, considering she didn't like me, and seemed almost resentful of me and dismissive by turns.

"Part of the day, anyway. Is that going to be a problem?" The edge in Grant's voice said the answer had better be *No*.

"We'll be fine." My rosy prediction for our shift together was about as realistic as my chore chart had been. I finished the last of my beer and put the empty bottle in the glass recycling bin under the kitchen sink. "Are either of you going to help me out at Grandma Gloria's this weekend, or is that hopeless at this point?"

"I can't this weekend," Grant said. "I'll see if I can make time next week."

"The store's closed on Sundays," I pointed out.

"Corporate's closed all weekend, but that's never stopped you from going in. You think I don't have enough work to get on with?"

I raised a hand in surrender. No need to get into a battle about overtime. Nobody came out a winner in that fight.

"What a time for Grandma to move into the retirement center." Rhett set his dirty bowl on the coffee table and tossed his feet up on the couch. "She's got to empty her house the same month we're busy with the store anniversary."

"She didn't plan it," I said. "Fiesta Village has a wait list, and her number came up. If she doesn't move now, they'll stick her back at the bottom."

"I kind of hate to say goodbye to that old house," Grant said.

"So do I." As much time as my brothers and I had spent with our Grandma Gloria and Grandpa Connor growing up, I had fonder memories of their house than I did the one we'd lived in across town. Grandma's decision to move into the retirement center had been a long time coming, but even with that level of foresight, it still struck a nerve. Every now and then, shockwaves radiated out, surprising me all over again. "But the house is too much for her. Too many rooms and too much yard."

I'd been helping her with her yard ever since I came back to Magnolia Ridge after grad school. We had a standing Saturday appointment of lawn maintenance followed by dessert and coffee. Even with everything I did for her, she couldn't handle a house that size. Sometimes, I wished I could take the house myself, but without a family to fill the rooms, it would be just as absurd for me to live alone there as it was for Grandma.

"Let her move to the retirement center, she'll love it." Rhett wandered into the kitchen—without his dirty dish, of course. "She already knows practically everybody in there."

"The point is, she needs help sorting through her things and packing them up. I expect both of you to stop in and do your part."

"Why don't you make a sign-up sheet?" Rhett called. "Or a color-coded calendar."

"Don't joke, he'll do it," Grant muttered under his breath.

"If that's the only way for you two to get over to Grandma's this month, I will." Joke around all they liked, my calendars got the job done.

The chore charts were admittedly a bust.

"We're not going to stick you with everything over there, don't worry your pretty little head."

"I expect you to keep your word."

"And I expect you to keep your word about doing a good job in the store and getting along with Eliza." Grant's knowing look held both challenge and skepticism.

"I'm not going to have any problems working with Eliza Webb."

Though she might have problems working with me.

dean

"REALLY GREAT TO SEE YOU today, Dean."

Wow. Ten minutes into my shift and I already had a *Screw you* from Eliza. After the way yesterday had gone, I supposed it seemed fair.

"Good morning, Eliza." I smiled, but she didn't seem to notice. I ran a hand over my face to make sure the impulse had made it from my brain to my mouth.

"How did the rest of your first day go? Get into any fistfights over sleeping bags?"

Her light teasing and that saucy little eyebrow twitch shot adrenaline straight through me.

"I was perfectly behaved all afternoon."

Only because I'd shadowed Grant the rest of the day. I didn't offer to assist anyone, and had deferred to my brother when customers asked questions. I wasn't about to admit to Eliza I used her *It's my first day* line several times to great effect.

She looked me up and down. "I seriously doubt that."

"I can be good."

"Let's see just how good you can be," she said in a low voice.

I held my breath, unsure if I'd heard her correctly. We stood close enough I could smell the fresh, minty scent that floated around her, and my pulse kicked. It took me a second to realize she wasn't looking at me, her eyes on the door.

A woman had just walked in and was examining the miniature tent display on the wall. Eliza's challenge was of the work variety, not the more fun variety. Not that *fun* was remotely on the table with her.

"Why don't you take this customer?" Her smile was syrupy sweet, like she'd just offered me the last bite of dessert. "Since you're such a people person."

Incredible how one minute she could make my blood turn hot, and the next minute freeze it ice-cold again.

An excellent reminder I hadn't come down here to chat up Eliza Webb. I'd been sent to prove a point to my father, however asinine.

I walked past her to the woman examining camp stoves and dug down deep for something like geniality. "Good morning, welcome to Irwin's."

"Oh, thank goodness." A light of desperation shone in her eyes. "I hope you can help me."

That intro didn't instill me with confidence. Something along the lines of *I'm looking for a Vireo 25* would have been my top choice in customer interactions. At least I knew where those were.

"What can I do for you?"

"Well, my nephew asked for camping gear for his birthday." She watched me expectantly, and I knew I should probably say something here, but for the life of me, I didn't know what that was. Grant or Rhett would have half a dozen suggestions and twice as many stories to go along with them, but I had nothing.

It wasn't lost on me that *this* was the whole reason I'd been sent down here.

"What kind of camping does he do?"

"I know he mostly hikes in to campsites." She paused again as if this might have inspired me to a great suggestion. Since I'd never hiked in to a campsite myself, I was no closer to a magical gift idea than she was.

Still, I nodded and tried to connect the dots. "So, he's a backpacker."

"That's right, but I don't know what to get him."

I looked at the displays around us for a hint, and gestured to the purple nylon stretched above the camp chairs. "How about a hammock?"

She glanced up at it as if I'd pointed out a hanging bat. "Oh, I don't know about that."

"Maybe one of these?" I nodded at an array of bundles in a corner. Sleeping pads seemed appropriate for a backpacker.

She flinched as if I'd offered to demo one with her. "No, not that."

"What about trekking poles?" I grabbed the closest handle, but she was already shaking her head.

"I don't think so."

My frustration cranked higher with every dismissed suggestion. At this rate, I could offer her the whole store and still come up empty. "Is there anything else you can tell me to narrow it down a bit?"

"Well, he's twenty, if that helps."

"Why would that—?" I bit back the rest, taking a deep inhale instead. This was it—I was going to lose my mind. I would break right here in the store. Day two: aneurysm.

Eliza stepped up beside us. "How are you doing over here?"

The woman visibly relaxed as soon as Eliza swooped in to save the day. Probably her good-natured smile set her at ease. I couldn't blame her. Eliza's smile loosened something in my chest, too.

Wait—had I even smiled at the woman, or did I just barge

in with questions? I smiled now, but too little, too late. I'd been completely forgotten in favor of Eliza's glow.

"I'm looking for a present for my nephew," the woman told her.

"Would you like some suggestions, or do you want to browse on your own?"

She probably talked to people this way fifty times a day, but nothing in her mannerisms were fake or sarcastic. She was either an excellent actress or she was genuinely this friendly to everyone. From all I'd seen of her, I guessed she was genuinely this friendly. And yet, somehow, the two of us had never reached the same kind of easy affinity she had with total strangers.

That knowledge rankled, even if it made sense. Grant was right, we were nothing alike. We rubbed each other wrong, like two and two making five every time. Still. I wanted her to shine a little bit of that Eliza glow on me.

"I'd like some suggestions, please," the older woman said. "I don't camp myself, and I don't know what anything is."

"My favorite gift idea are these buffs." Eliza led her to the nearby display rack. "They can be worn over the face in the winter, or over the head in summer, and they come in a variety of colors and fun patterns."

The woman looked the buffs over, intrigued.

"Dean's favorite gift idea are headlamps," Eliza said without missing a beat. "If your nephew doesn't have one, they do come in handy."

The woman looked past me to the headlamps Eliza pointed out. "Oh, that's nice, too."

"And if you're still not sure, you can't go wrong with an Irwin's gift card."

"You know, I think I'll do that."

They walked off to the registers to complete the transaction.

I closed my eyes and prayed to the retail gods to give me strength. How was I supposed to learn how to help people who had no idea what they wanted? I couldn't read minds. And all the endless cheerfulness? Not my strong suit, either. I only had so much patience for hand-wringing and waffling.

I really wasn't cut out for this.

Eliza had the gift card rung up and the woman out the door again within minutes. She sidled up next to me, and I could tell from the sparkle in her eyes I was about to get an earful on my latest botched attempt at customer service.

"Wow," she said, a huge grin dancing across her face. "That was something else. You really went for it. You just dove right in with *hammock*."

I sighed, already exasperated by her triumph. "Don't."

"Never really pictured you as a hammock guy, but you learn something new every day."

"I said the first thing I saw." Not that that made anything better. I'd just proved yet again I was in over my head down here.

"I think hammocks are wildly uncomfortable, by the way, but whatever floats your boat."

"They don't float my—"

"The guy who invented the two-person hammock probably had a touch of insanity, but you do you."

Her teasing chipped away at my frustration, loosening the hold of my customer service-induced bad mood. I leveled her a hard look anyway. "We can stop talking about hammocks any time."

"If you want."

She eased up on the gloating face, and I almost missed it. Now there was a sign these two days on the sales floor were getting to me—was I actually enjoying Eliza's exultation at my expense?

"You know, most people don't need you to hold their hand through the store. When they're really out of their element, go for the gift card. Nine times out of ten, it's a hit."

I nodded, wishing I'd thought to bring a pad of paper and a pen. Keeping notes on tips like this would help make my weeks down here easier, but I had a feeling if I whipped out my phone to start a file right now, I'd never hear the end of it.

Her grin returned. I liked that way too much.

"Seriously, though, your people skills are kind of rusty."

And there went my almost-good mood. I frowned at her. "You're full of observations."

She held her hands up in innocence, but that grin held a devilish glint. "I call them like I see them."

"Are you going to finish rubbing it in any time soon, or will this go on for a while?"

"I'm good. For now." She sobered up a touch. "I know you're the spreadsheet guru upstairs, but it's a different game in retail. If you're planning to be down here for a while, it's a good idea to go through the store and really look at all the displays. Get a feel for where things are. The better you know the store, the easier it will be."

Her encouragement instantly brightened my mood, as if it really could be that easy. How? How did she do that?

She walked to the registers, and I told myself it was wrong to let my gaze travel over her body even as I did it. She had nice...pants. With effort, I put my eyes back in my skull and followed her advice.

I spent the morning making slow circuits around the store, mentally cataloguing product displays. Examining items up close I'd only read about in spec sheets and sales reports, I scoured packaging for information I might use when asked infuriatingly vague questions. Now and then, I subtly dodged customers, leaving them in Eliza's far more capable hands.

Even if becoming a touch more familiar with the store gave a small, probably misplaced confidence boost, I couldn't shake the indignation I had to do it at all. Was this really fair punishment for my poor interview skills? Or just another reminder of my even worse people skills?

"How's it going?" Grant asked after what must have been my tenth lap through the store.

"Good. I think I've got it."

"Sure you do. Are you actually helping customers or are you letting Eliza do it all?"

I looked over my shoulder to watch her chatting with a young woman. Talking up the merits of different types of hiking socks as if nothing could be more interesting, she laughed, and something jumped to life in my chest.

I turned back to Grant.

"I've helped some."

His gaze hardened. "You can't be down here if you're going to be completely useless."

"I'm touched by your confidence."

"Hey, I've fired trainees who did nothing but lurk in the shadows while everyone else worked. I'm not above kicking you out."

"I'm working on it."

He dropped his voice. "How are things with Eliza? Did you bury the hatchet?"

I turned to watch her again. What was it about her that left people so relaxed and at ease? And how could I get her to turn that charm on me? Her smile as she rang up the woman's purchase sent little whirls of awareness through me.

Remembering Grant had asked a question, I faced my brother. "Eliza and I are good. We're going to do just fine."

"I'm glad to hear it, because I'm pairing you with her for your training."

Panic knives stabbed at my lungs as I imagined how that would go. A woman barely five-foot-five should not make me break out into a sweat. I held my own in seven-figure business negotiations—I did not get intimidated by sassy women.

Aside from this particular sassy woman.

"I thought I would be shadowing you."

"Can't. I'm too busy for it, that's the whole point. I actually need you down here. Between interviews, and Rhett and I planning out the anniversary celebration, I've got enough to do without walking you through how to do your job."

"This isn't my job."

"It is for now. Anyway, I don't think sitting around on your can and watching other people work would give you a very realistic experience of what it's like to be on the sales floor."

"So pairing me up with the cute girl who can't stand me is more realistic?"

Grant's mouth flattened into a thin line. "That's an interesting choice of words."

I squared my shoulders as if I could deflect the remark. "I didn't say anything revolutionary. She's objectively cute."

So much more than just cute, but now was not a great time for me to drill down to specifics.

"Yeah, she is cute. And she definitely can't stand you." He laughed at my grimace. "Yes, it would be much more realistic for you to work with someone who can't stand you, and *deal with it*, than it would be for you to trail me for four weeks and learn nothing."

I passed a hand over my eyes. "I can't believe this."

They wanted me to learn the basics down here, fine, but did Eliza have to be the one to watch every minute of that mess go down? I'd resigned myself to the indignity of wearing the vest, but knowing she'd witness it all poured on fresh humiliation. I'd rather have both my brothers set up camp chairs and take notes on my crappy customer service than have Eliza smirking over my failures.

"I'm doing it for you. Do you think Dad is going to be happy if all you do is sit on the sidelines and watch me work? He sent you down here for a reason."

I ground my teeth together rather than admit he was right. If our father caught the slightest whiff I hadn't done what he asked, he'd send me straight back to the sales floor for another month. Or worse, take the CFO promotion off the table indefinitely. I didn't think he'd take it away permanently, but I wasn't arrogant enough to assume he couldn't find someone better qualified than me if he set his mind to it.

"For the record, I agree with him. You'll do a better job in corporate for what you'll learn down here."

"What precisely do you think I'm going to learn down here?"

Grant gestured at me. "Maybe how to get along with people."

"By working with the woman who can't stand me? Am I hearing this right?"

He prodded me in the shoulder. "You could use some customer service skills. Maybe learn to be a tiny bit less of a control freak."

"I don't need customer service experience to be CFO."

Nobody made Rhett log sales hours so he could do a better job with our social media marketing. As General Manager, Grant's case was different, but fair to say he'd never been asked to prove himself proficient at something entirely unrelated to his actual job requirements or skill sets.

"No, but what happened the last time we took on an intern in accounting? I'm trying to remember."

My insides shifted at that little reminder, my guilty conscience getting me from all sides today.

"How many days did he last before he went home crying?"

"He wasn't *crying*." He'd been close, though. At the time, an honest assessment of his work had seemed the best course of action. In retrospect, maybe I'd been a little too thorough in my honesty. Sending employees packing after three days wasn't in the company's best interest.

"I get it," I finally said. "But I don't have to like it."

"Then get ready to not like this." Grant grinned, turning to the registers. "Eliza, could you come here for a minute?"

I froze, waiting to see how this would play out. She might refuse to train me. It wouldn't be the mark of a very good employee, but she hadn't had much of a problem speaking her mind so far. Maybe Grant would wind up stuck with me, after all.

Eliza walked over looking as casual as anything. "What's up?"

"I'd like you to take over Dean's training," he explained. "I don't have time for it, but I trust you to help him get down the basics. Train him on registers, inventory, get him acquainted with our top sellers, things like that. You know what to do."

She grinned up at me, a hint of mischief in her eyes. "That sounds really, really great."

Clearly, she was going to love holding her seniority on the sales floor over me. My ego would never survive the next few weeks.

eliza

"THESE BOOTS HAVE sturdy ankle support and a firm arch, which are important when you're hiking on uneven terrain."

I struggled to remember all the benefits of this particular style of boot—hard to focus with Dean staring at me from across the store. He wasn't good at hiding it, either. He'd spent the afternoon either skulking around like a Secret Service agent, or watching my customer interactions with a little too much dedication. All in the interest of getting the hang of the job, yes, but it felt more like he was judging my work than trying to learn anything from it.

I didn't like feeling like I was under a microscope on my best day, but when Dean was the scientist in the white coat doing the critiquing, it threw me completely off my game. No way would someone like him find anything good to say about me.

My customer tromped around the shoe displays, testing out the boots. He looked as if he teetered on the edge of a decision, so I gave him a gentle nudge.

"They're waterproof, with a deep grip in the soles for extra traction in wet weather. Plus, they're ten percent off this month."

"I'll take them."

"Sounds good." I put away the other hiking boots he'd tried on, and rang up his purchase at the counter. Dean stayed close by, seemingly absorbed by an array of dry bags even though he was clearly listening in on the conversation like some wildly amateur private investigator. "Thank you for coming in to Irwin's."

The man made unintelligible sounds in place of a goodbye as he walked away.

I waited until the door had closed behind him before turning to Dean. "Can you tone it down there, Creepy Joe?"

"What?"

He approached the registers affecting an unconvincing innocence. Right. Because *I* was the one acting weird in this scenario.

"You could try staring at me a little less."

"I'm not *staring at you*."

I didn't love the vehement denial. Not that I *wanted* him to stare at me, but he didn't have to act like the idea offended his very soul. "Sorry, I meant gawking."

A grimace twisted his mouth. "You're training me, remember? I'm supposed to watch you."

"Not like that. It's okay to break eye contact now and then. Encouraged, even." I opened my eyes wide and blinked several times in quick succession to demonstrate.

He huffed out a breath. "And you think you're the people person?"

Fine, maybe I made a good candidate for that anti-antagonism HR thing. I couldn't help it with him. I would never behave like this with Grant or any of my other coworkers, but something in Dean's buttoned-up attitude just made me want to wreck his whole day. Knowing I could do it with a single smirk made it all too tempting.

"I don't watch people like I'm eyeballing whether or not I'll fit inside their skin suit."

He laughed, and for just a second, I caught a glimpse of how he would look if he were ever enjoying himself. *Gorgeous.* Gorgeous is how he would look. A lost, lone butterfly skipped around in my belly. Best to trap that butterfly and get rid of it before it could even think about making babies.

"I promise I'm not going to make a skin suit out of you. You're much too small for me."

I rolled my eyes, ignoring the flush of warmth that swept over my cheeks. The starched suit was *not* flirting with me, and even if he were, I would never entertain the idea. I stuck to imaginary guys I had no intention of ever talking to, not real ones who were infuriatingly attractive despite their insistence on buttoning all the way to the top. At least he'd left the tie and suit jacket at home today.

"I learn best by observation." He looked solemn, as if he actually believed I might let him skate by just watching me do the work.

"Nice try. You need to learn by doing." I nodded over his shoulder at a guy who'd just walked in. "It's showtime."

He seemed to gather up his strength before approaching the customer. Fascinating that a man who had confidence bordering on cockiness could need to pump himself up just to chat with customers. He had no problem talking to me, so what was the big hang up about strangers? Dean wasn't shy, and yet he'd gone out of his way to avoid talking to customers as though he didn't work here. I couldn't understand it.

I wandered closer to listen in on his conversation, but less obvious about it than he'd been, arranging a stack of Texas Trails T-shirts while he tried to be helpful. He still sounded stiff and awkward, but he didn't push or get frustrated. That had to be worth something.

After finishing up with a monotone 'let me know if you need anything', he appeared at my side. He glanced down at me, eyebrows raised as though asking for approval. Then again, chances were equally good he was doing a silent *Look at me* brag about his success.

I gave him a thumbs up. The smile that spread over his face moved through me like liquid heat, his hazel eyes pure honey.

Nope. Not even slightly entertaining *that* idea. Tearing my gaze away, I turned around and went straight to the back of the store.

As he had all afternoon, Dean followed. To learn by observation, of course. Since his customer didn't seem to need anything yet, I let it go.

"Okay, let's talk gear." I ignored his luscious eyes and focused instead on a point just to the left of his head. Considering all the bad ideas those eyes brought to mind right now, going no-eye-contact seemed the safest option. "What's your poison?"

His eyebrows furrowed together, but I refused to look at them. He had really nice eyebrows.

Gah, this wasn't happening. Since when had I noticed *eyebrows*? Good eyebrows weren't even a thing.

"What do you mean?" he asked.

"Customers are going to ask what products you recommend, so you should have a few go-to items. What do you like to do, kayak, climb, camp?"

His brothers had racked up achievements in white water rafting and mountain climbing—it only made sense Dean had some secret talent hidden away under the suit, too. Maybe knowing his activity of choice would give me some insight into what made that brain of his tick.

His eyebrows relaxed, but now his mouth went tight. "What does that matter?"

"It matters for making suggestions to customers. What you like to do in your off hours is a good place to start for ideas."

He cleared his throat and glanced away as if he were late for a meeting. See, now I was back to wanting to strangle him. He didn't have to be so difficult; it wasn't a hard question.

"So which is it?" I pressed.

Still not looking at me. "I don't have many off hours."

"Everybody has off hours."

He shot a look that said he was completely serious. Huh. Sitting at his desk every day wasn't far off from what I'd imagined of him, but hearing him say it out loud, it felt wrong, somehow. Sure, his big-shot corporate job was important, but the guy deserved a break now and then.

Oh, no. Was I feeling sorry for Dean Irwin? Definitely time for another chorus of "Shake it Off."

"Who doesn't get time off?"

A muscle twitched in his jaw. "My job is very demanding."

"So are your parents' jobs, and they take time off. I know for a fact they went to Florida last month."

His stoic veneer faltered, switching over into something close to confusion. Weird that the concern in his eyes and the odd tug at his mouth could twist something inside me, too. Uncertain Dean appealed a heckuvalot more than Know-it-All Dean.

"How do you know that?"

"I saw your mom in Fine & Dandy the last time I stopped in."

His eyebrows furrowed again as if this revelation unsettled him.

"Don't worry, I'm not stalking you, I only said hello to your mother. Relax."

"I am relaxed."

"Yeah, you're a very chill guy."

He tensed his jaw until a muscle pulsed by his ear. *Oh so chill.*

"Okay fine, you're married to work. But don't you ever go hiking or biking? Anything?" He still watched me with that blank look, like those terms didn't make any sense. "You can't seriously do nothing active."

I'd glimpsed too much of his physique through his dress shirts and slacks to believe his body was purely an act of God. He had to do *something* regularly to earn it.

"I run."

"Finally, thank you." I could work with running. Knowledge about local trails would be something. "Where do you run?"

"On a treadmill."

I stared at him, incredulity seeping from my pores.

"Your family owns the biggest independent outdoor store chain in Texas, and you don't do anything active?" My voice raised an octave at the ridiculousness of the idea. It had to be a joke, but he wasn't laughing.

"I work hard." An edge of defensiveness crept into his answer. "I can't spend all my time playing around outside."

"Do you spend *any* of your time playing around outside?"

His mouth thinned into a sour frown.

"Wait. Let me get this straight. You've never worked retail before, and you can't possibly make time to use any of the gear we sell. Why did Grant even agree to let you work down here?"

"Trust me, I'm more than qualified to be working retail down here with you."

I sucked in a breath as the part he didn't say hit home. Who wouldn't be overqualified, right? Back here at Irwin's at twenty-six working the same job I'd had at sixteen—of course he thought I was nothing, that's exactly what I'd accomplished in life.

I didn't care what Dean Fancy Pants Irwin thought of me. I didn't. But he'd managed to shine a light on all my insecurities in one snide sentence, and I hated how small I suddenly felt. This was how he saw me—maybe how most people saw me—insignificant and inadequate. Those words etched themselves on my mind like acid, my stomach twisting over the truth in every letter. Hot tears stung my eyes, but I'd walk barefoot through a patch of stickerweed before I ever cried in front of Dean Irwin.

Swallowing down my regrets, I cleared my expression, counting on Dean to be too absorbed with himself to have seen how his comment affected me.

"Why don't you help the couple who just walked in? I'm sure you're plenty qualified for that."

I walked away from him, wishing I could put more than the width of a sporting goods store between us.

Permanently.

dean

ELIZA FINISHED out our shift like she'd turned her internal dial down to zero. Her voice lost its enthusiasm, and she only spoke to me when absolutely necessary. No more teasing banter, no more sarcasm, only a tepid professionalism. I couldn't regret the loss of her antagonism, but her indifference hit harder. The minute she clocked out, she disappeared through the front doors and down the street without a word to me.

A young woman with long braids pulled into a topknot walked in a few minutes after Eliza had left. I recognized her as one of the store's part-time employees, but we'd never met.

"You must be Dean," she said, holding out a hand. "I heard you'd be working with us down here for a while. I'm Nicole."

I shook her hand, dreading to think who she'd heard that from, or what else had been said. I didn't fool myself Eliza had anything positive to say about me. Frankly, I wasn't sure Grant would have anything positive to say, either.

"Good to meet you."

Grant joined us at the front desk. "Nicole's going to dental assisting school, but she's tossing me crumbs and picking up hours with us now and then."

"I do what I can." She flashed a bright white smile that made me want to brush my teeth. Then she turned to Grant. "Tell me about the jerk."

"What jerk?"

"I saw Eliza on my way in here, and she was practically in tears. I asked what was wrong and she said some jerk gave her crap for working retail. So who was it? I need to know, I'm keeping a list. For reasons."

Grant looked to me. "Do you know anything about this?"

My stomach turned sour as realization hit. Maybe *I* needed the HR training. I'd trampled Eliza's feelings without thought or realization. Disgust and disappointment filled me like a deadweight as I turned over my curt, bitter remarks in my mind. I'd been such an ass. And for what? Childish insecurity, nothing more.

"I didn't hear anything." Maybe that was the worst of it. I'd hurt Eliza enough to change her whole demeanor, and I'd needed somebody else to step in and point out what I'd done. Too consumed by my own frustration at having to change up my job, I couldn't see how cruel I was being to her. If she didn't think I was a dick before, she did now, and with good reason.

Grant's eyes narrowed. "You were here the whole time with her."

I made a vague gesture.

He interpreted volumes in that arm wave, and his nostrils flared. "We need to talk."

We moved to a corner of the store while Nicole went in the back to clock in and get her vest on.

"It was you, wasn't it?" Grant's tone came out sharp as knives. "I didn't pair you with Eliza so you could break her down."

"I didn't do it on purpose." I truly hadn't. Not much consolation, though, knowing now I'd sent her home unhappy and had no clue.

"You do realize half the store managers are terrified of you."

I didn't see how the two related. "They should be. Half of them can't get their reports in on time."

"I'm going to say this the nicest way I know how." He shook his head. "No, screw that, I'm going to be blunt. Sometimes, you're a real ass. You forget not everybody is made of the same steel you are. You might not have emotions, but other people do."

My ribcage grew uncomfortably tight, not just for the reminder people saw me as heartless, but for how little I'd done to challenge that conclusion. In my youth, my volatile emotions had been too much for me to handle. I'd spent years learning to level out the seismic ups and downs so I'd never feel so out of control again. I'd distanced myself from my temperamental nature, and with it, the bulk of my emotions. Given the way I'd treated Eliza, that distance hadn't served me as well as I'd thought.

I'd chafed and fought against her every attempt to teach me, treating her like an inferior when she clearly had seniority down here. I'd seen my time with her as a punishment instead of an opportunity, and lashed out without thinking. Shame ate away at my insides as I imagined how Eliza must feel. How I'd *made* her feel. I might hate the term heartless, but today, I'd lived up to every cold-hearted image people had of me.

The heaviness in my chest wore on me, but I kept my breathing steady. I needed to focus.

I needed a plan.

Grant jabbed a finger hard into my chest. "If you have anything like a heart in there, you'll fix things with Eliza."

I wasn't even sure if she'd let me at this point, but I'd be no kind of man if I refused to try.

"I know, and I will. I just need your help."

He glared, but listened to my idea that had sprung to mind from out of nowhere. Maybe I could prove to Eliza I wasn't the person I'd been down here so far.

Maybe I could prove it to both of us.

An hour later, I finished with Grant and went upstairs to check through the latest updates on the store builds. I needed a couple of hours of working through numbers to take my mind off of how I'd treated Eliza. It wouldn't ease the guilt—I'd need to ask for forgiveness first—but I needed a moment of calm to hold myself together.

Accounts and allocations had always proven a strong distraction. Nothing ever went exactly on time or under budget, and billing adjustments for the new locations were forwarded to me nearly every day. I sat down at my desk and pulled up my email. Sure enough, I had new notices from two of the builders.

I hadn't endorsed this rush to build, but I'd been out-voted. The timing was right, my father and the others had said, and the property was available. *If not now, when?* was my father's motto. My motto would have had a little more practicality and caution thrown in there.

Working for a family business, fundamental differences of opinion colored everything. I liked to have a step-by-step plan of action with cost/benefit analysis and pro/con lists before I made a move. The rest of my family could make decisions on a dime, relying on their hunches, hearts, and sheer whimsy to guide them. Among this group of impulsives, I sometimes wondered where my more logical brain had come from.

I'd gone through one of the updated invoices when my father stepped into my office and leaned against the doorframe. "It's late, you should go home."

"I'm working two jobs at the moment." I adjusted the projected budget for one of the new stores. "I'm not allowed overtime or weekends, but I need to work when I can."

"How's it going downstairs?"

My fingers froze over the keyboard. Grant obviously hadn't said anything about my coworker problems, because Dad wasn't the type of man to beat around the bush. If he'd known how badly I'd handled things so far, he would have already said so, at great length and high volume.

"All right." Nearly true, my missteps with Eliza aside. I'd heard plenty of stories about Grant's more colorful trainee failures. The bar sat fairly low. "I'm getting time on the sales floor and first-hand experience with customers."

Not that long ago, I'd exulted in saving Irwin's tens of thousands of dollars this fiscal year. Now here I was begging for recognition for enduring customers' questions and the occasional flippant attitude.

"Realistically, I don't think it's going to take me a whole month to learn the basics downstairs. I can be in and out in two weeks, tops."

Dad's knowing smile didn't convince me he'd fallen for that.

"What have you learned about the gear we sell? What have you learned about the people who choose to come into our stores, and the people who work there?"

So far, I'd learned that hiking socks sell remarkably well, half the people who came through the store were 'just browsing', and watching Eliza work was no great hardship. Mostly, I'd learned I was an insensitive ass who needed to show some common empathy.

"All you've learned is that you're not cut out for customer service, am I right?"

"No news there."

"This will be good for you if you give it a chance. Your mother's right. You do need a break from this office. Your brothers at least get out now and then. Rhett gets out probably more than he should."

I did not need the comparison right now. When my parents did get around to thinking about my personal life, it only came in light of what I hadn't accomplished compared to Grant or Rhett. They appreciated what I did for the business, no question, but my brothers' outdoor achievements *impressed* them. Big difference there.

"You don't get out nearly enough," Dad said.

My thoughts returned to Eliza, and what she'd said just before I stuffed my foot in my mouth. *You're married to your work.*

Yes, I was driven. I knew the value of my time and didn't want to waste it. I'd long ago given up the competitive nature that Grant and Rhett had, and traditional hobbies had never held much interest for me. Still, even under her barrage of questions, I hadn't been able to come up with one activity I enjoyed. It was that magazine interview all over again.

I had fun…didn't I? I knew what Eliza's answer to that question would be, but the fact that I had to ask in the first place said it all.

"It will be good for you to have the chance to fail."

I shifted under the weight of his words. "You expect me to fail at this?"

"No. If I know you, you'll drive Grant crazy with all the ways you find to improve operations down there. No, Dean, I'm saying you'll have the *chance* to fail."

"You're sounding like Gandalf here, Dad."

He spread his palms out as if his meaning couldn't be clearer. "When was the last time you tried something you didn't already know how to do?"

I cast about but came up empty. I hadn't exaggerated the other night when I said I worked fifty hours a week or more. My attempts at new things didn't come around often. Practically never.

Dad pointed at me as if he could see the similarity in my days written in my face. "That's what I'm talking about. There's growth in that uncertainty, in trying something without knowing in advance that you'll succeed at it. You might find more than you're expecting to over the next few weeks."

"We're still talking about working retail, right?"

"Yes, Dean, but if you give it a chance, you might find there's more to be discovered than just that."

That seemed an esoteric way of looking at a temporary job switch, but I wouldn't belabor the point.

Truth be told, though, I planned on doing more than just learning retail. I would suck it up and become the best damn employee Grant had ever had. I refused to add my name to the list of trainees who'd gone down in flames after a few days on the sales floor.

And if she'd let me, I would make things right with Eliza Webb.

eliza

DREAD SPOOLED in my stomach as I buttoned up my green Irwin's vest. Given the chance, I'd take a dozen back-to-back family dinners over this. Anything would be better than training Dean all day, with his crisp shirts and condescending attitude. Last night, I'd devoured a pint of ice cream, trying to read the latest Penny Reid rom-com while his snide remarks circled through my mind on a loop. *"I'm plenty qualified to be working down here with you."* If he was so high and mighty, he could just go back upstairs and leave me and the rest of the peons alone.

At my lowest point, I'd considered making his life so miserable on the sales floor he would be forced to cry uncle. I'd picked up a few things from the slew of nightmare coworkers I'd known in my various jobs. It wouldn't be difficult to apply a few special tactics. I could ice him out, withhold key information, give him a case of mild but completely untraceable food poisoning. All great opportunities right at my fingertips.

But as fun as it was to think about torturing Dean with expired yogurt, I would never do it. Cruelty and manipulation weren't my thing, especially after experiencing them myself.

And anyway, he was sort of one of my bosses. Bare minimum, he worked in corporate, and that made messing with him off limits, no matter how much he deserved it.

I walked out of the back office to find him hanging around in the stock room, fiddling with a foam roller. Bitterness bloomed inside me, but I wouldn't let him see me sweat. Not over him. He set the roller aside and straightened up as soon as he saw me, Mr. Businessman reporting for duty. I put on a tight smile, ready to get this shift started and ended as quickly as possible.

"Good morning, Dean." I tried to emulate the stiff voice he used with customers. See? I could be professional, no matter what he thought of me. "Today, I'm going to start by showing you how to ring up sales."

I moved to walk past him, but he reached out a hand. His fingertips brushed lightly against my arm, almost a caress as he stopped me. A shiver rippled across my skin at the unexpected warmth of his touch.

I shifted away, smothering that reaction. How could I think of him as *warm* when he'd burned me so thoroughly yesterday?

"Wait, please."

I faced him fully, puffing myself up with a deep, bracing breath, that fake smile still on my lips. "Yes?"

"I'm sorry, Eliza."

His voice held so much humility, for a second I wasn't sure it was really Dean Irwin standing in front of me. The aloof, cocky guy I knew had been replaced by one looking down at me with nothing but regret in his eyes. The sincerity there surprised me as much as his submissive tone.

"I shouldn't have been so rude to you yesterday. It was unprofessional, and I apologize."

Of all the scenarios I'd imagined for today, I honestly hadn't expected an apology. Honestly, I didn't think he'd have enough awareness to realize he'd needed to give one. Kind of a nice surprise, in a weird way.

I was tempted to accept his concession and move on, just forget it all and leave it in the past. But part of me wasn't quite ready to let it go. He'd apologized, and I appreciated the effort, but I didn't think he really knew what he'd apologized *for*. If this was just an empty HR display, I didn't want it.

"I don't care that it was unprofessional. You mocked me for working in a store your family *owns*. That's just low." I stood straighter, giving voice to the retort I wished I'd had the strength to say yesterday. "And it was a mean thing to say to me. This job might not seem like much to you, but I need it. I shouldn't be ridiculed for that."

He cringed as my words struck home, but he kept his eyes locked on mine. "You're right. It was mean and wrong. I've been acting like a jerk. I'm sorry."

I stared back at him, testing the weight of his words. In my admittedly limited experience, apologies from guys were rare, and actual sincerity even more so. He seemed to mean what he said, but I didn't have much to go on. I'd been suckered by the nice-guy act before.

"I'll do better. I wasn't taking this job seriously, but that's going to change. Really. I give you my word."

Nice try. The only man I trusted to keep his word was my father.

He splayed his hands, his wide eyes practically begging now. "I'll do whatever it takes to prove it, Eliza."

I wanted to believe him so badly, the impulse shocked me. I wanted to trust Dean Irwin? I'd lost my mind—the only explanation that made sense here. But his earnestness and increasing agitation at my silence made me want to have a little faith.

I breathed a small laugh. "Okay, you don't have to swear a blood oath or anything. I accept your apology."

His small smile almost had me smiling back like a fool. *No.* I was still kind of mad at him, despite his cute face and soft touches.

"Can we start over again?" He held a hand out to me. "I'm Dean Irwin. We'll be working together."

I managed not to roll my eyes as we shook hands—a Fresh Start Handshake seemed like a very Dean thing to do. But mostly, I tried to ignore how warm and right his hand felt wrapped around mine. As far as handshakes went, this one was pretty dang good. He didn't let go, but just kept shaking my hand, that tiny smile on his face growing more strained by the second, as if the handshake confused him even though he'd been the one to offer it.

Honestly, it confused me, too. A few minutes ago, I hadn't wanted to see his stupid handsome face much less touch him, and now I was thinking how awesome his handshakes were?

Not normal.

When I finally pulled away, he seemed startled, like he hadn't expected me to let go.

"We should really get out there." We weren't here to chat, after all, and our shift had started two minutes ago, but also, *What the heck was that?* We'd never touched before, never had a need, but now, I was ready to ask him to shake hands a second time.

I'm sorry, I messed that up, my hands weren't clammy enough, could we try again?

"Right. Yeah. Register. I should—" He hooked a thumb over his shoulder as explanation. His smile disappeared, and I immediately wished it back.

Ugh, no, this was not happening. Wishing to see a tiny twitch of a smile on this stoic man's face was *not* my style.

"I think I heard the door." He nodded and slipped out of the stock room onto the sales floor.

Once he was gone, I finally breathed easier. I was *so* not doing this. Liking Dean as anything more than an uptight coworker was strictly out of the question. Men were meant to be kept at a safe distance, enjoyed from afar but never engaged with. *Never* trusted. That went double for business types, and triple for ones who were kind of, sort of, my boss. My no engagement rule had served me well for years, and I wasn't about to break that now.

Never mind that weird fluttering going on in my chest and my utterly bizarre jonesing for a handshake. Who did that?

And anyway, his vow to do better might be short-lived. Promises were easy, but actions were tough. If I gave him a little more time, he would probably prove he hadn't meant his apology. Any minute now, he'd be back to staring at me like I had food stuck between my teeth. He'd have something snarky to say about my job history or my outfit or my college education. Hell, he might be arguing with customers right now.

On that note, I should probably join him out in the store.

I walked onto the sales floor to find him chatting with an older man. Actually *chatting*. I froze just outside the stock room door, watching the scene unfold in total confusion.

"Where were you camping when your stove died out on you?" he asked.

"Davis Mountains," the man said, his pale skin wrinkling with a smile. "And I wouldn't say it died on me so much as I dropped the thing and busted the valve. Wasn't much I could do after that but buy a new one."

They laughed as if it were the most natural thing in the world. I checked to make sure my mouth wasn't hanging open. Dean had said he would do better, but I hadn't expected he would do *this* much better this quickly.

The man pointed at a green camp stove. "How many BTUs does this one have?"

"I have to confess, it's only my third day in the store," Dean told him. "I'll have to check the label."

He actually admitted it. I kind of thought he'd never stoop so low as to declare himself a trainee.

He picked up the stove and scanned the package. "Ten thousand BTUs."

"That's the one. Just like my old one, but the paint's a little shinier. I'll take it."

"Sounds good." Dean carried the stove back to the registers.

Stunned, I followed, assuming he needed me to ring up his sale. He grabbed the scan gun and flashed a smile at me. A real, actual smile. That fluttering thing in my chest started up again.

"I've got it, thank you, Eliza."

What alternate universe had I fallen into? Dean scanned the stove, announced the price, and swiped the customer's card before handing the stove and receipt over with a polite nod.

"Thank you for coming in to Irwin's."

Traces of Awkward Dean peeked through in his interaction, but he'd handled the customer just right, start to finish. No resentment, no sullen attitude, no attempt to distance himself from the job. The man said goodbye and walked out the front door, his new camp stove tucked safely under one arm.

"What was that?" I screeched at Dean, unable to help it. "How did you learn to do that?"

He still stood at the register, barely concealing a proud little grin, so pleased with himself he was dang near adorable. Oh, this was not okay. I was not prepared for him to be competent, helpful, *and* adorable all in one go.

"I asked Grant to train me last night."

Some of my delight faded. "I was supposed to do that. He's got so much going on with the anniversary thing coming up, I thought he didn't have time."

Add it to the list of things I should have done but hadn't.

Train Dean on registers. Put it right under *Have a business plan for my soap company.*

"It's fine. He had some extra time last night after Nicole came on. I asked him to show me so you wouldn't have to."

"Oh." I hadn't loved training Dean so far, but knowing he'd gone out of his way to avoid that training still hit like an insult. Just more evidence he thought I didn't know what I was doing, and couldn't be counted on to teach him. "I get it. I've kind of been..."

I refused to say *incompetent.* That description haunted me the most.

"Antagonistic," I finished.

"No, it's not like that." He ran a hand through his hair, an awkward look pulling at his mouth and eyes. "I asked him to show me because I wanted to try to make things up with you."

That little confession sent an unexpected zip of pleasure through me, even though it didn't quite line up. "Why?"

He spread his palms in front of him, his uncertainty making him weirdly relatable, like maybe we were both adrift at sea just now. "A show of good faith. I meant what I said earlier. I haven't treated being down here like it's really my job."

"That's true. You've kind of had a stick up your butt about it."

His mouth quirked, but he seemed to accept the crass description. "Exactly. But I'm going to take it seriously from now on. I wanted to try to prove that to you."

Oh, no, Adorable Dean again. I couldn't handle it. "But what about all that just now when you were talking with Camp Stove Guy? You were great."

"Yeah?" His whole face lit up, as if my brief praise was all he'd wanted to hear. Who even was this man? "I asked myself *What would Eliza do?* So I asked him a few questions and tried not to push. I smiled. I blinked."

I'd noticed that, too. He wasn't completely at ease yet, but he hadn't talked through gritted teeth, either. His first two days down here, he'd scared off a couple of customers just by looking growly at them.

"Well, thinking like me might not always point you in the right direction. I have lost a lot of jobs following that protocol."

"Eliza, I'm sorry. I was being a jackass and shouldn't have said that. I'm not used to..." He grimaced as if he already regretted his explanation. "I'm not used to being around people all the time. I'm not good with them. You were right when you said my people skills are rusty. It's not a skill I ever picked up."

The glimpse of true Dean behind all his façades made my chest squeeze. This level of candor from him was unprecedented. If I said the wrong thing, I might jinx it. "You can always learn new skills."

He nodded, an echo of a smile on his face. "I'm working on it."

Two young women walked through the door. Dean moved toward them as though ready to put his new customer service skills to use again, but I stopped him.

"Don't worry about it, I'll take this one."

I greeted the two women while my brain whirred over this unexpected change. Dean had learned to use the registers to try to prove himself to me? As much as I liked the idea, it seemed like a big left turn from the guy I'd known. That alone should give me serious pause. Guys who changed their personality like throwing a light switch were a huge red flag. I'd been fooled by the Nice Guy routine before, and refused to get sucked in again. But something about his awkward confession told me this wasn't just a charade he was playing at. He really wanted to try harder.

The big question was, would he?

"We're getting ready to do some big-time hiking," one of the women said to me.

"It's just to Enchanted Rock, it's not out in the boonies," the other said.

"Whatever. We need a really good first aid kit, just in case."

I led them over to the first aid section and picked up a small pack. "This is what we recommend for a day trip. It's got all your essentials like remedies for stings, bites, burns, things like that. Anything you choose from there just adds more to the bag, so it's up to you what you think you might encounter."

I grabbed a small card from its display rack. "This is a list of Ten Essentials for anyone exploring the wilderness, just in case you've forgotten anything for your trip."

One woman took the first aid kit from me while the other looked over the card.

"Thanks," the second woman said. "I think we're missing most of this stuff."

"A headlamp?" The first woman craned her neck to read the card in her friend's hand. "We're not going to need that on a day trip."

"You never know."

I glanced over at Dean, who watched me with that cute, small smile I hadn't seen enough of. That smile alone could make me believe in the sincerity of his fresh start. He didn't usually share his smile, like he kept it stored away somewhere for special occasions. The fact he had it out on display now, no matter how small, seemed significant.

The women opted for the first aid kit and a small compass, just in case. I rang them up and watched them go with a little pang of longing in my heart. I hadn't been out on the trails in months. I loved going on a good hike or a bike ride, but since I'd started my soap business, I hadn't been able to get out as often as I liked. Most of my time was spent making, selling, and trying to market my soaps. Now with my job at Irwin's taking up even more of my time, day trips were harder to arrange than ever. I had plans to go paddleboarding with Harper on Sunday, but it would be the first time I'd had that kind of day off in almost six months.

Fresh guilt washed through me for teasing Dean about his lack of off hours. Sometimes, days off proved hard to come by. And goodness knows, being responsible for the finances of eight stores and counting had to be more demanding than my attempt to get my soap business off the ground.

I turned to find him hunched over the counter behind me, writing something down.

"What are you doing?" I stepped closer to see.

He straightened up and put his hands behind his back. "Nothing."

That reaction surprised me all over again. This self-consciousness didn't fit my impression of him at all. Dean was supposed to be the strict principal, not the guilty schoolboy. I don't know why, but it made me smile.

He relaxed again and brought his hands back out. He had a pencil in one and a tiny notebook in the other. "I'm taking notes."

"What kind of notes?"

"Work notes." He flipped the notebook open, and I just glimpsed the words *gift card*, *buffs*, and *ten essentials* before he closed it again. He slipped the notebook and pencil into his pocket, looking more awkward than I'd ever seen him.

"That's really..." I wasn't sure of the best word here. Taking notes on my conversations with customers came off a little weird, to be honest, but it also showed how hard he was trying. It was kind of sweet, too, like he thought what I said was important enough to remember. Nobody had ever taken notes on me before, even if it was only in a work context.

One of his eyebrows twitched, as if he were waiting for me to say something snarky about the notes. My heart pinched to see how he braced himself for whatever I might blurt out. Well, I had been doing that, hadn't I? Teasing, poking, and generally giving him a hard time ever since he'd started down here. Ever since we met, really. I wasn't innocent in our little clashes—there'd been plenty of jerkiness to go around.

I'd had a lot of jobs, but I'd never been a slacker or a bad employee. I didn't call in sick for no reason, and I didn't badmouth managers. So why had I always given Dean such a hard time? The fact that I couldn't think of a good reason sent guilt cruising around inside me. *He's too handsome* wasn't an excuse.

"That's a really good idea," I said at last.

His eyebrows relaxed, and his mouth shifted into the smallest smile. Some of the tautness in my chest crumbled away, along with a bit of the tension between us. Were the Automatic Enemies actually becoming friends now? I'd promised myself to stay away from guys like him, but we had to find some way to get through this brief stint as coworkers without completely destroying each other.

I smiled back. Being friends with Dean Irwin wouldn't be the worst thing in the world.

dean

I KEPT my word to Eliza. Over the next few days, I lost my attitude and did my best to apply my usual work ethic to this temporary position at Irwin's. Some aspects didn't overlap much, but professionalism, organization, and follow-through did. I greeted customers, rang up sales, and restocked inventory without a single grimace or sarcastic comment. This might be nothing like my actual job, but it was still my job for the time being. So I would dominate it.

Her attitude changed, too. She hadn't quite lost her impulse to tease me, but the bite had disappeared. I no longer felt like an annoyance whose presence she had to endure, but a genuine coworker, teaming up to get the job done. She dropped helpful hints more readily, too, little words of encouragement that made me think I would survive my mandatory weeks down here, after all.

I still eavesdropped on her conversations with customers, but I tried to be a little more discreet about it than I'd been before. She was so much better at that side of the job than I was, I needed her to set the example. And yes, I freely took notes when she wasn't looking.

I brought an armful of wool socks to restock the display rack, where I'd be close enough to listen in on Eliza and her customer in the camping section while I worked. I didn't see much point in being subtle about it—she already knew I needed all the pointers I could get.

"I'm heading to Taos next month, and I need a better sleeping bag," the older man told her. "Have you ever been to Taos?"

"No, never," she answered. "How low do you expect the temperature to get overnight?"

"It'll dip down into the twenties. I enjoy dipping into the twenties now and then, myself."

Wait, what?

I looked up to see the man grinning at Eliza, who seemed oblivious to either the gross insinuation or his brazen tone. Easily in his fifties, the man had longish, graying hair and a bright silver goatee. A lot of things about the guy seemed stuck in the past, from his shark tooth necklace and leather bracelets, to his blatant interest in younger women.

"These two bags are rated down to twenty degrees." Eliza pointed at the shelves in front of them. "You might want to choose a zero-degree rating, if you're looking to be extra safe."

"Oh, I'm safe, don't you worry about that." He shot her a wink. "Clean, too."

I stopped caring where the socks went, and shoved them on any hook available as indignation flared to life in my chest. This was the point I usually started my deep breathing exercises and soothing mantras, but today, I didn't even try. My attention stayed locked on the creeper coming on to Eliza.

"Well, if you're looking for a zero rating, this one is the best we carry."

When she moved to indicate one of the sleeping bags, the man shifted even closer to her. She slid away with a thin smile, clearly uncomfortable having him in her space. Blood pounded in my veins as I sized the guy up.

What was I supposed to do here? None of Eliza's customer service tips applied, and Grant had never mentioned a scenario like this. Waiting it out seemed wrong, but stepping in could get dicey.

"Come to think of it," he said, "I might need a double, after all. It gets cold out there, and I could use a warm up for a few nights. What do you say? You want to see Taos, honey?"

That ended my debate. Dropping the rest of the socks, I stalked over and put myself between the man and Eliza. Taller, fitter, and younger than the other man by a long shot, I wasn't above using that to intimidate him.

"Can I help you?" My voice sounded pretty damn friendly considering the way my insides simmered.

The man blinked at me, startled by the intrusion. Good. If he had any idea of the thoughts in my head, he would be a lot more than *startled*.

"This little gal is helping me just fine." He grinned again at Eliza but was smart enough to knock off the leer. I was one suggestive remark away from grabbing his collar and escorting him out the door.

"I'm helping you now." I shifted to block Eliza from his view. "Did you decide on a sleeping bag? Sir?"

His eyes dropped to find Eliza again, but I moved to keep myself front and center. If he wanted a chest to ogle, he would only find mine.

"I'm not too sure. She was showing me the options. I'd like to get back to that, if you don't mind."

"I can show you the options." I'd edged Eliza out of the conversation, and I had no idea how she'd react to that, but I wasn't about to stand by and let this lech hit on her. "Which sleeping bag did you want?"

"You can't just come in here and—"

"I can and I am. Are you here to buy a sleeping bag or not?" Grant would have had a conniption to hear me talk to a customer this way, but I didn't care. I'd endure every reprimand he could dish out if it meant I could get this guy to leave Eliza alone.

The man sighed, apparently resigned to my help. He gestured vaguely at the display. "The twenty degree one. Green."

"Terrific." I picked up the sleeping bag and nodded for him to go to the registers. No chance in hell would I leave him behind with Eliza.

As though against his will, he turned and tromped to the registers. I rang up the bag and passed it over. My smile couldn't have looked genuine. "Thanks for shopping at Irwin's."

As the man walked away, he paused near Eliza but glanced over his shoulder at me. I narrowed my eyes on him, conveying with one look that if he so much as breathed on that woman, he would regret it. The message must have been received. He walked past her and out the door without another word, thank God.

If Grant gave me a hard time about arguing with a customer when I was seventeen, what would he think if I'd assaulted one today?

My relief didn't last long. Eliza stalked toward me, both hands on her hips. "You didn't have to do that."

"That guy was a creep."

"He was my customer."

"Maybe you couldn't tell, but he was hitting on you. He needed to stop."

Unless...wait. Unless she *wanted* the guy to hit on her? That didn't seem possible, but what did I know about what Eliza wanted?

The grin that spread over her face filled me with a crazy, nameless hope.

"Did you just *rescue* me?"

I mirrored her stance, unsure now if I should admit the truth or not. She sounded both flattered and offended, and I couldn't tell which way she might lean more.

"Maybe?"

"Dean, I am a woman who currently works in a retail store frequented by men. Of course I knew he was hitting on me. It happens all the time."

"All the time?" How often did she mean? Every once in a while? Or closer to daily? More importantly, did Grant know? The idea she had to put up with this kind of gross behavior regularly disgusted me.

She shrugged as she came closer, and her spark of defiance winked out. "You get used to it."

"You shouldn't have to get used to it. This is where you work. That's harassment."

The way she watched me, I had the distinct sensation she was rearranging her opinions of me. I sent up a prayer they were changing for the better. Being offended by casual sexual harassment was a pretty low threshold, but maybe it was a start.

"It's not ideal. If he'd gotten any worse, I would have politely but firmly told him off."

"He invited you to his double sleeping bag in Taos. How much worse can it get?"

She gave me a *You don't want to know* look. As a young, good-looking woman who worked customer service, it probably got a lot worse. My insides crawled just imagining it. "I'm sorry, that's terrible."

"Plus, you stole my sale." She tried to sound like she was only teasing, but I knew better.

"I put it on your account."

Her eyes brightened. "You did?"

"I wouldn't cheat you like that." That I had to say those words at all proved how badly we'd started out. She actually thought I'd steal customers from her for the commission? "I only wanted to get rid of him."

"Just so you know, I don't mind that you stepped in with that guy. Sometimes, coworkers just stand around and let it happen."

Fire flashed in my blood. "That's not okay. If this is happening regularly, we need to adjust our training to make sure all our employees work together to put a stop to it."

"Wow. You're really mad about this."

I took a step back and checked myself. She didn't know what my *really mad* looked like, but I needed the reminder to ease up. Deep breaths. Calming thoughts. Plan of action. I would talk with Grant tonight.

"Hey." She moved closer, her eyes wide with worry. "I'm okay. Really. It's kind of sweet you're so concerned."

Her shy smile sent liquid energy coursing through my veins, washing away some of the anger. *Sweet* was definitely an improvement over jerk. Not that she'd ever said the word, but I'd bet money she'd been thinking it.

"You aren't the same guy who walked through those doors on Monday."

"Yeah? How's that?" I wanted to know for purely empirical reasons. To verify my efforts were working. Not fishing for compliments.

But I would eat those compliments out of her hand.

"You're laughing with customers over their camp stoves, stocking inventory like an old pro, and riding in on your white horse to stop old dudes from propositioning me."

When she put it like that, I had half a mind to run the man down and smother him with his sleeping bag.

She shrugged again. "I'm impressed."

I flashed a cocky grin. "So you're saying I'm not unnecessary in my job."

Slipping back into our old teasing banter seemed a much safer route than the dangerous paths we were skating around—and getting dangerous with Eliza grew more tempting by the hour.

She tilted her head from one side to the other, evaluating me. "There's just one thing."

On second thought, I wasn't sure just how far I wanted to revert to our teasing. A frank assessment from her just might lay me out, all my worst attributes summed up in a few sassy words.

She came closer until I breathed in her minty scent. Her bright blue eyes gazed up at me as though she were a swimmer checking for shark-infested waters. Electricity pulsed through my body on every heartbeat as she reached for me.

Her mouth twisted, and she bit her lower lip as her fingers worked the top button of my shirt. It was all I could do to keep my focus on her eyes rather than her soft mouth, and even that much drove me crazy. Her eyes were perfect sea blue, wide open and unsure.

When she pulled the button free, she smoothed my lapels down. That brief touch on my chest sent heat swirling in its wake, and I had to hold my breath for fear of doing or saying something stupid.

In that moment, *all* of my thoughts were stupid.

"There," she said. "That's better. You look more relaxed."

I wasn't relaxed at all. My whole body had gone to red alert. She moved back a step but stayed close enough I could still circle her in my arms if I wanted. And I did want. I didn't know quite where that urge had come from, but every molecule in my body zeroed in on this new desire to hold Eliza. I had to thrust my hands into my pockets to stop myself from acting on the impulse.

A couple walked through the store's front door. On instinct, Eliza called out a greeting.

Turning back to me, she said softly, "Thank you. I mean it."

Then she walked away to check in with the new customers.

I stood frozen in place a whole minute, breathing slowly and willing my body to settle down, but I'd already lost the battle. I prided myself on control, but Eliza managed to whittle it away, piece by piece.

eliza

MAGNOLIA RIDGE'S Saturday Market had been jumping all morning, and I'd already made back my booth fee, thank God. On rare days, I sat and watched the crowds pass me by without a glance, and fears of a repeat non-performance crept through me every time I laid out my soaps in their rustic wooden crates. With nowhere to go but up, I could relax as customers systematically sniffed all my bars.

"Well if it isn't my favorite soap maker."

One of my regular market customers bellied up to my booth to look over the bars. Lettuce and kale peeked out of the top of the tote slung over her shoulder, and even at this angle, it looked heavy.

"Looks like you've had success this morning, Lily."

"You should see what I made Steve lug out to the car! I told him I had to stop in and see you." She picked up a Citrus Burst bar and held it to her nose. "He said my soap budget is ten dollars, but I refuse to accept that kind of negativity in my life."

I laughed at her attitude. My favorite thing about working the markets was how many people I met, from awesome customers to supportive vendors. Sure, standing outside in the burning Texas sun could get sweaty and miserable, but I liked chatting with people here. For the most part, folks were positive, enthusiastic, and encouraging. Truly my ideal way to make a living.

Would have been even better if I were actually making a living.

"Everybody can use more soap," I said, passing change to a woman who'd bought three bars.

Lily mock-gasped. "You've added fall scents." She edged closer to the crate filled with bars scented of apple, pumpkin, and fig. "These are a dream, I'll take all three."

We exchanged cash and soaps, and she jaunted off again with her purchases. I'd barely had time to smile over my successful morning when another woman stepped forward to inspect my soaps.

"Are these made with harsh chemicals?" She turned her nose up like she'd asked if my hot dogs were made from real dogs.

"The ingredients are on the back of each label." I cashed out another customer, bracing myself for what was sure to come. People only asked about ingredients when they had an axe to grind. "I use sustainably-sourced palm oil, coconut oil, shea butter—"

"This says you use sodium hydroxide." She set the bar aside as if it might bite her, and didn't look where she put it. The bar tumbled off its display onto the table, denting one corner in the fall.

A few people looked sideways at the woman, and then suspiciously at the soaps. Listing things out by their chemical names made people jittery, but *everything* had a chemical compound name. Anything could sound scary if you made it more complicated than it needed to be.

"Sodium hydroxide is lye." I kept my cool, tucking the

dented bar behind the bins. I would have to slice it up and use it as a sample now. "All true soap is made with lye. It reacts with the oils to make soap, but by the time you use it, there's no lye left in the bar, just a rich, creamy lather."

That seemed to satisfy the man at the front of the line, who put forward two bars and some cash, along with a generous smile. I could have thrown my arms around his neck for the silent show of support.

Of course, that thought reminded me of Dean. Not that he'd been very *silent* in his support. He'd quickly gotten rid of the creepy sleeping bag guy and then seemed genuinely offended on behalf of everyone subjected to sexual harassment. I'd had the weird urge to throw my arms around *his* neck, too, but I'd just managed to control myself.

Then I'd turned around and unbuttoned his shirt, but we couldn't all be saints.

"I'm not going to put lye on my body," the woman said. "*Nobody* should."

I silently bid her good riddance as she huffed away down the crowded market aisle. Thankfully, most of the people hanging around my stall didn't follow her lead. Nothing like a Critical Cathy to spoil a good sales day.

"You get another anti-chemical lady giving you trouble?" Tanisha Hendricks moved beneath my awning from her booth next door, Dairy Kid. She sold goat milk, goat cheese, goat butter, and she even sold baby goats in the spring—although not at the actual market. Unfair no-livestock rules.

"You heard that? It's been a while since the last one. I was due, I guess."

I'd considered buying a sign that said *Everything is Made from Chemicals*, but that would probably just open me up to more criticism.

"I had a woman ask me this morning if my milk is fresh."

Tanisha shook her head crowned with gorgeous coils. "As though I'm out here selling stale old milk."

Considering her stall had a banner emblazoned with *Fresh Goat Milk* over it, I agreed the question was ridiculous.

Most people at the market came to appreciate locally grown food and handmade goods. Very few came to criticize and pick stalls apart. But just like at Irwin's, when someone did make a stink, I couldn't do much without risking alienating more customers. I still believed in putting customer service first, even when the customer in question didn't deserve it.

"You should tell them if they want to go all-natural, they can stop wearing deodorant and start brushing their teeth with a stick," she said.

"My soaps *are* all-natural. They have fewer ingredients than most soaps you can buy in a store. Some people just have a hang-up about lye."

"Yeah, and some people turn their noses up at goat milk." Her face split into a wide grin. "They're the ones missing out."

I grinned back at my friend. "Save me a pint today, okay? I'm ready to try a batch of goat milk soap."

"I can't wait. It's going to be so good, I know it."

Tanisha had been encouraging me to make soap from her goats' milk since we first became booth buddies. One of those additives that could make a good soap luxurious, goat milk sounded like the perfect mix for some of my bars—if I could get it right.

"Don't get too excited. From everything I've read, there's a chance my first batch won't even turn out." The thought of wasting ingredients still made my stomach creep, but I'd decided to start with a small batch for my trial run. "Milk soaps are harder to make than regular soaps."

"Look at all these beautiful bars of soap." She waved a hand over my display like a fairy godmother. "I've got every faith they'll turn out just perfect."

She went back to her booth, leaving me in a glow of confidence. The best thing about being next to Dairy Kid was that if I ever had an off day, Tanisha's infectious optimism could turn it right around.

"If you're making goat milk soaps, does that mean you're going to make honey soaps, too?"

On my booth's other side, one of the Oh, Honey! guys leaned across his crowded table to chat. Some weeks, I felt like a 1950's housewife talking to my neighbors over the fence, but I kind of loved it.

"I will, Miguel, I promise." Adding honey to soap could be just as disastrous as adding milk, but both had soothing properties I wanted to experiment with one day.

Miguel's partner, Ethan, put a hand on his shoulder so he could chime in. "We're starting to take the rejection personally."

I looked over their table stacked with jars of artisan honey in varieties from lavender to avocado. A goat milk and avocado honey soap bar would be dreamy. Unfortunately, ounce for ounce, the specialty honey would be the most expensive ingredient I'd ever worked with, and I didn't like rolling dice with that kind of money.

"It's not personal, it's more...financial."

We all knew most of us weren't making bank at the farmers market, but that didn't mean I got a thrill out of broadcasting my money woes, either.

Miguel leaned closer. "We'll sell to you at cost, honey."

He winked and turned back to his customers. My vendor neighbors were the best ever.

I stopped to retie my yellow apron and spotted two familiar faces walking my way through the crowd. My cousin, June

Evans, and her hunky beau, Ty Hardy, strode up hand in hand. June had moved back to Magnolia Ridge a few months ago, and her decision had everything to do with the man at her side. Well, almost everything. I couldn't blame her, though. The rancher looked delectable in his Stetson, button-down, and jeans. From the little bits June shared during our regular girl's nights, Ty was secretly a cuddly teddy bear, but from my vantage, he was all rugged man.

"How are the lovebirds?" I asked at full volume. A few people turned to look at the couple, and Ty's mouth twitched at the edges. He didn't like attention, which was why I always drew all eyes to him. I loved poking the bear, teddy though he may be.

"We're doing good." June's big smile said things were better than good. Glancing over her man, I could well imagine. "We haven't been to the market in a while, and I thought we should stop by."

I spread my hands out over my displays. "This is where the magic happens."

Ty stifled a laugh.

I leaned forward so only they could hear. "Dirty men come to me every week to satisfy their needs."

His laughter rang out loud and clear as he shook his head at me. "You better watch yourself."

June used to look shocked when I said things like that, but today, she just gave me an indulgent smile. It echoed my conversation with Harper last week—*You're all talk*. I was, but that didn't mean everybody had to know. Where was the fun in that?

"Your soaps have been flying out the door at Fine & Dandy," she said. "We're almost out already."

"Truly?" Sales had been steady, but they hadn't exactly been *flying* so far.

She nodded. "I guess word is getting around. I'll send you an email later with a fresh order."

Ty let go of June's hand and snaked it to her waist, pulling her close to drop a kiss on her temple. "I thought we were busy later."

"Gross." My faux-disgusted face seemed to amuse Ty, who looked thoroughly unashamed of his affection as he snuggled up on June.

"We're going riding," she explained.

I raised my hands. "I don't want to know what you call it."

She rolled her eyes and plucked up two soaps. "I'll take these before we go."

Ty pulled out his wallet and passed over a few bills while June tucked the bars into her bag.

"You should try the soaps, too, Ty," I said as I passed him his change. "Don't let June hog them all."

"Oh, we share." He looked down at her with so much desire in his eyes, it was a wonder she didn't burst into flame on the spot. She just soaked up his attention like she'd never get enough.

Was it completely wrong that my thoughts went straight to Dean again? Yes, that was definitely wrong. Wrong and slightly bonkers. Dean was my coworker of sorts, and while he'd been true to his word and improved his behavior over the last few days, I was not—*not*—about to let myself have a crush on him. I would just have to live with the way my skin tingled whenever he spoke to me. Or looked at me. Or existed anywhere in my general vicinity.

"This is a family establishment," I said to Ty. "I'm going to have to ask you two to leave."

They both grinned as they turned to go. They'd only taken a few steps when June looked over her shoulder. "We'll have a girls' night soon."

"Yeah, yeah. Don't forget, my soaps make great wedding favors!"

Her eyes went wide as people turned to stare at them again, but Ty just hugged her closer and pulled her away.

Lucky dogs.

Those two were so in love it made me want to vomit. For joy, of course. They were as bad as Eden and Booker. As much as I liked teasing them, I truly was happy for June. I'd never seen her so sparkly with delight. Content, too, like she had everything she wanted in the world: a great job, a fabulous family, and she'd found her man.

Of course, she only found him after she'd had her heart ripped out by his no-good, cheating brother. Just like Eden found Booker only after her long-term boyfriend told her he could do better after they finished grad school. What was that garbage they fed girls? *You have to kiss a few frogs before you find your prince.*

I had no intention of kissing any more frogs.

dean

I'D BEEN BROKEN by my own experiment.

After a full week, the only thing I'd proven to Rhett was that at some point, I would clean up his messes. I'd tossed out trash, wiped up spills, and disinfected all morning. I had mere hours before the place started drawing flies again, but for now, I'd made it livable, mostly because Rhett wasn't in it.

I looked around the place, searching for what to do next. Most Saturdays, I went into the office for a few hours at least. Sundays, too. I always had a report to finish or a project to start, anything to tide me over until Monday. But Eliza took Saturdays off, and since my hours in the store were now tied to hers, I had the day off, too.

I'd briefly considered volunteering to work a shift, anyway. The schedule said Nicole and the other college kid had it covered, but Grant would put me to work without a second thought. It might give me something to do, but the prospect of working the sales floor didn't seem much fun without Eliza there.

My usual visit with Grandma wasn't until later in the afternoon, giving me hours to kill. I picked up a book but couldn't settle into it. Nothing on television drew my interest. Only one thing I could do with all this useless energy—time to burn it off.

I changed into sport shorts, an athletic tee, and running shoes. Remembering my dad's advice to try something new, I took off down the street instead of hopping on the treadmill. Far too hot already for a solid run at this time of day, but I could log a few miles at least.

Running usually cleared my mind. One of the reasons I preferred to run indoors—aside from the air conditioning—was to limit the distractions. The pressures and expectations from work fell away with every step until I reached an empty, Zen-like state of pure movement. But not today. Today, my thoughts were crowded with Eliza.

These last few days since our truce, we'd worked side by side without incident. We'd settled into a work routine of friendly banter and mutual helpfulness. We were colleagues developing a successful and amicable rapport. Absolutely nothing untoward or unprofessional about it.

Except for every single one of my thoughts about her.

I'd been safer when she truly disliked me. At least then, I'd had nothing to hope for beyond a brief, pointed conversation whenever she came on staff. Now, the closer we came to true friendship, the more my thoughts tangled around her. I knew they shouldn't, knew she didn't have the same reaction to me, but that didn't stop the glimmer of hope.

I ran along Center Street, glancing into shop windows as I went. The smells wafting out of the diner had my stomach growling for a burger and fries. I passed a new craft brewery that looked interesting, and a yarn store that did not. I jogged by a thrift store and a yoga studio, a gift shop and a pharmacy, all the regular haunts of a thriving small town.

Close to the town hall, orange barricades blocked off the street, and people crowded beneath tents and awnings. I didn't usually shop at the farmers market, but I had an itch to stop in today. No big mystery why. I slowed my pace and strolled the busy aisles, casually checking out booths without any real interest. Most of the stalls held produce, preserves, and other foods, but crafters and artists popped up among them, too. In any case, I'd left my wallet in my apartment.

Eliza's laughter washed over me like a soft caress I wanted to lean into. I spun on the spot, craning my neck to search for her. At last, I saw her standing behind a table piled high with bars of soap, talking animatedly with another woman. My feet moved without a clear thought to do it, her face drawing me closer.

I should turn around, pretend I never saw her, and get on with my aimless weekend. The whole run here, I'd done nothing but tell myself I needed to keep my interest in check. Talking to her outside of the store could only inflame it.

And yet.

Where was the harm, really, in saying hello?

Another customer walked up to Eliza's booth, and the bright, open smile on her face decided me. If I could have nothing else here today, I wanted one of her smiles for myself.

She finally noticed me, and did a legitimate double take. Her gaze traveled from my sneakers to my loose shorts and damp shirt. If I'd given it more thought, I might not have approached her all sweaty from my run, but I couldn't walk away now. Not without looking like a complete jerk, anyway, and I'd had more than enough of that this week.

Her eyes roamed over my chest and arms longer than seemed necessary before they darted back up to my gaze. "What are you doing? You're all…"

Her eyes fell to my chest again.

"I know, sorry about that." I ran a hand down my shirt. "I've been running."

Captain Obvious, reporting for duty.

"I didn't think you owned casual clothes."

I relaxed a little. Maybe she wasn't pointing out my sweat-soaked shirt and desperate need of a shower. "You can't run in dress shirts and loafers."

Her smile encouraged me to move a little closer.

"If anyone can, it would be you. Did you see anything interesting on your run through the market?"

"A few vegetables I couldn't identify, but nothing too unusual. Tell me about all this." I nodded down at the array of soaps laid out in front of her. At least a hundred bars sat in neat stacks and wooden bins, with handwritten labels marking each variety.

"These are just, um..." She made a face, and her laughter sounded strained. "I told you I make soap."

"Sunshine Soul." I read the banner across the front of her tent. It had a stylized sun in the center with rays glowing all around it. Glancing over her soaps, it wasn't hard to catch the theme. *Lavender Luster, Rose Sparkle, Grapefruit Glow*. It fit that her brand would be so sunny and cheerful. That suited her. "I like it."

"Smell a few." She waved me closer before she shifted away to help someone else.

I smelled each soap in turn. Thick, chunky bars that probably appealed to both men and women, they had subtle colors, distinct but not overly bright. Their scents ranged from fruity to floral, spicy to hippie. I inhaled one, and my eyes shot straight to Eliza. This had to be the scent she used. *Rosemary Peppermint*. It smelled exactly like her. I brought it to my face again.

That scent called to mind Eliza unfastening my top button, her eyes unsure but steady, her warmth at once calming and pushing the bounds of my control. That moment stayed stuck in my memory, a brief delight I returned to more often than I should.

"Please don't make love to my soap."

Her pert voice woke me from my little reverie.

"I know it's tempting, but it bothers the other customers."

Her saucy smile sent heat spiraling through my chest. I stopped breathing her in, and put the soap back where it belonged. "How long have you been doing this?"

"About six months. I'd made soap before, but I'd never tried to sell it until this spring."

"And you're doing pretty well?" She'd made several sales in the few minutes I'd been standing by her booth, but I had no idea what kind of profit that correlated to. Considering the soap's price point, it couldn't be much.

"Things could always be better, right?"

"So that's why you had to come back to Irwin's."

She looked away, her mouth pulled down. "Right."

Idiot. I'd dimmed her spark with just a few careless words. Couldn't I keep my thoughtlessness in check for five minutes?

"These look great." I grabbed a bar and smelled it, and barely contained a groan. My hands had sought the rosemary peppermint without me realizing it. "How are they as, you know, soap?"

She smiled at my silly question, a big improvement from the frown I'd caused a second ago.

"They have a great lather, and they're very moisturizing. You should try one."

Against my will, I put the bar down. "I don't have any cash on me, but I will another time."

She shrugged as if it didn't matter one way or the other, but she probably heard empty promises like that all day long. If I'd had money on me, I would have stocked up on soap for the rest of the year.

"Where do you make all these?"

"In my apartment."

"You don't need a big set up?"

"Not for the numbers I make." She moved closer and leaned a hand against the table, her casualness chipping away at the walls I kept telling myself to rebuild. "It's not hard to do, it just takes time and a little know-how."

"Is that legal?" Some cottage businesses could be run from home, but I'd never researched the requirements. Since there were no health department concerns, it probably capped off at some arbitrary number, either sales or production quantity.

She gave me a look like I had a screw loose. "Yes, Dean, it's perfectly legal."

"Do you have to have a license?"

"No."

"What about insurance?"

"Dean." We'd come full circle, and she was back to glaring at me. "Why are you asking so many questions?"

"I'm just interested."

She didn't look like she believed me. Good thing she had no idea just how interested I was.

Her phone buzzed, and she pulled it from her pocket. Hooking a thumb over her shoulder, she turned away from me to take the call. "Go interest yourself in some goat milk."

I looked past her to the next booth over, where a woman stood surrounded by coolers beneath a banner that read Dairy Kid. Goat milk? Huh. I'd never seen that before.

A minute later, Eliza released a little groan of frustration as she put her phone away again.

"Something wrong?"

"My sister and I were supposed to go paddleboarding on Paintbrush Lake tomorrow, but she says some virus is going around Fiesta Village. She's not doing so hot. So I guess that's out."

She kept her tone light, but her *no big deal* grin wasn't very convincing. This meant a lot to her, even if she pretended like it didn't. I was starting to see a pattern.

"Can't you go by yourself?"

"I could, but it's like swimming alone. It's not the smartest idea. Plus, when my sister and I bought the paddleboards, my dad made us promise we'd never go by ourselves."

I liked her father already. Caution was a dying trait.

After half a second's pause, I said, "I could go with you."

Yeah, so much for caution.

Was it a smart offer? No. Could I have stopped myself? Also, apparently, no.

She stared at me and then looked around, as if maybe those words had come out of someone else's mouth. I hadn't fully thought it through—I only knew I wanted to save her day of paddleboarding. A crazy impulse, made all the crazier by my total lack of experience in the sport.

"Really?" She stared up at me as though I'd offered to grow a tail.

Her blatant incredulity only made me stick tighter to the offer. "Sure. It sounds like fun."

Eliza watched me like she doubted I knew what the word *fun* meant. Given some of our conversations, I couldn't blame her.

"You said the other day you've never gone before."

"I haven't. I'm basically guaranteed to fall in."

A little grin broke through her apprehension. "Now you're just trying to sweet talk me."

She had no idea.

"Whatever it takes for you get your time on that lake."

A wistful look came into her eyes. "You really want to go?"

"I absolutely do."

She stared hard at me for two long beats as she drew in a deep breath. "Okay. Sure. Let's go paddleboarding."

I gave her my phone number before jogging back through the market crowd and past Center Street's shops. As I ran, I told myself that really, I was only doing what my dad had asked. I would get some time on a lake, try a new sport, maybe even put some Irwin's gear to use. All in the name of business. My offer had nothing to do with the opportunity to spend time alone with Eliza.

I lied to myself the whole way home.

eliza

I PEEKED out my living room window every few minutes like I was waiting for the delivery guy from Channa Masala to bring me curry. Dean definitely had a *Five minutes early is on time* vibe. No way would he show up at exactly ten.

At first, I hadn't thought he was serious about going paddleboarding with me. He'd made a nice offer, but he would rethink it given enough time. When I texted him last night, I was half-convinced he would back out with a flimsy excuse. Any excuse. Instead, he'd agreed to meet at my place for our day on the lake.

A day on the lake with Dean.

I told myself this was perfectly normal, nothing to stress over. In the past, I'd gone on hikes, bike rides, and other little outings with my Irwin's coworkers and never thought twice about it. But in the past, none of my coworkers had made my stomach feel like it was turning inside out when they looked at me.

Gravel crunched outside. That had to be Dean, at nine fifty-five on the nose. I grabbed my bag and headed out the door before he could try to come up. I had no intention of letting him see my tiny, over-the-garage studio apartment crammed with soap at one end and my bed at the other. At least I'd made the bed this morning, but his ability to see everything I owned in one quick glance wouldn't do me any favors.

I jogged down the stairs to meet him. "Are you all set?"

"I'm ready."

Except for the little pull of uncertainty at his mouth, he looked pretty set. Naturally, he'd found the most sedate board shorts of all time. Slate gray, they could have matched the slacks he wore to work most days. He also wore a plain blue T-shirt and running shoes. Thankfully, this T-shirt left a little more to the imagination than the one he'd worn yesterday. Yesterday, I'd stared like I was trying to decipher a code in his chest muscles.

Good Lord, I missed that shirt.

I'd strapped the paddleboards to my Bronco's roof first thing this morning, and packed a simple lunch for after. Setting the cooler in the back seat, I gestured for him to climb in. He turned to walk around the car, and I caught sight of his backpack.

Oh, this couldn't be good. We hadn't even left my driveway and I was already irritated with him.

"You have a Vireo, I see." I buckled my seat belt with a snap.

He tucked his bag behind the seat. "I bought it from you this week."

I turned the key, but the Bronco's engine didn't roll over. "I very much remember *not* selling you that pack."

"I put it under your sales number when I bought it."

"Why would you do that? Why didn't you use your employee discount?" The Irwin's discount was one of the perks that kept me coming back. That, and at this point, it was my longest-running job.

He shrugged, apparently unbothered he'd spent more

money than he needed to. Must be nice. "Your sales pitch convinced me. It's only fair."

He'd paid full price just so I could get the commission? I wanted to believe he'd done it out of a sense of fair play, but his reasons probably leaned more toward guilt. Giving me a big commission to make up for his remark about working retail felt like a very Dean thing to do.

"You didn't need to do that." I tried the ignition again. Of course it would act up today in front of Dean, like everything I touched turned to crap.

He stared at the dash like Superman busting out his X-ray vision on the Bronco's crummy engine. "Does it need a jump?"

"It's just got a tricky ignition, it's fine." Encouraged by my confidence, the engine finally fired up. "It's just old."

"It sounds like you should take it to a mechanic."

I backed out of the driveway past Dean's car. A sensible sedan, as I'd expected, and electric to boot. "My dad usually fixes all that, but he's busy vaccinating everybody's calves right now."

Dean's eyebrows shot up.

"He's a large animal vet. Anyway, I'm afraid if I tell him about the ignition issue, he'll just want to buy me a new car."

"You need one. This one's on its last legs."

I pointed an accusatory finger at him. "First, I love this Bronco, so don't talk that way about it. Second, that's not the point. My parents try to do too much for me as it is."

"Like what?"

Their never-ending acts of helpfulness paraded through my mind. "Anything. If I stop in for dinner, they have a week's worth of groceries delivered to my door. I mentioned once I needed new jeans, and they bought me three pairs."

"You're lucky to have people who care so much about you."

"I know they only want to help," I said, trying not to sound like a little ingrate. "The problem is, the more they help, the more helpless I feel. I'm not their baby anymore. All their advice and offers to take care of me just reinforce the idea that I can't handle life."

I'd been avoiding this particular hard truth for a while now, but for some reason, I gave voice to it in plain language to Dean. I couldn't tell you why. Maybe because he watched me without expression, an indifferent outsider to my family drama. Or maybe I just figured his opinion of me couldn't get any lower. Rock bottom had some benefits.

"You seem like you can handle plenty to me."

A disgusted sound came out of my mouth before I could stop it. "How can you say that with a straight face? I've had eight jobs in the four years since I graduated college, I live over somebody's garage, and my car is older than I am."

"That's not saying much."

"How old are you, then?"

His eyes shifted to me. "Thirty-one."

"Five years isn't that much older, Father Time."

He laughed for a minute, a deep, rumbling sound in his chest that seemed to echo in mine. Had he ever truly laughed around me before? Now that I'd heard a hint of his laugh, I was greedy for the whole thing.

"How did it go at the market yesterday?" he asked after another minute. "Did you sell a lot of soap?"

"A pretty good amount, yeah. My sales aren't as high as they were in summer, but I'm still holding on to strong numbers." Tanisha had told me to expect a drop until winter, when the markets would be packed again for the holidays. Seasonal changes were just one aspect of many I hadn't considered when I dropped everything to go into business for myself.

"Is that the only place you sell your soaps?"

I hitched a shoulder. "For now. I have a website, too, but it hasn't really taken off."

"What about wholesale opportunities?"

"I've tried." Sort of. I hadn't tried again since Countryside said *Thanks, but no thanks.* I had a feeling if I got very many more rejections, my veneer of confidence would crumble away entirely. Better to hold on to what I had than risk even more disappointment.

"No luck?"

I flashed a wide grin. "Basically, I'm broke."

"What's your plan for your soap business, if you don't mind me asking?"

"I do mind you asking." I gripped the steering wheel tighter, fully embracing my snippy tone.

Dean just sat in the passenger seat with his head turned toward me as though waiting for me to confess my sins. I had plenty, although very few of them were the fun kind. Mostly, they were the financial and career-killing kind.

"So there's no plan," he said after a while.

"Nope."

I drove in silence, hoping that would be the end of it. I didn't want more questions that would shine a light on just how blindly I'd rushed into this whole soap-selling thing. I'd quit my day job with no plan, no agenda, just the lure of working for myself. Without a solid long-term goal, no wonder I was stuck treading water now, but I'd never been the best at thinking long-range.

"You know," he said after another pause, "I could help you figure out a business plan."

I exhaled a laugh. "That's a bad idea."

"Why?"

"I don't think I can..." *Rely on you. Trust you. Need you.* "That would be weird, don't you think?"

"Why is it weird? I don't know much about soap, but I know a few things about business plans. I have an MBA."

I faked a gasp. "You don't say."

"What?"

"Everybody knows you have an MBA, Dean. It basically makes you Eligible Bachelor Number One in Magnolia Ridge. All the moms I know are dying to set you up with their daughters."

"Huh." A short little pause, and then, "Where does your mom stand on that?"

"She's probably first in line, but I have a strict No Businessmen policy."

"Why no businessmen?"

I shifted in my seat as Magnolia Ridge's residential areas faded into farmland. "I'm allergic to starch."

A heavy silence settled over the car. I felt like I'd said the exact wrong thing, and yet I couldn't for the life of me believe he might care what I thought about businessmen. Dean wasn't interested in me, right? Just like I wasn't interested in him. Right?

Right?

"Is this what you really want to do as a career?" he asked after a few minutes. "Sell soap?"

"I don't know. I love the creativity of making the soaps, designing them and mixing them. And I like working for myself. There's no competition, no worry about what happens to my work when I let go of it, no one waiting to stab me in the back."

"Is that what happened in your other jobs?"

His voice had gone gentle, and that alone killed me. How pathetic must I sound to bring out Dean Irwin's soft side? I turned to him again, but had to look back at the road. His open, curious eyes could make me confess everything if I let them. If anything could make him think even less of me, that story would.

"That's enough Dean questions, now it's time for Eliza questions."

He grumbled but didn't argue. He put both his hands on his knees as though preparing himself. "Let's hear it."

"What's with all the suits?"

"Excuse me?"

I waved a hand over him. "You know what I mean. Nobody else around town wears a suit every day."

"Maybe that's why I do it."

"Ah." I nodded as if he'd given away something important. "They're a protective shield you wear to give everybody that Dean Aura."

"What *Dean Aura*?"

"I'm asking the questions now. Why don't you ever eat at Homegrown? I never see you in there."

"You're not looking at the right time. I'm a big fan of the bacon burgers. Next question."

"What is your office like? I'm thinking stark white, sharp smell of disinfectant, people go in, but they never come out."

"You've thought about my office a lot."

"It helps me sleep."

"So you go to sleep thinking about me in my office."

I heard the smile in his voice, but when I turned to catch a glimpse of it, his face had gone neutral again.

"Interesting," he added.

"You're not in the office when I think about it." *Lies.* "You've just stepped out, probably to fire someone, and I rummage through your desk."

"Not that it matters in your imaginary scenario, but I've never fired anyone."

"No? I'd think you were made for firing people."

"You don't know me as well as you should."

I refused to think about what that little jab meant, and focused instead on the seriousness of his voice.

"Have you always been this intense? I'm trying to imagine you as a kid and it's just not working."

"Yes, I've always been this intense."

The edge to his voice made me think I'd crossed a line in my rapid-fire teasing. I held my breath, debating what to do, but when he spoke again, his voice had lost that tension.

"I had anger issues when I was a kid. I wasn't very good at controlling my temper. Anything could set me off. Arguments, disappointments, frustrations. Sports were the worst. If I lost a game or got less than first place, I just...lost it."

I stayed very still, like if I pretended I wasn't here, Dean would keep talking. This revealing moment seemed fleeting, and he might clam up and go straight back to icy stares if I said or did the wrong thing.

"My brothers were both great at sports, and that only made my outbursts worse. I was good, too, but I wanted to be the best. It was harder, in that way, being *almost* as good as they were. As I got older and learned ways to control my anger, I found it easier if I didn't compete with them. I stopped going out for sports. I stopped biking with them so it wouldn't turn into a race. I stopped climbing with them in case I couldn't climb as high or as fast. It took a long time, but eventually, I got to a place where I didn't even miss it anymore."

My heart fluttered to hear this usually stoic man so open and vulnerable. I reached over and took his hand, a silent thanks for being willing to share anything at all with me. Holding his hand felt right and good, like our restart handshake had—like nothing in the world could be more natural. I didn't let go, but kept hold as I drove, enchanted by the warmth of his skin.

"I threw myself into school." His words came out soft but unashamed. "Tests and grades had a predictable outcome that sports didn't. I could control all of that if I put in enough effort, enough hours. Work is pretty much the same. I guess I'm still competing, but just with myself."

"I'm sorry for what I said the other day, that was so mean of me." I'd blurted out horrid things about his lack of outdoors experience, never guessing anything tender could be hiding just beneath his impassive veneer.

"You didn't know."

His thumb traced a pattern over my fingers, and I had to bite back a sigh at the sweetness of his touch.

How was this happening? Two weeks ago, I would have never thought he could be so gentle, even with me. Maybe especially with me. Now, the soft little touches sent shivers up my arm and into my chest, lodging there like they intended to stay.

I swung the Bronco into the lake access parking lot and found a spot, my hand still enveloped in Dean's.

"Do you still deal with anger issues?" I asked softly. He'd stepped in pretty quickly when that sleeping bag guy was being a creep. He hadn't been angry exactly, but I'd seen the tension coiling beneath the surface.

"I've learned ways to keep it in check. Running is one." He lightly squeezed my hand. "I can still be intense, though. About certain things."

His low voice hummed through me. The Bronco's cab had never seemed this small before. Shouldn't there have been more space between us? For safety's sake? My heartbeat raced in my ears even as I told myself this nervousness was ridiculous. I wasn't looking to kiss any frogs, and I wasn't yet convinced Dean was a prince.

But the longer we sat in silence, the more I wanted to lean closer to see what might happen next.

I did not lean. My skill set was pushing away, not drawing close. So why was I still sitting here looking into Dean's eyes like I'd found something important and wholly unexpected there?

"Thank you for telling me."

His tiny smile stirred up a warm breeze in my chest.

"Thank you for asking."

Finally, I pulled my hand free from his. There was only so long we could hold hands in my car before it got weird, and we'd passed that mark a few miles back. He let my fingers slip through his without a word.

"Are you ready to get your paddleboard on?" I asked too loudly, then clapped my hands together for good measure, in case he didn't know I was the most awkward woman ever. Thankfully, I managed not to finger-gun him again.

He parted his lips to answer, and I had to look away. If I looked at his mouth one second more, I really would have leaned in, and how dumb would that make me? Businessman, suit, and coworker, all rolled into one? I'd ridden that ride, burned the T-shirt.

Kissing Dean would be the biggest mistake I could make.

The biggest, best mistake ever.

dean

I'D MADE A HUGE MISTAKE.

I knew it when I climbed into Eliza's hulk of a car and her fresh, heavenly scent surrounded me. I knew it when I confided about my anger issues, something I never relived if I could avoid it. I knew it when she took my hand and something deep in my chest shifted into place.

My mistake became even clearer as Eliza shimmied out of her shorts and T-shirt at the lakeside. We'd carried the paddleboards down to the water's edge, where she was losing her clothes in a pile. Her floral swimsuit wasn't skimpy or especially revealing, and yet every inch of skin she bared felt like a miracle. She tugged a rash guard on over the suit, concealing everything and nothing. I could die a happy man for having seen that suit.

"Ready?"

I swallowed hard, willing away all the delightful images that sprang to mind. "Ready."

We let the paddle boards float, cool water washing over our feet and calves. Though already late in September, chilly autumn weather was still months away. The day was hot, and after watching Eliza get ready to swim, the lake water wasn't nearly cold enough.

"We should probably go a little way out before you climb on your board." She sat cross-legged on hers as she paddled, and quickly lost me while I waded through knee-deep water.

"What is this?" I asked, peering at something pale in the shallows.

"What?"

"This lobster thing. Is this a dead lobster baby?"

She turned her paddle board around. "It's a dead crawfish, but you're morbid."

"You're the one who brought me to a lobster baby grave-yard." They littered the lake bottom, spurring me to climb on my board and remove all possibility of accidentally stepping on one of the disgusting things.

She shook her head at me, muttering, "The man doesn't even know what a crawfish is."

I threw a leg across my board and paddled after her, my legs dragging through the water. It'd been years since I'd last paddled anything, and I struggled to find a steady cadence.

"You'll want to start on your knees."

She demonstrated by going first to all fours and then rising up to her knees with the agility of a yoga instructor. My stomach clenched as I drank her in. I could watch her do that move all day.

"I don't think I caught that. Could you go to all fours again?"

She looked surprised for a second, as if she wasn't sure if this was me flirting or not. But when she caught my mischie-vous smile, she echoed it.

"I think you've got the idea, Mr. Sassy."

Denied a repeat viewing of the most glorious thing I'd seen in ages, I shifted onto all fours. My board keeled back and forth beneath me as I tried to keep my balance. No matter how still I tried to be, it shook and wobbled like a bad carnival ride.

"You're doing great." Paddling wide circles around me, Eliza made it look like nothing could be easier. "When you're ready, move to your knees."

"I don't think it's going to go so hot." Maybe I should have given my genius plan to spend the day with Eliza a little more thought. I'd wanted to save her day, sure, but at the total expense of my ego? That ego always seemed first on the chopping block with her.

"You can do it. Just get up."

Her confidence encouraged me to go for it. I shifted a leg from beneath me, the oar gripped tight on the board, but as soon as I moved to stand, I lurched and fell into the lake. I bobbed to the surface, inhaling sharply. The water wasn't all that cold, but it still shocked my system. I reached for my oar, swam the two strokes to the board, and laid my arms across it.

Only then did I realize how much harder getting on the board from the water would be than it had been on shore. With no purchase beneath me, I had to slither up on my belly like a fish. Thank God I managed to get on the board and keep my shorts above my hips at the same time. Eliza had already given me plenty of nicknames—losing my trunks would surely earn a new one.

She paddled closer. "How's the water?"

"Just get up?" I sputtered at her.

"Think of it like tackling a really tough spreadsheet."

I barked a laugh, and she just grinned back. Now *this* side of her, I would take.

"You can sit on it like a kayak and paddle if you don't want to try standing again."

I ran my fingers through my sopping hair, shaking it out. "You're giving up on me already?"

"I'm giving you an out. There's a difference."

I didn't want an out. I went through the process again, moving from wobbly all-fours to a successful kneel, but as soon as I tried to stand, I fell in. Groaning, I pulled myself onto the board for the second time.

Whatever delicious thoughts I'd entertained about Eliza at the water's edge, I couldn't possibly be inspiring similar thoughts in her. Nothing about my failed attempts to stand on the board, or my clumsy process for getting back on it, could be considered sexy. I spent a full fifteen minutes just learning how to stand without dumping myself in. To her credit, she didn't laugh at me, but I was pretty sure she came close a time or two.

I finally managed to stand, but then froze. Any attempt to paddle would surely land me straight in the lake, and I needed at least a few seconds to enjoy this victory.

"I would have expected you to have more ab strength," she said, drifting a few yards away.

I raised my eyebrows at her.

"What? You've got a whole washboard thing going on over there."

"I didn't think you'd noticed."

"You showed up at my booth yesterday in a skin-tight shirt. I noticed *everything*."

The confirmation she *had* entertained sexy thoughts about me threw off my precarious balance—I overcompensated and fell right back in. This time, she did laugh, but probably only because I was laughing, too.

"You're enjoying this," I said, pulling myself onto my board.

"I'm enjoying parts of it."

Her wicked grin heated me up until I wished we weren't separated by fifteen feet and a whole lot of water. What would it be like to kiss that grin? To taste that mouth?

I cupped my hands in the water and doused my face, but I'd grown immune now to the chill.

After a little more trial and error, I figured out how to stand on the board and keep my balance well enough to paddle. Eliza offered words of encouragement whenever I needed them, and I needed plenty. There was nothing graceful about my movements out of the water, and it didn't take much to send me straight back in, but I managed. We coasted a safe distance from the rocky shore, startling ducks and the occasional fish rippling beneath the surface.

"This is peaceful." Even after all the careening into the lake, I couldn't deny the serenity of the place. "I can see why you like it so much."

I'd spent years creating a safe harbor for myself, a way to control my temper through meditation and running. Out on the lake, I was starting to realize there was more than one way to reach that shore.

She paddled close enough I could see the dimple near her mouth when she smiled. "You're an old pro now."

I wasn't anything close to it, but I'd accept her compliment. "I've got the best teacher."

Her smile went crooked, as if my words didn't quite ring true. Considering our first rocky week, I guess I understood her skepticism. Regret for all my careless words sank through me yet again, but I decided that from now on, when I complimented Eliza, I'd make sure she knew I meant it.

By the time we returned to shore, I needed the break. I'd never had a workout quite like that, as unexpected little muscle aches reminded me. Eliza, on the other hand, somehow looked *more* energized, as if she could paddle all afternoon. We dragged the boards to a grassy area near a picnic table, and she ran to her Bronco, returning a minute later with beach towels and her cooler.

She tossed one of the towels to me. "You look like you could use this."

I ran it over my hair. "You're not even wet."

"Aw, you did great, though. I've seen people give up on standing, but you refused to let it beat you."

"It's all that intensity."

She twisted her lips as if she were biting something back, and I would have bought all the soaps in the world to know what she was thinking. Whatever it was, she kept it to herself.

She sat down across from me at the picnic table and opened the cooler. "I've got water bottles, granola bars, and sandwiches in here. Nothing fancy, but I figured we'd be hungry after."

"It sounds good to me."

We ate in silence, looking out across the lake. Other paddle boarders and kayakers skimmed the blue-green waters, and the play park at the lakeside had its share of visitors, but it wasn't crowded. Even kids' shrieks ringing out now and then couldn't spoil the peace of the moment. If I could go back and redo my interview with Explore Texas, I'd tell them my favorite spot was right here.

"How is your sister doing? Have you talked to her today?"

Eliza spun on the bench to face me. "I visited her yesterday after market ended. She was in pretty bad shape. I feel for everybody at the retirement center if that's what's going around."

"I'm sorry she's sick, but I'm grateful you let me take her place."

"She was sad to miss it. We've been talking about it for weeks."

"Do you come out here a lot then?"

"Not as much as we used to." She picked at her sandwich bread. "Not this summer, anyway. I've been busy with all my soap stuff and working the market on Saturdays. Before that, we had my oldest sister's wedding to deal with, so we haven't had a lot of chances."

"All the more reason I'm glad I could join you."

Her mouth twisted. "You say that like people are beating down my door to go paddleboarding with me."

"Aren't they?"

"No. I only got Eden out here a couple of times. She's one of the ones who gave up trying to stand, FYI. I'd ask my cousin June, but she's been pretty tangled up with her man. Most of my friends are that way now, honestly, so Harper's kind of my only option when I want to go out."

She dropped her chin into her hands. "That came out a lot more pathetic than I thought it would. Let's talk about you again, that will cheer me up."

I raised my eyebrows.

"Because your social life is more pathetic than mine, obviously," she added.

"Obviously."

Her expression turned curious, her eyes alight. "Do you really work weekends all the time? Never go out, never do anything fun, just work all the time?"

I figured we'd eventually circle back here, and yet, I hadn't come up with a better answer since the last time we'd talked about it.

"That's taking it a little far, but yes, I usually work weekends."

"So yesterday after I saw you at the market you just, what, ran to the office and started in on those spreadsheets?"

"Again with the spreadsheets."

"It's the only thing I know."

I fought back laughter. "No spreadsheets. Yesterday, I spent the afternoon with a woman."

Her friendly smile disappeared, and she straightened like she'd been stuck with a cattle prod. "Oh. That's nice."

Her odd tone didn't sound like she thought it was very nice.

"Yes, she's very nice." Wrong of me to tease her, but I hadn't expected to get a rise out of her. "She loves to make dinner for me."

Her mouth turned sour. "Lucky you."

"She calls me her special boy."

Her eyebrows pulled down as she glowered at the table. "I don't need to hear about this."

"Eliza, it's my grandmother."

She looked at me for a second as she processed that. Then she leaned over the table and smacked me on the shoulder. "You're a jerk."

I risked a smile, rubbing my arm. "What did I do?"

"You know what you did."

"I was simply telling you about my day with my grandma." The little flash of jealousy that had brought out? Just a bonus. "She's moving into the retirement center in a few weeks, and I've been helping her clear things out."

"Don't tell her about the stomach bug over there."

"I'll keep it to myself."

She gathered her lunch trash into a small bag. "It must be hard to downsize your whole life like that. I can't imagine having to get rid of most of my stuff."

"It's just stuff."

Her eyebrows twitched higher. "So you wouldn't mind throwing out all your things? I could just back a dump truck up to your house and throw it all in?"

"I'd hope you'd use some discretion, but no, I wouldn't really mind."

She stared at me as if searching for the lie.

"I'm not sentimental about things. I don't hold onto something useless just because it once belonged to long-gone family members."

"You're cold."

A chill doused my good mood. Not the first time someone had said that to me, but it might have been the first time it bothered me. It hit too close to how I figured she truly saw me —cold-hearted, efficient, and brutal.

"I suppose you still have all your stuffed animals from childhood."

She hitched a shoulder. "My apartment's too small, but yeah, they're all still over at my parents' house."

"Getting rid of things that are holding you back can be very freeing."

She batted her eyelashes at me. "Even Bun-Bun?"

"Especially Bun-Bun."

Our drive home from Paintbrush Lake went by faster than I expected, with Eliza peppering me the whole time with questions about my grandma. Probably the safest topic she could think of, after her uncomfortable talk of work and my bizarre confessional on the drive out. By the time she pulled into her driveway, she knew all about my grandmother's eagerness to move into the retirement center, her long list of friends there, and the short list of items she planned to take with her.

"Are you really going to let her sell all her old furniture?" Eliza said as she climbed out of the Bronco. "You've got to take something."

I grabbed my backpack and joined her at the other side of the car where I'd parked my Prius. "Where would I put it? My townhouse doesn't have room for secretary desks and old hutches."

She sighed, and the sound made my stomach tighten.

"I love a good secretary desk. It's heartless of you to make her sell all that."

I stilled at her offhand remark. The h-word. Again, not the first time I'd heard it, but I didn't love hearing it come from her lips. "I'm not making her do anything. Simple math says she can't keep it all when she moves into Fiesta Village."

"It's still a shame. I'd probably cry if my parents ever sold their house and parceled off all their belongings."

I said nothing. If she was waiting for me to tell her I was equally cut up about my grandmother's move, she would keep waiting. Losing the old house would be an adjustment, but logically, it had to happen one day. If some of my more fanciful hopes for my future were tied to it, well... I needed to be realistic.

"Anyway," she said after a minute. "Thanks for coming out with me today. I had a really good time."

"You sound surprised."

"I am."

Her warm smile softened the sting of how thoroughly she'd written me off. She shifted forward, and for one glorious moment, I thought she was moving in for a hug. I wasn't idiot enough to think she would ever kiss me, but a hug seemed appropriate. Instead of closing the distance, she caught herself and shuffled backwards, as if to prove she hadn't leaned forward in the first place.

I refused to be denied all possibility of touching her, and held out a hand. She glanced down at it, and for a second, I thought she might slap it away. Then she laughed, the sound awkward and strained, but placed her hand in mine and shook it.

It would be so easy to tug her to me and hold her tight, to kiss her like I'd been wanting to do all day. Longer. But I still saw that fleeting uncertainty in her eyes that said while she might like me a little more than she had, she didn't yet trust me.

Now more than ever, I wanted to earn that trust. I wanted her to see me as more than an uptight coworker.

I wanted her to see *me*.

The longer we shook hands, the wider her eyes got, filling with something I couldn't name. Finally, she pulled her hand from mine, as if she knew I had no intention of letting go first.

"I'll see you tomorrow," she blurted, and turned to dash up the stairs to her apartment.

I watched her go as I climbed into my car, stretching my fingers as though I could ease away the shiver that thrilled through them from her touch.

SIXTEEN

I WALKED into Irwin's back office Monday morning ready to get out on the sales floor. Maybe I hadn't expected to enjoy this job a week ago, but now, the idea of working all day with Eliza had me eager to conquer some retail mountains. I'd spent most of Sunday with her, and it hadn't been nearly enough. It seemed we were on the verge of something here, and I was ready to go head-first over the edge.

But instead of my chipper former nemesis, I found Nicole in the back office suiting up in her green vest. I checked the schedule on the whiteboard and confirmed it read *Eliza & Dean*.

"Hey, Dean." Nicole flashed a big, dentist office smile as she walked past me to the sales floor.

I echoed her greeting and turned to Grant, who sat at the desk typing on his laptop.

"Where's Eliza?"

He didn't look up. "She called in sick, so I asked Nicole to fill in with you today."

"What's wrong with her?"

"Some stomach bug. I told her to stay home for a couple of

days at least. If anyone else here gets it, we'll have a disaster. We can't close in the lead-up to the anniversary celebration."

A stomach bug. She'd probably caught it when she checked on her sister over the weekend. Of course, she'd just had to stop by when a text would have been more prudent.

"Did you talk to her? How did she sound?"

"Pretty out of it."

Whatever she was sick with had come on in the last twelve hours. She was probably in the worst of it right now.

"Did she happen to say if she needed anything?" I asked, slipping my vest on.

Grant finally looked up. "Why are you so worried about Eliza?"

"I'm not worried, I just want to make sure she's being taken care of." Avoiding my brother's eye, I snapped the vest cabinet shut. "I'm going to go help Nicole."

Yes, fine, I was worried. Eliza could take care of herself, and yet everything about her said she wouldn't ask for help unless it came down to an emergency situation. I didn't like the idea of her just lying in her apartment, suffering valiantly on her own. But she had family nearby—they would probably take care of her.

That *probably* ate at me all day.

I talked with customers and rang up sales, but couldn't muster more than a half-hearted *Thanks for shopping at Irwin's*. Nicole kept me entertained with a running stream of horror stories of customers past and dental assistant school present, but it wasn't the same. I missed Eliza's teasing smile. I missed how she lit up the whole place. I missed *her*.

In the afternoon, I finally texted her.

Dean: How are you doing?
Eliza: Not awesome

Dean: Do you need anything?
Eliza: I'm okay

That didn't answer my question.

Dean: Can I stop by after work to check on you?

She didn't respond right away. As the minutes ticked by, I worried I'd gone too far.

Eliza: You'll just get sick, too

Still not a no.

Dean: I never get sick. I'll see you after my shift

As soon as I clocked out, I swung by the grocery store. Eliza didn't admit to needing anything, but I picked up a few essentials just in case. I didn't want her to get her appetite back after being sick and have nothing suitable to eat.

I parked behind her Bronco with the two paddleboards still strapped to its roof. I texted a quick *I'm here*, grabbed the grocery bags, and climbed the stairs to her apartment.

Shifting from foot to foot on the small landing, I started sweating under the afternoon sun. No sound came from inside. I knocked. Agonizing minutes went by. I was contemplating the logistics of kicking down her front door when the deadbolt turned. Eliza swung the door open and slumped against the frame.

Dark circles ringed her glassy eyes. "You're going to regret this."

Her voice came out hoarse and achy, like just forming words was too much to bear. Wobbling on her feet, she clutched the doorjamb to steady herself. I dropped the grocery bags on the landing and put an arm around her before she swayed again. She only wore a tank top and pajama shorts, but her skin was on fire. A fever flush stood out against her cheeks, and her hair hung in sweaty tendrils, pink and blond tangles stuck to her neck and shoulders.

I peeked inside her apartment. An attic studio, it was all angled ceilings and whitewashed walls, with a tiny kitchenette near the door and a bed at the other end. In between, one whole wall of shelves stood stuffed full of soap bars.

"Let's get you back in bed. Is it okay if I pick you up?"

It wasn't that far to walk, but she didn't look like she had the energy. She nodded, and I scooped her into my arms. Nestling against my chest, she rested one hand on the nape of my neck, a little ball of fire on my skin. I carried her across the small apartment and laid her down in her bed.

"You shouldn't have come." Her voice came out thick, as if tears might spring to her eyes. "I don't want to get you sick, too."

"I told you, I never get sick." I gently smoothed her hair out of her face. "I'll be fine."

"I'm gross, don't look at me." She covered her face with one hand. "And don't look at my apartment, it's a mess."

"I won't look at anything. I'm going to bring the groceries in, okay?"

She pulled her hand away from her eyes. "You brought stuff? You weren't supposed to bring stuff."

I didn't bother acknowledging that. No way would I come over here empty-handed when she was sick. Grabbing the bags I'd left on the landing, I made space in the fridge and coun-tertop for the things I'd bought. Not much, but it might help when she felt a little better. I wet a clean washcloth in the tiny bathroom and brought it to her.

Sitting next to her on the bed, I laid the cool cloth across her forehead. She looked up at me as if seeing me from far away. Seeing this lively woman so wretched set an ache deep in my heart.

"What did you bring?"

"Gatorade, Seven-Up, saltines. A quart of plain chicken soup for when you're ready. Do you want anything now?"

She shifted her head to the side. "Just some water."

I found a glass in the kitchen and filled it with cold water. Returning to her bedside, I helped her sit up and eased the glass to her lips until she'd swallowed a few sips. I made room for the glass on her nightstand crowded with books. *Grow Your Own Business, Start Small, Grow Big*, and *Easy Entrepreneur* stood out among other titles. She was probably getting conflicting and potentially damaging advice from that stack of easy-answer hack jobs.

She slumped back into bed, her hair splaying across the pink polka dot pillowcase.

"How can I help you?" I whispered. Bring her ice chips, spoon-feed her broth, research her best marketing plan—she could have asked for anything, and I would have done it.

"Go back in time and tell me not to visit Harper."

Some of the squeezing in my chest eased. "At least you have enough energy to joke. That's a good sign."

"I came up with a lot of zingers on the bathroom floor this morning."

I laid the washcloth back over her forehead. "Have you taken your temperature?"

"A little while ago. One-oh-two point seven."

Higher than I would have liked, but not high enough to need medical attention. Nothing to do but treat her symptoms as best we could.

"I'm cold."

She reached for her covers, but I only tugged the sheet over her. "It's already pretty warm in here. If you get too hot, it could make your fever worse."

Shivering beneath the thin sheet, she pulled the washcloth off her forehead.

"El, you need this, you're burning up." I took the cloth from her and tried to put it back in its place, but she blocked me with a trembling hand.

"I have to get up." She struggled uselessly against me like she was treading water.

"You need to rest."

"I'm going to barf."

I pushed off the bed and helped her to the bathroom, and she slammed the door closed as soon as she made it inside. She probably wouldn't want me to wait by the door while she was sick, so I tried to make a little noise in the kitchen.

I had no loss of things to do in the small space. I filled the sink with soapy water and washed her stack of dirty dishes, placing them in the drying rack. Beneath the sink, I found a bottle of cleaner and some dishcloths, so I wiped down her countertops and dining table. The label didn't say it was germ-killing, but still better than nothing. I wiped down most of the hard surfaces in the apartment for good measure.

Still waiting for a sign from Eliza, I examined the soaps on her shelves. Hundreds of bars of twenty or more varieties of soaps sat neatly spaced and labeled. The bottom row of each shelf held different sized tubs and bottles carefully laid out, along with pots, bowls, and spatulas.

It wasn't hard to see she'd maxed out her space. She needed two bedrooms, let alone one. Better yet, she needed a workshop where she could concoct, create, and store soaps to her heart's content. There had to be a better place for her to live and work in Magnolia Ridge. But she'd told me on our drive to the lake that she was broke. If she was struggling enough to need a second job, no way could she afford to rent a bigger place.

Eliza opened the bathroom door looking worse for wear. I went to her and wrapped an arm around her waist. She leaned into me, her skin fire everywhere we touched. I helped her back into bed and slipped the sheet over her again.

"Can I have that washcloth now?"

I found it and replaced it on her forehead. Brushing her hair out of her face, I let my hand rest against her soft, flushed cheek.

Her eyes drifted closed. "You're being so nice."

"Weird, I know." I hadn't made a very good impression on her in the past, but I hoped I'd changed her mind about me.

Her weak smile tugged at my chest, encouraging my heart to come out to play.

"I'm sorry I give you such a hard time. It's just easier."

"Easier than what?"

She opened her eyes. "Liking you."

Even if she was sick and miserable and strung out with fever, her soft little confession wound its way around my heart, shattering the walls I'd built up brick by brick. I stroked her cheek with my thumb, my mind racing, searching for something to say that wouldn't screw this moment up.

"I don't have a great history with nice guys," she said softly.

I could hear the air quotes around *nice guys*. She didn't like businessmen either. I wanted to know who she meant, what had happened, and how to track the guy down. Now wasn't the time to question her, though.

"But I don't think you're a nice guy. I think you're a good guy."

My chest swelled to hear her say that, but I probably shouldn't encourage more sweet disclosures in her state. She might have serious regrets about this conversation tomorrow.

"I think you're delirious."

She nodded, almost nuzzling against my palm. "That must be it."

"I should let you get some sleep." I didn't truly want to leave, but figured she would rest easier without me watching over her.

Her chest rose and fell in deep, slow breaths. "Okay."

Without thinking, I leaned in to kiss her forehead, but the impulse died when someone knocked on her front door at the same time they opened it.

"Eliza, baby, how are you doing?"

A middle-aged woman who could have been Eliza fast-forwarded in time walked through the door, stopping cold when she caught sight of me. I was sitting on Eliza's bed, caressing her face while she lay there barely dressed. Sick as a dog, yes, but still barely dressed.

I scrambled to my feet but didn't leave Eliza's side. Her eyes darted to the door, and her mouth contorted into a not-quite-smile. She made a broad gesture at me, her fingers brushing mine before she dropped her hand again.

"Mom, this is Dean Irwin. He's a coworker of mine."

Frozen with one foot over the threshold, her mother took in the scene. A second later, she recovered herself, and her shocked expression smoothed into one of polite interest, her manner almost regal as she walked across the room toward me. I still hated to leave Eliza, but I met her mother halfway.

"Darlene Webb," she said as we shook hands.

"Nice to meet you. I just stopped in to check on Eliza."

"That's very kind of you."

Her friendly smile eased away my fear she might call the cops after finding me on the bed with her practically-incapacitated daughter. Now if it had been her calf-vaccinating husband, all bets would have been off.

She went to Eliza's side and placed a hand on her pink cheek. "Oh, baby, you're hot as Hades. Have you had anything for the fever?"

"She can't hold anything down yet," I told her.

Darlene nodded, her eyes glued to me as if I might have further insight into Eliza's condition. She waited a beat, but I just stood there not knowing what to say. I really didn't have the right bedside manner for this.

"I just came by to check in on her," I said. Again. I wasn't handling this unexpected meeting with her mother like a pro. "Eliza, the soup and drinks are in the fridge when you're hungry."

She nodded, and her mouth eased into a soft little smile. "Thank you for coming by."

"Anytime." I needed her to know I meant that without question.

"It's so good of you to look after my baby girl," Darlene said. "When she's feeling better, you should come over for dinner with our family as a thank you."

"I'd like that." I held up a hand in a brief goodbye to Eliza, who lifted her fingers in return. "Rest up."

I nodded to her mother. "Mrs. Webb."

"Darlene, please."

"Okay. Darlene."

I walked to the door and cast one last glance back at Eliza. She smiled faintly as I pulled the door closed, that tiny smile twisting and tugging inside me.

Yeah. There went all hope for putting a stop to my growing affection for Eliza Webb.

eliza

PRETTY SURE THE fluttering in my stomach wasn't puke anymore.

Life wasn't fair. I'd just experienced the sweetest moment with Dean, and I was the grossest I'd ever been. He'd been so kind to me, bringing food and helping me to the bathroom. Oh, sweet Lord, the bathroom. On second thought, maybe it *was* puke swirling in my stomach. If seeing me in all my snarky glory at Irwin's wasn't bad enough, he'd been ten feet away while I emptied my guts.

You go, little rockstar.

When Dean was safely out the door, my mom turned to me with a serene smile. "He's awfully handsome. All those Irwin boys are."

I groaned and shut my eyes. I hadn't done anything to deserve this. Only my mother could intrude on...well, whatever had been happening with Dean, and then gloat about it. "We just work together."

"How nice of him to bring you *soup*." As though soup were some rare luxury item he'd had imported just for me. "So thoughtful."

I made a noncommittal sound. It *was* thoughtful, but the less my mom knew of these whatever-they-were feelings, the better.

"When did this start up?"

"Nothing's starting up."

Probably.

Was it?

No.

Maybe.

"It sure looked like something from where I was standing."

"Mom, please. I'm sick." I didn't want her asking questions. I had basically zero answers right now, for her or myself.

"Baby." She sat on the bed next to me, but it wasn't quite the same as when Dean had done it. "First Harper and now you. What am I going to do with you girls? Do you want a sip of water?"

I shook my head. That hadn't gone so well the last time. My stomach still felt like it'd been filled with razor blades. Just the thought of trying to eat or drink something had me twitching to get up for the bathroom again.

"It's stifling in here." Mom went to the thermostat and fiddled with the buttons until the air conditioning kicked on higher. I shivered beneath my sheet. "Maybe you would be more comfortable in your own room at home, just until you're recovered."

I'd been puking my guts out all night. I didn't think I'd feel any better even if I were in a first-class hotel suite with full wait staff. "I'm fine here."

Mom *tsked* my answer away.

"An attic is no place for a sick person." Her hands went to her hips as she inspected my little studio. "It's no place for a healthy person, either."

I rolled over, turning my back to her. I couldn't stop shivering even though I was horribly hot, I'd just sort of confessed to kind of liking my maybe-not-awful coworker, and I might throw up again at any minute. Really not the best time for commentary on my shabby living conditions.

I heard the soft sound of the refrigerator opening and my mom rummaging around. "Chicken soup, clear drinks. I'm guessing he brought the crackers and white bread on the counter, too. Your Dean knows what he's doing. I like him."

I covered my eyes with one hand. He wasn't *my* Dean, but Mom was on a roll. Maybe if I faked a coma, she would leave me in peace.

She walked back across the apartment, and her hand came to rest on my shoulder, cool and soft. "We'll have some groceries delivered to you tomorrow. There's not enough in here to live on."

"It's lucky I can't eat anything then."

She *tsked* again. "You need to keep your strength up. If your Dean hadn't brought that food, there wouldn't be anything in your refrigerator but ketchup and lunch meat."

There it was again. *My Dean.* Mom's head had already started spinning with schemes of weddings and babies, I just knew it. Probably best to ignore her hints.

"Baby," she said gently, "wouldn't you rather come home? You don't have to stay here."

I rolled over to face her. "Harper said she's starting to feel better today. I just have to get through another day or two. I'll be okay."

Her smile turned sad as she pulled her fingers through my stringy hair, smoothing it out on the pillow. "I meant you could come home to stay."

I opened my mouth, but she kept talking.

"You don't have to answer now. I know you're not feeling so good, and it's not the time to make a decision like that. But think about it. Your father and I would be happy to have you back for as long as you need. It would give you a chance to get back on your feet again."

Back on my feet. Sometimes, that concept felt so far away, I wasn't sure what it even meant. As far as I could tell, I was still trying to get on my feet for the first time. Scrambling to hold down jobs, just scratching by with this apartment—my feet were sliding beneath me like slipping on ice.

I couldn't keep letting my parents carry me along, helping me out with everything I needed. Every time they brought me gifts or slipped a check in my purse was one more reminder I wasn't where I needed to be. Long past time I sorted out my adulthood on my own. Moving back in with them would save money, but losing my pride in the bargain was too high a price.

"I think I just want to sleep now."

After a few generous goodbyes and promises to check in again tomorrow, Mom finally closed the door behind her. I squeezed my eyes shut but couldn't stop the tears from falling.

That was just because I was so sick, that was all. I wasn't crying because of how desperately my parents wanted to help me, or how badly I wanted that help. And it definitely wasn't because I needed, more than anything else, to stand up and do this on my own.

dean

"CAN YOU STOP PACING?" Grant stood at the registers, juggling General Manager duties with store operations duties.

"I'm not pacing, I'm checking stock."

I was pacing.

I'd showed up too early for my shift and now had nothing to do but wait. Eliza had been out sick four days. That bug had knocked her out, leaving her weak and feverish even after the stomach nastiness subsided. She swore last night she felt well enough to come back today, and here I was too early. Waiting.

I hadn't visited her again. I'd wanted to, but being caught by her mother had only amplified the shadow of worry that maybe I'd overstepped. She hadn't strictly asked me to come by, and I'd done it anyway. But I'd convinced myself it couldn't hurt to text.

It had started out gradually, just a simple check-in to see how she was, but by last night, we'd exchanged so many messages, it had become a habit. We didn't share anything earth-shattering or reveal our deepest secrets, but I got a crazy little thrill every time my phone pinged with a new message.

Speaking of—I pulled out my phone and scrolled through last night's texts again.

Eliza: Is watching sixteen straight hours of Netflix a sign of a problem?
Dean: Depends on the show
Eliza: True crime documentaries
Dean: Should I be worried?
Eliza: Of course not
Eliza: Come back over, I'm all stocked up on zip ties and bleach
Dean: You can't have my skin
Eliza: But you'd be so cozy

"What are you smiling about?" Grant asked.

Clearing my face of the traitorous smile, I slipped my phone back into my pocket. "The NASDAQ."

He narrowed his eyes. "Who is she?"

"You think I know someone named NASDAQ?" He could squint at me all he liked, I wasn't ready to confide this yet. "What are you working on?"

He glared at the obvious topic switch, but relented. "Just finalizing a few things for the big anniversary party. As soon as Eliza gets here, I have to go upstairs for another meeting with Rhett."

"You could go now. Don't you trust me to run the store for a few minutes?"

"Is there any reason I should?"

Probably not, but I still didn't like to hear it.

"Have you found time in your schedule to help at Grandma Gloria's?" I asked instead.

"I'm working on it. You're not the only one who cares about her move going smoothly, you know."

"Aside from Mom, I'm the only one helping her pack."

Grant's shoulders slumped. Rhett had been right, the timing for her move couldn't have been worse. We all had enough going on in a normal month, let alone the month of the big anniversary. I hated to guilt him into it, but I needed help over there.

"I'll find time," he finally said.

"Hey, guys."

I whipped my head around so fast, I probably pulled a muscle. Eliza walked up the center of the store, all bright and smiley. My heart slammed against my ribcage, trying to convince me to move in for a hug. She'd said she was feeling better, but seeing it for myself eased some of the tension I'd been carrying since first finding her so miserable. I'd never thought of myself as much of a worrier, but that question of *How is Eliza doing?* had echoed through my skull on repeat all week.

Grant closed his laptop and walked around the counter to greet her. "I'm glad to see you're feeling better."

"I am, thank you." She glanced at me and away again, a hint at shyness that only sped my heart rate faster. "I'm sorry I was out so long."

"Don't worry about it. You needed the time off, and Nicole was fine with the extra hours." He turned to address us both. "I'll be upstairs in a meeting. If there's an emergency, you know where to find me."

As soon as he left, Eliza moved closer to me, and I willed myself to stay in one place. I would *not* sweep her into my arms again, no matter how badly I wanted to.

"Well, did you miss me?"

I held up one hand, my index finger and thumb a centimeter apart. "A bit."

She grinned. "I'm a highly missable person."

"Hey, you should see my blog."

We passed our shift catching up on everything that had happened at Irwin's during her absence. I told her stories about indecisive customers and how Nicole put the fear of God into me about the need to floss my teeth nightly.

"I guess you see some things in dental assisting school." I could have done with fewer details about the perils of gingivitis, but it got the job done. I'd bought a fresh pack of floss that same night.

Eliza sat down on the stool behind the counter, and the delicate way she moved brought me straight to her side. "Are you feeling okay?"

"I'm just a little tired. I'm good."

She'd been on her feet shuttling around the store for hours, and her fatigue was showing. Her overly bright smile couldn't hide the lingering dark circles beneath her eyes. "Are you sure?"

"I thought I'd be over it by now. I just need a minute."

"You look pale." I placed my palm on her forehead to check for fever, and her eyelids fluttered shut. Her skin felt cool but clammy. Not feverish, but not one hundred percent, either. "You shouldn't have come in. We could have handled another day without you."

She opened her eyes to glare up at me. "Stop, you'll make me blush."

I smiled down at her, drawing my hand away with reluctance. "That didn't come out right. You needed to rest longer."

"The shift's almost over now. I'll go home and sleep some more."

"Are you going to be up for tomorrow's farmers market?"

"I don't have much of a choice. After missing Wednesday's market, my income this week is kind of shot." She winced as if she hadn't meant to reveal quite so much. A second later, she replaced her dismay with another big smile. "I'll just bring a chair, it will be great."

Her brave face wasn't fooling me. I couldn't guess how much she'd lost in sales this week, but it must have been significant.

"I'd still like to help you with your business plan."

Her dark look let me know I'd said the wrong thing.

"A business plan wouldn't have stopped me from getting sick."

"No, but it could help you prepare for those kinds of eventualities." She clearly had no cushion to make up for sick days, not that I needed to point it out.

"I can handle it on my own."

"I know you can handle it, that's the whole point. I just want to see you succeed."

Some of her irritation melted away, but she still pursed her lips like an angry librarian. "I'll think about it."

I stared down at her, knowing damn well what that meant. "You're not going to mention it again, are you?"

Her saucy grin said it all. "Nope."

"Fine. What about tomorrow at the market? Do you have anyone who can help you?"

"I can't afford to pay anyone to help run the booth. It's a one-woman show right now."

"What if someone was willing to help you out of the goodness of his heart?"

Her eyes narrowed to slits. "I would say someone is being very nice but had better forget it right now."

"I don't mind."

"Oh, we're talking about you? Then definitely no." She gave my arm a quick squeeze. "I appreciate it, and it's really sweet of you to offer, but I'll be just fine tomorrow. I promise."

I leaned closer until she sucked in a little breath. Her eyes grew wide, but she held my gaze with a bold look that heated up my blood.

"Your willfulness is infuriating, do you know that?"

She turned her nose up. "I don't know what you're talking about."

"Sure you don't."

I still stood way too close to her when a man walked in and headed straight for us. I stepped away, knowing Grant would tear into me if he heard about my flirty behavior in front of customers.

"Miguel, hi," Eliza said as he joined us at the counter. "I haven't seen you in here in a while."

"My free time is dictated by the bees these days. Those queens are demanding." He shot her a wink. "I didn't know you were working here again."

Her smile strained at the edges, like she could have done without the reminder. "Back again. What can I help you find today?"

"Just a bite valve for my hydration pack. I've got it."

Moving past us to the backpacks, he grabbed a small package out of a bin and brought it to her at the counter.

"Do you know Dean, Miguel?" She swept her hand to indicate me. "He keeps Irwin's finances humming."

We nodded at each other, but his attention stayed focused on Eliza. "Where were you Wednesday? I hope you're not giving up on the mid-week market."

She rang up his sale, and he handed over a few dollar bills. "Nope, I was just a little sick this week."

"That's too bad. Are you back up to speed?"

"Completely." Her guilty eyes darted to mine, but she ignored my stern look.

"Do you have anything going on tomorrow night?"

Her eyes cut to me again, and that little hesitation set my heart to pounding. Would *we* have plans together if I asked her?

"I don't think so."

"Tomorrow's Ethan's thirty-fifth birthday, and I'm throwing a big party. Big. Think out-of-control college party, but without the college students. Want to join us?"

Eliza paused, the softest, slightest sigh as she considered.

Miguel's eyes moved between her and me like he was doing a whole lot of math in a hurry. "Dean, you're welcome, too."

I doubted I'd know anybody at this party aside from one woman still recovering from being sick who probably shouldn't attend. She also happened to be the one woman I kept telling myself I needed to stay away from. If visiting her at her apartment had seemed like a step too far, seeing her at a party wouldn't be any better.

"What do you think?" Eliza asked me. "Want to help Ethan celebrate in style?"

"No presents," Miguel added. "Just come have fun."

She glanced from him to me. Her little eyebrow bob had just enough sass in it to be a challenge. "I'll be there."

That decided me. "Count me in, too."

dean

"YOU WANT to take over for a bit, honey?" Grandma said.

I set another box of old photographs on her dining table. I'd spearheaded the effort to organize some of her moving chaos, but the process dragged. Each room held stacks of boxes labeled *Trash*, *Donate*, *Sell*, and *FV*. All of her photo boxes had been labeled for Fiesta Village, but downsizing from a four-bedroom to two, it just wasn't feasible to take them all.

Willing to give myself a short break from sorting through her things, I joined her in the kitchen.

"What do you want me to do?" I asked even though I could guess. While I'd been inventorying her belongings, she'd sliced apples for pie filling and worked up a dough for crust. She pulled a disc of dough from the fridge and set it on the counter.

"Put on an apron, for starters." She nodded to the hooks on the side of the refrigerator.

I picked a teakettle-print apron and slipped it over my head, tying it at the back, then struck a pose in the over-the-top thing with lacy frills along the hem and neck. "Better?"

"Much." She sprinkled flour on the clean countertop and passed me her old wooden rolling pin.

As a kid, I'd used the same one to roll out crusts and cookies during countless after school visits in this very spot.

"It's too hard for me to roll out crusts these days. It needs a young man's hands."

I pressed and rolled the dough under my grandma's watchful eyes. It had been a long time since I'd made a pie, and my skills hadn't weathered the break well. The dough pulled up and tore as I rolled it, spiking my frustration, but I silently repeated a calming mantra to keep myself in check.

At the moment, the calming mantra mostly consisted of Eliza's name, which quite frankly left me anything but calm.

"How are you handling it?" Grandma asked.

"I'm a little rusty, but I don't mind rolling out dough."

"I mean being banned from your office." She knew all about the little deal with my father, and had declared herself a great fan of the arrangement.

To restrain myself from going to the farmers market and helping Eliza in her stall after she'd told me not to, I'd gone in to work this morning. For the last two weeks, I'd split my time between the Irwin's store and my office above it, but someone always seemed to find me out when I went in on the weekends. I'd barely gone over the latest budget adjustments when my office phone rang—my mother, demanding I go home. I'd resisted, considering the workload piling up, but her threats to send Grant upstairs to kick me out convinced me I'd rather leave of my own volition.

"We're in the middle of an expansion. It doesn't make much sense to tell me I can't do my job."

"They're not telling you not to do your job, they just don't want you to do it on the weekends."

"They never minded all the weekends I worked before." Occasionally, one of my parents would chide me for not taking days off, but they had never gone so far as to actually make sure

I wasn't in the office. They'd always seemed to approve of my work ethic before, but now, I was being punished for it.

"This time in the store could be a good thing," Grandma said. "It might be good for you to learn a few new skills, become a little more well-rounded."

Again with the refrain I was missing something. Everyone from my dad, to Grant, to my grandma had an opinion on what I lacked and the best way for me to go about getting it. Even Eliza had pointers for me, although she was meant to be training me, so I let that slide. I'd be willing to let a lot of things slide when it came to Eliza.

"What skills are you talking about?" I knew Grandma didn't care how well I could sell day packs or first aid kits.

"It couldn't hurt you to be out among the living a little more."

I thought about Miguel's offhand party invitation, and Eliza's eager interest in my response. Or at least, I'd thought it eager. Grandma was right, it had been too long since I'd last been out among the living. I might be misreading Eliza's friend-liness as something more than she meant. I didn't think I was off base, but I didn't like to assume, either.

"I'm out of practice."

"Oh, I know, honey. But it never hurts to get back in the game. If you don't use a skill, you lose it. I used to knit beautiful hats and scarves when you boys were little, but I hadn't taken up my needles in years. I joined a knitting group over at the senior center last spring and realized I'd lost all the skill I once had. So you know what I did?"

I shook my head.

"I started again."

She brought the glass pie pan over, and I folded the crust, picked it up, and laid it out in the dish. I fumbled a clumsy pinching maneuver around the edging, frowning at my completed work. The crust looked like it'd been thrown together by a chimpanzee.

She patted my shoulder. "Not bad." She dumped the apple filling into the dish, followed by a crumbled mixture of flour, brown sugar, and oats, and popped the whole thing into the oven.

"Sit," she said, wiping her hands off on a dishtowel.

Pulling off the apron, I replaced it on its hook. The mountain of work left to do in this house called to me, but I sat back down at the dining table, where she took the chair next to me.

"You remember when I first taught you how to roll out crusts?"

"Vividly."

In the throes of my angry outbursts and childhood temper tantrums, Grandma had decided I needed to help her bake pies. I'd resisted at first, wanting instead to burn off my anger with activity, but she'd never been good at hearing the word no. She patiently instructed me with gentle guidance and soft words, helping calm my mind after frustrating days at school. Sometimes, the attempts made me more upset than whatever I was trying to calm down from, but mostly, what I remembered from those days was a sense of peace.

The same sort of peace I'd felt during my day on the lake with Eliza. Like I didn't have to keep such a tight leash on everything. I could just *be*.

"You were such a perfectionist," she said. "You'd get so upset over every little thing that went wrong. I guess I hoped I could show you that even if the pies didn't look perfect, they still tasted delicious. You don't always have to get it perfect, Dean. Sometimes, the beauty is in the attempt."

I loved my grandmother, but I'd had enough cryptic life advice from my elders lately. "We need to get you a scanner and save all these pictures to a flash drive."

She shrugged, letting my topic change go. "Whatever you say. You still haven't told me what furniture you want. You'd better decide before I move, or I'll sell it all."

The plan was to move her and her most vital possessions out of the house and into Fiesta Village, leaving anything sellable for an estate agent. Whatever didn't sell would be donated, and once the house was empty and cleaned, we'd list it for sale. My mother had chosen a few things she wanted from her childhood, but my brothers and I hadn't yet gone through the remaining items.

I couldn't decide what I wanted to keep, if anything. It wasn't any one thing that stood out, but everything taken all together. The old brass mirror over the fireplace that greeted me when I walked through the door. The secretary desk where I used to do my homework after school. This dining table where my brothers and I had dinner when our parents worked late nights at the store. All laced with memories that made the items feel more important than they really were.

If I had a family or a wife, I might have asked to buy the house already. But for just me on my own, the impulse seemed wrong, somehow. Like I'd get blasted for my presumptuousness. Grant had built a house for him and his fiancée, and now had to live in it all alone. I didn't envy that kind of heartache.

"This old place has been a big part of your life," Grandma said. "It's okay to miss it."

I shook off my train of thought. "I'm not sentimental about the house, just the times we had here."

"That's the same thing, honey." She patted my hand. "Now, what are we going to do to get you out socializing a little more, eh?"

She rarely put on her meddling hat, but when she did, she committed.

"Grandma, I'm doing just fine."

She pinned me with her sharp gaze. "You got yourself a girl?"

My thoughts went to Eliza, who most definitely was not my girl, no matter what I wanted from her. "Not at the moment."

"I'm never going to get great-grandbabies at the rate you boys are moving. Grant's nearly thirty-five and gun-shy after that girl jilted him, and I'm not sure Rhett's ever going to grow up. I was counting on you to settle down and start a family."

I put on a thin smile even as she echoed my own thoughts about everything I lacked. "No pressure or anything."

The soft lines in her face deepened as she laughed. "I think of it as a gentle nudge in the right direction."

"I don't know about settling down, but I'll see if I can socialize a little more."

She heaved a dramatic sigh. "I suppose that's all I can ask."

eliza

"MRS. LEWIS BROKE her wrist in a fall this week, but she refuses to stop knitting. I keep telling her she needs to take it easy but she just doesn't listen. It's an obsession."

Harper's voice barely registered over the bass drum thrumming in my bones.

I only had half an ear on my sister's exciting tales of the elderly. We stood crammed together in Miguel and Ethan's house along with what looked like everyone in Central Texas under the age of forty. When Miguel said big party, he really meant *big party*.

Harper and I had been here an hour, mixing it up with the rambunctious crowd. I recognized a couple of people from high school, but a lot of the guests weren't quite in my age range, and mostly, we'd just wandered around. We'd made s'mores at the firepit, played darts in the garage, and beer pong in the dining room, where I forfeited my forfeit and was banned from further rounds. I'd hurled too much in the last week to take the triple shot of Patrón the winner had challenged me to. If I never got to play beer pong again, so be it. I'd find a way to survive.

I'd positioned myself in the living room to have a full view of the front door. Dean had said he would come, and I'd passed on the details from Miguel, but he hadn't shown. Apparently, the whole five minutes early thing didn't apply to parties. After a while, though, I had to accept that he wasn't coming.

No big deal. The sinking sensation in my chest like a kid who'd just been told our trip to Disneyland had been canceled? Unrelated.

"So then I just rammed the knitting needles straight into her ribcage."

I blinked hard and turned to Harper.

"What's going on with you?" she said. "You're staring at the door. Are you ready to leave?"

"No, I'm fine."

I glanced to the door again without thinking, and took a sip of hard lemonade. I'd figured one drink wouldn't kill me, and I'd nursed it the whole hour. The boozy sweetness should have relaxed me, but it only made me more wound up than ever.

She nudged closer. "Are you waiting for someone?"

"I'm not waiting for anyone."

Because fate loves a good laugh, Dean chose that minute to walk through the front door. I couldn't stop the smile that broke across my face as relief and happiness tumbled together inside me. Holy cow, did he look good. He scanned the room and when his eyes caught mine, his grin set my skin alight.

Harper followed my gaze, that snoop, and spoke right into my ear. "You are such a liar. What is going on with you and Dean Irwin?"

Pushing her away, I grinned stupidly at Dean. He walked straight to me, a six-pack of beer in each hand.

"Dean!" Miguel zoomed out of the crowd, ready to be a good host. Ethan was somewhere outside, a glittery plastic Birthday Boy crown perched on his blond head. "Thanks for coming."

"Thanks for the invite." He lifted the six-packs. "I wasn't sure what to bring, so I split the difference."

"You're a keeper." Miguel winked at me, then took the six-packs from Dean. "Make yourself at home."

Dean snagged a bottle before Miguel disappeared to deposit them with the rest of the stash in the kitchen. I couldn't think where he would put them, since the dining table was already littered with every kind of alcohol I'd ever heard of, and some I wish I'd never seen. Bacon vodka? Gross.

"I wasn't sure you were coming," I said without thinking.

"I'm just fashionably late." His eyes never left mine.

I'd given him a hard time about the staring early on, but I was super into it now.

He twisted the cap off his beer and took a long drink, watching me with a boldness that sent ripples from my scalp to my toes. Every time I saw him, a slightly different version of him took center stage. Or maybe they were all partial glimpses at one whole I hadn't yet discovered. I didn't quite know how to read him, but more and more, I found I liked every possible version.

Harper shifted against my arm, snapping me out of my dreamy gaze. Right. Introductions. "Dean, this is my sister, Harper. Harper, Dean Irwin."

"The soup guy," she said.

I gulped my drink. I never should have told her anything about him. I hadn't gone into details, but hard to avoid using the word *sweet* when describing a guy who spontaneously brought me soup when I was sick. I might have also used words like *handsome, thoughtful,* and *protective.* Possibly *sexy as hell.* I couldn't be sure.

"I've been called worse." He looked at me. "Recently, I'd imagine."

I screwed up my face and put a finger to my lips. "I think the worst I called you was jerkwad. Is that as bad as you were thinking?"

"That's pretty tame. I expected more expletives in there."

"I was feeling generous."

"Thank you for your generosity." After a second, he turned back to Harper. "You're the physical therapist at Fiesta Village, right?"

"That's me."

"My grandmother, Gloria Bailey, is moving in next month."

"I look forward to meeting her. Not that I hope she needs physical therapy. Just...you know what I mean."

"She can be a little prickly, but she grows on you."

"That must run in the family," I said. Dean turned to me, and we stared at each other until heat tingled down my spine.

After a while, he nodded at the crowd pressed around us. "Looks like they succeeded with their over-the-top party plans."

I hitched a shoulder. "Ethan's a people person."

He raised his eyebrows at my little joke, but I outright started giggling. He nudged me with his arm, making me laugh more. Stupid hard lemonade.

"Yeah, I'm going to see if any sandwiches are left in the back." Harper disappeared into the swaying and gyrating party crowd, leaving us alone. Well. Relatively.

"How did the market go today?"

I'd half-expected him to turn up to help me out, in spite of my declarations I didn't need him to. I'd watched for him with sad puppy dog eyes all morning. Not that I would cop to it.

"I did really well, better than I have the last few weeks. Maybe my customers missed me when I was gone."

"I know I did."

That crazy fluttering started up again in my ribcage. Were

we really doing this? Were we flirting now? I could roll with that.

Yeesh, maybe.

I gazed up at him, committing to memory the five o'clock shadow along his jaw and the way his hair looked all tousled and delicious. Wearing a simple gray T-shirt and jeans, he seemed even more relaxed than he'd been on our day on the lake. Something about that relaxed attitude made me want to snuggle up against him. Although that was probably the hard lemonade talking.

The hard lemonade needed to keep its mouth shut.

"What about your day? I hope you didn't go into the office on your day off."

His gaze shifted away from mine. "I had to take care of a few things."

"Dean."

He shrugged, taking another drink from his beer. "There's a lot going on. Store expansion, sales reports, new product contracts."

The glow of his steadfast responsibility shone a bright light on my own irresponsibility. I'd only had his level of dedication to one job, and despite all my best efforts, it had slipped from my fingers anyway. After that, I'd never been entirely sure the effort was worth it.

Tonight was *not* the time to think about that mess.

"What?" he said when I'd stared up at him too long.

"You're a really good businessman."

His mouth sank into a frown. "You don't like businessmen."

"They're probably not all horrible human beings."

"When I die, I want that on my gravestone. *Not a horrible human being.*"

"*Probably* not a horrible human being," I corrected.

A slight curl at the edges of his lips made me want to press mine there. I hadn't even finished the one hard lemonade, and here I was imagining kissing him. Though it wasn't a bad image.

I really, really liked that image.

"I hope you make your mind up before I die."

Staring up at him way too long, tendrils of warmth curled through my belly. Had I made my mind up? And was I willing to say so if I had?

"Ah, speaking of dying, my Bronco finally quit on me this morning. My dad had to tow it from town after the market. That's why I asked Harper to drive me here."

His brow furrowed. "You could have asked me to bring you. I'm happy to give you a ride."

Dean's offer filled me with gooey warmth. He didn't ask for anything in return—he just wanted to give me a ride because I needed one. Doing good guy things. Hard to get used to that.

Sad that a guy offering to do the bare minimum had become such a huge shocker for me. But again—tonight wasn't for thinking about old mistakes.

"I wasn't sure you were really going to show up. I hoped you would, but I thought you might have found something better to do."

I cringed over my own stupid mouth. See? Drunk-girl conversation.

"You think I could have something better going on than this?" He gestured around the crowded room, encompassing a group of people making fun of the 90s song blaring through the speakers, two guys comparing pictures of dogs on their phones, and someone wandering around in a silky smoking jacket. Miguel and Ethan had the most interesting assortment of friends.

"I know it's hard to believe, but there's probably something better out there."

Staring straight at me, he ticked his head to the side. "Not from where I'm standing."

Dean was definitely flirting now. He couldn't seem to look away from me either. Or maybe that was just me staring too much at him. Hard to be sure. A lot of mutual staring going on right here.

But what did we do after staring? I hadn't even really flirted with a guy in forever; I wasn't sure I knew how to act at this stage of the game. Should I touch his bicep? Compliment his spreadsheets? Look up at him through my eyelashes the way romance novel heroines always did, even though it was physically impossible?

Yeah, I'd be doing none of that.

"Anyway, it's good for Harper to get out a little. She never goes out, she practically lives at the retirement home. She's basically an old lady hermit at twenty-eight."

Yes, I was shamelessly throwing my sister under the bus, but my mind had gone haywire beneath Dean's unbroken gaze. I'd never thought swooning a real thing, but I was seriously tempted to swoon into his arms, and he only had to look at me.

"Do you go out a lot, then?" He bent his head closer, like he didn't want to miss my answer.

I licked my lips, and his eyes tracked the movement. "Not all that much, really."

"Neither do I."

Oh, Lord, when had his voice become so husky? I wanted to swim in this growly, sexy version of his voice.

"Then it's probably good we're out now. Together. The two of us." Ah, yes, Awkward Eliza had showed up right on time, joining forces with Drunk Eliza to embarrass the hell out of both of us.

Someone bumped into me, and I stumbled against Dean. He put one hand on my waist to steady me, and my free hand went to his chest. My stomach bottomed out as bursts of energy zipped through me like I'd been tasered. My nose was practically at his neck, and his delicious cologne made me want to sigh. Bergamot something. I'd need to figure out what that something was so I could turn it into a soap. I'd never sell it, though. Just hoard it all for myself.

Mine.

Maybe I'd had more alcohol than I'd thought.

We stood frozen like that for a minute, as though staring into each other's eyes in the middle of a crowded party was normal behavior. Heat prickled up my neck and across my cheeks until I must have been fire engine red.

"I think I need some air."

He nodded, and we moved through the house, his hand guiding me at my waist. I didn't even process the rooms we walked through or who we passed, my whole focus zeroed in on the warmth of his hand through my shirt. Outside, the huge back yard was as crowded as the house, but Dean turned, leading me to the far end of the wraparound porch. How he knew where he was going, I couldn't guess, but he seemed to have a destination in mind. When we were sufficiently far away from the others, he leaned back against the porch railing, his hands at either side of his hips.

"Feeling better?"

The night air wasn't cool yet, but the scent of lavender moved on the slight breeze. Much better than the overwhelming smell of beer and sweat in the stifling party.

"I just drank too fast." Speaking of, we had both set our bottles down somewhere along our journey through the house. Probably for the best. "It was really hot in there."

He nodded once, his eyes locked on mine.

So far, this escape outside hadn't helped anything. Instead of staring at each other in a crowded party, we were staring at each other alone in the dark. My heart beat like crazy until it rivaled the bass beat pulsing from inside the house.

"What else did you do today?" I said. "It better not have all been work."

"I visited my grandma this afternoon. She's convinced I need to be more well-rounded. I spent most of the day in her kitchen, up to my elbows in pie crust."

"You bake?"

His head ticked to the side again. "Not really. She taught me to roll dough when I was a kid, and decided I needed a refresher."

The thought of him in his suit, dusted in flour and rolling out dough, proved all kinds of enticing. I really needed to get a handle on that, but the idea already stuck in my mind. Dean baking pies with his grandma sounded cuter than anything. I needed to see it.

"What else is involved in becoming a well-rounded man?"

"How much time do you have? She's got a long list."

I laughed, swaying closer to him. "It sounds like you have a lot of deficiencies."

"Too many to count." His voice went all husky again, deep and rumbly and seductive.

I shook my head. "I don't think so. You're plenty well-rounded to me. I think you're pretty great."

"I think you're pretty great, too."

Even though I'd drifted close enough we were nearly sharing breath, he hadn't moved. His hands gripped the porch rail behind him, and I caught the strain in his voice. His relaxed attitude covered a tension that practically vibrated through him. He wanted to kiss me, I was sure of it, but he held himself back. Structured, in control Dean had shown up at exactly the wrong time. If someone were to make the first move, it looked like it would have to be me.

I could do this, right? Dig down deep, find every last scrap of my tough-girl swagger, and just lay one on him. The idea almost made me giggle—me, kissing Dean Irwin? But then *that* idea sounded so, so good, and his mouth was right there, soft lips haloed by dark stubble, waiting for me. *Me.*

Gathering up my courage, I closed the last trace of distance between us and met his mouth with mine. I pressed soft kisses to his warm lips, tasting him, breathing him in. Dizzying to be so close to him, enveloped in his warmth. My fingers twisted in his T-shirt, my body pressed to his.

In my brain's muddled state, I spent too long swimming in my own enjoyment before I realized he hadn't responded to my kisses. He stood frozen, enduring my affection but not returning it. Finally, his hands touched my waist, but instead of pulling me in close, he gently pressed me away.

Alarm bells blaring at my mistake, I sprang back, pushing his hands off me. In the dim porch light, Dean's face contorted with emotions I couldn't sort through. The only thing I knew for sure was that I'd kissed him, and he'd done nothing to reciprocate.

I'd got it all wrong. He'd held back, not because he was so in control he couldn't be the one to kiss me, but because he hadn't *wanted* to. My stomach bubbled and twisted as humiliation burned through me.

"I'm sorry, I shouldn't have done that. I'm just..." Horrified. Appalled. An embarrassing train wreck of a person. He could take his pick.

"El." His voice had lost its husky wonderfulness. Now he sounded apologetic and a little sad. Whatever he might say, I didn't want to hear it. I could lecture myself on my own.

"No, I'm—" I gestured at my head as if he could see the alcohol sloshing around inside it. "I had one too many. I don't know what I'm doing."

"El." He reached for me, but I stepped out of his grasp.

"It's probably time I let Harper take me home anyway. She's got to get up early to get over to the retirement home. Work, work, work, you know how it is." My shrill laugh probably made me look more ridiculous but at this point, that was unavoidable. "I'll see you Monday."

I turned and barreled across the porch and back into the house, not stopping when he said my name again in that same soft voice. I staggered through the crowd, telling myself what a complete idiot I'd been while I searched for my sister. This was what impulsive decisions got me: humiliation and heartache.

How many times would I have to learn that particular lesson? And why, why had I made such an epically impulsive decision with *Dean Irwin*?

I finally spotted Harper drinking a root beer in the corner while a much younger guy gawked at her. Miguel had said no college kids, but it looked like one had snuck through. She seemed to have no idea the effect she'd had on the poor kid. He could get in line, I was first on the Unrequited Train tonight.

I grabbed Harper's hand. "We need to go, now."

"Hey," the guy complained as I tugged her away.

I rolled my eyes. "Dude, it was never going to happen."

"What's the matter?" she said from behind me.

"We need to get in your car right this minute. Now, please."

Grateful we'd already wished Ethan *Happy birthday*, I bolted through the door, scrambled down the front steps to the driveway, and across the gravel.

"Are you going to tell me what happened back there?"

No, I was not. I'd spent years avoiding guys I could possibly have any real interest in, brushing off advances and telling myself I didn't need that kind of trouble. I'd been made a fool of by someone promising love and togetherness once—never again. I would put my energy into myself, my life, and my family, not some random guy. I wouldn't get sucked in by lies and manipulations again.

Tonight, I'd put all that aside and thrown myself at Dean Irwin. I'd kissed him, and he'd just *stood there* like a mannequin. What a nightmare.

If I had my way, I would never talk about this again, ever.

dean

"WHAT IS YOUR PROBLEM?" Grant asked Monday morning.

I strode up and down the length of the store, looking at displays without seeing them. Grant and Rhett stood at the registers talking anniversary party plans, but I couldn't focus on that. Not even the local news crew RSVPing to the celebration could interest me.

"I'm eager to start the day." More like eager for one particular start to my day.

"You ran longer than usual this morning." Rhett twirled a pencil between his fingers as he watched me make my laps with amused interest. "Had to be at least five miles."

"Ten." I hadn't slept well, tortured by slick, sweaty dreams ever since that kiss Saturday night. When Eliza had pressed her sweet mouth to mine, I'd had to call on superhuman strength not to kiss her back. I'd tried to do the right thing by her, but she hadn't seen it that way.

Eliza had run out of that party like she thought I might chase after her. Fighting the impulse to follow, I'd stayed where I stood, even though in my heart I knew letting her go only confirmed her fears. Texting had seemed like a weak way to discuss what had happened, and a phone call wasn't much better. Going to her house, on the other hand, had felt like pushing things too far, so I'd waited.

I was sick to death of waiting.

The bells on the door jingled. I spun my head around to see Eliza walk through the doors with a bright smile on her face.

"Good morning, everyone." She tossed up a beauty queen wave just before disappearing into the back room.

That was not how I had expected her to act after Saturday night. Then again, there was a slim chance she didn't remember Saturday night very well. If that was true, I should have felt better about the choice I'd made, but the idea she truly hadn't meant to kiss me only made me feel like more of a tool.

"The lights were on in the offices last night," Rhett said. "Anyone know who was working all day Sunday?"

Grant looked over at me, little scowl lines embedded around his mouth. "You can take days off, you know. There's no prize for working yourself into the ground."

Ignoring my parents' calls, I had spent most of the day and part of the evening catching up on everything I'd let slide while working the sales floor during the week. I'd needed the distraction, but it hadn't made a difference. Nothing would get Eliza out of my mind now that she'd kissed me.

"Sure there's a prize, it's CFO," Rhett said.

"CFO isn't the only reason for living," Grant said.

"I don't need this lecture right now."

"Should I pencil you in for another time?"

Eliza walked back out onto the sales floor, and my eyes snapped to her. She straightened her name tag as she approached us at the registers.

"How are things, Eliza?" Rhett asked.

I wanted to wipe away the flirty smile on my brother's face.

Even if he smiled at all women like that, this particular woman was off limits.

Presumptuous? Maybe. But she'd kissed me, and until we'd talked this out, I didn't want Rhett getting ideas about her.

Actually, I would *never* want Rhett to get ideas about her.

"I'm doing great."

She flashed her own broad smile. A little too perfect and calculated for me to believe the ease she tried to convey. I'd watched her with customers enough over the last weeks to know when she was relaxed and natural. Right now, she was anything but. She kept her eyes fixed on Rhett as though willing me into nonexistence.

"Have you conquered any new rivers lately?" she asked.

"I've got a trip up to Tennessee next month that will add another notch to my bedpost."

She *tsked* over that. "Those poor rivers. You just love 'em and leave 'em."

"I'm not a one-river man." He flashed her a devilish grin.

I clenched my jaw. "Don't you and Grant have someplace to be?"

"I'm not busy." He gazed meaningfully at Eliza, clueless to how close he was to getting punched right now.

"He's right," Grant said. "We need to get these last details settled. I don't want anything left to the day of."

"I'll see you around, Eliza." Rhett saluted her as he and Grant left the store.

I reminded myself his flirting was meaningless, but it still took a minute to slow the simmering in my blood.

Once my brothers were gone, the cheery smiles Eliza had been flashing at them completely winked out as she turned to me. "We need to talk."

That was supposed to be my line. I moved closer, my hands

stuffed into my pockets so I wouldn't reach out to touch her. "Okay."

"About the party," she said, her mouth twisting. "And that kiss."

So. She did remember. Just the word on her lips made my heart jackhammer in my chest.

"Let's just pretend it never happened."

Now my heart sputtered as if the power had flickered out. "What?"

"It was nothing, right? Just one kiss. No big deal." Embarrassment flashed in her eyes, but she tried to cover it with bravado the way she did so many other things in her life. Her tiny apartment, her troublesome car, her struggling business—she put that same attitude over all of them. Her brave face was admirable, but completely unnecessary.

"It was a big deal to me, El."

She raised her hands between us. "I get that, and I'm sorry. I didn't respect your boundaries. It won't happen again."

"*My* boundaries?"

"I'd had a little too much to drink, and I misread the room." She shrugged. "I blame it on proximity to hotness."

"Hotness?" I cringed at my own stupid mouth, parroting her words back like I didn't have a brain in my head.

"Nevermind."

A customer walked in the door, and Eliza called out her usual greeting. Lower, to me, she said, "I really am sorry. We can just leave that in the past and forget it, okay? We'll be like it never happened."

She flashed a tentative, false smile before walking away to offer the woman assistance.

I wanted to put the *Closed* sign on the door and usher the customer out of there. The eight-and-a-half minutes while she wandered the aisles seemed an eternity of me standing on one side of the store watching while Eliza did her level best not to look at me.

When the woman finally left, empty-handed, no less, I stalked over to Eliza. She put on her brave smile again, but I saw the uncertainty behind it now. She wanted to act like everything was normal between us when it was nothing of the kind.

I leaned close until I crowded her space, breathing her in. That fresh, minty smell drove me out of my mind. She stood close enough for me to touch, but I wouldn't. Not yet. "What if I don't want to pretend that kiss never happened?"

Her indifferent façade slipped. "What? Of course you do."

"No, I don't."

"Yes, you do." She scolded me as though I was being needlessly difficult.

"Eliza, I know what I want. I can't pretend that kiss never happened, because it's all I've been able to think about for the last two days."

She goggled up at me. "You—you didn't kiss me back. In fact, you pushed me away." Her chin jutted up a little higher. "I can read signals loud and clear."

"I'm not sending signals, El, I'm telling you straight out. I didn't kiss you back because you were drinking and I wasn't completely sure you knew what you were doing."

"I wasn't that drunk." She straightened, apparently offended by the implication she had been intoxicated, even though she'd used the same excuse on me.

"It's not a risk I'm willing to take." I moved in closer, her gorgeous blue eyes staring up at me. "The next time we kiss, you will be sober, and I promise I will leave you with no doubt of what I'm feeling."

A rosy tint swept over her cheeks. "Oh."

"Do we understand each other?"

"Yes."

"Good. Can I take you to lunch later?"

Her mouth twisted up into a smile. I'd just laid my cards on the table with this woman, and she would revel in her power. "I suppose."

"You're killing me, El."

eliza

THE LUNCH DATE with Dean turned out to be a scam.

As soon as we gave our order to the pizzeria waitress, he knocked his knuckles on the table. "Let's talk business plan."

Was a full-body eye roll a thing? Only Dean could turn a spontaneous would-be date into a business meeting. "You're relentless, you know that?"

"I'm aware." He pulled out his notepad and pencil, and flipped to a blank page. "What's your vision for your company?"

"We are not doing this."

"Why not?"

"I'm barely prepared for a lunch date with you, I can't talk work plans, too."

"You kissed me." A smile quirked along his mouth. "It's fair to say you're prepared for a date with me."

My stomach swooped at the return of Cocky Dean. I'd sort of missed him. "Fine, then I'm not prepared to talk work plans."

"Why not?"

"It's...too intimate, don't you think?" I was grasping, but it could work. "Like getting naked on the first date."

Bad analogy.

His smile notched a touch higher as though no part of that scenario bothered him. "When you think about your soap business five years in the future, what do you see?"

Groaning, I sank lower on the hard plastic bench. I liked the underlying flirtation there but could do without the business talk. My dreams were just that, dreams. Everything I wanted and hoped and wished for my little soap venture, I'd kept to myself. Even my family didn't know the full scope of those dreams. Bringing them out into the stark light of day under Dean's keen gaze? No, thanks.

He reached across the table, wrapping my hand in his. "El. You can tell me."

His warm touch and sweet, curious eyes worked on me like some kind of truth serum, and I caved.

"I want to see my soaps in local stores, little displays of them in gift shops and grocery stores. I like doing farmers markets, but I want to get into wholesaling so I'm filling regular orders and receiving regular checks, too. It would be nice to have a little she-shed in my back yard, where I make and cure all my soaps."

He smiled as I talked, and embarrassment lumbered in to squash out the rest of my thoughts.

"It's silly, I know." I didn't even have a back yard for a she-shed, let alone all the other stuff. At this rate, I was more likely to be living in my parents' house in five years than a place where I had room for a separate work space.

"It's not silly," he said, caressing my hand as he soothed with his words. "You know what you want. It sounds perfect for you."

Our pepperoni pizza arrived, and we started eating. I thought the business portion of the lunch date was over, but Dean had just started.

"Who is your ideal customer?"

I worked a long string of cheese into my mouth with my fingers. "Are we really doing this right now?"

"Yes." He ate a slice with one hand while his other gripped the pencil, ready to write down my answers as if this were a real business meeting. As if he actually took me seriously.

His persistence could be a little annoying, but I also liked how he acted as though I deserved the full attention of his businessy brain.

"My ideal customer is a woman, aged twenty to fifty, who has simple tastes and isn't too fussy, but is willing to splurge on herself now and then."

"So you have thought about it, that's good."

"I was just describing myself."

He subdued a smile I'd rather he unleashed on me. Wasn't that a normal thing for lunch dates, big stunning smiles and flirty looks, not five-year plans and business models?

"Which stores have you approached about wholesale opportunities so far?"

"Fine & Dandy stocks my soaps. I also approached Countryside, but they said no."

Dean wrote down the names in his notebook, a check next to one and a minus sign next to the other. "Where else?"

My stomach clenched. "Nowhere else."

He looked up at me. "Just those two?"

"Yes."

"If wholesaling is one of your business goals, why haven't you talked to more stores?"

I glanced around the pizza place as though I might stumble on a believable answer. "I don't think it's the right time."

"Can you explain to me why?"

My stomach twisted tighter. Why did talking with him always have to illustrate just how badly I was running my life? I stared daggers into his skull, but he didn't even flinch.

"This is part of your business plan, you just said so. Why are you sabotaging yourself by not approaching more businesses?"

He made it sound so easy. For a guy like him, it probably was. Me? Not so much.

"I'm not sabotaging myself, Dean, I'm trying to keep everything together for as long as I can." My voice got squeaky, and probably loud enough for the other pizzeria customers to hear. "If I go out and get rejected by all the other stores in town, that's it. I'm done. It will prove I need to shut everything down, pack it all away and move on to something else. I'm not ready to do that yet, even if it's coming."

"Why do you assume they would all say no?"

"Countryside is the big guns around here. They know what they're doing." I left the rest unsaid. If my soaps weren't good enough for Countryside, should I really keep pitching them to businesses around town? My farmers market customers were great, but that didn't mean I had the potential to go big. And if I couldn't go big, soon this whole enterprise would collapse like a house of cards in the slightest breeze.

"There are dozens of local stores that could stock your soaps that aren't Countryside. I hate to see you give up before you even try."

I exhaled a groan, my frustration with his easy answers maxing out. He truly had no clue.

"Have you ever lost a job, Dean? Have you ever applied to a job you really wanted and didn't get it?" He snapped his mouth shut rather than answer. "You have no idea how hard that gets after a while."

His shoulders sagged a bit, and his expression softened. He looked almost...impressed? By me? That didn't add up.

"You're right, I don't know how hard it is. You're a lot tougher than I am."

I rolled my eyes, but he took my hand again. "Seriously, El.

My parents hired me out of grad school. There was no interview process, no chance I might not get the job. I never ran that gauntlet of interviews and waiting to hear back and dealing with rejections. I never started my own company from scratch, either, or had to do everything on my own. You're a *lot* tougher than me."

My heart seemed to lift like a little balloon at those sweet words. He managed to make my last few years sound like something I'd grown from, instead of just stumbled my way through.

I bobbed a shoulder, pretending at an arrogance miles away from the doubts that threatened to crush me like a bug. "I am pretty great."

His mouth quirked up at the corners. "Don't I know it."

We spent the rest of our lunch break expanding the list of stores and shops I should approach for wholesale opportunities. The thought of getting a stack of *No, thank you* notes from them made my stomach cramp, but Dean wouldn't let the issue rest. If nothing else, I would have the list when I was ready to use it. When exactly that would be...well, let's just say I didn't commit to anything.

He talked marketing strategies for a while, and offered to research ways to help my website stand out in online searches. I needed a way to differentiate myself from all the other soap companies out there on the web—I just hadn't lit on the right idea.

"What you need is a niche nobody else is filling." He jotted something down in his notebook. "A unique way of looking at what you do."

He sounded ready to devote himself to the cause as soon as lunch ended, as if piling a dozen more tasks on his over-filled plate was no big deal.

"This is going to take up a lot of your time, don't you think?"

I looked over the pages he'd filled in the notebook. "You're already working two jobs."

"I don't mind."

That was the weirdest part. He didn't seem like he was helping me out of obligation or even as a way to get into my good graces—he just wanted to help because he could. I suspected some of his busyness had to do with our conversation on the way to the lake last week. Maybe he kept moving to help him focus his energy into something useful, instead of the negativity of his old patterns. The rest of it, though, pointed to a kind heart beating beneath his crisp façade. My own heart got a little giddy over his selflessness. Workaholics weren't supposed to be this endearing.

When the check came, Dean laid down a twenty and we left. Walking back down Center Street to Irwin's, he laced his fingers in mine—just like that. No hesitation, no playing it casual out in public. A tremor of affection surged through me. Guys like him didn't come along every day, that was for sure.

Trying to squash down those gooey feelings before they took hold too tight, I rummaged in my purse with my free hand for my wallet. "I can split lunch with you."

"It's on me."

"I do have ten dollars to my name." *Last I checked.*

Speaking of, my Irwin's paycheck should have hit my account this morning. I pulled out my phone and opened my banking app to double check the balance. I needed to buy a few more soap supplies soon, but that would go a whole lot easier if I actually had money in my account.

When the number came up, I nearly dropped my phone.

"Everything okay?" His eyebrows tugged together as he took in what had to be my freak-out face.

"No. I mean, yes. Everything's fine."

That only made his eyebrows tug more. Could a man make his eyebrows touch just from being irritated? Time would tell.

"Are you sure?"

I put on a tight, absolutely-not-sure-at-all smile, and nodded.

Back at Irwin's, I asked Dean to cover registers while I went in the office to talk to Grant. Better to deal with this immediately than wait around while I tried to sort it out. He swiveled away from his laptop to face me. He'd been so busy with all the preparations for the company celebration, I hated having to add a payroll issue to his to-do list.

"What's going on?" Worry furrowed his forehead, and I hadn't even described the problem yet.

"There's something wrong with my paycheck. There's way more commission than there should have been. I don't know what went wrong, but these numbers are off."

Unlike the managers at some of the other jobs I'd had, I liked and respected Grant. Everyone knew I'd taken this job because money was tight. I couldn't bear it if he thought I'd intentionally misrepresented my sales to get a higher commission. I kept a tally of my daily sales and knew approximately how much would come to me each pay period. This number nearly doubled it.

He didn't look alarmed when I described how much the amount was off. No eyebrow raise, no *How could this happen?* expression. If anything, he looked like he'd been expecting it.

"I double-checked the sales records before I cleared them," he said. "If there's a problem with sales numbers being misallocated, you might want to take it up with a coworker."

A coworker? But—

"Or the accounting department." Grant gave me a significant look.

I drew in a deep breath, my spine turning to steel. What the actual heck?

Had Dean seriously given me his commission behind my back? Choice words for him exploded to life in my brain. Arrogant. Presumptuous. Dickweed.

A few for me followed right behind. Flat broke. Pathetic. Incompetent. But I'd focus on him for now.

I stormed onto the sales floor to find the accounting department finishing up with a customer. As soon as the man walked out the door with his green Irwin's bag, I turned on Dean.

"Have you been ringing up your sales to my commission number?"

He glanced sideways as if he could see Grant through the walls. A sigh rippled through him, but when he turned back to me, he looked anything but apologetic. "Yes, I have."

"Why would you do that?"

"You deserved it." He sounded as if nothing could have been more obvious.

"The Vireo bag was one thing, Dean, but all of your sales? I am not a charity case."

"I don't think you are."

"You obviously do if you would give me your commission like that. I don't want anybody's pity, especially not yours."

I wished that last part back, but I meant what I'd said. I might be a hot mess, but I wasn't so bad off I needed Dean to toss money at me. I could handle a lot of things, but I hated pity, most of all from people I cared about.

I rocked back on my heels as that realization hit. Oh, I was *not* caring about Dean Irwin. I'd promised myself two things: no dating coworkers, and no dating businessmen. And now, I'd fallen right into that trap again.

"It's not pity or charity, Eliza. It only makes sense for you to have the commission money."

Somehow, his steady patience in the face of my rising anger poured gasoline on my simmering fire. Thank the Lord nobody else was in the store at the moment, because they would have been in for quite the show.

"How does that possibly make sense?"

He paused as if searching for the right excuse from a mental file cabinet. "You're training me. I wouldn't be able to make a single sale if it weren't for you."

"That's not how commission works, Dean. If it were, I should be signing all my money over to Grant, who trained me."

He clenched his jaw until it looked like his muscle might snap. Whatever other explanation he had, if he even had any, he could save it.

"I'm going to cash it out and give it back to you."

Crossing his arms, his expression went hard. "I won't take it."

"Do not be a dick about this, not right when I'm liking you."

"How is giving you money being a dick?" His low voice strained with frustration. Maybe even a touch of Dean-style low-key anger in there, too. If he was angry, good. I sure as hell was.

"Do you even hear yourself? 'Giving me money'? What makes you think any part of that is okay?"

"I don't need the commission money, and you do."

I could have screamed. One more person stepping in to help poor little Eliza, who couldn't keep it together on her own. Our lunch date-turned-business meeting made me even angrier now. I blew out a breath, pressing my fingernails into my palms.

"Scaring off creepy guys is one thing, but this is completely different. I don't need you to rescue me."

A man and woman walked through the front doors. I stared at Dean, gathering whatever calm I had left to do my actual job.

I turned my face and offered the couple as cheery a greeting as I could before looking back at him.

"Don't you dare put another sale on my account," I seethed.

He clenched his jaw, probably debating the wisdom of continuing this argument. Half a minute later, he ground out, "Fine."

"Good."

I went to help the customers, wishing for the millionth time my life wasn't such a pathetic mess that even the man I liked felt the need to step in and fix it for me.

ELIZA WORKED through the last of our shift in enough of a storm, I wasn't sure how close I should approach her. Everything I said in my defense only made her angrier. She didn't yell or rage, but her furious exhales and cold shoulder got the point through clear enough. When she clocked out and left the back room without her vest, I tried again.

"El." I reached for her hand but didn't take it. She didn't draw away, which I took as a good sign, but that only got me so far. "Can we talk more about this?"

"I can't right now. Harper's out front to give me a ride home."

"I can drive you."

She hesitated but shook her head. "She rearranged her schedule to come all this way. We can talk tomorrow."

Not what I wanted, but I would take it. She walked out the store and climbed into Harper's car at the curb. I locked up the front door, watching the red taillights disappear into the night.

In the back office, I slumped into a folding chair across from Grant. "Well, that didn't work."

He didn't look up from the laptop. "I could have told you."

"She needs that money."

"Probably."

"I thought I was doing a good thing."

"Giving her your commission just told Eliza you don't think she can take care of herself."

I sagged against the chair. That was exactly what she'd said about all the ways her parents tried to help her. Too much interference had left her feeling coddled and powerless, and I'd turned around and done the same thing.

It was easy to want to help Eliza. Her charm and big heart made her immensely loveable. I wanted to help her succeed. But not at the expense of her self-respect.

"It was the wrong move," I said.

"By a long shot, yeah." Grant turned with a strange look on his face. "Honestly, I'm surprised it bothers you this much."

He didn't know the half of it. I hadn't said anything about Eliza to my brothers yet. Still way too soon to invite that kind of color commentary into my life. Anyway, I had too much going on right now to add fielding inappropriate questions about Eliza into the mix.

"Why are you surprised?" I asked, hoping my voice and face remained reasonably neutral. "I can't take the commission; I'm not in retail. She's a good coworker, and she deserves the money."

"It's nothing about Eliza. You just don't normally take an interest in other people's problems."

My back stiffened at the casual slight. "What is that supposed to mean?"

He shrugged indifference as if he hadn't just characterized me as an insensitive ass. Again.

"You're usually too absorbed in work to pay attention to what other people have going on."

I didn't need this particular mirror held up to me just now. I stood. "Good talk."

"Hey, wait, let me rephrase." He seemed to consider his words this time. "I'm glad you care enough to have tried, that's all I'm saying. It's a good thing."

Frankly, that wasn't better. It still sounded like my own brother thought of me as an unfeeling man, even when I was trying to do something good. Being accused of heartlessness never got easier to hear.

eliza

ANOTHER NIGHT TO drown myself in ice cream.

I slumped on my couch next to Harper, recounting the lowlights of my rollercoaster of a day. From my embarrassed apology for drunkenly kissing Dean, to him assigning me all of his commissions, my day had been just packed.

"You have to admit, it was really sweet of him to try to give you his commission money."

I turned to my traitor sister. "That is not the takeaway of this story."

She laughed. "It kind of is. Most people wouldn't do that."

"That doesn't make it okay."

"And everything he said about kissing you again?" She fanned herself. "That conversation alone is more action than you've had in ages."

"Shut up." She wasn't wrong, though. Just hearing Dean tell me how badly he wanted to kiss me again—really kiss me this time—had left me hot and agitated right there in the middle of Irwin's. When he finally touched me, I'd probably explode.

But then he had to go and give me all his commission money like he was stuffing cash into the office fundraiser jar.

"I thought he was different."

She cut me a sideways look. "I know what you're going to say, but Dean doesn't sound anything like Carter."

"But he's..."

She waited, but I couldn't draw a strong parallel. A shared affinity for suits hardly condemned the two men to the same personality defects.

"Carter took, but Dean gave. Maybe he gave clumsily and without your knowledge, but he was still trying to give."

I released a deep sigh. The day had been an exhausting tangle of emotions I hadn't finished sorting through. Humiliation, excitement, then back to humiliation again. Dean hadn't been up front about it, but he *had* been trying to help. That had to be a point in his favor, even if I disliked his methods. Mostly, I hated that he knew how badly I needed *any* help.

"The way Carter used you was awful. It was cold and calculated, and when I think about that guy, I want to track him down and punch him in the face."

I smiled at Harper's protective MMA-wannabe side.

She laid a gentle hand on my arm. "But Dean doesn't sound like that at all. I know you don't want to let anyone take care of you—I get it. But not everyone who shows interest in you is trying to take advantage of you."

Slumping lower against the couch, I scooped a huge spoonful of chocolate chunk ice cream into my mouth. "So you think I overreacted?"

"No. That was a totally inappropriate thing for him to do, and you were right to call him out on it. All I'm saying is, I don't think it came from a place of trying to hurt you. Dean likes you. Don't miss that point in all of this."

That reminder fired up the cozy feelings in my chest again. Dean had meant well—he'd just chosen a crappy way to make his nice gesture. I could relate. I'd had good intentions with crappy outcomes plenty of times, today included.

"So I should apologize?"

She gestured with her spoon. "Probably, yeah. If you want things to move forward with him, anyway."

I did want things to move forward with Dean. As terrifying as that thought was, I couldn't pretend I felt anything else. He was a businessman and he could be a little stuffy sometimes, but the glimpses he gave me of Sweet Dean, of Soft Dean, made me want to get to know him better.

But getting to know him better held risks. Risks were usually my jam, but not ones that had the potential to involve my heart. Not ones that could smash me into a million little pieces. I put myself back together once. I didn't know if I could do it again.

"Okay," I said, ready to push aside my little woe-is-me jag. "That's enough of that. What's the latest gossip at Siesta Village? I want to hear about those old ladies who make trouble for everyone."

"Bonnie and Vivian? You would be their number one fan." Harper laughed, but it sounded strangled at the end. "It's not news about them, but uh, Sam Donnelly started volunteering at the Village today."

I whipped my head around to her, my eyes probably gigantic. "Sam Donnelly? Why didn't you lead with that?"

"Maybe because you were in full freak-out mode when I got here?"

I ignored her. That freak-out was well within my rights. "I didn't know he was even in town. When did this happen?"

She shrugged as if she didn't know or care, but I knew my sister better than that. Sam had been her big high school boyfriend after being friends for years, and she'd totally fallen head over heels. They'd had perfect couple written all over them, right up until he dumped her and took another girl to prom two weeks later. Talk about *ouch*. It'd been ten years, but still. Not like she'd forgotten.

"He hasn't been back long."

I scrolled through all the gossip that had swirled through town about him. After high school, he'd gone off on an adventure and never looked back. I wasn't sure I'd even seen him in town again. Apparently, things had changed.

"Last I heard, he was in New Zealand, wasn't he?"

"Colorado." She clamped her mouth shut tight, as if ashamed of knowing that tidbit. Then she shrugged. "His grandfather, Glen, lives in the Village. He talks about Sam sometimes."

My eyes were glued to her, waiting for everything she refused to share. "And? Why are you making me ask? What does he look like now? What's he doing in town? Are things weird between you two? Spill it!"

"He looks like a man. Glen says he's back to stay, but I have my doubts. And things aren't weird between us, because we're not seventeen anymore. We're not even going to interact, anyway. He's working with the activities' director, not me."

She took a big scoop of ice cream and stuffed it into her mouth, still not meeting my eyes.

"'*He looks like a man*'? That's the best you can do?"

Her cheeks went bright pink, what she called the Curse of the Redhead—from anger to embarrassment, all her big feelings colored her face.

"When it comes to Sam Donnelly, yes. That's all you're getting from me. You'll see him in town soon enough, I'm sure. Irwin's is right up his alley."

From all the adventuring he did, this was totally true, yet

not likely he'd confide any juicy gossip in me. That was supposed to be Harper's job, and she'd decided to hold out.

"Yeah, but it's kind of a convenient coincidence, don't you think, him volunteering where you work?"

Sighing as if she wished this conversation were over, she grabbed another scoop of ice cream. "I told you, his grandfather lives there. Whatever you're thinking, it's not that."

Still sounded pretty convenient to me.

"What's he volunteering as?"

Harper looked physically pained. "Yoga instructor."

I sucked in a breath, ready to ask a thousand questions about *that* piece of information, but she finally swiveled her head to me. Her expression had turned to steel, despite the red splotches still staining her cheeks.

"I think you've had more than enough gossip for one night."

I pouted at her. "But you have so much more to tell!"

"Yeah I do, like how Mom's been asking about your soap business."

I froze, all my delight in her *convenient* reunion with her high school boyfriend turning to dread, that old familiar weight settling in my stomach. "What's she been asking?"

"How serious you are about it, do I have any idea how much you're making, ballpark estimate of how much I think you might need for a small business loan."

"A small business loan?" I nearly choked on my chocolate chunk. Jeans and groceries were one thing, but trying to interfere in my work? Too far. "What?"

"She tried to play it casual, but you know Mom, she doesn't do innocent questions well."

I splayed my hand. Harper had become the queen of Not Enough Information tonight. "What did you tell her?"

"I told her she would have to ask you."

Breathing a sigh of relief, I eased back into the couch. "Thank you."

She turned to face me. "But that means she's going to ask you."

eliza

WALKING around with this much cash made me feel like some kind of mafia boss ready to whip out a wad of bills at any minute. I didn't hate it.

At Irwin's, I found Dean talking with a customer in front of the water bottle display. Of course, he'd showed up early for our closing shift. Come to think of it, he was always in the store before I clocked in, and didn't leave until after I'd clocked out. He wasn't kidding about not wanting off hours. I could admire his work ethic, but I wished he wouldn't push himself so hard.

Okay, fine. Yes. I cared about Dean Irwin. He'd grown on me, despite the smart suits and sometimes aloof attitude.

He watched me with a wary expression, as if he expected me to lash out again any moment. Between misunderstandings and overreactions, I'd given him plenty of cause for uncertainty. I flashed a smile, finding satisfaction at the relief that shone in his eyes.

By the time I clocked in and put my green vest on, Dean's customer had left the store. My heart raced, but I took a deep breath, determined to get through this as quickly as possible.

"Here's your money." I held the cash out to him, hoping this wouldn't turn into another battle of wills.

He hesitated, glancing between me and the money. Finally, he took the cash and slipped it into his pocket.

"You didn't have to do that." His voice held no trace of bitterness in his soft rebuke. He seemed to understand he wouldn't change my mind.

"I did, actually. But I'm sorry for how I reacted yesterday. It wasn't the best."

It wasn't the best. Kind of the theme of a lot of my choices lately.

"You don't have to apologize. I'm sorry I didn't talk to you about what I wanted to do."

"I know you're only trying to help." If I could stop saying that to everyone in my life, that would be great.

"Maybe you were right. Maybe I did want to rescue you again." He watched me with those kind, hazel eyes, and a small smile curved along his lips. "I'm realizing you're the kind of woman who rescues herself."

That compliment swelled through me until I thought I might burst. He saw through the wreck I was to the woman I was trying to be. That right there was worth more than any commission.

We worked through our shift, taking customers by turns. Dean had become comfortable enough chatting people up about trekking poles and camp kits that I no longer spied on his conversations to make sure he wasn't about to lose his cool. His demeanor still held a bit of stiffness to it, but I suspected that was just his way. Kind of endearing, actually, now that I understood him better.

"We recommend this first aid kit as a good base kit," he told a young man. "And here's a list of Ten Essentials to have with you on your trip if you need a starting place for your pack."

I hung back as he rang up the kid's purchases, leaning my elbows on the counter behind him, and watching his shoulders move as he worked, mentally mapping out his muscles. The memory of him in his wet T-shirt and board shorts at the lake had kept me humming for a whole week now. It could probably maintain me for a lot longer, but I wanted more. More of that tenacious Dean who refused to let the paddleboard get the best of him. More of that open Dean who confided about his struggle to learn control. Mostly, I just wanted more *Dean*.

After seeing the young man and his first aid kit off, he turned around to face me. I grinned up at him like a goof.

"What?" he said.

"It's cute to hear you use phrases you borrowed from me."

He leaned back against the opposite counter, squaring off against me. His stance reminded me of the night of the party, but today he looked much more relaxed as he watched me.

"Cute, huh?" He didn't seem impressed by the description.

"I like how you've embraced business casual, too. No top button, sleeves rolled up and everything. It's nice."

Still overdressed in my opinion, but he'd lost his CEO-on-a-firing-spree air. And those forearms he kept flashing me with? Delicious.

"Nice?" He shook his head. "Now we're spiraling down."

"Nice can be good."

He pushed off the front counter and bent forward until he rested his elbows on the counter across from me, mirroring my pose. "Nice isn't going to work for me."

With our faces inches apart, his fingers lightly stroked my elbows. I'd never thought elbows could be an erogenous zone, but everything in my body focused on them now.

"Gentlemanly?" I offered.

He shook his head, his eyes never leaving mine.

"I can bump you up to cordial, but that's the best I can do."

"I'm going for sexy or nothing at all."

Just hearing him say the word *sexy* made my insides squirm in the best way. I'd locked all that up long ago, but Dean had found the key. He'd unleashed something new, tempting, and entirely too dangerous.

Only my good old swagger could see me through this conversation. I didn't have a clue what I was doing, but he didn't need to know that. "I'm going to need a lot of convincing."

His mouth quirked. "I'm up for the challenge."

"Dean, Eliza," Grant said, walking out of the back room.

I launched myself away from Dean so hard, I sent T-shirts swinging on their hangers around me. His eyebrows hitched up, confirming I'd proven myself ridiculous. Whatever we were doing, I wasn't ready to have Grant walk in on us practically kissing on the sales floor.

Luckily, Grant didn't seem to have noticed my supreme display of weirdness.

"Can you close out your shifts with some tagging?" he asked. "We got two big deliveries this morning I haven't been able to get to."

"No problem."

Dean's husky voice and heated look left me no doubt his mind was still on the gauntlet I'd casually thrown down. I was playing with fire now, and wasn't sure I wanted to put it out.

We followed Grant into the stock room where he showed us the boxes full of assorted gear, along with the price sheet he wanted us to use. Dean's eyes still had a smoldering fire in them that made my stomach flutter. Good thing I was already a pro at tagging, since I didn't hear a word of Grant's instructions.

"I appreciate this," he said. "I'll watch the registers while I finish up our monthly sales report. The head of our accounting department can be a real hard-ass."

Dean didn't seem amused by the joke.

Grant disappeared again, leaving me alone with a mountain of items to tag and a man who had probably never seen a sticker gun in his life. After a quick demo on how to use the sticker guns and the best way to apply them to the tags, we set to work. The stock room seemed more cramped and confined than usual tonight. Not even the clacking of the guns could drown out my decidedly one-track mind.

I tried to keep my focus on the task at hand, but it wasn't easy. If I happened to look up, I met Dean's eyes staring into mine with a heat that curled my toes and made my elbows tingle.

This wasn't normal. Women who had been kissed properly in the last four years probably didn't get tingly elbows. Sloppy midnight kisses on New Year's Eve at the Broken Hammer didn't count for much. Those brief kisses and the guys who'd bestowed them hadn't meant anything, but Dean held a category all his own. Right now, that category was deeply distracting me from my work.

"I bet you never thought you'd be tagging Texas Trails' maps when you got that MBA." I glanced up to see amusement curl along his mouth.

"It's not what I had in mind."

"New experiences might be good for you."

"I agree."

His coarse voice snaked through my chest. This was not okay. He had me in grave danger of melting in a puddle at his feet. I needed to find some leverage.

"You never told me what else your grandma thinks you need to learn to turn you into a well-rounded man."

"I have a feeling you would use that information against me if I did."

"Me?" I grinned at him, loving the direction of this conversation already. "I would never."

"Baking is a big one for her. I need to be able to do more in the kitchen."

I nodded like a freaking fount of wisdom. "This is true. Women love a man with kitchen skills."

"I have skills in other rooms."

Tendrils of heat whirled through my belly and curled up my spine. He thought he could turn my teasing against me? If he thought I'd back down, he didn't know me nearly well enough yet. I would turn it right back. "Do you mean bedroom skills? Are you saying you can fold fitted sheets?"

His eyes locked on me so hard, his gaze tingled over my skin.

"It's okay if you can't," I said. "Some people never get the hang of it. It's like kissing in that way."

His gaze turned so hot, it could have sparked tinder, and the muscle in his jaw twitched. I would *so* win this little game. Pretty sure the prize was watching the other person's control break. Tonight, that wouldn't be me. Tonight, I wanted to see neat, buttoned-up Dean go a little wild.

"I'm guessing that's part of why you stopped me the other night. It's totally fine. You don't know how to kiss. It's no big deal." I couldn't help the smile tugging at my mouth. He had frozen like a cat getting ready to pounce.

"Lots of people don't know how to kiss," I plowed on. "Some people go their whole lives not knowing how to kiss. It's a lost art, kissing."

Dean dropped the sticker gun on the counter and moved closer until he stood in my space. His body pulsed with barely-contained energy, his gaze all fire, heating my body like I'd walked into a solar flare.

"Say *kiss* one more time." His voice had gone low and dangerous in his challenge.

My heart pounded like mad, and my breathing turned shallow. I was about to win, in so many more ways than one. No sense backing down now.

"I'm sure there's some sort of remedial kissing class you could—"

His hands were on the sides of my face in an instant, his warm mouth covering mine in retaliation. His lips pressed, caressed, and nudged mine open as my body came to life in his arms. Had I ever been kissed like this before? The forgettable midnight kisses of my past had never awoken this kind of storm, and all I could do was hold on.

His punishment was thorough, his tongue sweeping across mine until I groaned against his mouth. He still cupped my face like I was a delicate work of art while my grabby hands explored the expanse of his broad chest and shoulders, a sea of muscle beneath crisp linen.

He shifted slightly and I followed, pressing my mouth back to his. I delighted in this intensity, and my only thought now was that I didn't want it to stop. He wrapped me up in his arms like a Dean cocoon, cozy and perfect.

I wanted to stay here forever, please and thank you.

When he finally broke the kiss, we barely moved. Pressed snug against him, I breathed him in, my heart doing endless cartwheels in my chest. He sighed against me as if he felt the same contentment I did, and I nestled even closer.

"I guess you don't need that class, after all," I said.

The sound of a throat clearing drew our attention away from each other. Grant stood in the doorway to the sales floor, his eyes fixed on Dean in a murderous glare.

dean

I RELEASED ELIZA, letting her slip from my grasp to put a respectable distance between us. Just a moment ago, I'd been immune to everything else in the world as I savored the wonder of this woman. My name and location? Unknown. The only certainty was the overwhelming want tumbling through me like an avalanche.

Now, speared by Grant's icy stare, regret shoved all my desires aside.

"Your sister's out front." His words were for Eliza, but he stared at me as if he could turn me to dust.

She snapped out of her daze. "I lost track of time."

I stood frozen in place while she scrambled to clock out and hang up her vest. She turned to me, a blush still touching her cheeks, a mix of embarrassment and pleasure in her eyes. "I'll see you tomorrow, Dean."

Her saucy tone made my pulse tick up, but beneath Grant's unblinking gaze, I couldn't do anything but nod in return.

To Grant, she said, "I'm sorry, I probably shouldn't have..." She gestured helplessly, as though to encompass everything:

me, the kiss, the stack of products we hadn't fully tagged in our distraction.

To hell with the abandoned work—I hated that once again, she'd apologized for kissing me.

Grant's brief smile was at least sincere. "It's not my business."

The tension drained away from her face, and I knew she'd expected a reprimand for our little indiscretion. She needn't have worried. Grant's frustration would only be aimed at me.

"I'll see you tomorrow." Behind Grant, she turned to me at the doorway, and the look of longing in her eyes set my chest on fire all over again.

My brother stood stock still after Eliza had left. I could practically hear him counting down from ten in his head. When he finally turned to me, his eyes brimmed with barely-contained anger. "What do you think you're doing?"

I spread my hands out wide, unsure where to start. "I like her."

"I can see that. Is that why you signed your commissions over to her?"

"No, I started that before anything between us—"

He held up a hand. "What are you doing with her?"

His frustration went beyond anything I'd expected of him, and I willed myself to stay calm. I did not need to turn this into a full-blown argument. Not when I wasn't sure I would win.

"I'm getting to know her better."

He ran a hand through his hair. "I can't believe you. Dating an employee right under my nose."

"It's not against the rules. I'm not her boss."

"Because that would be wrong. But it's not wrong if you're an executive about to become CFO of the company where she works?"

Ice water doused all the lingering heat from my time with Eliza.

I had no good explanation for my actions. I'd known all along my interest in her could be a conflict, but I'd managed to convince myself the risk was minimal. At first, the idea of her returning that interest had seemed so out of reach, I'd thought I was the only one who stood to lose anything. Lately, I'd forgotten just how problematic our relationship had the potential to be.

More to the point, my interest in her had completely overtaken my rational mind until I no longer cared about the potential conflict.

Our relationship wasn't strictly against company policy. Coworkers could date, although our situation wasn't so simple. As far as I knew, my brothers had never dated an employee, but whether that came out of noble intentions or lack of interest, I didn't know. If I were to do things right, I would need to report the relationship to my superiors. That meant my parents. Coming to Mom and Dad with a new girlfriend who happened to be a regular on the sales floor could only further tangle this already complicated beginning with Eliza.

"I have no problem with two employees dating," Grant said. "I have no problem with you dating Eliza. Hell, I'd be happy for you if I weren't so mad at you for keeping all this from me. I had no idea you had taken your interest in her this far."

I sank against the stock room table. "You want me to end things with her?"

His eyes narrowed. "Is that all it would take? Me asking you to?"

The thought of being nothing more to Eliza than a coworker made my chest constrict. One kiss—two—and I already couldn't see myself going back to that space of casual indifference. "No. I couldn't even if Dad asked me to."

"Good. I don't want to find out this was just a fun fling for you."

I took a step toward him, my anger boiling to life. "That's not what this is."

He raised both his hands, finally relaxing a bit. "She's a nice girl, is all. I've known her a long time. I don't want to see her get hurt."

I didn't want Eliza to get hurt, either. That Grant seemed to assume that was where this relationship was headed only gave a new name to my frustrations. Leaving a trail of women behind him was Rhett's M.O., not mine.

"What do you suggest I do?"

He made a face like there were no good answers. "Just be careful."

I worked in the stock room, tagging all the gear Eliza and I had abandoned, and thinking over Grant's warning. *Be careful.* I had been careful for years now, safe and controlled, keeping everything in neat little boxes. I didn't want that kind of safety anymore, not with Eliza.

When I finally went home to my townhouse, I was too wired for sleep. I changed into workout clothes and went into the garage, switched on a box fan for a little circulation, pulled up what Rhett called my Angry Mix on my phone, and started pummeling the punching bag hung in one corner. Before I discovered running as a way to ease my *intensity*, as Eliza called it, my parents had bought me a punching bag as a teen. It had been a safe way for me to release some of my pent-up anger and frustrations. Tonight, I had plenty of both.

I had someone I wanted to share my heart with, and Grant's immediate conclusion was I intended to use her. No *Congrats*, no *Happy for you*, but *Don't hurt her*. Did I really give off such an overpowering air of indifference that my own brother assumed I couldn't care for Eliza?

I jabbed at the bag, letting some of that resentment go with each strike.

Eliza.

I couldn't cling very tightly to my irritation when we'd shared a devastating kiss that quickened my pulse every time it crossed my mind—which was nonstop. The memory of it lived in my skin, reminding me of every touch of her hands, every sound she had made.

I wouldn't sleep at all tonight.

"Yes, let the hate flow through you."

I turned to see Rhett smirking in the doorway, his fingertips together in his best impression of Emperor Palpatine. He walked across the garage floor, pulled a beer from the fridge, cracked it open, and gestured at the bag. "What's going on?"

"Nothing." I turned back to the punching bag and struck it a few more times. "Just working a few things out."

"Maybe you should talk about it."

Bitter laughter escaped me as I punched the bag. "Are you saying I need therapy?"

I'd been through plenty growing up. I'd needed to learn to control my anger, to call into line those wild emotions that threatened to overtake me. I still saw my therapist occasionally to make sure I was finding healthy ways to cope when everything else became too much.

"I mean maybe you should talk to me, idiot."

I glanced at my brother but went back to punching the bag. "I'm fine."

"Is it woman problems?"

Whatever incriminating thing my face did made Rhett grin wider. "It is a woman. Damn."

I slammed the bag harder. "Damn what?"

"It's been a while for you, that's all."

"Just what I wanted to hear, thanks." I ignored his smug

smile, focusing instead on the sound each punch made as it landed on the bag.

"So who is it?"

I flicked my eyes to him but said nothing.

"Don't make me follow you around until I find out. And I will find out."

Rhett was skilled at that. I liked my privacy, but his persistence knew no bounds.

Stepping away from the bag, I swiped my forearm across my sweaty face. "Eliza."

He paused, his beer bottle halfway to his mouth. "Eliza *Webb*?"

"Obviously." I pulled off my boxing mitts and unwound the tape from my knuckles.

"That's not a real likely match, is it? You two are—" He drew his hands apart to indicate just how different we were. "You're not exactly peas in a pod."

"This is why I don't want to talk about it." I laid aside my boxing gear and grabbed my neon green water bottle, downing half of it in one go. I didn't want commentary on what Eliza saw —or didn't see—in me.

"And she, uh...she reciprocates?"

Rhett flinched under the weight of my glare.

"Yes, she reciprocates." My blood pulsed all over again with the memory of her enthusiastic reciprocation.

"Good, good. Good for you, man."

I shook my head, unsurprised he didn't get it. "Not good. She's one of our employees."

"Who cares about that?"

"Grant does. Mom and Dad might."

He nodded and gestured at the bag. "So that's the source of tonight's punch-a-thon?"

I shrugged, tugging one hand through my hair. "Among other things."

Rhett's grin flashed again. "You dog."

"I'm going to bed." I brushed past him, ignoring his laughter.

"Sweet dreams," he called.

They would be.

THE WEDNESDAY FARMERS market went by in a blur. Honestly, it was a wonder I could make proper change with the memory of Dean's touch echoing through my body. I'd tossed and turned in bed the night before, wired on his kiss like caffeine. Now, a post-kiss fog had settled over me, coloring all my interactions in a dreamy kind of haze. I'd become as bad as Eden and June.

That thought made me sit up a little straighter at my booth. I needed to get a handle on this thing before it turned my head to mush. Badass businesswomen did not let their brains go all fluffy just because of one kiss.

One scorching, phenomenal, elbow-tingling kiss.

"Eliza, how are you?"

Sarah Daniels had snuck up on me in my dreamy Dean-contemplation. She managed to stop by most weeks, if not to purchase, then at least to say hello. Customers like this, who came by just to see me, made the farmers market one of my favorite places.

"I'm super, thanks." My face was probably still all flushed from constantly reliving that kiss, but I could blame that on the heat. I gestured at the bulky bag she carried. "What have you found?"

Since I worked every farmers market without anyone to cover for me, I hadn't actually browsed the market stalls in months. I kind of missed walking through the gauntlet of goodies collecting special treats.

"I bought up a bunch of beautiful pears." She opened her market bag, and I caught a peek of the light brown fruits piled inside. "I think I'll make pear tarts for tomorrow's guests."

Sarah and her husband Mark ran the Bluebird Lodge, one of Magnolia Ridge's upscale bed and breakfasts. They had a giant log house-style main lodge, with several tiny log cabins scattered around their property. I'd never stayed there, but from all I heard, it had become a popular honeymoon destination.

"Pear tarts sound delicious. Do you make everything yourself?"

She nodded, swiping her hair from her forehead. "We make everything from scratch each morning. It's a bit more work than having food delivered or heating something up, but I think it's important to give customers that special touch, don't you?"

"Absolutely." I had no interest in trying to outsource the manufacture of my soaps, as some sellers did. If I didn't make them myself, what was the point?

"I buy locally as much as I can for the same reason." She looked over my display. "Why are soaps so addictive? I know I have bars at home I haven't even used yet, but I'm just itching to buy another."

I filed that compliment away to remember later. "I think it's because they appeal to our senses. They smell good, they look pretty, they feel great on our skin. If I could eat them, I would."

She picked up a bar of Lemon Luster and sniffed it. "This one certainly smells good enough to eat. I'll take it."

She handed me a few bills, and I'd just wished her goodbye

when a man rolled a hand-truck up to the Oh, Honey! booth next door. Miguel and Ethan loaded three crates onto it, an envelope exchanged hands, and the man carted the honey off. A little curl of envy worked through me as he walked away. That had to be the biggest purchase I'd ever seen someone make in one go at their stall.

I moved closer to catch Miguel's attention. "What was that about?"

He didn't mask the pride in his satisfied expression. "Texas Gift Works out on Highway Thirty-five put in an order. If this goes well, they could become a regular customer for us."

"Congrats." That was the kind of big-time deal I needed to snag. Somehow. "How did you get a deal like that, if you don't mind me asking?"

He shifted closer until sunlight shone on his deeply tanned skin through the gap between our awnings. "Two words: Hard work."

"Wow. Thank you, I'm writing that down. That's good stuff."

His grin grew wider. "We got a lot of rejections before we got our yeses. That one big Yes represents about fifty Nos. Are you trying to get into wholesale?"

"A bit, yeah." I still hadn't taken any real steps that direction, but I'd taped Dean's action plan to my dresser mirror. That was kind of a step.

"There's your problem right there: *A bit.* Go big, or go home."

Flashing a teasing grin, I said, "Going home's not so bad."

Miguel arched an eyebrow. "Home isn't where the success is at, honey."

I waited until he'd turned away to let my face fall, all the cocky attitude inside me deflating with those few teasing words.

I wanted the kind of success they had—I just wasn't sure I could handle the crushing failures he said went hand-in-hand with it. *Fifty nos?* I'd cry like a baby over that kind of rejection. I'd specifically started my business so I *wouldn't* get rejected all the time.

Harper showed up when the market ended at one to help me pack my booth. We dragged boxes to the vendor drive-up line, sweating in the afternoon heat. I'd perfected a minimalist set up specifically for this reason—carting heavy displays through the market would be the worst way to close out a five-hour shift.

"I don't have a lot of time," she said as we crammed bins into her trunk. "I'm technically on my lunch break. Do you mind if I drop you off early at Irwin's?"

"Totally fine. You are the best of all possible sisters." I hated trespassing on her good will, but with the Bronco out of commission, I didn't have a lot of options for getting around. "I'll find a way to pay you back."

Her uneasy smile sent guilt and shame chasing each other through my stomach. How many times had I said that phrase to her? I'd turned IOUs into a skill like no other. Dinners, beers, movie nights—I owed my sisters plenty through the years. This soap venture was supposed to change all that, and somehow, I'd fallen into a worse hole than before, unable to even get to my job without help.

We loaded the last tote bin into Harper's car when my phone buzzed with a text.

Dean: Need a ride in today?

I grinned over the offer, tiny butterflies zooming around in my chest. Carpooling with Dean sounded much better than making my sister go out of her way during her lunch break. A simple matter of convenience, that was all. It had nothing to do with the man making the offer.

Nope. Not a thing.

Eliza: My hero

"Your problems are solved. Dean offered to take me to work this afternoon."

Harper climbed into the driver's seat. "Praise the Lord. Are you two dating now, or...?"

I scrunched up my nose even as those happy butterflies froze over and dropped into my stomach. "I think it's still *Or.*"

Probably should add *Figure out relationship with Dean* to my never-ending to-do list.

I clasped my hands together in my lap, feigning a Sunday school reverence. "But we did kiss."

She whipped her head around. "You did what now?"

My grin radiated pure bliss. "He kissed me. It was spectacular. You should be jealous."

She pulled out of the vendor line and headed toward my place. "This isn't one of those *I'm pretending to get it on with a biker but really I stayed home and watched K-dramas all night* scenarios, is it?"

I full-on gasped at the insinuation. "I never pretended to get it on with anybody."

"You kind of did." She lightly smacked my leg. "So how was it?"

Every time I thought about how Dean had taken my face in his hands and claimed my mouth, wildfires sparked inside my body. I never would have guessed Dean Irwin would be the one to turn me into an inferno of longing, but here I sat, burning away.

"It was the single most incredible experience of my life."

She sighed. "I need to get out more."

"Staying in Siesta Village all the time might work in your favor now that Sam's hanging around there, too."

She scowled at the road. "He's cutting into my workload, if you can believe it. My patients would rather take yoga with him than do PT with me."

"Well, you know, yoga's popular, right?"

"It's because he's young, hot, and a total flirt."

A slow grin spread over my face even while hers darkened as if her own personal storm cloud followed us around. "So you're saying he's hot?"

Her mouth twisted. "He's annoying."

Oh, yeah. She thought he was hot.

After she took off again for Fiesta Village, I lugged my bins up to my apartment, leaving the front door wide open to let in a little fresh air. Any day the temperatures stayed below eighty demanded an open window or two. As much as I loved the smell of my soaps individually, the scent of hundreds of them could be smothering. I had just set the last box of soaps back in its place on my shelves when Dean's shadow loomed in my doorway.

A smile crossed his face while my brain scrambled to assess the situation. Were we at the kiss hello stage? Should we hug? A handshake was right out of the question. Although he did give good handshake, that wasn't close to what I wanted.

He walked through the door looking as professional and handsome as ever. His neat green Oxford had the top button undone, revealing the barest glimpse of his neck. My pulse quickened as my eyes devoured the cords of muscle there. I used to want to strangle that neck, and now all I could think about was kissing it.

He walked closer, resting a hand on my hip as he brushed a kiss against my cheek. "How was your morning?"

"Getting better." Disappointed he hadn't gone for my mouth, I kept the petulance out of my voice as he stepped back out of my space. "How did things go with Grant last night? He looked pretty unhappy when I left. Did he say anything to you about...us?"

He paused, and fear bloomed in my chest like a giant, ugly flower. He'd come to his senses. He was about to tell me there was no "us". We were just Dean and Eliza, two coworkers who needed to keep things professional and very, very separate.

"He's concerned."

"Oh." I took a step away from him, bracing myself against the kitchen counter. Wrapping my fingers beneath the edge of the Formica, I tried for a casual calm even though my insides felt like they were circling a drain. "Concerned. What about?"

He frowned just enough to notice. "I'm an executive at Irwin's, and you're one of our employees."

"Right. That."

Somewhere in the last two weeks, I had lost track of that little detail. Honestly, I'd never given his title much thought except to mentally disparage whatever it was he did upstairs in the corporate side of things. He'd always just been Dean, gorgeous grouch in a killer suit. That our relationship, or whatever this was, might be against Irwin's rules had never occurred to me.

That it expressly went against my own rules had occurred to me plenty of times, but I'd become skilled at ignoring that.

"I'm not concerned about it if you're not. I should report it to my superiors, though."

My eyes darted to his. "You mean your parents?"

He nodded.

"It's not prohibited or anything?"

He pulled his mouth to the side as if debating how to phrase his answer. Whatever it was bothered him at least a little.

"There's nothing in company policy against two employees choosing to date."

"Are we doing that? Choosing to date?"

Maybe it was a forward question, but I needed to know what we were doing. I didn't need a marriage proposal, but if he just wanted to get something out of his system, I would take a pass on that right now.

"Can I take you out to dinner Friday night?"

Elation sprang up in my chest but subsided again like waves crashing against the shore. His invitation was exactly the right response, and exactly the wrong one.

"No."

He furrowed his eyebrows in that little show of frustration I found so adorable.

"No?"

"We don't have to go out." Going out to dinner would just be another thing I should pay him back for and couldn't, one more IOU to add to my list. His efforts to help me out with my business plan had been awkward enough, and the commission thing even worse. I didn't want to owe Dean anything.

He nodded as if I had said all that out loud. "What if I make dinner for you?"

"I thought you couldn't cook."

"I'm a great cook. It's baking I'm lost at."

"Baking's just following a recipe."

His eyebrows twitched. "So they say. Is that a yes to dinner?"

"Sure, it will give me a chance to check out your place like you checked out mine." I hadn't missed the fact he'd tidied my apartment during his brief visit. If my mother hadn't interrupted, he just might have done my laundry.

"I thought I would make dinner here."

"What's wrong with your place?"

He scrubbed a hand over the back of his neck. "My living situation is complicated."

That sounded like a line if ever I'd heard one. All kinds of awful *complications* danced through my head, one in particular worst of all. "Do you have a girlfriend?"

He froze, lines etched around his eyes. "What? No, of course not. Do you really think I would ask you out if I had a girlfriend?" Blowing out a breath, he stepped closer, his bergamot cologne swirling in the air. "No, El, I don't have a girlfriend. I live with Rhett. If I fix you dinner at my place, he will show up no matter how clear I make it he's not invited."

I nodded, wishing I hadn't sounded like a jealous weirdo, but pleased all the same by what he'd said. "I'm sorry, I shouldn't have accused you of having a girlfriend."

A little smile touched his mouth. "I don't mind the idea of having a girlfriend."

The grin that popped onto my face eclipsed his. Yeah. We were really doing this. "I guess we can eat here, then."

"Love your enthusiasm."

* * *

The main thing that made my Wednesday evening shifts at Irwin Outdoors bearable after working at the farmers market all morning was that the store was usually a graveyard mid-week. Dean and I had relieved Nicole of her post at the registers, but customers rarely trickled in during the hours since. I'd planned to finish the tagging Grant had left for us the night before, only to discover everything had already been done.

"Did you do this?" I assessed the neatly organized inventory. The tidy stacks and perfectly centered price stickers had his fingerprints all over them.

"I had the time."

"How long did you stay after our shift ended?" He must have done an hour's work or more past closing.

"I didn't pay attention."

"Dean, you have got to rein in this obsession with work." I was only half kidding. The man had business on the brain twenty-four seven.

"After the way we finished our shift," he said, his voice gone low, "I needed something to keep myself busy."

Heat washed up my neck even as my stomach flipped over. Any number of responses came to me, none of which were appropriate in our workplace. Before I could get written up for kissing a coworker's face off, I spun around and walked onto the sales floor.

Out among the tent displays and camp chairs, I saw the one thing I hoped I would never have to face while wearing my Irwin's vest. The warm flush from Dean's flirtatious remark turned chilly, and I contemplated running straight back to the stockroom. Maybe I could escape out the delivery door.

My mother stood admiring a rack of hydration packs, her silver-blond hair in flawless waves. She wore cropped khakis and a sleeveless blouse as if she'd spent the day golfing and drinking mojitos. I could have used a mojito just about then. Two, to be safe.

Mom caught sight of me before I had a chance to dive behind one of the clothing displays. I adored her, but some things didn't mix well—like work and overly-interested parents.

A satisfied grin lit her face. "It's so good to see you again."

Okay, weird greeting from my mom. But...no. Realization sank through me like a weight, dragging shiny-new dread behind it. She wasn't talking to me—she'd spoken to Dean. *Dean.*

Kind of wished I was back at home throwing up again.

He shook her offered hand. "It's nice to see you, Darlene."

"What are you doing here, Mom?"

She barely glanced at me, her eyes still glued on Dean. Her obvious mooning made me antsy, and I hoped whatever she wanted, she'd make it quick.

"I was in the neighborhood and thought I would stop by. Say hello, you know." She stared up at Dean as if meeting a superhero in the flesh. "I wanted to thank you again for looking after my baby when she was so sick last week. It was so kind of you."

He glanced to me, a slight smile on his lips. "There's no need to thank me, I was happy to do it."

Mom melted a little at that perfect answer. Dean was rocking Parental Interaction 101. Of course he was.

Two men walked through Irwin's door, and I called out my usual hellos. I turned to my mother, who gazed at Dean in adoration. She had all the subtlety of a New Year's Day parade float.

"It's good to see you, Mom, but we have customers."

"Oh, you can take care of them, can't you? It will give me a chance to talk to Dean, here."

I tried to telegraph to him he should run away now while he had the chance, but he seemed to have no idea what awaited him. Mom waved me off as if *I'd* interrupted *them*. Against my better judgment, I left to help the new customers. I tried to keep one ear out for their conversation, but the two men had so many questions about Irwin's return policy, I couldn't focus on it.

By the time I finished up with the men and saw them safely out the door, Dean was agreeing to something that clearly delighted my mother. *Oh, that can't be good.* I joined them, prepared for the worst.

"We'll see you at seven on Sunday, then," Mom said.

Every muscle in my body cringed. Yep, that would be the worst.

She turned to me with a small, content smile, but she might as well have shot a confetti cannon in the store. "See you this weekend, baby."

Waving at each of us, she sashayed back out of the doors, aggressively happy with herself.

I turned on Dean. "Did you just agree to come to our family dinner?"

"Yes."

"Why would you do that?" My high-pitched question rocked him back on his heels.

"I didn't realize it would bother you. I can cancel if you'd rather I didn't go."

Realizing how that must have sounded, I ran a reassuring hand along his bicep, fighting the urge to grab and squeeze. For a runner, his arms were seriously muscled. "It's not that. You have no idea what you just signed up for. My parents mean well, but their brand of love is just...relentless."

He looked entirely unimpressed. "People who love you too much are the worst."

"They're just so encouraging."

"That's it, I'm canceling."

I sighed, wanting to make him understand. "When your parents genuinely believe you're capable of anything and then all you accomplish is a big fat nothing, their encouragement becomes criticism all on its own."

His eyes went all sweet and sympathetic, and I wished I'd been a little less honest.

"El, you have not accomplished nothing."

"My sisters are both very successful in what they do, and I —" I opened my palms. There was no good way to finish that sentence.

I had a degree but hadn't found a way to put it to use. I had a string of jobs to my name but nothing like a stable career in sight. I made soaps but couldn't live off their profits. My parents' constant reassurances that I would find my footing soon only heightened how shaky I truly felt.

"You're still figuring things out," he said. "That's nothing to be ashamed of."

"That's not what you said two weeks ago."

"I was a different man two weeks ago. You said so yourself."

Now I did squeeze his arm. "This isn't going to work if you're going to remember things I say and quote me on them."

"You also said you think I'm hot."

I scowled up at him, knowing it had no bite when I was basically copping a feel at the same time. The man had glorious biceps. "You're infuriating."

"Infuriatingly hot."

All too true.

eliza

FRIDAY NIGHT COULDN'T COME SOON
ENOUGH.

I spent hours of each day with Dean at Irwin's, plus time going to and from work in his clean, electric, decidedly non-junker car, but it didn't compare to the prospect of our date. We lightly flirted on the sales floor and stole back room kisses when we could, but work hours demanded we maintain a certain level of platonic professionalism that our date would not.

Nerves multiplied in my stomach every time I checked my watch. I knew he wouldn't be late, but the butterflies swarming around in there made it hard to settle down. I'd dated in the past, but it'd be fair to say I had never experienced anything quite like what Dean and I were doing. *Choosing to date.* Those words kept popping up in my mind, their intent crystal clear and yet oh so murky. We were dating, but what did it mean? And how, at twenty-six, could I be this out of my depth in the dating world?

For all my talk, my experiences with guys didn't tally up to much. My high school boyfriend had been a bit of a dud, cute and great at football, but lousy at doing anything that didn't involve kicking field goals or pressuring me for sex. In college, I had taken all the evasive maneuvers I'd learned from dating him and built an increasingly impenetrable shield around myself, warding off frat boys and the stray teacher's assistant with ease. Whatever I'd had with Carter counted for exactly nothing, since it had all been a lie.

But Dean was no overeager boy looking for a conquest, or a scheming coworker looking for a path to advancement. He was a kind, successful, extraordinarily smart man, and he wanted to *date* me. If I dwelled on that thought too long, I just might spiral into a panic.

"Who wouldn't want to date you?" I said into the mirror. My reflection showed a woman who didn't buy what she was selling.

Dean knocked at my door, and my stomach dropped down to somewhere near my knees. I would either dazzle him with my patented swagger, or run screaming from the room, I wasn't sure which. Taking a deep breath that did nothing for the galloping in my chest, I crossed the apartment and opened the door.

My heart was racing before, but the sight of him sent it into overdrive. He wore jeans and a dark green short-sleeve Henley with the top *two* buttons undone. He needed to show off that glorious vee every day.

No, wait. On second thought, I'd rather keep that all for me. The man made me greedy.

"Hi." My voice came out ridiculously breathy. His well-worn jeans and sneakers reflected casual comfort, but it was his tousled hair that knocked me out. Like he'd just run his fingers through it on the way up. The same way *I* wanted to run my fingers through it.

"Hi."

He smiled, and my insides exploded into goo. Oh, I'd definitely become as bad as Eden and June.

My eyes snagged on the canvas Irwin's bags that weighed him down, and I stepped out of the way to let him through.

"Come inside. I'm sorry, my brain just kind of…" How to explain without having to say *I was wondering what your skin tastes like?*

He set the bags on my small dining table and turned to me. A wicked grin lit his face. "Don't apologize. I like it when you look at me that way."

I stood taller, uselessly trying to gain height on him as he drew closer. "This is the way I always look at you."

"No, it isn't," he said when his hands finally found my waist. "I wish it was."

He leaned down and pressed a brief, heated kiss to my mouth. Two minutes into the date and I was already willing to throw all those groceries out the window if it meant we could keep doing this.

He broke the kiss. "Are you ready?"

A little dazed, I opened my eyes. "Mm-hmm."

He wore the smuggest smile.

I pulled out of his arms, trying for some composure. "I'm ready for dinner. Obviously."

Yes, girl, rock that swagger.

He laid out ingredients across the table—dry noodles and healthy veggies the likes of which had never graced the inside of my apartment before. Out of a second bag, he revealed a wok and other utensils like a magician pulling a family of rabbits from a hat.

"I wasn't sure what you'd have," he said when I stared at the wok too long.

"Yeah, I don't have a wok." My kitchen held the bare minimum of pots and pans, but nothing fancy or single-purpose. My meals stuck to tried and true categories, like *easy* and *cheap*.

He held up a bottle of white wine. "What about a corkscrew?"

"That, I have." I found it in a drawer and passed it to him. When he'd poured me a glass and I took a sip, I made a yummy sound. This was *not* the cheap stuff I bought for myself.

Another smile tugged at his lips. "Sounds like I made the right call."

Watching Dean make dinner was how I imagined spying on Gordon Ramsay at home would be. He moved with precision and intent, as though he'd planned out each move in advance and knew this routine by heart. His dicing skills nearly made me giddy. Awkward and Unsure Dean could be adorable, but Expert Dean just might leave me breathless.

"You really are a good cook," I said, watching him sauté thin strips of chicken. "Usually when I cook, there are curse words, sloppy spills, and charred food involved."

"You can swear if it will make you feel more comfortable."

My kitchen had never smelled so good. At least, not from something actually edible.

"You said you don't have any hobbies, but you've obviously practiced this."

He hitched a shoulder. "It's not really a hobby, more of a life skill that keeps me from eating too much fast food."

It didn't seem like the right time to confess I practically lived off of fast food. "You're so disciplined."

He glanced over at me. "Not always."

That longing bloomed through my chest again, filling me up until I wanted to do something stupid with it. I sipped at my wine but set it aside again. Whatever happened tonight, I would be completely aware of it and in control. And if not *totally* in control, then definitely fully aware.

"I feel like I should be taking notes on your technique. Do you have your little notepad on you?"

The saucy look in his eyes made my insides tumble.

"You can check."

Emboldened by this unapologetic flirting, I decided I was game. "Okay."

I moved behind him, snuggling right up until my front pressed against his back. My greedy hands slid from his waist around to his stomach without shame. I rested one cheek against him, heat rising over my neck and face at this boldness, but unwilling to stop my exploration just yet. Eyes closed, I breathed him in, his light cologne working on my senses until my head spun. I laced my fingers at his stomach, content with the quality firmness there.

"Find anything?" he asked, amusement ruffling his voice.

"Give me a minute." Or a few hours. Days. Forever.

"Do I have to turn out my pockets?"

"I'll just do a visual inspection." I pulled away, letting my hands smooth across his sides as long as possible while my eyes traveled over all the faded parts of his jeans. He needed to wear jeans all the dang time. "Yeah, you're good."

"You're tempting me to let our dinner burn while I return the favor."

"Better not, I love chicken and whatever those green things are." I wiggled my fingers at the vegetables sizzling in the pan.

His hot look turned incredulous. "Snow peas? You don't know what snow peas are?"

"I'm just kidding."

"I don't know, I've seen what you keep in your fridge."

"Hey, I was sick that day. Anything you saw in here can't be used against me." It had probably been a pretty accurate snapshot, though.

He nodded benevolently. "I'll give you a pass for the sick day."

"Where did you learn to cook? Did your parents teach you?" Mom was forever trying to give me pointers and expand my dinner repertoire, but that just opened me up to even more life advice.

He pressed his lips together but kept his eyes on the food as he stirred it around in the pan. "I taught myself in grad school. My parents weren't around a lot when I was growing up."

"What do you mean? I thought they were here."

"They were busy running the store, and couldn't be home all the time. I spent most of my days with my grandparents."

He sounded so matter-of-fact about it, as though his parents' absence couldn't possibly be a big deal, it made my heart ache. I ran one hand over his bicep. "I'm sorry."

He drained the noodles and served some onto two plates, then deftly slid sautéed chicken and vegetables drenched in a spicy sauce he'd made on top. After a minute of this silence, I supposed that was the end of what he was willing to confide for the night.

Finally, he turned his eyes to me, wiping his hands on one of my dishtowels. "They didn't neglect us, if that's the way it sounded. They were there for important events, they took care of us in all the usual ways. But the store ate up most of their time. Getting it off the ground, keeping it open, and later expanding it into a chain, it all took a huge amount of time and effort. There was no ill-will behind it. Everything they did, they did for my brothers and me."

"Didn't it bother you having them gone so much?" My dad was in and out on vet calls all year, but my mother could always be found nearby when my sisters and I needed her. Sometimes, the less she was needed, the more she hovered.

"Maybe, but I'd never regret all that time with my grandparents, either. There's no sob story there, if you're looking for an explanation for how I became such a work-loving monster."

I pinched his arm. "I don't think you're a monster."

"Good. Let's eat."

We sat down at my blue dining table. Suddenly, sitting there with Dean, every little dent and nick stood out. Mismatched chairs, a collection of plastic big box store dishes —tonight, everything in my apartment struck me as shabby. I wished I had ever thought to buy a tablecloth and nice plates. Should I own fancy dinnerware? It had never bothered me before, but just now, my tiny apartment full of dollar store buys felt like an overgrown dorm room. I guessed the Asian-inspired meal Dean had prepared should have been eaten with chopsticks, but I didn't have those, either.

At the first bite of noodles, my eyes rolled back in my head. "This is amazing."

"Thank you, it's one of my favorites. I like to bring it out for special occasions."

I told myself not to go all mushy over him calling our date a special occasion, but the damage was already done. The night felt special to me, too, full of potential and possibility, but comfortable. We'd spent so much time together over the last weeks, this didn't feel like a first date. It felt...*normal*. Exciting, yes, but normal. Natural. Good.

"You really should have considered a career as a chef." I tried to pace myself. It might spoil the specialness of the occasion if I scarfed dinner down in one giant slurp the way I wanted to.

"Who says I didn't?"

"Did you?"

"No." His mouth spread into a smile as he teased me. "No, I was pretty set on finance from the start."

"What is it you love about it?"

He shifted in the tiniest shrug. "It suits me."

I moved a stray strand of hair from my eyes. "You have to give me more than that."

He set his fork on his plate, his eyes intent on me. Of course Dean would completely focus on his answer.

"I like keeping things organized and in control. Making sure our expenditures, contracts, and practices don't get out of hand. I can identify potential problems and make changes before they become a reality. My more...analytical nature is put to good use. Like I said, it suits me."

"Wow. You really like being in control."

"So do you."

I made a strangled sound. "Excuse me, I've never held people's careers in the palm of my hand."

"That's not what I do, by the way, but that's not the kind of control I'm talking about. You want supreme and total control over your life."

"Doesn't everybody?"

"I agree, everybody wants to have a say in how they live their own life, but your independent streak should be studied for science."

I stared at him. "What are you talking about?"

His smile returned. "I don't understand why you're trying to deny it, it's not something you take great pains to hide. Do I have to spell it out? You started your own business so you would be beholden to no one, you resist my efforts to help you with said business—"

"*Said business*, really?"

"You refuse to tell your father your car needs to be laid to rest, and, I suspect, you color your hair so brightly to prove to the world that *you* are in charge of you. I'm only surprised you don't have a tattoo."

I tilted my chin higher. "I do."

His eyes narrowed as they drifted over me before they snapped back to my face. "Where is it?"

"It's in a very secret place."

His curious expression warmed. "I'm going to need to see it."

"After everything you just said about me? I don't think so."

"Was I wrong?"

I opened my mouth but had to shut it again. Nothing he said was inaccurate. If anything, his list was incomplete. My past was riddled with things I had done in my quest to prove I listened to nobody but myself. That contrariness was the main reason I had quit so many of the jobs on my spotty resume. I'd just never thought of independence as being a facet of control before.

"Your independence is one of the things that makes you so attractive to me," he said. "Don't change a thing."

TWENTY-NINE

WE CLEARED away dinner and washed up the dishes side by side. Eliza had tried to do them herself, because of course she had. I couldn't just tell her to her face I thought she was willful and then expect her to let it slide. When we dried the last plate, I refilled our wine glasses, and we sat together on the couch. Across from us stood three shelves of soaps and a television that centered on neither the couch nor the bed.

I tried not to let my eyes wander in that direction, but I struggled. Eliza's bed sat mere feet from us, spread with a bold floral coverlet. Far too inviting. Better not look at the bed.

Get a hold of yourself.

All in all, it was a cute little apartment. She didn't have much artwork or decor, but evidence of her was everywhere, from the chunky strands of necklaces looped over a hook on the wall, to the precarious stack of library books on the floor, to the bulletin board covered in polaroids. Somehow the swirling scent of hundreds of soap bars tied it all together.

"Do you ever get headaches from how strong these soaps are?"

"Sorry, I should have opened a window." She darted off the

couch and cranked open a skylight in the sloped roof. "You're going to go home reeking of soap."

"I don't mind," I said as she returned to take her place next to me. She left a little more room between us than had been there only a minute ago, and I kicked myself for mentioning the smell at all. "I didn't mean that to be a criticism, I was just concerned."

"Oh. No, I don't get headaches from them. It's a lot some-times, but it doesn't bother me that way." She leaned forward to take a sip of wine, and I laid my arm across the back of the couch behind her. "You should be more concerned about me when I mix up the lye. It gets boiling hot and creates toxic fumes."

"I am concerned now that I know about the toxic fumes."

She smiled, took another sip, then leaned back against the couch. I ran my fingers along her shoulder, light little nothings just for the sake of touching her. I wasn't being subtle, but I no longer thought I needed to be.

She darted her eyes sideways at me. "You left me hanging at dinner."

"That's not how I remember it. You can't just tell me you have a secret tattoo and think that will be the end of it."

She still didn't look directly at me, but the edge of her smug smile drove me crazy.

"I'll show you another time." Then she turned and raised one finger between us. "Maybe."

"Maybe. All right." In with a chance. I could live with that. "How did I leave you hanging?"

"You said my independence is one of the things that makes me attractive to you. What are some of the others?"

This woman. Prodding me to tell her more about all the reasons I wanted her. So confident, and yet wanting reassurance at the same time. Every mystery I unraveled only produced another. "You think I've been keeping a list?"

"I know you like to take notes." She shifted toward me on the couch, tucking her feet beneath her, ready to listen. If she tilted her head a few degrees to the side, it would rest in the crook of my elbow.

She raised her eyebrows, waiting for me to get on with it.

"I like how forward you're being right now, for starters."

The curve of her mouth increasingly distracted me from my train of thought. And my current train of thought proved distracting enough already.

"I like how charming you are."

Her lips twisted. "I haven't been all that charming to you."

We'd had a few bobbles, but nothing I would ever bring up again. "This is my list. I like how you started your own business. You saw what you wanted and went for it."

I shifted my free hand to brush her knee with my fingertips. She wore cropped jeans and a billowy white sleeveless shirt I also wanted to touch but wouldn't yet dare.

"I like the way you sass me."

Her grin looked nothing short of triumphant. "That's why I do it."

"Maybe now, but you've given me attitude for as long as I can remember."

She tilted her chin to the side until her hair brushed my arm. "I think that's why I've always done it. To see if I could get a reaction out of you."

That settled it. I couldn't sit and do nothing with the suggestion she'd been trying to catch my attention all this time. I traced the angle of her jaw from her perfect pointed chin with the tiny scar on the tip, to her ear, my blood racing as her lips parted at my touch. I slowly leaned closer to claim her mouth, and her eyes drifted shut, waiting for me. Her explicit trust made me ache for her. *This woman.*

I finally reached her mouth, and she sighed against me. I wove my fingers into her hair as her hands wandered over my arms and back. Her open appreciation of my body spurred on my need to explore hers, but I would be patient. We had time.

I pulled her closer, and she swung one leg over mine to crawl into my lap. She might not have liked me describing her as wanting to be in control, but it looked good on her now. Her eyes sparked with a mix of desire and mischief, confirming her total control over me.

She trailed her hands over my shoulders and down my biceps, mapping out my muscles as if preparing for an expedition. Her hands glided down to my stomach and up over my pecs, dawdling on their detours. A wash of pink swept over her cheeks, the mischief entirely gone now. Darkened eyes followed the paths of her hands like this was serious business, until she stopped at my neck.

"Should I tell you all the things I find attractive about you?"

The combination of the question and her husky voice made me tighten my grip on her waist. "If you want."

Her mouth twitched as if she recognized that casual response for the lie it was. It wouldn't take much before I'd throw aside my control and crush her to me.

"I like how composed you are." She leaned closer until her lips brushed against my ear. "I like even more when you break."

I would die right here on this couch. My blood churned for her, but I didn't dare move. I wanted her to go on.

She drew back, a playful smile on her face. "I like how you're helping out in the store because your brother needs you."

Guilt wove icy little threads through me. I wasn't nearly that selfless. I never would have stepped onto the sales floor if my promotion hadn't been on the line. I would have to set her straight, but this wasn't the moment. Tucking that confession away for another time, I focused on the here and now.

"I like how you take notes on what I do in the store, like what I say matters."

That sobered me a little more. She should always know what she said mattered.

"And this," she said, stroking the hollow at the top of my sternum. "I can't get enough of this spot here on your neck. It drives me crazy."

She bent down and peppered kisses across my neck. I might have groaned, I couldn't say for sure. The only thing I knew with any accuracy was the softness of her lips, and the heat that rose up inside me, threatening my plans to take things slow.

"You're a very naughty businessman, sir."

I took her arms and pressed her gently away so I could see her face. "What's that about? Your *No businessmen* rule?"

The spark in her eyes dimmed a touch. "That's a story for another day. I'll tell you," she said when I opened my mouth to protest. "But not right now. Not when I'm in your lap and enjoying myself so immensely."

"Immensely?"

She leaned forward to press a soft kiss to my mouth. When she spoke again, her lips brushed against mine. "Very much so."

dean

"IS THIS EVERYTHING?" I scanned the items in my trunk, stuffed back to front with Eliza's Sunshine Soul tote bins. She had hundreds of soaps tucked away in their displays, ready for this morning's farmers market.

Her hands rested on her hips as she counted the bins. "That's it. You really don't have to keep driving me. Harper would have—"

"Shh. I want to do it."

She drew back a little, a deep furrow between her brows. "Did you just *shush* me?"

I cleared my throat, painfully aware of my mistake. "Yes?"

Her mouth shifted to the side. "That's your one and only shush right there, pal."

"You're right, I'm sorry, that was patronizing."

"Yeah, it was."

"Forgive me?"

The twist of her mouth transformed into a saucy smile, and I wondered if I could kiss my way to forgiveness. Probably not, but I would be willing to try.

"It's hard to stay mad at you when you're flashing me like this."

I glanced down at my jeans, mortified for one agonizing second that I'd shown up at her house this morning with my fly down. But no, everything looked fine. "How?"

She stepped closer and ran her hand over the base of my throat. "Here."

"You've got a curious fascination with my neck."

And I'd exploited it. After her confession last night, I had intentionally worn a V-neck T-shirt today. It looked like my gambit had paid off.

She moved closer until her body touched mine, the minty smell that hovered around her filling my senses. She framed my neck with her hands, her arms resting against my chest.

"Your ties used to drive me crazy, you always looked so perfect and business-like. I much prefer your casual side."

I circled her waist with my hands, loving the feel of her. "You're tempting me to give up suits."

She tilted her head. "I guess you can keep wearing them. You do look incredible in them." Leaning up on her tip-toes, she gave me a playful peck on the lips. "Now let's get going, there will be a long line of vendors in the drive-up, and I don't want to be today's rotten egg."

Climbing into the car, my mind searched for my calming techniques. I had only ever used them to quiet anger or frustration, but this morning, I needed them to distract me from a very different overwhelming emotion.

I'd gone home late last night completely wound up. We had kissed and laughed and cuddled on her couch for hours until I'd finally said goodnight. Even though leaving Eliza had been a kind of torture, it was the right decision. Whatever her past issue was with men in general and businessmen specifically, I needed to be sure she understood I didn't see anything in our relationship as transactional.

"Am I still invited to your parents' house for dinner tomorrow?"

She exhaled a little sigh. "Oh, yes. My mother has been sending subtle reminders twice a day."

"Are you busy before that?"

"No. What do you have in mind?"

"I was thinking about a hike."

She shifted toward me in her seat. "I'm in."

The excitement running through her voice had me humming with satisfaction. I'd hoped she would be pleased with the idea, and clearly, she was without knowing more about my plan.

"I've been researching the Leavenworth trails. It's a bit of a drive, but we would have a few options for the hike, and the wildflowers should still be in bloom."

Her grin ignited an answering spark deep inside me.

"Yes, absolutely. Let's do that."

"How about nine?"

"Perfect."

She reached over the console and laid her hand on my leg. The simple show of affection squeezed at something in my chest. More and more, I was realizing my affection for Eliza was far from simple.

"I thought you said you didn't hike either." Her voice held no trace of teasing, only curiosity.

"I haven't in a long time. Lately, I want to again."

She made me want to again. On my own, hiking a few hours through the Leavenworth trails didn't sound like much of a draw. But spending the day in a reportedly remarkable area, at the side of a beautiful woman who had an even more gorgeous soul? Couldn't miss out on that.

In the center console, my phone pinged a calendar reminder notification. My mind raced through dates until I remembered what it signified.

"What was that?"

"I've got a financial statement due Monday. It slipped my mind." I'd forgotten the quarterly Profit and Loss Statement was due, and marveled a little at that. I had every report with color-coded due dates on my calendar, and usually had them created, double-checked, and filed before the day arrived. The reminder app was supposed to be a back-up contingency only. I'd never actually had to rely on it before.

"Do you want to do the hike another time?"

"No, it won't be a problem." The P&L wouldn't be hard to draw up. Our accounting software did most of the work, although I would still verify everything in it before submitting it.

I pulled up to the vendor line and waited our turn to unload Eliza's bins. She hadn't been kidding about the long line-up. Cars and trucks snaked around the block as vendors carted off crates of vegetables and baskets of flowers.

She gave my leg a gentle squeeze. "Are you sure you don't want to do the report tomorrow? I don't want you to mess up your job because of me."

The worry shining in her eyes slayed me. "Are you saying you want me to work more?"

"I don't want to distract you from your work."

I pressed a kiss to her lips. "El, you can distract me any time you want."

DEAN PARKED his car and made it back to my stall just as the market officially opened. We'd cut it close, what with all our morning banter and me mindlessly spouting off about how hot I found him. I wasn't even trying to contain the crush now.

He strolled over and stood in front of my booth like he had the first day I'd seen him at the market, looking at my soaps as if they were an entirely novel concept. I sold one to a teenager before turning my attention to him.

"Can I help you?" I asked in my most prim and proper voice.

He stuffed his hands in his pockets. "I was just thinking I need some soaps."

I winked. "Feeling dirty, are you?"

He tilted his head down, his eyes intense. "El, you have no idea."

Flirtatious Dean, hello. You rule them all. "Then you've come to the right place."

"I'll take one of each."

"Ha ha. Now step aside. You're blocking the paying customers' views."

"I'm serious."

I looked from him to the soaps, and back again, tallying up what that would come to. "No you're not."

"I am."

I crossed my arms, intending to shut this down quickly. "That's twenty-five bars of soap, Dean."

"I realize that." He smiled back, all placid and normal, as though people offered to buy *one of each* every day. I still did a mental happy dance when someone bought more than one at a time.

When I didn't move, he started picking up soaps from each labeled bin.

My heart raced, and I sweated up a storm in my casual T-shirt and jeans. "What are you doing?"

"I'm buying soap," he said in that same easygoing voice.

I darted around the table and grabbed the bars from his hands. "You do not need twenty-five bars." Flattery and indignation duked it out inside me, but I returned the soaps to their bins. "You're being ridiculous."

"Maybe I have a lot of gifts to give."

"No. You're not allowed to buy my soap, I'm sorry."

His mouth curled a little, as if he found my reaction amusing. "You're cutting me off?"

"I'm not cutting you off. You never bought a bar to begin with. I'm banning you."

His smile peeked out a bit more. "El, I really need the soap."

Unfair of him to use his nickname for me that way when I was trying to hold my ground. He had to have figured out how it made my silly heart skip every time he used it.

I drew up to him until I was nearly in his face but kept my voice low to avoid a scene. "You do not need twenty-five bars of soap. It would be completely weird for me to sell a whole batch of soap to my boy—"

I gulped down the rest of *that* word. We hadn't talked about this in anything close to an official capacity; we hadn't labeled anything between us. Choosing to date had a lot of definitions, and I wasn't sure yet where we had landed, if we'd landed anywhere. For all I knew, we were still in a holding pattern mid-air.

"Your boy...?" he prompted, his eyes sparkling with tiny stars.

I straightened my spine and jutted my chin up at him. "My boy who is banned from buying my soaps. That's you. If anything, I should give you a bar for driving me around all week."

"You know you don't owe me."

"I do. So." I swept a hand over the display. "Choose."

He stared down at me as though telepathically trying to sway me to his generous but totally inappropriate offer. Twenty-five soaps? No way. That was only slightly better than the whole commission thing. He definitely stood a chance to actually use the soaps eventually, but it was the principle of the thing. I couldn't let him buy my stock.

He shifted closer, reaching behind me. His body brushed against me, and my stomach clenched at the contact. His eyes never left mine, until finally, he presented me with a single bar of soap.

"I'll take this one, then."

I glanced down at it. *Rosemary Peppermint Radiance.* "Is this your favorite?"

"Yes."

"Mine, too."

His mouth quirked, and he tilted his forehead closer. "I know."

Heat wound its way through my insides at those half-whispered words. The man had me. I was absolutely lost.

I glanced to the side and realized a few people had walked

up behind me to smell and admire my soaps. Snapping out of Dean's spell, I stepped away from him and got back behind my table. It was all for show, though. A couple of feet wasn't nearly enough distance to settle me down, when what I really wanted to do was leap into his arms and see if he'd catch me. Because I had gone completely and totally insane.

"Go," I said, shooing him away. "Explore the market. Look around. Don't distract me from my work."

With one last glance that said he had every intention of distracting me, he walked away.

Trying to settle my Speedracer heart down, I made a few sales before I discovered Dean hadn't gone very far. He stood beneath Tanisha's awning, listening to her talk about the benefits of goat's milk, nodding now and then as if intrigued. She turned behind her, poured a tiny paper cup of milk from a glass bottle, and passed the cup to him.

A certain percentage of market patrons walked away at this point. They'd thought they wanted to try goat's milk, but with the cup in their hands, they just couldn't do it. Dean held the cup up and seemed to examine it.

Please, please don't chicken out.

I had to turn away to answer a customer's question before I could risk a glance back at him. He sipped the milk, his eyebrows bunched up, staring at nothing in particular. As he drank, his confusion turned to surprise, maybe even pleasure. He said something that made Tanisha clap her hands.

Leaving my browsing customers, I walked to the edge of my booth. "You tried the goat's milk?"

He looked at me as he drank the last of the cup of milk. "It's sweet. Like cow's milk, but...better."

Tanisha squealed, her grin proving just how much he'd won her over. "I knew I liked you when I saw you."

He bought a bottle of milk from Tanisha, but didn't stop

there. While I craned my neck around customers to see what he was up to, he bought a jar of wildflower honey from the Oh, Honey! guys, fresh salsa, a dozen organic eggs, and enough fruits and vegetables to fill two grocery bags. Eventually, he walked back to my stall, clearly proud of his bounty.

"I'm going to run all this home so it doesn't spoil, but I'll be back at one to pick you up."

"You are really adorable, you know that?"

He walked around my table and leaned down to press a sweet, soft kiss to my mouth. "I know. That's my Dean Aura."

Laughter burst out of me. As he walked away, I called out, "That's not your Dean Aura."

I leaned my palms on the table, stretching to watch him go until he disappeared in the crowd. I straightened back up, trying to wipe the moony grin off my face before some unsuspecting market patron thought I was flirting with *them*.

"Honey."

I jumped and turned around to find Tanisha standing between our booths.

"Is that little cutie patootie yours?"

"He's...we're just..." My brain searched for a good and plausible excuse, but from her expression, one probably didn't exist. She had just seen us kiss. No sense keeping secrets when we both knew the truth.

"Yeah," I finally said with a grin. "He's mine."

* * *

"Who had the great idea we had to be mature and go out for dinner instead of drinks?"

I scanned Lupe's Escape's menu, debating between the enchiladas and chimichangas. Harper, Eden, and June rounded out the table for our long-awaited girls' night out.

We hadn't been able to get together much since Eden's summer wedding, and I wanted to make the most of it. I would have to trade beers for guacamole tonight, but that could work.

"We can't go to The Broken Hammer every time we get together for the rest of our lives." Eden closed her menu and laid it in front of her. "There's a lot to be said for girls' nights that don't involve going home smelling like a dive bar."

"You're no fun."

"They have a dozen margarita flavors to choose from," Harper pointed out. "I'm sure you can live on tequila just as well as beer."

I scrunched my nose at her, but Lupe's margaritas *were* good. I could only handle one, and I'd have to nurse it all night, but I supposed it was a fair trade.

Our waitress came by to drop off chips and salsa and take our drinks orders. I chose the watermelon margarita, Harper the peach, and June the mango. Eden ordered a plain lemonade. The rest of us stared at her as the waitress left the table.

Eden carefully unrolled her napkin and laid it across her lap. She straightened her silverware, ran a hand over her hair, and generally avoided our eyes for a whole minute.

"Do you have something to tell us?" I finally said.

She looked up at us, a shimmer of excitement in her eyes. "I didn't plan on doing it this way, but y'all had to go for the margaritas."

She'd barely finished her sentence before we erupted into shrieks of congratulations. June and I moved in for hugs, and Harper leapt out of her seat to reach her.

When we finally settled down, she said, "You can't tell anyone yet, not even Mom and Dad. It's still really early."

June ran a hand over her shoulder. "Everything's going to be just fine."

Eden's smile was bright but watery, like she might burst into happy tears. "We're so excited, though."

"How much did Booker cry when your pregnancy test came up positive?" I asked.

Her smile got bigger until a couple of tears splashed down her cheeks. "So much."

After the waitress came by with our drinks, June raised her wide margarita glass, and Harper and I did the same. "To Eden and Booker."

"To the love child." I winked at my sister and took a big gulp of the margarita I had intended to nurse all night.

Eden was pregnant. Soon, there would be a baby in the family. I would be an *aunt*. I was delighted for my sister and Booker, but this new change was hard to imagine. Wait, no it wasn't. Imagining Eden as a mother, shuttling around with kids in tow—yeah, I saw it perfectly. She would be a fantastic mom, her purse would always be full of snacks, she would master the art of the loving time out, and her kids would be the luckiest little munchkins in the world.

But this unexpected news highlighted just how stuck my own life was. Not that I needed a husband and a baby at twenty-six, but I still lived like a college kid, moving from job to job like cycling through majors, eating ramen noodles out of plastic bowls, and relying on other people to drive me around. Even if I didn't want or need exactly what Eden had, the total absence of *any* of it left me feeling like less than an adult.

No wonder my parents still coddled me like a child. I still acted like one.

Shaking myself out of the existential crisis waiting for me at the bottom of my watermelon margarita, I said, "What about you, June? Any wedding bells in your future?"

She nearly choked on her drink, but the question couldn't have been a surprise. I asked her every time we got together.

"We've only been together four months."

"Sure, but Ty's been pining for you for years."

I loved that little tidbit. Big, burly Ty had fallen for June hook, line, and sinker two years ago when she was dating his stupid brother. He'd had to push down his longing, convinced he could never have her, and had nearly fallen into despair all alone out on his ranch. Or so I imagined. She hadn't given us a whole lot of details, but I had enough to go on. Bottom line was, the dude had wanted her long before he got her.

She rolled her eyes but still looked pleased, like just the reminder that Ty loved her made her giddy. She was queen of the doe eyes, all sappy and beautiful and madly in love.

"That doesn't mean we need to rush into anything." She didn't even try to deny how long Ty had cared for her.

"But you'd still say yes if he asked you," Harper said.

"Hell yes, I would." She grinned over her giant margarita glass, practically sparkling in all her moony loveliness.

I had barely scooped a huge bite of salsa-coated tortilla chip into my mouth when Harper said, "What about you, Eliza? Anything going on in your love life?"

Daggers might have shot out of my eyes. Harper was really thriving on shoving the spotlight on me with pointed questions lately. I swallowed down the bite. "Not really, no."

She mouthed *BS.*

Eden had a little more class, and only rolled her eyes. "Mom already told us Dean Irwin is coming with you to dinner tomorrow night."

I groaned. Of course our mother had told everyone. Their neighbors probably knew by now. "It's no big deal."

"That's not what Mom says."

June glanced around the table as if she were watching the most confusing tennis match ever. "What's going on? Are you *dating* Dean Irwin?"

"Why did you say it like that?" I said. "Like you're asking me if I've murdered a guy?"

"Have you?" Harper asked under her breath.

"Shut up."

"No, I'm sorry, I didn't mean it that way." June looked at each of my sisters for help. "I just had no idea you and Dean were... Rhett, you know, maybe, but Dean..."

"*Are* you two dating?" Eden asked. "Mom was coy about it, but she mentioned something about him taking care of you when you were sick a few weeks ago."

June's eyes went round. "He did?"

"He brought her soup and everything," Harper said.

I crossed my arms and made a sour face. "If you guys already know everything, why are you asking so many questions?"

"Just tell us already." Eden busted out her bossy oldest sister voice. "Are you dating him or not?"

"Yes, I'm dating Dean Irwin. Yes, he's amazing, and I'm happier than I've ever been. Are you satisfied?"

"Of course we are, you goof. We want you to be happy." Her smile had an edge to it that didn't entirely reassure me. "It's just surprising, that's all."

"Why is it so surprising I would like Dean?"

"You do talk about bikers an awful lot," Harper said.

I brushed her off. "Just the one."

"Dean's always seemed so reserved and professional, and you're..." Eden apparently rethought the rest of what she wanted to say.

I slumped against my chair. "And I'm not."

June grabbed my hand across the table. "That's not it at all."

"You have to admit, you are pretty different," Eden said. "I'm just trying to picture you standing next to him in his power suit, with your crazy hair and bright blue cowboy boots."

I forced a laugh, as if my insides weren't shriveling up. "We are kind of a weird match, aren't we?"

June squeezed my hand. "If you care about each other, that's all that matters. If you work, you work."

"I just want you to be smart about it," Eden said.

"Be smart about it," I repeated. "Okay. Thanks. I'll do that."

Our meals arrived, and conversation scattered from one topic to another. I smiled and laughed and tossed out random *You go, girls* to hide the hollowness aching inside me, a black hole ready to swallow me up.

They didn't think I matched well with Dean.

Even though I wouldn't have predicted the match, either, now that we were together, I at least expected support and encouragement from my sisters and cousin. Not veiled commentary on how ridiculous we must be together. How unlikely, how *surprising* it was we were dating.

Sadness and a little bit of self-pity hid behind my empty smiles. My life had become such a dumpster fire of failures and false starts that even the people who loved me best couldn't imagine me with a guy as together as Dean.

dean

"I DID NOT PICTURE you as an emo rock guy."

Eliza sifted through the CDs in my center console as I drove us the hour's ride out to the Leavenworth trails. I couldn't believe it had taken her this long to snoop through my car after days of regular commutes together. She'd been disappointed by the run of the mill items in my glovebox and had moved on to commenting on my musical taste.

"I prefer the term indie rock."

"These Weezer CDs beg to differ." She popped one into the player, turning it low. The first song came on, and she swayed in her seat. "I suddenly feel the need to write bad poetry in my college dorm."

"I would read that poetry."

She grinned, and my heart laid down in surrender. For our day on the trails, she'd worn cropped athletic pants I praised almost as highly as whoever had made her swimsuit, and a sporty plaid camp shirt. Her hair was in a messy ponytail, its pink tendrils splashing down her back. She was relaxed, at home, and utterly Eliza.

I returned my eyes to the road—I had to pull myself

together. If I spent too much time appreciating how lovely she was, I would swerve into the ditch and ruin our day in a big way.

"Should I ask how girls' night went, or is that a Fight Club type situation?"

"It was good. Everyone's doing well. I ate an entire bowl of salsa by myself, so you know, it was a good night."

"Their salsa is pretty good."

"It's life-changing, and I won't hear otherwise."

I laughed at her tough-girl attitude. "I won't fight you on it."

"Good."

I cleared my throat unnecessarily, figuring it best to just dive right in. "So, are you going to give me some kind of cheat sheet on everyone who will be at your parents' house tonight?"

I wasn't nervous per se. I'd met every member of the Webb family at some town event or another, but conversations with people I didn't know well—particularly people I hoped to impress on a personal level—had never come easily. A contract negotiation wouldn't faze me, but dinner with Eliza's family? I could use a few pointers.

"I don't think so. I'm just going to throw you to the sharks and see what happens."

"From all you've said, there's a good chance I could be encouraged to death."

"You're in for a serious maiming." She stretched out in the passenger seat as we sped past farmland and cattle pastures. "Okay, so my mom and dad are pretty standard stuff. You've met my mom, she's basically like that all the time. Chatty, pushy, mother hen type. My dad is just this nerdy cowboy vet. You never know if he's going to talk John Wayne movies for an hour, or tell a gross story about blackleg."

"What's blackleg?"

"You won't ask him if you want to keep your dinner down."

My stomach crawled with the possibilities. "Noted."

"You met Harper at Ethan's party. She's pretty chill, but she's got a bit of a Mama Bear streak, and will protect the people she loves to the death. Eden is a sweetheart but she will slice you open with her honesty. Booker is Eden's husband, he is the easiest of easy-going. He's the least of your worries."

"I'll stick close to him, then."

"Good call."

I darted my eyes to her. "Does your family get together for dinner every Sunday?"

"We do."

"Really? That's—"

"I know," she said, scrunching her nose in an adorable way. "It's pretty old fashioned."

"I was going to say it's pretty fantastic."

"Sure. You wouldn't say that if it was *your* family finding new and glorious ways to embarrass you every week."

"The last time my whole family got together for dinner was Christmas."

She turned until she sat nearly perpendicular in the seat, her soft lips dropped open. "Seriously? But that's almost a year."

"We'll do Thanksgiving next month, but that's about it."

She sputtered as if too many arguments came to mind, and she couldn't decide the best way to scold me.

"But you all live here in town. How can you get together only a couple times a year?"

I affected a nonchalance that didn't quite match up with the regret her question dragged into the light. "Who needs dinner when we see each other every day in the office?"

"That's not the same."

"I live with Rhett, and we have regular dinners together. Of a sort." Me sitting at the table while he forked food into his face on the couch wasn't quite how I imagined her family dinners going.

"But what about your parents?"

"They travel a lot to meet with manufacturers, visit each of the branches regularly, go to trade shows. They're not around as much as you'd think. They're in Corpus Christi this week to meet with the construction company handling the new store we're building there."

"Wow. My dad is away a lot making house calls, but he's hardly ever *gone* gone."

She stayed silent a minute, probably out of respect for my tragic upbringing.

"So you guys really don't get together?"

My family dynamic had never bothered me that much. My parents traveled, my brothers were always off doing their own things, and I liked my solitude. We weren't estranged, but we weren't close, either. We'd never been any other way, even growing up. But confiding that to Eliza only brought home how odd it was my family didn't spend more time together.

"It's just not a priority." I pressed my lips together, disliking the bitter aftertaste of those words. I'd never said it outright to anyone, but sometimes, that's how it had felt as a kid. My brothers and I weren't the same priority for our parents as the store. They loved us, I knew that without question, but I couldn't pretend we were the most important things in their lives.

"Is togetherness not a priority for you, either?"

Her tone sounded strange. I glanced sideways at her but couldn't pinpoint what she was getting at.

"It doesn't trouble me, if that's what you're asking."

Although, right now, *togetherness* had jumped to the top of my priority list, but not with Grant or Rhett. I wanted all the togetherness with her, but this drive was probably not the time to lay it all out there.

She stared straight ahead for a while. "Are your parents going to be back for the big anniversary celebration Friday?"

"They plan to be. That reminds me, Friday will be my last day in the store with you."

"Friday's your last day?" She shifted away just enough to notice. I felt more than saw the change. "Oh."

That soft, disappointed *Oh* worked its way through my ribcage to settle over my heart. "Are you going to miss me down on the sales floor?"

She smacked my arm. *Not* the reaction I'd hoped for.

"Of course I will. Why didn't you tell me before?"

"I never thought about it. I'll just be upstairs from you. When you're on shift, we can have lunch together in my office."

That thought toppled into others, like dominoes in my brain. Eliza, in my office, rummaging through my paperwork. Sitting on my desk. Finding new and glorious ways to distract me from my work.

"I didn't know Grant already hired someone to replace you."

"He hasn't." Last I'd heard, he had found one solid interview prospect among a handful of promising candidates, but he hadn't signed anyone on yet.

"But you're going back upstairs anyway?"

Her chiding reminded me no part of my deal to work retail for a month qualified as selflessness. It barely qualified as helpful. I was working down there to prove some ridiculous point to my father, not to round out Grant's schedule gaps indefinitely. But admitting any of that would likely give Eliza more reasons to reprimand me. We'd had a rocky enough start these last few weeks—tossing out a casual *Actually, I'm working here against my will* wasn't the way to go.

"That was the original plan," I said, "but I might stick

around a while longer. There's this girl I have my eye on at work."

She leaned closer over the console, seriously tempting me to pull onto the side of the road and kiss her senseless.

"Is it Nicole?"

I chuckled softly, lacing my fingers with hers. "I only have eyes for you, El."

* * *

An hour into our hike, I wished I'd chosen a different spot for our day together. The wooded paths were pretty enough, and the trail wasn't all that taxing even with the high humidity, but the area turned out busier than I would have liked. Hikers passed us in both directions, along with mountain bikers who had no concept of how to share the trail. Occasionally, a runner dashed by wearing little more than a sheen of sweat.

I'd had better ideas.

"I didn't know it was such a popular spot," I said after the second scantily-clad runner sped past.

Eliza took a drink from her water bottle. "I'm sure the wildflowers are worth it."

Another hour or so from here, we would reach the wildflower meadows, and a little farther on, a long, narrow lake. Or so my map said. "They had better be. That was a lot of skin I just saw."

"Are you opposed to seeing skin?" The mischief in her eyes had me contemplating the logistics of wandering off the trail for a private detour. A completely stupid idea, given all the poison oak, but she would be worth it.

"His? Yes. Yours?" I stepped closer to her. "I'm all for it."

"How do you do that, exactly? How do you smolder like that?"

I willed my smile not to turn smug and ruin the effect. I couldn't remember any woman telling me I'd *smoldered* before. "I was smoldering?"

"Uh, yeah. Big time."

"I wasn't trying to. I was just looking at you, thinking about your skin..." I ran one palm down her arm, distracted from everything around us by the softness of her.

"There it is again."

I pulled her in for a quick kiss. "Clearly, there's a link. You're very much required for the smolder."

"On your left," a man's voice called behind us.

I shifted Eliza to the side as a jogger trotted past. The paths weren't wide enough for the kind of traffic out here today.

The man glared at us over his shoulder. "Get a room."

I looked down at Eliza, still close enough I could kiss her again. "Now there's an idea."

She took her hands off my chest and looped them beneath her backpack straps. "Come on. One thing at a time."

We walked at a steady pace, hiking up and down scrambles between long stretches of level pathway, stopping to take pictures of the oaks and elms just starting to shift into their autumn glory of yellows and oranges. Now and then, a squirrel chirped at us from behind a tree. In the quiet moments between bikers and joggers, it felt almost peaceful. Yet another place I could find a small slice of serenity.

I heard the bikes coming up on us, the low whirr of tires on the dirt path the only indication they were there. I jumped back as the first biker passed me with inches to spare on the narrow path. I wasn't quick enough with a warning, and a few feet ahead, his elbow struck Eliza's shoulder. She stumbled to the side, clutching her arm, but he continued on unfazed.

"Jackass!" I shouted uselessly, but the guy was already gone.

The second biker, however, heard me, and skidded to a stop just ahead of us. "You got a problem?"

I put myself between him and Eliza. "Your buddy just ran into my girlfriend."

The guy craned his neck to get a look at her. I couldn't tell for sure what he was looking at because of the reflective sunglasses he wore.

"Prove it." He pedaled off in a blur of neon.

I stared after him a second, anger flooding my system like a hurricane rushing in. If the guy had been a few feet closer, I would have punched him without a second thought.

Holding back the poison rising inside me, I turned to Eliza and looked her over. I ran my hand along her arm as if I could assess her injuries by touch. A small red bruise was forming on her upper arm where the biker had made contact, but it didn't look bad.

"Are you okay?"

"I'm fine," she said as I examined her. "I'm more surprised than anything."

"I'm sorry, we shouldn't have come here. We can go back if you want." She wasn't badly injured or even all that shaken, but the incident had soured me on the day. Plus, if we ran into those bikers again farther up the path, I wasn't sure what I might do. I hadn't completely lost my temper in a long time, but hurting Eliza was a sure way to trigger it.

"No, I don't want to quit. Let's keep going."

We trudged on, but I walked next to her in the middle of the trail, just in case another inconsiderate mountain biker came by. I still couldn't believe their reactions to the collision, but thinking about them too much risked sending me to a dark place.

I silently went through my calming exercises, slowing my breath and soothing my mind. Eliza twined her fingers with mine, stroking my hand as though she knew I needed the help.

"You called me your girlfriend back there." Her eyes stayed on the path ahead as if she had remarked on the weather and not our as-yet undefined relationship status.

"Is that okay?" I'd thought so, but worry rushed in anyway. I didn't want to take anything for granted with her.

Her smile radiated joy and relief. Had she doubted my intentions? I didn't want her to feel any uncertainty with me, but I loved these glimpses of the soft woman beneath the brash exterior she usually affected. She wore her heart closer to the surface than most people guessed.

"Well," she said, squeezing my hand. "It's only fair. You are my boy."

We grinned at each other like fools until we bumped arms. She winced at the contact, and some of my anger with those mountain bikers resurfaced like a diver coming up for air. "I wish I had an ice pack for you."

She shrugged it off. "You should have seen me after I quit my job in San Antonio. I went home, changed clothes, and headed straight for the hills. You know, such as they are. I was a little too much in my head and took a pretty big tumble. I bloodied both knees, one hand, an elbow, and this little spot here."

She leaned closer, pointing to a pale, shimmering scar I'd noticed on the tip of her chin. "I looked like I'd been attacked by zombies. A little bruise is nothing."

"Sounds like a bad fall."

"I fell in front of a whole squad of new soldier recruits loaded down with their packs out for a training run. They had bandages on them, so that was good, but talk about making a fool of yourself in front of an audience."

I was grateful they'd been there to patch her up, but her

embarrassment over her fall wasn't the point I'd fixed on from that little anecdote. "Why did you quit your job in San Antonio?"

She stiffened, the light in her eyes winked out, and her lips pressed into a thin line. "It's a long story."

"I have time." I wouldn't try to make her tell me anything if she didn't want to, but I needed her to know I was there for her.

A few seconds later, she glanced sideways at me and blew out a breath. "After I graduated college, I got an internship with a PR firm in San Antonio. There were four of us interns basically in competition for one entry-level position, shadowing staff members, and getting lots of valuable on-the-job experience.

"We were supposed to create a portfolio for one of their existing clients. We made all these publicity campaigns and PR strategies, media content and press releases. It was so much work to do for practically no pay at all, but I don't know, I kind of enjoyed it."

She let go of my hand to adjust her pack, looping her fingers in the shoulder straps when she'd finished. "There was this guy —Carter."

Hot anger erupted in my chest all over again. Hurt, resentment, and temper simmered together when she said that name, and I knew already the guy was no good.

"He was one of the other interns, a few years older than the rest of us. He was a go-getter, he dressed to impress, he had mastered the firm and decisive handshake. You know the type."

I did know. *The Businessman.*

"Early on in the project, he kind of singled me out. He was very complimentary, very flattering. Very *nice*. Lunch together in the staffroom turned into dinners alone."

She grimaced as if the memories turned her stomach. "I thought we were dating."

That short, bitter sentence told me everything.

Her knuckles stood out white where she gripped her pack straps. "One night at my apartment, I showed him my completed portfolio. I was so proud of it, but he didn't seem all that interested, to be honest. He said I should probably work on it longer."

We came around a bend where the trees gave way to wildflower fields. Blues and purples dotted with red spread like a sea across a huge meadow bordered by old oaks blazing orange. Eliza stopped and stared as though she didn't see it.

"I waited another week, toiling away to make my portfolio that much better. As soon as I turned it in, my supervisor called me into her office. She said there was evidence I had plagiarized my entire portfolio. It almost exactly matched someone else's work. You can guess whose."

Rage coursed through me, ready to boil over on Eliza's behalf. I clenched my fists at my sides, wishing uselessly for something to punch. Some*one*.

"Carter had stolen everything I'd done, made a few changes here and there, and turned it in as his work. I heard he got the job, so I guess my portfolio was pretty good." She laughed, but it rang hollow.

"How did he get that kind of access to your work?"

She looked to the side, but her eyes didn't reach me. "He'd stayed the night at my place a few times. I assume he did it sometime in the night. I don't really know."

I had more questions I wouldn't ask, like what was Carter's last name, and where I could find him.

"My supervisor said I could explain myself, or I could pack my desk and leave. So I left."

"You could have proven you had done the work. Your software had timestamps that his wouldn't—"

"Dean, do you really think I wanted to explain to the entire lineup of executives that I'd been fooled into dating—" She looked to the skies, regret written across her face. "Into *sleeping* with someone who only wanted to steal my work, and hope that they believed me? It would have killed me to tell them all that."

My urge to somehow fix this died away. She was right, of course. She wouldn't have been able to defend herself without some explanation for how he had accessed her work. Telling her bosses any of that would have heaped more humiliation on her when she'd already been broken down.

She stood just out of my reach, refusing to look at me.

"Eliza."

"I hate that it happened. I hate that I didn't realize what he really wanted with me. I hate that I was so easily sucked in."

"El, that wasn't your fault. You trusted the wrong person, but that doesn't make it your responsibility. It's his fault, and only his."

"I thought I was this rockstar tough girl who couldn't be fooled, and all it took was a few sweet words to break all that down."

The tears shimmering in her eyes cut me open like a knife. I wanted to pull her in close, crush her to me and soothe away her hurts, but I couldn't. Not after what she'd shared. I opened my arms for her and hoped she would choose to come to me.

A few excruciating seconds later, she stepped into my arms. I wrapped her up, pack and all, wishing I could take away her hurt and humiliation. She pressed her face against my chest, inhaling deeply as if she could breathe from my lungs. Anything I had that she needed, I wanted her to take it. She could take it all.

After several long minutes, she sighed against me, finally relaxing into my touch. I stroked her hair as a heron flew by in the distance. Other hikers and bikers passed us where we stood just off the trail, but for Eliza and me, nobody else mattered.

"So," she said, her cheek against my chest. "That was my first and only corporate job, my first work betrayal, my first...*first*. That's why I've stayed away from businessmen. Until you."

I hugged her tighter. I wanted to hunt that guy down and... well, I didn't need to think too hard about what I would do to him. I would rip the guy apart. What kind of person would take advantage of someone that way, intentionally misleading and manipulating her into giving up *everything*? That guy wasn't the only one out there, I knew that. Plenty of people went after what they wanted without caring about the consequences, in relationships and business. I hated that she had come away thinking everyone in a suit was like that guy. I was no saint, but I would never treat someone that way.

She pulled out of my arms and pressed the heels of her hands to her eyes. When she drew them away, she shook them as if she could physically shake away the memories.

"Anyway," she said, a hint of forced laughter in her voice, "that is the story of why I quit my job in San Antonio."

She still hadn't looked at me. Her eyes darted everywhere—the ground, her shoes, over my shoulder—except to meet mine.

"El."

Finally, *finally*, she gave me her eyes. She inhaled sharply, but held my unwavering gaze. "I should have known better."

I cupped her face in my hands and ran my thumbs over her cheeks. "No. That was an awful thing that guy did to you, and I'm sorry it happened, but that story isn't about you failing at something."

"But I—"

"*No*. That's not on you. You are *more* than that, El. So much more. You are filled with more life, and heart, and goodness than anybody I've ever met."

She smiled up at me, and my heart thrummed in my chest

to see a glimmer of real joy in her again. I pressed a soft kiss to her forehead.

"How do you know exactly what to say?" she asked.

"I've been taking notes."

She shook her head at me, but that soft smile didn't leave. "I'm going to need you to be less perfect."

"I'll see what I can do."

"Okay," she said as she took one last deep breath, "confession time's over. If we don't keep moving, we'll never make it to the lake."

I laced my fingers with hers. "Lead the way."

THIRTY-THREE

EVEN IF MY experience hadn't proven many existed, everything pointed to Dean being a genuinely good man. I'd confessed the worst parts of my life, and he had held me, comforted me, and generally made me feel better when all evidence said I had acted like the most gullible of fools.

I never talked about Carter, and now, I'd spilled it all to Dean. Among my closest friends and family, only Harper knew the full story. The others would have been outraged on my behalf, and I could appreciate that anger, but they would have been disappointed in me, too. I couldn't take my mother or Eden knowing what I had done, what I had let happen. But somehow, I'd opened up with Dean.

I'd been afraid when I finished the story he would look down at me with that same reproving gaze he used to. I would find him judgmental and distant again, and definitely rethinking us *choosing to date*. But instead, he'd pulled me closer, and I'd relaxed into his arms, letting all my mistakes and failures retreat to the past where they belonged.

We'd spent the rest of the afternoon exploring the wild-flowers and the lakeside before we had to turn around for home. Dean had dropped me off and given me time to shower and change before he picked me up again. Now we climbed the steps to my parents' front porch to endure what would surely be the most excruciating Webb family dinner of all time.

"I really should have brought something."

Dean fidgeted next to me. He'd put on a navy polo and khakis, and although I thought it made him completely over-dressed for a family dinner, I wouldn't complain when he looked so scrumptious.

"You're not supposed to show up to a dinner party empty-handed."

I kept my smile in check. "It's not a dinner party, it's just dinner. And my mom would lose her mind if you brought something. You're our guest."

He twisted his mouth, and I could tell he was calculating whether or not he had time to run to the nearest grocery store to pick up a hostess gift.

He didn't. I threw open the door.

"We're here!" I shouted my usual phrase to alert my family of our arrival. "Webb family dinner can officially commence."

Eden and Booker were putting the final touches on the table setting while Mom served up side dishes in the kitchen. Harper shuttled platters of food to the table, and Dad sliced up a pot roast. The whole scene was so normal, I could have cried for gratitude. I'd been half afraid we would walk in to find everyone posed in a fake tableau around the fireplace like an awkward family Christmas card.

My family hadn't affected a staged casualness for Dean's benefit, but there was a lot of staring and craning of necks going on. To be honest, I kind of got it. I'd never brought a man home before. Fine, my high school boyfriend had come to dinner plenty of times, but comparing Dean to him was like comparing big, dashing apples to silly little oranges.

And for the record, my mother had invited Dean. If they wanted to get technical, him being here had nothing to do with me.

Except for the little part about him taking care of me when I was sick, which my mother had apparently relayed to everyone in a seventy-mile radius. So there was that.

I led him into the dining room for a quick round of introductions. He shook hands and had smiles for everyone. I caught glimpses of Awkward Dean, but my family would probably never notice.

"How was your day hiking out on the trails?" Mom asked.

I shot Harper a look. She hitched a brief shrug of apology, as if blabbing my plans to our mother had been unavoidable.

"It was a good hike," Dean said. "But the trails were more crowded than I would have liked."

He said nothing of my little injury, the wonderful man. My mother would have put out an APB for the mountain biker herself if she'd known about it.

"I'm more wiped from the sun than the trails," I said, inspecting the platters on the table. "Once you get to the meadows, there's not much shade."

"Your nose does look a little pink." Mom paused dishing up roasted potatoes. "If you don't have sunscreen, take an extra tube from the front bathroom. We've got plenty."

"I have sunscreen, Mom." They would send me home loaded down with rolls of toilet paper if I let them.

"That's good, baby." She handed the last dish off to Harper. "I think we're ready to take seats at the table."

No big surprise Dean wound up seated next to Mom. At least she'd put me on his other side. I figured she was half in love with Dean herself. My father said a quick grace, and for a few minutes, it was nothing but passing food and groaning over how good the roast had turned out.

"Did you get your varsity team nailed down yet, Booker?" my father asked.

Now that Booker was part of the family, we had a deep, personal investment in the high school boys' basketball team.

"I posted the roster Friday," he said between bites. "It'll be a good mix of seniors and juniors, with one outstanding sophomore I expect to lead the team next year."

"And your Trekkies?" I asked.

He attempted a stern look that didn't quite work with his good nature. He could probably stir up a scary glower for his high school students, but with the family, he just didn't have it in him.

"They're the Sci-Fi Enthusiasts, and they're planning a mini-convention in the spring."

"With cosplay and everything?"

"That's kind of the point."

I had to giggle over that. I could not get over this brawny basketball coach being a Star Trek nerd. I loved it.

"Are you going to dress up?"

His look turned smug. "I might have something in mind."

At his side, Eden said, "You do look good in uniform."

I covered a snort behind my hand. Pretty sure a Star Trek uniform was not what most women meant when they said that.

"You're so good with those kids over there." Mom's voice had gone all ooey gooey. "I wonder when you'll want some of your own."

"When the time is right, Darlene." The man looked serene as anything, as if Eden wasn't cooking up a little Trekkie already.

"There's no right time. You want to do it, you do it. We didn't plan on Eliza, and look at the joy our baby has brought the family. We weren't expecting her, but we love her anyway."

"She's been impulsive since before she was born." Dad laughed at his old joke.

"Gee, thanks," I said.

"Dean, I noticed some signs in town today." Mom thankfully left off the talk of my unexpected arrival in the family. "I didn't realize it was Irwin's thirtieth anniversary this year. It must be an exciting time for y'all over there."

"We're proud of the accomplishment. My parents have put a lot of hard work into the store through the years."

"I'm sure they have. Joel's been in practice nearly that long, and there were some days early on I wasn't sure how it was going to go."

Dean nodded. "My parents went through the same thing. Starting your own business can be tough."

Mom cut her eyes to me, probably itching to jump in on that opening, but she held back, thank God. "It looks like you're having a big celebration on Friday."

"Yes, ma'am. My brothers have planned out a few activities to celebrate my parents a little bit, and thank Magnolia Ridge for being so supportive of us through the years."

"That's wonderful all you boys have a place in the family business."

Pretty sure at this point, anything Dean said would earn a *that's wonderful* from my smitten mother.

"I tried to get the girls to go to veterinary school, but every last one shot me down." Dad looked around the table at us, grinning even though we hadn't followed in his footsteps. "They each spent just enough time working with me to realize becoming a vet was the last thing they wanted to do."

"I could handle the cute side of it," Harper said. "The calves and the foals would have sold me, but all the vaccinations and treating rotten injuries?"

We collectively shuddered.

Dad just laughed. "You get the point, Dean."

"I've been warned not to discuss certain illnesses at the table," Dean said.

Dad turned to me. "You would ruin my fun?"

"Honestly, I saved us all."

Conversation drifted from vet troubles to Eden's library budget woes to the general condition of Harper's various patients at Fiesta Village. The longer people talked, the more my stomach twisted in on itself like origami. Just as I'd suspected—Dean fit in perfectly with my family. He talked, laughed, and listened as though he'd always been part of the table dynamic.

Watching him and Booker compare the merits of NBA players as though they were putting together their own roster, my heart seemed to swell up until it popped with a million little confetti pieces in my chest. Dean fit. It didn't matter that he fit with my family, he fit with me. We worked. Emotions spun through me so fast, my world seemed to tilt on its axis.

I think I love him.

As that thought crystallized, the happy confetti pieces inside me turned to tiny shards of ice. I gulped at my glass of sweet tea to douse the panic spreading like wildfire.

How could I have fallen in love with Dean? A few weeks ago, I wasn't even sure I liked the guy. Okay, fine, he had intrigued and irritated me by turns, but love? I didn't do love—I had vowed to never fall for anything masquerading as love ever again. And now here I was, nearly hyperventilating at the rush of tenderness gearing up to remake me into a woman with permanent heart eyes.

"Everything okay?" Dean's soft voice pulled me from my panic.

"Uh." I drew my eyes from my hands, where I'd been staring while the *What is love?* crisis raged through me, and looked into his face. His hazel eyes were full of affection and more than a little bit of concern. Well, the concern made sense, considering I was probably mooning at him like a slightly unhinged fangirl. But the affection hooked right into me, drawing me closer.

"Everything's great." Not very high on the swagger scale, but it would have to do for now.

He took my hand beneath the table, anchoring me to him. He couldn't possibly know about the crazy tumult of longing and angst spiraling inside me, but yet again, he had done exactly the right thing. His clear source of calm in the midst of my chaos was just one more thing I loved about him.

The cringe factor on my internal monologue ran off the charts tonight, but at least I was the only one who knew it.

"Eliza," Mom said as dinner wound down, "any change in your soap business?"

That shut my swooning down right quick. I should have known they would get around to my work eventually. Not even Dean's presence could shield me from their well-intentioned questions.

"June and Marilyn almost doubled their last order for Fine & Dandy." That had come as enough of a shock I'd called June to make sure the numbers were right. After she confirmed it, I made her swear it wasn't a pity move.

"I love that place," Eden said. "I can't go in there without spending money."

Booker laid his arm across the back of her chair, his fingers playing over her shoulder. "We've got enough throw pillows to last a lifetime."

She shot him a sideways look. "Not a *lifetime*."

He leaned closer to give her a quick peck on the cheek. "Honey, thirty's enough for anybody."

After dinner came the Helpfulness Olympics. We jostled each other to bus dirty dishes, load the dishwasher, and in all other ways prove ourselves grateful for the meal. Everything I tried to do, Dean took over for me, leaving him drying pans after Booker rinsed them, while I did nothing but watch the procession.

Mom slid up beside me, an envelope held in front of her. "Your father and I have been thinking. We didn't do near enough for your birthday last month, and we wanted to make it up to you."

Warning bells rang in my head, but I took the offered envelope. "That's awful sweet of you."

She waved me on. "Open it."

I tore open the envelope and pulled out the card. It read *To our baby girl, so you can follow your dreams*. A check fell out, made to me for several thousand dollars.

My stomach dropped through the floor, straight into the depths of the earth. I thought I might vomit right there in front of everyone. They had good intentions, but they had no idea how much their generosity hurt. Swallowing hard, I replaced the check in the card, put it back in the envelope, and laid it on the kitchen counter behind me. Plastering on my best fake smile, I drew in a deep breath.

"Thank you, Mom, but I can't take it."

She looked to Dad for back up before turning her big eyes on me again. "What? Baby, that's for you. For your *birthday*."

Her emphasis on the word made it perfectly plain the money was for no such thing. That money wasn't meant for me to indulge in birthday fun—it was meant to keep me afloat before I sank straight to rock bottom.

"It's really generous of you, but I can't."

The others stole glances at us over their shoulders. With the whole family crammed in the kitchen, our conversation couldn't be classified as private, the water running in the kitchen sink not nearly loud enough to drown out this awfulness.

Mom picked up the envelope and tried to hand it to me again. "Of course you can take it."

I put my hands straight down at my sides. "I know you only mean to help me out, but I want to do this on my own."

"Think of it as an investment in your company."

I didn't take the bait, and Mom's broad smile slipped. "You could do so much with it. You could buy more soap supplies, pay for your pretty labels, rent a bigger apartment. Anything you want."

"I'm sorry, but I can't." The more I said *I can't*, the stronger my voice grew. "I know you mean well, and you're only trying to help, but I have to do this on my own. I can't keep taking gifts from you. I started this business by myself, and I'm going to keep it going by myself. I want to stand on my own two feet."

Mom drew back with pursed lips and grim eyes, the embodiment of *disappointed but not surprised*. She turned her face away. "Dean, you know about business. Tell Eliza it makes good sense to accept investment money."

Somewhere in the center of the earth, my stomach finally burned to a crisp. I hadn't fathomed my mother would try to use Dean against me like that. Worse, as often as he had clumsily attempted his own version of helping me whether I wanted him to or not, he would probably side with Mom and Dad. Why wouldn't he tell me to accept investment money freely given? Wasn't that every small business owner's dream?

Dean turned from the sink and wiped his hands on a kitchen towel, glancing from Mom to me. I willed him to understand me. Maybe it wasn't logical for me to refuse the money, but I couldn't accept another handout. He'd said he liked my independence—I just hoped he liked it enough to know I needed to keep my business going on my own. I couldn't bear it if my last refuge of support in this left me now.

The soft expression on his face made me hold my breath, waiting to see if he truly understood me as well as I'd hoped.

He turned to my mother. "Darlene, I'm afraid I can't tell Eliza that. Sunshine Soul is her company. She has a business plan for moving forward, and she knows what she wants. If she says she doesn't need the investment money, then she doesn't need it." He turned his big, beautiful eyes back to me. "I believe in her."

His every word made my heart rise higher, sweeping away my lingering fears and doubts.

I love this man.

Ignoring the confused sounds coming from my mother, I stepped across the kitchen and grabbed Dean's hand. Pulling him along behind me, I wove through my sisters and Booker, past my father, and out the back door onto the porch.

Safely away from the rest of my family's prying eyes, I turned to face him.

"What are we—"

I interrupted him by leaping into his arms. He grabbed me by the waist, and I wrapped my legs around him, holding on tight as I poured all my gratitude and affection into our kiss. It was cheating, trying to convey all these big, tender feelings without putting them into words, but it would be enough for tonight. He returned my kisses with just as much ferocity, whole conversations exchanged in every touch and caress.

I finally pulled away just enough to nuzzle against his neck. "You're the best."

He made a sound of disagreement as he shifted to find my mouth again, and I happily took up where we'd left off.

"Eliza, if you—"

Dad's voice forced Dean and me apart. Caught red-faced

and red-handed, Dean let my legs slip down until I had my feet again, but he kept an arm around me, like he didn't want me to go far. As if I was going anywhere.

Frozen at the sight of us tangled together, it took Dad a minute to find his voice again. "I wanted to say, your mother and I understand if you don't want to take our gift right now. If sometime down the line you decide you'd rather have it, you're always welcome to it."

My heart swelled with gratitude for their kindness and generosity. Even though their helpfulness hurt sometimes, they really did mean well. They only wanted to take care of me because they loved me so much. I truly did know that. But that didn't mean I could keep taking their money.

"Thank you."

A jet could have landed in the deep crease between his eyebrows as Dad looked between me and Dean. "I was going to ask if you're coming in for dessert, but it looks like you need another minute."

He turned and disappeared into the house, leaving us alone on the porch.

As soon as he was gone, I cuddled back up against Dean. "Thank you for having my back."

He wrapped me in his arms, tracing circles on my skin. "I meant what I said. You can do this. I believe in you."

Those words were written like neon lights in my heart, *Dean Irwin believes in me!*

"Are you ready to go back in?" he finally asked.

"Nope. My sisters will never let me live this down."

He hugged me closer. "I have no regrets."

dean

"GOOD NEWS. Looks like this should be the last day I have to ask you to ferry me around."

Eliza pulled off her Irwin's vest after our Monday shift. Nicole had relieved us at the registers, and Grant was puttering around somewhere with Rhett. Down to the last few days before the anniversary celebration, my brothers were constantly double-checking each other's plans for the party. All of their secret meetings and whispered conversations reminded me of when they used to team up against me as kids.

I didn't love it.

"How is that good news?" I hung my vest next to hers, glancing her over out of the corner of my eye. She wore a simple outfit of cargo pants, a plain gray T-shirt, and sturdy shoes. Nothing out of the ordinary, and yet taken altogether, it had been hard for me to focus on our customers.

"My dad texted me he's coming by this afternoon to fix the Bronco. You'll be free."

"I don't mind carpooling." The more we shared those little moments, the more I wanted to hold onto them. The everyday activity of driving around together had become a comfort I wasn't prepared to give up just because her car ran again.

"I have to deliver soaps to Fine & Dandy tomorrow after our shift, and Wednesday is the chaos that is the farmers market. It will be easier if the Bronco's up and running."

Her argument made sense, but I still didn't like the idea of losing those hours together. "What are you doing right now?"

"Clocking out?"

"After."

She gave me a flirty sideways look. "Are you scheming up another plan?"

"Probably. I do like plans."

Her grin lit me up until I had enough electricity coursing through me, I could have powered the whole city.

"I guess I'm in."

I held my hand out to her. She slipped her hand in mine, and I led us through the store and out the front doors. "I thought we could get spiced ciders at The Busy Bean."

She crinkled her nose. "Spiced cider? It's eighty degrees out."

"Seventy-eight."

"Oh, sure, seventy-eight is downright chilly." Tugging on my hand, she flashed a smile. "Fine, yes. Cider sounds great."

We walked up to the little cafe with its elaborate chalk board out front listing two dozen varieties of coffees, teas, and ciders. I bought our drinks and kept walking. She looped one arm in mine while she sipped at her cider, watching me as if she thought I was about to change color or do a backflip.

"Why are you looking at me like that?"

Her mouth curled at the edges. "You are a curiosity."

"I'm flattered?" I turned up Third Street, past the pharmacy and the Post Office to where businesses thinned out and neighborhoods took over.

"I'm just wondering where you're taking us."

I nodded straight ahead. "Aileen Park."

Towering oak trees provided canopy for the classic town park boasting an old wooden gazebo in the middle and a recently refurbished playground at one end. Still early yet for the big show the oaks would put on later in the fall, but pretty enough to visit.

"What are we doing here?"

Her hesitation was making me second-guess my decision to bring her. Impulsive decisions were still new for me. Maybe this one hadn't been a hit.

"I wanted to see the park from here on the ground." I turned to face Center Street, hidden by blocks of buildings and trees. "I can see the tops of these trees from my office window. I know there's a park here, but I never visit it. Before I go back to sitting at my desk from eight in the morning until eight at night, I wanted to come here with you."

Her eyes softened the longer I talked, growing wider and a little bit sad. She looked like she might cry, or bare minimum say *Bless your heart*. Instead, she threw one arm around my shoulders and kissed me hard.

"That's the sweetest thing I've ever heard."

If Eliza liked stories of me being cooped up in my office all day, sweeping her off her feet wouldn't be a problem.

"I love that we're here. Thank you for bringing me."

Arm in arm, we sipped at our ciders and pretended it felt like fall. We strayed off the path to walk through the grass, crunching twigs and bark beneath our boots.

"Look at how many acorns there are this year." She bent down and scooped up a handful. "Don't you just love acorns?"

I didn't, but I tried to look like I might.

"There's so much potential inside them. They might never get planted, or a squirrel might eat them, or they could get crushed under our feet. But they *could* be something huge. Isn't that incredible?"

She marveled at the three acorns in her hand as if she were gazing at a baby, open and full of wonder. Her way of viewing the world was so different from mine, sometimes I hardly understood it. She carried so much more hope and optimism than I did, my heart ached to see it.

"When I was a little girl, I used to believe that you could tell an acorn your wish, and if you planted it and it grew, your wish would come true."

She raised an eyebrow at me and turned away, whispering into her cupped hand where she held the acorns. I died a little when she kissed each one, her rosy lips touching their brown shells.

"Are they like birthday wishes?" I asked, wishing her lips were touching mine instead of the acorns. "Does it spoil the wish if you share it?"

"Probably better not risk it."

I held out my hand, and she dropped the acorns into it with a soft clatter. "Where do we plant them to see if they'll come true?"

What I really wanted to ask was if her wishes were anything like mine. Visions of the two of us together on a more permanent basis. Too soon to confess to those sweet hopes and dreams, but I held onto them for later.

She looked up at the massive tree overhead and the branches that practically blocked out the sky. "Where is there space for an oak? Mom always pulled ours up every time my sisters and I planted our wishes in the back yard. Just think what I could be today if all my wishes had come true."

"You're doing pretty well from where I'm standing."

Cupping my jaw with one hand, she gave it a gentle pat. "You tell the sweetest lies."

She kissed me again until I tasted the cider on her tongue. From that moment on, apple cider would remind me of Eliza, sharp and sweet.

Shouts from the nearby skate park finally broke us apart, and we continued our walk.

She nuzzled against me in the shade of the trees. "How are things coming with your grandma's downsizing?"

Grandma was *not* on my mind after that kiss.

"We're making progress. Grant decided to take a few things, so that helps."

"And you?"

A twig snapped underfoot. "I don't think I need anything."

"There's got to be something you want to keep just for the memories."

"Nothing comes to mind."

"You can think through all the time you spent at your grandparents' house, from when you were a kid until now, and there's not one teeny, tiny thing you might want? Something that reminds you of a special moment? There's really nothing?"

I sifted through memories of the house, little moments with my grandfather or grandmother, searching for one thing I could possibly need to keep the image alive. A pointless endeavor. I would never forget that old house, or all the time I'd spent there growing up. It had been my most constant safe harbor from the storms in my own heart. I didn't need any of my grandma's furniture to remind me how special it was.

"Ha, I saw that," Eliza said, triumph lighting her eyes. "You thought of something."

"I didn't. I was thinking about my grandparents. They, and their memory, are more precious to me than anything inside an old house."

Her gloating melted into a tender look that spun through

me like sweet, shimmery strands of cotton candy. "Oh. That's so sweet. I didn't know you felt that way."

Those warm strands dissolved. "You didn't know I might care about my grandparents?"

She flinched, her eyes gone wide. "I didn't mean it like that. You just keep everything so buttoned up, it's nice to hear you talk that way."

Her naked surprise gnawed at me. She wasn't the first woman to think my reluctance to put my emotions on display meant I didn't have any feelings at all. The image of the unfeeling, strait-laced accountant made me want to punch something, no matter how apt it could be.

"I'm not a robot, Eliza. I love my family as much as you love yours."

"Hey." She stopped and lightly tugged my hand. "I'm sorry, I didn't mean to sound like I thought you didn't care about your grandparents. It was just a really beautiful thing for you to say."

Her sincerity soothed away my frustration. Didn't I know by now she wouldn't judge me that way? Shaking my head at my knee-jerk reaction, I squeezed her hand. "Thank you."

"You're welcome." She glanced sideways. "We should probably head back, though. This trip through the acorns is fun and all, but I don't want to be late for my dad."

Dread rose up through my chest like a snake. "You're not wrong there. I'm already on his list."

Her soft little smile confirmed it. I had never before experienced the absolute terror of having a woman's father walk in on us while she was wrapped around me, and never wanted to again.

"If I can't drive you to work anymore, at least let me take you out this weekend."

Her smile dimmed a touch. "You mean out, out?"

"Yes, to a restaurant and everything. How about Thursday?"

She scrunched her nose. "Why Thursday?"

"Friday night is going to be a madhouse after the all-day extravaganza at the store, and I don't want to wait until Saturday."

She grinned. "We could do Saturday, too."

Saturday, Sunday, and every day after. I wanted to hoard Eliza's time. *All mine.*

"I like the sound of that."

eliza

I NUDGED FINE & Dandy's door open with my hip and maneuvered through, careful of the cardboard box I carried. The store's air conditioning carried the sweet hint of jasmine, and soft music played overhead. I preferred a little more boho in my chic, but I couldn't knock the style in here. They had sleek modern coffee tables decorated with milk glass vases, plush armchairs in rich jewel tones, and Eden's beloved throw pillows sprinkled everywhere like fairy dust. I didn't usually browse too much when I visited, but only to save myself the pain of finding something I loved without the money to buy it.

Marilyn Wells, the owner of the shop and June's daddy's sweetheart, walked around a cozy-looking couch to greet me. "Is this what I think it is?"

"Sure is. I double-checked the numbers, your order's all here."

I moved to the space at the end of the front counter that had been set up with my soap display these last few months. But instead of finding my soap bars at the ready for an impulse buy, the space held a wicker basket filled with hand-painted ceramic tiles. My heart squeezed at the change. Maybe the soaps weren't selling as well as June had said. Even though I figured she might overhype my sales, I hadn't thought Marilyn would.

"You moved them." I tried to sound only mildly curious, pretending raw disappointment wasn't eating up my insides. I had to be grateful Fine & Dandy stocked my soaps at all, no matter where they chose to put them.

"Oh, honey, they needed more real estate." Marilyn gestured behind us.

I turned to see a gorgeous wooden hutch on the opposite wall, whose shelves boasted welcoming rows of soaps. *My* soaps. Their muted colors and soft scent drew me closer. I knew every last bar, but I still marveled over them as if I'd never seen them before. This simple showcase made my soaps look sumptuous.

Pride filled me up, warm and bright, until I might have been a little robin ready to burst into song.

"They were doing so well at the registers, I decided they needed to be showed off. We've had them here the last two weeks or so, and you can see by how few there are left they're doing well."

Some of the scents only had one or two bars on display. They'd really sold this many in a month?

"I kind of thought June was just sweet-talking me."

"No, dear, you're currently our number one impulse buy." Marilyn's smile faltered as she looked me over. "Are you all right?"

"I'm just..." My thoughts swirled, tangled, and straightened out again. I would *not* cry and let Marilyn see me for the basket case I was. No. "I *love* this. This is exactly what I'd hoped to see some day."

"I'm glad you like it. Have you had any luck getting into other stores? I know I should encourage you, one businesswoman to another, but selfishly, I kind of like having the run on them."

One businesswoman to another. Now I truly might cry. Nobody had called me that before. The title still didn't seem to fit quite right, like a little girl slipping on her mama's fancy dress, but for the first time in a long time, I thought maybe I really could grow into it.

"I haven't really..." I hesitated, and then just went for it. "Honestly, I've been afraid to try to sell them anywhere else. After Countryside passed, I guess my confidence has been kind of shot."

"Oh, I know how that feels."

"You do? How? This place is so great." I waved around at all the gorgeous items artfully arranged through the store. Fine & Dandy was one of the town's most popular shopping draws, and consistently won small business awards throughout the region. Now that June had come on staff to do interior design, its star had risen even higher. Marilyn lacking for business confidence just didn't compute.

A motherly sort of affection shone in her smile. "It wasn't always so great. The first few months—the whole first year, really—I wasn't sure how long I could stay in business. Every sale I made felt like a miracle. Some days, I didn't get a single miracle at all. It was tough going. But I kept at it, and I refused to give in.

"Anything worth doing is going to be hard. It's up to you to remember why you want to do it, and hold on tight to that dream." She leaned in a little closer. "Can I tell you a secret about Countryside? They're not the beginning and end of people's taste in this town."

The pride that had been swirling around inside me from seeing my soaps so lovingly displayed burst into a fireball of gratitude. I threw my arms around Marilyn. "Now I know why June loves you so much."

The hug might have been a little weird, one businesswoman to another, but her eyes glowed at the compliment.

"I'll cut you your check for the soaps. And Eliza, if this month is anything like the last one, you'll be hearing from us again soon."

Fizzy elation rushing through my blood, I climbed into my Bronco at the curb and headed to my apartment. Dean was right. I had been sabotaging myself, convinced more failure waited right around the corner, afraid to try again. Was I really going to let one rejection kill my dream of becoming a badass businesswoman? Hell no.

At home, I moved like a whirlwind. I opened up my laptop and emailed an updated price sheet to myself, along with the scent list I'd created for my website. I gathered up a selection of soaps and business cards, tossed it all into one of my farmers market display crates, and topped it off with a long list of businesses to visit this afternoon. Like Miguel had said, go big or go home.

I was going to go big.

dean

I SHOULD HAVE KNOWN Eliza wouldn't let me take her out to dinner.

She claimed there was no point in going someplace fancy on a weeknight, but I suspected she still didn't want to feel she owed me anything. Her fears of being indebted to anyone were understandable, but totally misplaced with me. She had no idea just how much I would give her, if only she would let me.

Instead of going out to the Thai restaurant that had recently opened in town, we made dinner together at her place. Pasta carbonara was no culinary masterpiece, but the chance to work side by side with her in her small kitchen more than made up for any deficiencies.

"I love watching you cook," she said as I dished up the pasta. "You should make dinner for me every night."

"Yes, I should." I spooned sauce over our spaghetti and added slices of garlic bread fresh from the oven to round out our meal. I'd brought another bottle of the white wine she'd enjoyed last time and poured us each a glass. Not quite the finery I wanted to give her, but still a pretty good date.

"Am I ever going to get to see your off-limits townhouse?"

"It isn't off-limits," I said, sitting down across from her. "There's just a little too much Rhett in it for my taste."

"You two don't get along?" She twirled pasta around her fork and took a bite.

The little groan she made would have brought out sinful thoughts in even the holiest man, and I wasn't all that holy to start with.

Drawing my eyes away from her obvious enjoyment of our dinner, I tried to get back to her question about Rhett. "There's no bad blood between us. We're just two very different men."

To put it mildly. Of my two brothers, Rhett and I were the least similar, and the most likely to have volatile reactions to each other. Grant and I had our differences, but with Rhett, it was like looking at myself in a negative image, all my traits reversed and blown out of proportion.

"Like how?"

"Rhett doesn't mind a mess. He's loud and scattered. Privacy isn't a big concern for him."

She bobbed her eyebrows. "You mean he walks around naked?"

"I mean *my* privacy isn't a big concern for him."

"Oh." She blushed, and suddenly, the only thing in the world I wanted was privacy. "What else?"

"He's a pack rat. The garage is filled with boxes of things he's had since he was in high school. Awards, trophies, baseball cards, everything."

"That goes against your *No mementos* rule."

Exactly, but I wasn't going to be drawn into another conversation about sentimentality and holding onto relics for the sake of history. "We're neither one's first choice in roommate."

"How did you wind up sharing a house, then?"

"It was mine at first. About a year and a half ago, Rhett broke up with his girlfriend and needed a place to stay." More like she threw him out cold, but I would spare Eliza the details. She didn't need to know the finer points of Rhett's inability to commit, or his loose definition of monogamy. "Couch surfing turned into a roommate situation, and here we are."

"What about Grant?"

"Grant bought a house a few years ago on a little bit of land on the outskirts of town." I thought it best not to say more, considering the details.

"Oh, I remember now. He had a fiancée." Her eyes turned soft and sad. "How do you leave somebody at the altar?"

"No idea." I would never forget Grant's face slowly crumbling as whispers roared through the church, waiting for the woman who had opted to leave town without a word instead of marry him. "My brothers haven't been very lucky in love."

"What about you?" Her curiosity seemed mixed with shyness, as if she both wanted the answer and regretted asking.

"I haven't been very lucky in love, either."

"Why not?"

I tried to pull a smile but felt the grimace on my face. "I'm not that easy to get along with."

"That's not true."

Her sweet vehemence made me laugh. "Think back a little."

"You can be a little prickly sometimes. So can I, so what?"

I focused on my wine glass. "Women I've dated have found me too...well, distant might be the nicest word. Heartless might be the worst."

Eliza stood and walked around the table to my side. She gestured for me to scoot my chair back, and I obeyed without question. Stepping over my legs, she sank down onto my lap and wrapped her arms around my shoulders. I had no choice but to stare into her ocean blue eyes so full of affection, I could drown in their depths.

"You're not heartless, Dean. I know by the way you're taking care of your grandma and helping out your brother. The same way you took care of *me*. You've got a big heart in there, you just don't show it to everybody."

Her gentle words soothed those old hurts like a balm. She pressed soft kisses to my mouth, one after another, as though she wanted to wipe those other memories from my mind. Her kiss held so much trust and tenderness, I could almost believe she was trying to tell me something else with every sweet touch. I finally broke, pulling her to me hard as I stood from the table. She clung to me as she had in her elation at her parents' house the other night, never breaking the kiss while I moved us to the couch and sat down.

"Better?" she whispered against my mouth.

"Much." I wouldn't push or press for more than she was ready to give, but I couldn't pretend I didn't want her. She drove me crazy in the best way, and I didn't want it to end. I didn't want any of it to end.

After minutes, hours, days, Eliza finally pulled away. "We keep winding up like this."

She slid off my lap and tucked herself up against my side. I wrapped my arms around her, content for now just to hold her close. "You're irresistible."

She laughed, a rippling sensation that echoed in me. "You didn't always think that."

"You can be a little prickly sometimes."

She smacked a hand against my chest at the way I'd echoed her. "What did you really think of me? Before you had to work with me the last month?"

"I thought you were beautiful," I said, to a satisfied if somewhat skeptical sound from her. "And irritating."

She swiveled around to glare up at me. "Irritating?"

I hugged her closer, and she tucked back down against me. "You hardly ever talked to me, or shared your gorgeous smiles with me. You had joy and laughter for everyone in town but me. Yes, I found that irritating."

Her hand returned to my chest, but to caress this time. "I thought you were brutally handsome but not remotely my type."

A chill worked its way through my blood. "Not your type."

Whatever emotion I tried to keep from my voice, she must have heard it. She pushed up until she faced me on the couch. "I didn't think you were my type because you seemed so together and successful. I didn't think I could offer much in the face of your achievements."

I cupped her cheek, stroking my thumb across her jaw. "El, I will take anything you want to offer me. Anything. And I'll be grateful."

I moved in for another kiss, but she drew back before I could reach her. Taking my hand in hers, she slipped it under the edge of her shirt. My heart stilled like time moved in slow motion as she guided my hand to rest on her ribcage beneath her arm.

"I want to show you something." Holding the front of her shirt down, she pulled the side up, exposing my hand.

I didn't have time to marvel at the sight of my hand against her skin or how soft and warm she felt. Something gray peeked from behind my fingers. *Her tattoo.* I looked into her eyes to find unwavering trust looking back at me.

I pulled my hand from her side. A heart with a swirling sunburst inside adorned the side of her ribcage. I traced my fingertip over the delicate black and gray lines, amazed at how much detail had been packed into a space I could cover with my palm. As vivid and lovely as any piece of artwork I'd ever seen, made even more so because it was a part of her.

"This must have hurt a lot."

She exhaled a laugh. "It hurt so bad, I could hardly stand it."

"But you still did it."

"I got it after everything that happened in San Antonio." Her voice was soft and quiet in the stillness as I reverently admired her tattoo. "I wanted a reminder to be true to myself, no matter what."

My heart swelled and ached in my chest as though her tattoo had been imprinted on my flesh. I vowed right then to cherish Eliza—just as she was—for as long as she would let me.

"It's beautiful. I love it."

I love you.

I barely caught her smile before she leaned in to press her mouth to mine. "Will you stay?"

That sweet whisper shot through me like a bottle rocket. I ran the backs of my fingers along her jaw, down the side of her neck. "Are you sure?"

She nodded and grazed my mouth with her soft lips. "I want you to stay."

"Then I'll stay."

eliza

IF ANYTHING WAS BETTER than being in Dean's arms, I hadn't found it.

We lay snuggled under my covers, Dean big-spooning me with one arm holding me tight against him. He'd spent the evening replacing every word in my vocabulary with his name, the overachiever. Even my elbows had been fully satisfied. We both hung on the verge of sleep, but I didn't quite want to let go of our night together.

"I don't know why I told you to be less perfect." My words blurred together, half-drunk on him. "Go on with your perfectionist ways. I applaud them."

He pressed his mouth to the nape of my neck, sending shivers down to my toes.

"I changed my mind. I don't care how crazy the party is, I want to see you tomorrow night." He kissed me again. "And Saturday." And again. "And Sunday."

"You're really filling in my social calendar."

"I want you all to myself."

I grinned wildly in the darkness. I could just make out the shape of his arm where it pinned me against him. His body heat warmed me up, back to front and outside in. The scent of his cologne wound through my hair and danced on my skin.

"I'm good with that."

We breathed in time with each other as we had all night, a drowsy coda to the earlier crescendo. Even in my half-asleep state, a tremor twisted through my belly remembering the tangle of arms and legs we'd made.

"I'm just going to say it again: Wow. You really know your stuff."

His laughter rumbled against my back. "It's all that intensity."

I giggled and lifted his hand to my mouth so I could kiss his palm once, twice. "You put it to good use, my friend."

He groaned. "Calling me your friend right now is cruel."

"My good chum."

He chuckled against my skin. "No."

"My old pal."

"You're really hitting me where it hurts."

"My lo—" I sliced the word in half with my teeth. Calling him *my love* stepped one shade shy of telling him I loved him, and it was way too soon for that, no matter how much I wanted to set the words free. Instead, I swallowed it down for another time. "My long-lost buddy."

He laced his fingers with mine, snuggling me as close as he could. "One more, but that's it."

"My compatriot."

His breath tickled my neck. "Go to sleep, El."

"Goodnight, Dean."

Best night ever.

THIRTY-EIGHT

IRWIN'S BLOCK party had to be drawing in record-setting crowds for Magnolia Ridge. Grant had arranged for a taco truck to park in front of the store, and put tables covered in sale and clearance items out front to draw customers from the food through the door. Rhett had raffle prizes going every hour. A woman made balloon animals for the kids. Local athletes and outdoor enthusiasts gave talks throughout the day on everything from kayaking to ice climbing to hiking the Appalachian Trail. It made for a crazy, exciting celebration of the outdoors, the store, and the family that ran it.

All through the aisles, staff picks had been marked down in honor of the day. Early on, I'd laughed over Dean's pick when I saw his name next to the hammock display. He had probably seen my choice of headlamp coming a mile away. Customers wandered from the crowded sidewalk through the store, talking with sporting experts and snapping up deals.

My next paycheck's commission would be significant.

"This is a better turnout than even Rhett expected." Grant refilled the receipt tape in the machine next to mine at the registers. "It usually only gets like this the two days after Thanksgiving."

"Are all the other branches having such a good day?"

"They are, my phone's been blowing up with calls and texts from the other managers."

"You should have anniversary parties every year."

"Maybe we should." He checked his watch. "You can clock out if you want. Nicole's out front now, and with the rest of us on deck, I think we've got it covered."

"You think I'm going to leave without a piece of cake?" A huge chocolate sheet cake emblazoned with *Thirty Years* in dark green frosting sat hidden safely away on Grant's desk. The snacks and cookies laid out in the front of the store were all well and good, but I needed to try that cake.

He laughed. "You're welcome to stay. My parents should be here soon."

"They're cutting it close." Rhett passed the registers, his arms full of clearance items to restock the sidewalk tables. "I thought they would have been here an hour ago."

He walked between shoppers and out the front door to greet people milling on the sidewalk.

"Is it worrying they're late?" I asked Grant.

"No, they stopped in at the Austin store on the way back from Corpus Christi. Double-dipping on celebration parties is what they're doing."

Dean came up to the registers, talking with a customer. He briefly touched my waist as he slipped past, and a thrill rippled through me at that small acknowledgement. Other than a quick breakfast together before he left my apartment, we hadn't had much chance for a moment alone.

"At least take a break if you're going to stay," Grant told me as he beckoned the next customer forward. "It's going to be a long night."

"I'll just go check on things in the stock room." I hitched a thumb over my shoulder, backing away from the registers. "I'd better make sure everything's all tasty and delicious in there."

He shot me a warning look. "If you sneak a bite out of that, so help me."

I laid on my best innocent look before hightailing it to the back room. The stock shelves looked a lot emptier than this morning. Which would sell out first—my headlamps or Dean's hammocks? We should have put a bet on it. Then again, after last night, I would have played to lose.

In the office, I snuck the cake one longing look before I sat in Grant's chair and checked my phone. We'd been so busy, I'd had it silenced all day. I'd only missed one message, though—a text from Sarah Daniels.

Sarah: Call me

My stomach squeezed over that vague note, but I tapped the *Call* button. Better to get this over with now and keep moving forward than to delay and agonize the way I'd been doing.

"Eliza, thank you for getting back to me," Sarah said as soon as she picked up.

"This was my first chance, it's been busy at Irwin's."

"Right, the big anniversary celebration, I saw the signs."

She took a deep breath, and my body stilled, preparing myself for the inevitable rejection. Maybe I'd aimed too high with my proposal. Maybe I should have started smaller.

"Mark and I talked it over, and we would absolutely love to contract with you for our hotel soaps."

My breath hitched in my throat as though my heart had lodged itself there. That...couldn't be what she'd said. "You would?"

"He asked me why I hadn't thought of it before. I *love* your soaps. What better way to show a little bit of Magnolia Ridge pride to our guests?"

I struggled to form actual words instead of the shrieks that wanted to erupt from my mouth. "That's great news."

Great. Wonderful. Fantastic. The best news.

"I'm thinking we should do a mix of the full-size bars as part of the welcome kit, and your mini bars for the guest toiletries." Sarah tossed out a number that made my head spin. "Do you think you could manage that many bars each month?"

Each month? That would match my income from the farmers markets with a single client. Money wasn't the most important thing—but it ranked pretty high up there. Plus, my soaps would be in one of the nicest hotels in town. "I could absolutely do that many for you."

"We're comfortable with the prices listed on the sheet you included." Sarah huffed happy laughter. "Send us a contract and let's get started."

We hung up a few minutes later, and I put my phone in my pocket, my mind in a daze. This was happening. This was really happening. *Eliza Webb, Badass Businesswoman.*

I rushed through the stock room onto the sales floor, where only one person waited to be rung up. I shot straight over to Dean and grabbed his arm.

"Can I borrow him?" I asked Grant. "I'll bring him back in two minutes, I promise."

Grant glanced between us like he might argue, but he gave a reluctant nod. "Two minutes."

"Thank you for shopping at Irwin's," Dean said, passing a bag over to his customer.

I took his hand and pulled him through the store into the stock room, my feet barely touching the floor in my excitement. "I have something to tell you."

He eyed me warily. "Okay."

"It's huge. I wanted to tell you earlier, but I wasn't sure if it would be huge, but now I know that it is, and I have to tell you. Because it's huge."

He raised his eyebrows. "So, we're talking huge?"

I clasped my hands in front of my chest. "Tuesday after work, I took a bunch of sample soaps and price sheets to about a dozen businesses in town for wholesaling, and Sarah at Bluebird Lodge just called to say she wants to contract with me for soaps for all their guest rooms!"

I barely got the whole thing out before Dean caught me up in his arms and lifted me off the floor. I couldn't have asked for a better congratulations than his warm, tight hug.

"That's great news, El. I knew you could do it." He set me back on my feet and pressed his mouth to mine in a quick kiss. "I'm so proud of you."

I grinned back. "Me, too. Now get back out to the registers before Grant comes looking for you."

We walked out of the back room just in time. Grant was headed our way, but seemed relieved he didn't have to risk catching us making out in the stock room again.

He tilted his head toward the doors. "Mom and Dad finally made it."

Nathaniel and Patricia Irwin stood at the front of the store chatting with a woman while a photographer took pictures. A small crowd had gathered inside, spilling out onto the sidewalk as people craned their necks to catch a glimpse of the small-town couple made good on their special day.

"Mayor Collins is here?" I asked Grant as I eyed the elegant Black woman dressed in a red pantsuit.

"She's presenting them with the Key to the City."

"People still do that?"

He lifted a shoulder. "Apparently."

I wrapped one arm around Dean's waist. "I didn't realize how huge this was for you guys. This is amazing."

"I've heard even better news today."

His bright smile held so much tender sweetness, I wanted to whip out a beach towel and just bask in it.

I stayed through Grant's speech honoring his parents, and the Irwins' humble words of thanks for the people of Magnolia Ridge. I even stayed after the last slice of sheet cake had been devoured. Long past regular closing time, with the taco truck still out front and customers cycling through the store, they hadn't bothered to close up. The atmosphere had become like a party nobody wanted to leave.

Dean and I stood in a quiet corner of the store, finally enjoying a little one-on-one time as the crowd thinned. I tugged on his shirt sleeve. "I love that you went with hammock."

"I've heard they're terribly comfortable."

"That's not remotely what I said."

His gaze was all heat. "You haven't been in one with me."

I grinned stupidly at him, a thrill of delight skimming over my skin as I considered the possibilities. Anything involving two people in a hammock still sounded like the makings of a tragedy, but if Dean was that second person, I would be willing to give it a shot.

"Dean." Nathaniel Irwin had come up behind us while we talked. He clapped his son on the shoulder, looking every bit the outdoor company exec in his plaid travel shirt and wrinkle-resistant pants. "You've done a good job the last few weeks."

Dean ticked his head to the side as if brushing off the compliment when really, he deserved so much more. Sure, he'd been a pill about it at first, but he'd become more than just *good* down here. He'd become vital.

Vital to *me*.

"I've tried."

Nathaniel laughed as though Dean had said something else. "Oh, I know you didn't want to come down to sales, but it's important you see the store from every angle. You're a good sport for humoring me down here."

Dean's mouth pulled into a tight smile. "It wasn't a problem."

"I hope you tried new things like we talked about, eh? Moved a little outside your comfort zone?"

Dean's eyes darted to me, and Nathaniel finally noticed they weren't alone. He reached out and shook my hand.

"Eliza, from all Grant's said, Dean owes his promotion to you."

The moment seemed to slow to a stop, the noise of the lingering crowd pressing in on my ears. I was so far out of my depth, I couldn't even feel my hand in Nathaniel's, I was just a blank smile without a body. *What promotion?*

I tried to swallow, but my throat caught. Confusion made my skin creep until I itched. "I don't think I did anything."

Nathaniel laughed, oblivious to my flat tone. "Grant said you trained him. Taught him everything he needed to know about retail."

I looked to Dean for some kind of explanation, a denial, anything. Instead, I only saw confirmation in his eyes. Confirmation of what, exactly, I still didn't know, and couldn't bring myself to ask.

Nathaniel clapped him on the back again so hard, Dean took an awkward step forward. "Now that he's run the gauntlet down here, he's ready to be our Chief Financial Officer."

Chief Financial Officer? He'd never said a word to me about it. Probably the biggest promotion of his career, and he hadn't bothered to share it with me? Disoriented from a rushing surge of embarrassment, I plastered on an even bigger smile.

"I'm glad I could help him out with that. Congratulations on the store's thirtieth anniversary." I turned to Dean. "Can we talk for a minute?"

He nodded once, a stiff, bleak confirmation of everything he'd never said.

I turned and took a straight shot for the back door, ignoring everyone we passed. Five minutes ago, I would have celebrated right along with them, but now, I'd gone too off-kilter to listen to stories about outdoor adventures.

"El."

In the back parking lot, I turned around to face him but wished I hadn't. Under the pale light of the street lamp, he looked tortured and miserable.

No, not that. That was reading too much. He looked guilty, nothing more.

"Congratulations. Why didn't you tell me about your promotion?"

The moment I had good news this afternoon, I'd rushed in to share it with him—I'd needed to include him in my excitement. But he'd kept this to himself for weeks. The question of *why* spun through my head, making me dizzy.

"I didn't think it was important."

"Right. You didn't think becoming Chief Financial Officer of your family's company was important."

"Of course I think that's important, I just..." He shook his head, seeming to dismiss every possible end to that sentence.

"Oh." My heart dropped until I was sinking through the ground. Falling, falling, with nothing beneath me. "You didn't think telling *me* was important."

"El, no, there was just never a good time. My father wanted me to get the full experience of what it's like to work in one of our stores, that's all."

"Yeah, you really got the full experience," I said, my voice flat. The conversation with his father echoed through my head, leaving the sting of fresh humiliation behind. Nathaniel hadn't spoken to me as anything more than an employee. "You didn't tell your parents about us, did you?"

His hesitation made me want to scream for everything it said. His parents didn't know about us, because we weren't important enough to mention, either. Maybe there was no *us*.

"I haven't brought it up yet."

So diplomatic and tactful, but his polite words made my stomach churn. He hadn't accidentally forgotten—he'd intentionally kept them in the dark. Kept *me* in the dark.

"What was that crack he made about trying new things?" My skin crawled as realization wormed through me. "Is that what the paddleboarding and hiking were all about? Part of the promotion package?"

"Maybe at first, but it became more than that."

Maybe at first. My lungs felt stuffed with cotton until I couldn't breathe. He'd spent time with me just to fulfill some weird promotion stipulation? My heart collapsed in on itself like a dying star, winking out with a pathetic *pop*. I wanted to shout, run, let the hot tears waiting behind my eyes stream down my face. Mostly, I wanted to go back and undo everything that had happened with him in the last few weeks.

"Was everything just about this job? Was everything between us a lie?"

He reached for me, but I backed away.

"I never lied to you, Eliza."

I shook my head, sifting through conversations, searching for evidence to confirm or deny his words, but everything was tainted now. His father had sent him to the sales floor on a work assignment, and boy, he'd committed. And I'd bought into it completely.

Eden's advice lit up like neon in my mind: *Be smart about it.*

If I'd been smarter, I would have remembered the hard lessons I'd learned and bitter promises to myself, but instead, I'd flung them all aside for Dean.

"I should have known there was a reason you were spending so much time with me."

His brow furrowed, his mouth set into that subtle show of just-beneath-the-surface anger I'd seen before.

"Did it ever occur to you I spent so much time with you because I was falling in love with you?"

I froze, suddenly back in San Antonio four years ago. *"I think I'm falling in love with you."* Carter's words echoed through Dean's until they became one voice, telling me what I wanted to hear, but I couldn't let myself believe those words. Not again.

Last time, Carter had left me humiliated and alone. This time, I would be the one to walk away.

"Well, I'm not falling in love with you."

Dean flinched, and some terrible part of me triumphed that I could hurt him like he'd hurt me.

He worked his jaw as though struggling for the right response. "What about last night?"

I couldn't think about last night. If I remembered his soft caresses, the tender words he'd spoken, I would forget myself all over again. I focused instead on the promise I'd made in that tattoo studio in Austin as the needles imprinted their ink in my flesh.

Be true to yourself, no matter what.

"You're not my type, remember? I want a guy with a heart." The tortured look in his eyes twisted through me like a knife, my cruelty turning back to cut me. I wished my words back, but what would be the point? Maybe it wasn't being true to myself, but if the lie could protect my heart even just a little, that would be something.

He took a step backwards as though I'd shoved him. "Is that really the way you feel?"

It wasn't the way I felt, that was the whole problem. I'd chosen to put my heart and soul in his hands. But I'd proven time and again I didn't make good choices. I'd leaped without a glance down, and only now, mid-air, could I see the fall that waited for me.

I wasn't sure I'd ever recover from this one.

"Goodbye, Dean."

He stood like stone as he watched me, a look of sorrow contorting his face, until he finally turned around and walked back into the building. I put a hand on my side, over my tattoo, as though I could keep myself from breaking apart, but it didn't help. Every step he took seemed to tear me up until my heart was nothing but tatters in my chest.

I LAID into the punching bag, each blow landing harder than the last. My lungs burned, and my hands cried out in pain with every strike. Sweat dripped down my forehead and into my eyes, blurring my vision. I pulled the back of an arm across my face without pausing my annihilation of the bag.

Damn my father's scheme to put me on the sales floor. Damn everyone's advice that I should try new things I could fail at. I had tried new things all right, and I'd sure as hell failed at this one. I would never get over the look in Eliza's eyes when she told me goodbye, like she never wanted to see me again. That look would haunt me.

Maybe it should.

"This isn't good," Rhett said.

I didn't turn from the bag, just kept throwing punches. "Now's not the time."

My brothers walked across the garage and hovered near me, close enough to scrutinize but out of reach if one of my punches were to go rogue.

Grant sat on a stool beneath the dartboard. "You want to talk about it?"

He would understand this misery. When his fiancée had left him at the altar, he'd been a ghost of a man, his broken heart on display for the whole town to see. If anybody could commiserate with my situation, he could. But commiserating would mean talking about it, and I could not bear that right now. I wanted to destroy something as surely as I was being destroyed.

"No, I don't want to talk about it."

Rhett moved closer, worry furrowing his brow. "Look at your hands."

I didn't stop pummeling the bag. "It's nothing."

Grant hopped from the chair and got into my space. "Stop this. Use one of your calming techniques or something."

"This *is* one of my calming techniques." I moved to throw another punch, but he grabbed my arm. We struggled, but he finally held my hands up in front of my face.

"This isn't calming."

I hadn't bothered to tape my hands or wear gloves tonight —I'd just come home and gone straight for the punching bag. My knuckles were nothing but a mass of spreading purple bruises. Red scrapes covered my skin, blood oozed from where the first knuckle on each fist had split open. Looking them over, I felt nothing. They were nowhere near as flayed and battered as my heart.

I pulled out of Grant's hold and stepped away from the bag, my chest heaving with every breath.

"What happened?" Rhett asked.

"Nothing," I spat.

"Come off it, we're not idiots," Grant said. "We saw how you and Eliza left the store, now we find you doing this? What went wrong?"

I moved to walk past them, but they blocked my path.

Grant laid a hand on my chest to hold me back. "If you don't talk about it, you'll just wind up tearing this whole place apart."

"I really don't want to lose the deposit on that." Rhett gave a false laugh that didn't lighten the mood.

"I'm good for it." I stepped away from them, but there wasn't much sense trying to avoid my brothers. They would find me wherever I went. They were right, anyway. If I didn't calm down now, I was in serious danger of causing damage to something other than my hands. I hadn't done anything like that in years, but I might not be able to contain the hurt and anger tearing through me this time.

I tried to even out my breathing, but all the mantras, all the soothing images were of *her* now. My attempts to find peace only heaped on more heartache.

I released a low, guttural sound like a wounded animal. "Dad told Eliza about the promotion. She thinks all our time together was just for show, and now she doesn't trust me."

Grant frowned. "You never told her about the promotion?"

"I don't need a lecture about that right now."

"What did she think you were doing in the store?"

I exhaled a bitter laugh. "She thought I was doing it because you needed me to, and because I'm a good man. I wasn't in any hurry to spoil that image for her."

"It can't be that big of a deal," Rhett said. "You got a promotion, what does that matter?"

"It matters to her."

I wouldn't explain to them the humiliation she had been through at the hands of a coworker. I wouldn't tell them how the hurt and shock in her eyes had turned to something like hatred as she equated me to the man who had betrayed her years ago. That she thought I had intentionally used and lied to her the same way left me hollowed out inside until I thought I might crumple in on myself.

"What are you going to do?" Grant asked.

"What can I do? I told Eliza I'm in love with her, and she said she doesn't feel the same. That's all there is to it."

They exchanged a look.

"Do you believe her?" Grant asked.

Did I? Even as her words had left me raw and bleeding, I'd seen the truth hiding in her eyes. Her hurt had made her lash out and turn to the false front she so often relied on. She had used it against me often enough for me to recognize it.

"No," I finally said. "I don't."

"So go to her," Rhett said. "Convince her she's wrong. Show her how much you want her."

I shook my head. "I can't do that."

"You can't care about her very much if you're not willing to try," Grant said.

I got up in my brother's face in a heartbeat. "You think I don't care about her? I've never loved a woman like this in my life. Hearing her tell me she didn't feel the same split me open. I want to go over to her apartment, break down her door, and convince her she's meant to be mine."

I stepped away from Grant. "But if I did that, I'd just be doing the same thing her parents are doing, telling her I know better than she does. Trying to barge in and fix everything because I think she can't make her own decisions. I can't add to that. If she says she doesn't want to be with me, I have to accept it, no matter how much I hate it."

"Accepting things you don't like isn't really your strong suit," Rhett said.

It wasn't. But what kind of man would I be if I told the woman I loved I knew her heart better than she did?

dean

"THIS IS the last of the boxes from the bedroom." Rhett tromped down the stairs with his chin resting on top of the two cardboard boxes he carried. "I think we've just about wrapped it up."

"I'll do one last walk-through," Grandma said. "I don't want to have those estate people sell something I need, like my heart pills." She shot me a wink as she headed for the kitchen.

My family had spent Sunday morning loading Grandma's personal belongings and a few select pieces of furniture into the moving truck. My parents had mostly directed the action from the sidelines, arranging the boxes in the trailer to make sure everything fit. Grandma supervised the proceedings from her recliner until the moment we had to strap it in the truck.

Mom peeked her head in the front door. "The truck's locked up and ready to go."

Grandma came back out of the kitchen. "You go along in the truck, honey. Grant can drive my car over to the Village. I want to ride with Dean in his space age car."

She loved to tease me about my silent car.

"We'll meet you there, then." My mother disappeared from

the doorway, and in another minute, the rental truck engine fired up and faded in the distance as they drove away.

I stood with Grandma in the oddly silent house. Even the usual ticking of seconds passing by had faded, the grandfather clock loaded securely into the moving van with the rest of her most precious things. Seeing the house like this unsettled me, each empty space where a piece of furniture had been like an empty space in my heart. Logically, I knew she was only moving across town, but the change in the rooms left an ache of longing inside me that wouldn't ease.

Hollowed out and raw, I'd walked through the last two days unsure whether I should go to Eliza's and try to convince her we were meant to be together, or take up drinking as a professional sport. I had never felt this powerless before. Rhett and Grant kept their distance as if I were an unpredictable animal that might lash out at any moment. They weren't far off.

Grandma touched a hand to my back. "Are you all right, honey?"

I tried to shake off my melancholy, but it wouldn't budge. It cemented in place with every loss of the last few days. "Of course. Why wouldn't I be?"

She shrugged. "No reason. Just your grandma moving out of the house you practically grew up in. Thought you might be having a moment."

"It's just a house."

Her knowing smile cut right through me as if she'd opened me up and exposed my secret pain.

"You're just like your grandpa. I can read you like a book, because I've seen all the pages before."

I frowned at her. "And what are you reading now?"

Her eyes sparkled. "Your grandpa was direct. I liked that about him. Always said what he meant. I never had to question where I stood with him. He was quite forward, unafraid to go after what he wanted. *Unless* he thought he might not get it. Then, he would plot and plan and scheme until he could see a way to his goal. If he decided the goal was out of his reach, he could get like you are now."

She rubbed her hand on my back, soothing me even as she called me out.

"He'd be a little more stern, a little more closed off as he hid away all his sadness for those goals he decided he'd lost before he ever tried to get them. I don't like to see it in you, honey."

I inhaled sharply through my nose, sorrow coiling through me as if Grandma had conjured it with her words. Or maybe it had always been there, and I hadn't seen it for what it was.

"What is it you think you've lost all hope of having?"

I looked around us, memories rushing in from every room. Happy, sad, they all blended together, all the best, most important memories of my life contained in this old house.

"I always saw myself living in this house. I thought I—" I swallowed down the rest.

"Oh, honey." Her voice was barely a whisper. "You thought you what?"

I drew in a breath as though I could draw courage into my lungs to speak the words.

"I thought I'd raise my family here. But you're moving on, and I'm..." I was further away from that goal than maybe I had ever been. At least before, I had never loved someone I could see that kind of a future with. I'd never known what I was missing out on. Now I knew, and I almost wished I didn't.

"You're a planner like your grandpa, but honey, you don't have to know how everything's going to go. You *can't* know it. You want to have your next week, next month, next ten years laid out in advance. But life doesn't work that way. If there's something you want and all you know is that first step to getting it, it's okay to reach for it, even if you don't have all the in-between steps worked out yet.

"You want this house for your family? Take it. The family will come in its own time. You don't have to know the end from the beginning." She squeezed me a little tighter. "Now tell me the rest."

She always had seen right through me. Time to be brutally honest—with her, and with myself.

"I'm in love with a woman, Grandma, but I messed up. I kept something from her, and I hurt her. I don't know how to get her back."

She rubbed a circle on my shoulder and then gave me a gentle smack. "Aren't you listening? It's okay to go after what you want, even if you only know the first step to getting it. That includes your woman. All you need to know is if what you want is worth chasing after."

Was it?

Without a doubt, what I wanted was worth chasing. Eliza was worth everything—I just hadn't given myself permission to go after her. And the house, the life, the future I wanted was worth it; I just needed to reach for it. The rest would figure itself out.

"Grandma, I'd like to make an offer on your house."

She beamed up at me. "My boy, I thought you'd never ask."

eliza

SIMPLICITY HAD SEEMED the best course of action.

I had texted a basic *I'm not feeling well* to my mother and left it at that. Incoming texts from my sisters were left unread, my phone stuffed away so I wouldn't hope for a message from Dean. I still wore the pajamas I'd changed into after yesterday's farmers market, and planned to cry sloppy, possibly drunken tears over any movie where the couple was guaranteed not to wind up living happily ever after. Maybe something where they both died in the end. The last thing I wanted to see right now was somebody riding off into the sunset madly in love.

I had just started debating my Netflix options when a knock came at my front door. My stupid heart started up, wishing and hoping for foolish things. Watching too many rom-coms had at least a small part of me convinced Dean had showed up on a white horse, ready to make up. Hope swirling through me, I crossed the room and pulled the door open.

Instead of a desperate man ready to grovel, I found my sisters and cousin crowded on the landing. Eden held plastic bags from my favorite Chinese restaurant, and June held up two bottles of wine.

"What are y'all doing here?"

Harper shook her head as if the question were silly. "When you didn't show up to dinner and ignored all our texts, we decided we needed to come over immediately."

They filed inside, wrapping me in quick hugs and surrounding me with so much love I wasn't sure I could handle it. We moved to the couch, all four of us crammed together on the cushions like we used to do when we were little girls. And just like I used to do in those long-ago days, I spilled my guts.

While we ate, I told them everything, from the Irwin Outdoor's celebration party to my argument with Dean in the parking lot. They listened quietly, not asking a single question until I'd finished, letting me get all my hurt and anger out in the open.

"He kept this big, important thing from me, and he didn't tell his parents about us. I don't know if we really had anything at all. I'm angry with him, but I'm more angry with myself for falling for it again."

"What do you mean *again*?" Eden asked.

Time to come clean, I guess. I shifted so I wouldn't have to look my big sister directly in the eye. "That job I had in San Antonio, the one that ended so quickly? One of my coworkers stole my project. We were dating, or at least, I thought we were. He said he was in love with me. I gave him *everything*, but...he was just using me."

Humiliation echoed through me all over again. I was sure Eden would scold me for my behavior, or tsk over my poor judgment, or *something*. Instead, she took my hand.

"Why didn't you ever tell me this?" Her gentle voice soothed away the sting of admitting the truth.

"I didn't want you to think less of me."

"Eliza, never. Never. I love you, I want you to always come to me with anything you need to talk about. You're my baby sister." She hugged me sideways, shifting everyone else on the couch toward us. "I could never think less of you."

"But it's like you said at dinner the other night," I said when I pulled away. "I'm kind of a mess."

Her eyes flashed. "That is *not* what I said at dinner the other night."

"Do you think we're not messy, too?" June asked.

I gave a little hitch of my shoulder. Honestly, no, I couldn't see how their lives were anything other than put together.

June made an indignant sound. "Every day, I worry my interior design business is going to crash and burn, and bring Marilyn's store down with it. I feel guilty for liking my dad's new love, because I still miss my mom. And I am currently navigating a brand-new relationship with my ex-boyfriend's brother. Are you *sure* I don't have any mess?"

I had to laugh at the way she'd laid it all out there. "I mean..."

"I've already bought seven baby books," Eden blurted out. "I'm happy to be a mom, but I'm scared, too."

"That's kind of normal—"

"Eliza, I've *read* all seven baby books and I'm two months pregnant. I've highlighted hundreds of passages with little sticky flags, and Lord help me, I've been transcribing those passages into my own document file. I am *terrified* I'm going to get it wrong."

I gave her hand a squeeze. "You're going to be the best mom ever."

She smiled back at me, but the uncertainty in her eyes jolted me. She really was afraid of screwing this up. My big sister *didn't* have everything together? A weird thing to take comfort from, but it made me feel like less of a disaster.

"I think I'm spending all my time at Fiesta Village instead of actually…living." Harper's awkward smile pinched at my heart, and my eyes filled with tears.

"I tell myself it's all in the name of my career, but I'm kind of hiding, too. It's safe and cozy. I don't have to take any risks, or try new things, or do anything remotely uncomfortable. If anything, I need a little mess in my life, Eliza. Real living is all about the mess."

I kissed her temple. Wow. We were all a little bit messy, after all.

"I want to say something," Eden said. "And I want you to listen, Eliza. What that guy did was horrible. Truly. You've used it all this time as an excuse to not meet men, to not date, to never let anyone in again. But Dean got in, didn't he?"

Her words twisted and sunk like a corkscrew worming its way into my chest. I had been hell bent on never getting hurt again, never letting anybody in again. But Dean got in. Somehow, stiff, prickly Dean got inside my heart and made himself a home. He'd barged in and set up shop, and I had welcomed him with open arms. He was still in my heart now, even after I'd pushed him away and told myself I'd lost him. I had a feeling he would stay in my heart always.

"I don't know if I can trust myself to make the right decision."

That was the real trouble here. Dean's secrets had hurt, but it hurt more to think I'd fallen into the same old trap again. I wanted to trust Dean, and that alone made the impulse suspect. How was I supposed to know what to do when I'd made enough mistakes to fill the Grand Canyon?

"I understand that," Eden said. "And I can't tell you if you should trust Dean or not. But don't let that other guy stop you from ever trusting again. Don't give him any more power in your life. You need to make the best choices for *you*, and only you."

She was right—but I'd never been known for making the best choices.

eliza

MAYBE I SHOULD HAVE CALLED in sick. I'd begged off Webb family dinner under the same flimsy pretext, I could do it again for my job at Irwin's. But if I called in sick today, I couldn't see an end to it. I would stay holed up at home, avoiding everyone and everything in Magnolia Ridge that could possibly remind me of Dean. And even that would never work, since echoes of him followed me around my apartment.

And anyway, my time at Irwin's had an end date now. With another wholesale contract signed, the time had come to leave Irwin's again. I could get through two more weeks, couldn't I? And then, well—I would have to charge on. Dean and I had avoided each other well enough before his little experiment in working retail. I imagined we would go back to how we used to be, distant acquaintances who gave each other strained smiles whenever polite society forced us to.

The thought of Dean faking smiles with me twisted my insides until my stomach ached.

I found it surprisingly easy being in Irwin's once I got here. So what if Dean worked upstairs in his office? What did I care? I wasn't even thinking of him. Except for every time my heart beat. A tiny part of me had thought he would show up during my shift to confront me and try to explain away his actions again, but he hadn't turned up.

That was worse.

Working my shift in the store was a lot like working the market on Saturday had been. I stayed pleasantly anonymous, safe behind my customer service smile. Nobody knew my heart was broken, nobody asked how I was coping. Not a single soul suspected I had fallen miserably in love with a man but didn't know if I could trust him or myself.

The bells on the Irwin's door jingled as Rhett barged through. "Eliza, how the hell are you?"

I flashed my best killer smile. "Excellent as always."

He returned my grin and nodded like we'd had a meaningful conversation. As soon as he passed by, my smile collapsed. So far, Grant hadn't hinted that he knew anything between Dean and me was off, either. Well, if Dean hadn't told his brothers, I wouldn't do it for him. I could pretend everything was just peachy for another hour, clock out, and go home to cry in my soap some more.

Maybe I could use that as a selling point. *Now with real tears!*

"What do you think I should do?" Rhett asked Grant. "Should I advertise for a new roommate, or just enjoy the place Dean-free for a while?"

I whipped my head around. "Dean-free?"

The words were out before I'd given any thought to butting in on their conversation.

If Rhett found it rude, he didn't show it. "Dean's moving out. I'll have the place to myself."

"He's moving out? Where is he going?" I wasn't playing it cool *at all*, but the conversation made no sense.

He shrugged indifference, but Grant answered for him.

"Dean is buying our grandparents' house. He'll be moving in there."

I walked closer to the registers, completely failing to mask my pathetic surprise. "He's buying your grandma's house?"

"He's such a sap." Rhett rolled his eyes as if Dean's sweet gesture were ridiculous.

"He's always loved the place." Grant glared at his brother. "It makes sense."

"But Dean said he didn't care about the house. He told me he's not sentimental that way." Specifically, he'd said he wouldn't think twice about throwing out old mementos and relics from his past.

I wilted a little inside—had he already done that with his memories of me, just threw them out so he could start fresh?

"Dean doesn't *think* he's sentimental. That doesn't fit with his image. But he keeps things that are important to him. When he holds onto something like that, you know he'll never let it go again."

"I didn't see it coming," Rhett said.

Grant scoffed. "Have you learned nothing from living with him? He visited Grandma and took care of that house every Saturday for years—Dean's all about showing his heart in tangible ways. He doesn't put in time and energy where his heart isn't in it."

I walked between carrels of rain jackets and fleeces, my mind reeling from Grant's casual remark. How many times had Dean shown his heart to me in a tangible way? Taking care of me when I was sick, passing along his commission money, supporting me with my parents, and helping me with my business plan—hadn't he shown me I was a priority all along?

My heart bounded in my chest as the words I'd had on repeat echoed again. *I'm falling in love with you.* Could he have possibly meant it? Carter had said those words to wheedle and manipulate, to get what he wanted from me and nothing more. But what did Dean have to gain by telling me he loved me now, *after* the promotion? *After* we'd made love? The only thing he could have gained was...me.

I froze as that thought shivered through me, waking up the hope I'd been trying to smother all weekend.

He had told me once I was sabotaging my business because I was afraid to try. Maybe I'd sabotaged my relationship with him, too. Because I *was* afraid. Easier to think he'd never really cared about me than to consider he might truly love me. Easier to push him away than reveal *my* heart to *him*. My tattoo had been meant as a reminder to be true to myself, and I'd done the exact opposite.

I'd told him he didn't have a heart, but *I* was the one who'd said hurtful things. *I* was the one who'd been heartless.

My chest thudded and thumped, my thoughts whirling. Were we shattered beyond repair? Could I fix it? Finding out was scary. But I was done being afraid. I needed to know if I'd ruined everything with the man I loved.

"Grant, is Dean in his office?"

I heard the words before I realized I'd said them.

He looked over. "Should be."

"Could I go on break for a few minutes? Dean and I left a few things...unsaid."

Grant and Rhett exchanged a look that sent panic careening around my ribcage. If they thought it was a bad idea for me to visit Dean, maybe it was already too late. Maybe I'd already lost him. No more than I deserved, after the awful things I'd said.

"No problem." Grant's generous smile eased some of those fears. "Take all the time you need."

"Thanks." I turned to go but spun a full circle. "I've, uh, never been to the offices."

Rhett grinned. "It's easy, just go through the door on the

street and up the stairs. His office is the second door on the right."

"Okay, thanks."

He raised an eyebrow. Maybe he'd heard my voice crack from the nerves writhing around inside me. It didn't matter. I would do this. Creaky voice or not, I was ready to share my heart with the man I loved.

FORTY-THREE

dean

I LOOSENED my tie as I finished up the monthly financial report. I'd worn a tie to work every day for eight years, but today, it felt stifling. Maybe the business casual attire downstairs had grown on me.

I shook my head at my feeble attempt to lie to myself. That wasn't what had grown on me.

Working at my desk had been a kind of torture today, knowing Eliza was just downstairs, and not being able to go to her. She haunted my days, always somewhere in the back of my mind, ready to make my heart ache with a single thought.

The way she'd loosened my shirt buttons.

How she'd shone on the lake.

The memory of us in what should have been the first of hundreds—thousands—of nights together.

I was stewing, obsessing even, but she wouldn't leave my mind. I didn't want her to. What was more, I didn't want her to be just a thought in my head, but a person in my life, *the* person to talk to every day and come home to every night. But somewhere in the midst of those thoughts, her words barged in.

I'm not falling in love with you.

I still held onto hope she hadn't meant it, but that couldn't ease their sting.

I'd become miserable, unproductive, and completely powerless. If this was what missing her would be like, I didn't want it. She needed time, I would give her time. A few days maybe, and I would try to make her see how much I loved her, that we belonged together.

If I could get through that long without her.

A soft knock sounded on my door. I looked up, and my heart caromed in my chest, unprepared for the sight of her. Eliza stood in my doorway, so beautiful and perfect, my throat tightened just to see her. My impulse was to leap over my desk, crush her to me, and beg her to trust my love. Reason prevailed, but barely.

"Eliza." Against my will, her name on my lips conveyed all the tender feelings she didn't want to hear.

"I don't want to bother you if you're busy." She moved as if she would leave again, and I nearly jumped out of my chair.

"No, I'm not busy." Nothing in my job description could possibly be more important than this.

She stepped closer to my desk, but a deep line furrowed her brow. "What happened to your hands?"

I'd bandaged the worst of my injuries, but a mass of thin red scratches and whorls of purple bruises stood out on my knuckles and down my fingers. I shifted them self-consciously, as though I could conceal the injuries. "I got a little overzealous with the punching bag. It's fine."

She stared at my hands, that worry line never easing. "I wanted to tell you I gave Grant my two weeks' notice."

My heart seemed to still in my chest, shutting down like a watch I had forgotten to wind. She wasn't just leaving *me*, she was leaving *here*, leaving Irwin's behind. I didn't want to go back to watching for her around town again, resigning myself to catching glimpses of this wonderful woman I couldn't have.

I nodded acceptance, a lie if ever there was one.

"He hired two associates over the weekend. I guess the anniversary celebration was a success in more ways than one."

"I hadn't heard." I hadn't talked business with my brothers at all, and had forbidden them from talking about Eliza.

"Also, I got another wholesale contract over the weekend. I won't be able to keep both jobs anymore, anyway."

My heart kicked back to life, brimming with pride. She had finally grabbed for what she wanted, and she was making it happen. Even if she didn't want me there to help her and cheer her on, I would always be proud of her. "Congratulations. That's great news."

She looked around my office as though cataloging it, marking down the differences between imagination and reality. Not much to see. For all the time I spent in here, I had never given it much personality. No degrees framed on the wall, no plaques of achievements, no photographs. No life.

"I also have a wedding coming up."

That random statement lodged in my brain. "What wedding?"

But also *What wedding?*

"I advertised smaller soaps as wedding favors in some of the bridal shops around town, and got a hit on that right away. A Christmas wedding with Christmas soaps. They're going to smell really good."

I breathed easier knowing Eliza wasn't set to marry some unknown man. An absurd idea, but a terrifying one. She was meant to marry *me*. I sucked in a breath, trying to calm my rapid-fire thoughts, but utterly unable to when she stood this close and still so far away.

"That's wonderful, El. I knew you could do it."

Her smile beamed like a ray of sunshine lighting up my day. She'd shone that light on me, until I never wanted to be anywhere else. I loved this woman, plain and simple. I might have stared at her a little too intensely, and she glanced away, flustered all over again. A rosy sheen washed over her cheeks, and a strange expression crossed her face. I followed her gaze to my desk—

Her acorns.

Maybe it had been foolish to bring them here, but how could I have known she would ever be standing here to see them? I'd set them on my desk Saturday morning, and if seeing them caused me a little pain, the memories they recalled were worth it. My walk with Eliza beneath the canopy of oaks. Her lips pressed against the acorns. Her lips pressed against mine. A small memento of the woman who held my heart in her hands.

"You kept my acorns?"

Her soft voice barely reached my ears. I might not have heard her if my eyes hadn't been locked on her mouth. I swallowed hard, my answer unnecessary.

She nodded as if deciding something.

"The other thing I needed to tell you is that I'm a terrible liar." She took a deep breath. "I told you I wasn't falling for you, but I'm actually kind of super in love with you."

Her words exploded through me, wrapping around my heart and spurring me to action. Out of my chair and around the desk to her in a second, my hands found her waist of their own accord, my head tipped down nearly to hers.

"El?"

She threw her arms around my neck, pulling me in for a kiss. Every touch held sweetness and affection like I had never known before. *This woman. My* woman, now and always.

She drew away just enough to whisper against my mouth. "I'm so sorry for what I said. You are my type, you are exactly my type. You're so thoughtful and kind and supportive. You see more in me than anyone else ever has. You believed in me even when I didn't believe in myself. I don't want anyone else but you."

I cupped her face in my hands. "I should have told you about the promotion, I'm sorry I kept it from you." I stroked her hair from her face, taking her in, memorizing this moment. "El, I love you so much. I've never felt this way before. You fill my days with heart when I'm too much in my head. You make me want to try new things and explore the world outside my office. You make me want to be a better man."

"You don't have to be anything else, you're wonderful just as you are. I love you so, so much." She pressed her mouth to mine, confirming her words again and again.

The sound of a throat clearing finally made us pull apart. We turned to see my family gathered at my open office doorway, staring in and grinning wildly. I hugged Eliza closer. What explanation could I give when they'd seen the truth right before their eyes? I loved her, and she loved me right back.

Grant leaned in to grab the office door handle, pulling it closed with a smirk. Our parents' inevitable questions could wait until later. Hopefully much later.

Eliza grinned up at me. "We might have to declare our intentions."

"I intend to love you for as long as you'll let me."

She went up on tiptoe to kiss me again. "I like that plan."

ELIZA

Eight months later

I PUT the finishing touches on the soap I'd just poured, set the lid on tight, and moved it onto the curing shelves. A dozen fresh batches waited their turn on the cutting block this week, and from there, I'd transfer them to the staging shelves. I washed the bucket and utensils in the sink and put everything away, then stepped back to just marvel for a minute.

I had my very own she-shed, one-hundred-fifty square feet of soap-making goodness. More than enough room to prepare and store my soaps before I delivered them around town or shipped them across the country. Working in here always gave me a little thrill of pride to see how far I had come. Dean had even special-ordered a sign for over the door.

Badass Businesswoman.

Stepping out of my shed, I closed up for the night. Twilight was just settling in, tinging the sky in pink and purple. The rosemary and mint I'd planted around the shed filled the air with their dreamy scent, and crickets snapped in the yard. All told, I had a pretty damn fine work environment.

Dean walked out the back door of the house in all his suited-up glory.

Did I mention the views from my office were excellent, too?

He came straight to me and wrapped me in a warm hug. Nuzzling his face into my neck, he spoke against my skin, making me shiver.

"Good day?"

"Two more weddings confirmed and a bunch of random website business."

"Gotta love that random website business."

I laughed as his nuzzles turned into blatant kisses. "Did you get all your spreadsheets done?"

"So many spreadsheets." His hands found my waist, my hips, my back, lighting me up with every caress.

"I've got this month's rent for you," I said against his shoulder.

"Good. I'd hate to have to evict my girlfriend's business from my property."

"You're so strict."

He pulled back to flash a naughty grin. "Only when I need to be."

Dean had encouraged me to build my soap shed in his backyard the moment he'd taken ownership of his grandmother's house. I made a point of paying rent on it, and although he'd argued with me at first, now he accepted the money without complaint. He'd encouraged me to move in with him, too, but so far, I'd held onto my over-the-garage apartment. He wasn't likely to accept my share in a mortgage payment any easier than the meager rent he consented to take for the shed. We spent most of our time here at the house, and it was getting harder to go home to my apartment at night, but I still clung to that shred of independence.

"Are you ready for dinner?" I had the fixings for fancy ramen laid out on the kitchen counter. We cooked together most nights, and while I wasn't a pro at it yet, my skills had certainly improved with a little guidance from my personal chef.

"Not yet. Come here." He laced his fingers with mine and led me to one of our favorite spots in the yard.

"This is becoming a problem. Do I need to arrange an intervention?"

He just smiled as we crawled into the double hammock he'd set up beneath an old oak. I curled up next to him, amazed as always we could be so comfortable in a *hammock*. Dean stroked his hand over my shoulder and down my arm as I breathed in the smell of him.

"I've decided what I'm going to spend your rent money on."

"Mm-hmm." I pressed my nose to his neck. The man smelled better the longer I knew him. That didn't make any sense.

"I think it should go toward our honeymoon."

I laughed, still focused on how delicious he smelled. "Right, our honeymoon."

"I suppose there's a chance you'll say no, and I'll have to spend it on something else."

"What do you mean, say no?"

He slipped his hand into his pocket and when he pulled it out again, something shimmery rested on the first knuckle of his index finger. "Will you marry me?"

My body stilled, my brain crashed to a stop. "Wait—what?"

He grinned down at me even as he hugged me closer. "Eliza Emmeline Webb, will you make me the happiest man in the world and be my wife?"

I tried to sit up, but between his strong arm around me and

the total lack of purchase, I only rolled onto his chest. "What are you doing?"

"I'm asking you to marry me."

My heart stopped. I was dead. I had definitely died. "Did you just propose to me in a hammock?"

He laughed softly. "It seemed appropriate."

"You're serious?" My voice went small. He sounded serious, and the ring looked real, but I needed confirmation.

He flipped our positions so his face hovered over mine. "El, you are the bright shining center of all my days. I want to live with you, and love you, and cherish you forever. You make everything better, including me. I love you, and I want to marry you. Will you marry me?"

My eyes swam with tears until I couldn't see his face, but I knew where it was. I answered him in the spaces between kisses. "Yes. Yes. Yes."

He slipped the ring on my finger, and I cuddled into him, letting him kiss away my happy tears as they fell.

"You have my whole heart, El."

I stretched up to meet his mouth. "It's the only heart for me."

THE END

Thank you so much for reading my sweet starchy man paired with the hot mess express. As soon as I got the idea for matching Eliza with Dean, they wouldn't let me go! This was such a fun ride, thank you for taking it with me!

acknowledgments

Thank you for reading Have a Heart! It means so much to me to have readers getting to know these characters and enjoying my books! Your time is precious, and I appreciate you spending some of that with me.

Big thank you to everyone who beta read this book—Neely, Britt, Ashley, Allison, Chandra, Amanda, and Claire, your feedback helped me whip this baby into shape!

Thank you to my editor, Zee, for helping me iron out the last of the wrinkles. These characters shine so much brighter with your input!

Thank you to Melody for an absolutely stellar Eliza & Dean! I love this cover & can't thank you enough!

And special thanks to my husband and kids, who let me put on my writer cap while I lose track of things like dinnertime and laundry. Love you!

Genny Carrick is a sucker for an HEA, especially if there's a whole lot of laughter along the way. She writes romances and rom-coms about stubborn women and the men who fall for them.

When she's not lost in swoony reads, she's probably up to something crafty or trying to get her dog and two cats to love her.

Genny recently moved to Texas after a lifetime in the Pacific Northwest, and lives with her brilliant husband and two hilarious kids.

Stay in the know with book news at gennycarrick.com